PRAISE FOR 1
QUINN

C000090575

"Brilliant and heart pounding"

JEFFERY DEAVER, *NEW YORK TIMES*
BESTSELLING AUTHOR

"Addictive."

JAMES ROLLINS, *NEW YORK TIMES*
BESTSELLING AUTHOR

"Unputdownable."

TESS GERRITSEN, *NEW YORK TIMES*
BESTSELLING AUTHOR

"The best elements of Lee Child, John le Carré, and Robert
Ludlum."

SHELDON SIEGEL, *NEW YORK TIMES*
BESTSELLING AUTHOR

"Quinn is one part James Bond, one part Jason Bourne."

NASHVILLE BOOK WORM

"Welcome addition to the political thriller game."

PUBLISHERS WEEKLY

THE UNKNOWN

ALSO BY BRETT BATTLES

THE NIGHT MAN CHRONICLES

Night Man

Insidious

Mercy

THE EXCOMS THRILLERS

The Excoms

Town at the Edge of Darkness

City of Nope

Blinded by the Night

THE REWINDER THRILLERS

Rewinder

Destroyer

Survivor

THE LOGAN HARPER THRILLERS

Little Girl Gone

Every Precious Thing

THE PROJECT EDEN THRILLERS

Sick

Exit Nine

Pale Horse

Ashes

Eden Rising

Dream Sky

Down

THE ALEXANDRA POE THRILLERS

(Cowritten with Robert Gregory Browne)

Poe

Takedown

STANDALONES

Novels

The Pull of Gravity

No Return

Mine

Novellas

Mine: The Arrival

Short Stories

"Perfect Gentleman"

For Younger Readers

THE TROUBLE FAMILY CHRONICLES

Here Comes Mr. Trouble

THE UNKNOWN

A JONATHAN QUINN NOVEL

BRETT BATTLES

1

AUSTRIA

Snowflakes whirled in the halo of light outside the train's window, all but obscuring the dark countryside.

Snow.

In October.

An obscenity as far as Darius Kincaid was concerned. Last he checked, back home in San Diego it was a sunny eighty-three degrees, a more civilized temperature for this time of year.

It wasn't that he didn't like snow. It just had its place.

And October was not it.

He checked his watch. Twelve forty-two a.m. They'd be stopping in Innsbruck in about fifteen minutes. After that, the Nightjet train wouldn't halt again for another two and a half hours, giving Kincaid some time to relax.

He headed through the sleeper car and turned into the alcove for cabins 14 and 16, then took the short set of steps down to the cabins' doors. He rapped lightly on number 14 and pushed open the unlatched door.

Edgar Clarke, his colleague on this mission, lay on the only bed, hands resting on his chest, eyes closed.

"Wake up," Kincaid whispered.

"I am awake," Clarke replied without moving.

"We're almost to Innsbruck."

Clarke sat up and looked at his watch. "Right on time."

Kincaid stepped over to cabin 16 to check on their package. Unlike the other cabin, this one was locked. Using the conductor key he'd obtained prior to mission start, he unlocked it and eased it open far enough to peek inside. Like the last time he'd checked, the lights were off, and deep, steady breaths came from the dark lump on the bed.

Earlier that evening, in a library conference room at the University of Zurich in Switzerland, Kincaid and Clarke had taken charge of Thomas Brunner from an older man named Stefan Ferber, the mission's client.

Misty Blake, head of the Office—the agency coordinating the job—had warned Kincaid the client would be there and would probably be on edge.

"First timer," she'd said.

Great, Kincaid had thought. He much preferred working with people who'd used services similar to his in the past. First timers were…unpredictable. The less of that in Kincaid's line of work, the better.

Sure enough, Ferber had been jittery, eyes shifting side to side, and hands unable to remain still for more than a second. "He needs to be there on time," the older man said.

"He will be," Kincaid answered in German, his voice calm and reassuring.

"You *must* take extra care."

Kincaid had smiled and told Ferber they would. What he really wanted to say was "That's why you hired us," but he kept that to himself.

Kincaid was a professional courier. His area of expertise: escorting individuals in need of protection. He was equal parts bodyguard and logistics expert. Clarke, it turned out, made a living as a generalist, fitting into jobs wherever a competent body was needed. This was the first time they had ever worked together. Misty had been the one who paired them.

They had twenty-four hours to deliver Brunner to an office building in Hamburg, Germany. Normally that would be enough to get there and back again, with time between legs to get a good night's sleep. And by air, it would take only an hour and a half to get there.

But Kincaid had been told no one could know Brunner was even making the trip, let alone what route he would be taking. Using a direct route was out of the question. They would be taking a longer, less obvious, and lower-risk path to Germany that no one would know about other than Kincaid, Clarke, and Misty.

As for why Brunner needed an escort in the first place, Kincaid had no idea, nor did he care. Brunner was the cargo; that was all the information he needed.

After leaving the library, he and Clarke had escorted Brunner to an apartment building a half kilometer north of the university.

Outside the entrance, the cargo had paused and said, "What are we doing here? Where's your car?"

"Just go inside," Clarke said.

Brunner's brow furrowed, and he shook his head. "No. We-we're supposed to be going to—"

"Quiet," Kincaid snapped.

Brunner jumped at the sharpness of Kincaid's tone.

"Don't *ever* say anything about a destination. Understand?" Kincaid pulled the door open and stepped inside the building. "Move it."

Warily, Brunner entered.

They took the stairs to a second-floor apartment, and once they were inside, Kincaid looked at his watch and said in a calmer voice, "Make yourself comfortable. We've got about an hour to kill."

"An hour until what?"

"Until we leave."

Brunner's gaze switched back and forth between his two bodyguards. "I do not understand. Why are we wasting time here? We should be on the way to—" He stopped himself. "We should be on the way."

"We *are* on the way, Herr Brunner," Clarke said. "Now, sit down."

"Is that an order?"

"Of course not," Kincaid said. "It's a suggestion. If you prefer to stand for an hour, that's your choice."

Brunner walked over to the sofa, but then turned back. "I would really like to know how you are going to get me...there."

"And you will. Soon enough."

"I don't understand why you can't just tell me. It's not like I can share the information with anyone."

Kincaid had taken Brunner's phone at the library, removed its SIM card and battery, and put the parts in a lead-lined film bag, to be returned to the cargo upon arrival at their destination.

"I'm not telling you because you don't need to know. If you're not happy with that, you're free to leave." Kincaid motioned to the door. "If, on the other hand, you stay, I will expect you to accept there are some things we will keep from you, and that you will do everything we tell you to do." He locked eyes with Brunner. "What's it to be?"

"I-I-I never said I was going anywhere."

"Good."

They left the apartment fifty-five minutes later and took side streets to the Zurich Hauptbahnhof, Zurich's main train station.

"Graz?" Brunner said when he saw the digital sign above the platform, denoting the train's destination. "That's not even in the right di—"

"Don't," Kincaid whispered. "Remember what I told you."

They boarded the train and made their way to cabin 16 in silence.

As soon as Brunner was in his tiny room, he said, "Austria is *not* Germany!"

Kincaid grimaced at him from the doorway, his XL body almost filling the opening. "I'm well aware of that."

"Then why are we—"

Kincaid narrowed his eyes.

"Right," Brunner said. "No questions."

Kincaid held the man's gaze for another couple of seconds before he said, "Get some sleep. We'll wake you in plenty of time before our stop."

Brunner snorted. "How do you expect me to sleep? I'm too wound up."

"I could get you a beer if you think that would help."

A brief pause. "Two would be better."

The beers had done the trick, and now, almost two hours later, Brunner was still sound asleep.

Kincaid stepped over to the cabin's window and pulled the edge of the curtain back. A smattering of buildings had begun to litter the countryside, signaling the nearing city.

He shut the door and turned to find Clarke standing just inside cabin 14.

Without a word, the two men headed up the steps to the main corridor. There, they stopped in front of the alcove, and played the parts of two normal passengers stretching their legs.

In theory, none of the new passengers boarding in Innsbruck would need to enter via this sleeper car, as all its cabins and those of the other two sleeper cars between this one and the front of the train were occupied. But people didn't always operate in a logical manner, hence the need to guard the entrance to Brunner's cabin.

Kincaid watched through the windows as more and more buildings appeared, marking the train's official arrival in Innsbruck. At first, other than a car here and there, the streets were empty, but the number increased as the train neared the station. Not by a lot, but enough to lead Kincaid to believe there would soon be at least a couple dozen people joining them onboard.

His hunch proved correct, as his hunches often did. As the NightJet pulled along the platform, Kincaid saw approximately thirty people waiting. The moment the train stopped, the new passengers moved toward the doors.

Kincaid monitored the car's entrance to his left, toward the back of the train where things would be busiest, while Clarke did the same to the right.

A young family of three climbed into the next car down, the child passed out on the father's shoulder. They were followed by an older man, and then two middle-aged women who appeared to be traveling together. None of these passengers entered the sleeper car, nor did any give Kincaid the sense he needed to worry about them.

"Company," Clarke whispered.

Kincaid casually swung his gaze toward the front of the train.

A woman and a man, in their late twenties or early thirties, had entered the corridor, each wearing a backpack.

"See, I told you," the man said in German. "We are farther down."

The woman frowned but remained silent.

Nothing in the demeanor of either of them set off any alarms, though Kincaid did note the walking stick strapped to the man's backpack. A meter and a half long, it had a curved top, like a shepherd's crook, and was covered with carvings that gave it more of an art-piece feel than that of something used to climb hills. In the right hands, it could be a dangerous weapon.

As the couple neared, the woman said in German, "Pardon us."

Kincaid and Clarke pushed themselves tight against the wall.

While the woman easily slipped past Clarke, maneuvering around Kincaid was not so simple. He was larger than Clarke, six foot three and well muscled, and was wearing a protective vest under his shirt that bulked him up even more. So it wasn't surprising that, as the woman squeezed by him, her backpack bumped against his chest.

"I'm so sorry," she said, then, after looking up at him, repeated the apology in English.

He flashed her a smile. "Don't worry about it," he replied in flawless German.

This received a surprised look from both the woman and the man. Apparently, they hadn't met a lot of people of African descent who spoke their language. On one hand, Kincaid took some satisfaction at upsetting their worldview a bit. On the other, their reactions could've implied they'd thought that language skill was beyond his abilities, and that pissed him off.

After the couple exited at the other end, no other new passengers appeared, and within a few minutes, the train began moving again.

"Walk-through?" Clarke said.

Kincaid nodded. "I'll do it. You keep an eye on our friend."

With a smile and a shrug, Clarke said, "Hey, you want to pass up a chance to relax, that's fine by me," then descended the steps to cabin 14.

"It's not nap time," Kincaid called after him. "Stay alert."

"No shit, dude. I got this. Don't worry."

Clarke may have been a little looser than Kincaid would have liked in a mission partner, but Kincaid had worked with far less competent agents, so while he grimaced at the back of Clarke's head, he said nothing more.

He checked his watch and set an alarm for twenty minutes. That should give the new passengers enough time to settle in and get comfortable. And hopefully, if anyone had boarded intending to interfere with Brunner's trip, the person's guard will have slipped a little by then, too.

Kincaid watched out the window as the city fell away again, replaced by countryside and mountains of western Austria. The snow was still falling, though lighter than before, as if the storm was just reaching this area. Maybe they'd get ahead of it and he could pretend, for a little while, that winter was still two months away.

When his watch alarm began thumping his wrist, he turned it off and headed toward the back of the train.

The next car was also a sleeper. As he moved down the empty

corridor, he listened at every alcove for unusual noises, but the only thing he heard was the clacking of the tracks.

After that, he came to the first of the seating-only cars. Like the sleepers, the corridor passed along the side, not down the center. The difference here was that instead of cabins with seats that converted into beds, there were glassed-in compartments with two rows of seats facing each other, like a booth at a restaurant.

Most of the people in these compartments were asleep or at least giving it a try. Occasionally, he'd spot someone reading or looking at a phone or staring out the window.

So far, no one had registered as a problem.

Onward he went, car by car until he reached the end of the train. Not once did he get the sense there was anyone onboard he needed to worry about. Either the circuitous mission route to Hamburg had gone undiscovered, or the client had overestimated the danger to the cargo.

Kincaid had a feeling it was the latter. It certainly wouldn't be the first time he'd done a job where his services weren't really needed. Not that he was complaining. He and Clarke were making good money for this run. And as important as his fee was the fact he was working for the Office again.

Several years earlier, Peter, the late head of the Office during its first iteration, had given Kincaid his break in the business. He hadn't even realized the Office was back in operation, so he'd been both surprised and pleased when Misty called him about this job. Hopefully it would translate into even more work.

He turned and headed back toward the front of the train, giving the passengers a second look as he did. Right before he reached his sleeper car, he paused.

The young couple who had squeezed past him and Clarke in Innsbruck.

He hadn't seen them on either pass.

There were several empty seats, so it was possible they had been using the toilets, getting ready to sleep, when he went by the first time. But they needed to be accounted for. He'd alert Clarke to be on the lookout in case the couple was indeed a problem, then would go back to find them.

He entered his car and hurried to the alcove for cabins 14 and 16. When he swung around the corner to go down the steps, he jerked to a stop.

The doors to both cabins were open, the lights on in each room.

"Clarke?" he said.

Not a sound from below.

Kincaid reached under his jacket, pulled out his Glock, and attached the sound suppressor.

"Clarke, you in there?"

Still no answer.

He took the first two steps down and stopped to listen.

The hum and jostle of the train and nothing more.

He moved onto the lower landing and crept forward until he could see into both rooms.

Both beds were empty.

He leaned through the doorway to Clarke's room and found it deserted.

He leaned into Brunner's room.

Same story.

What the hell—

Behind him, the sound of a footstep, then a familiar voice saying, "Oh, shit."

Kincaid turned around and found Clarke standing at the top of the stairs, staring down at him.

"Where the hell did you go? I thought something had…" He realized Clarke was alone. "Where's Brunner?"

Clarke came halfway down the steps. "I thought you'd be gone longer."

"What?"

Kincaid prided himself on his reaction time, but Clarke's words confused him enough that he didn't see the gun in his partner's hand until it was pointed at him.

"Sorry, Darius," Clarke said.

A bullet hit Kincaid in the chest, slamming him back against the wall between the two cabins. He rolled and fell to the floor facedown, halfway into cabin 14.

Pain radiated across his torso, and he barely felt Clarke put a hand on his shoulder to turn him over.

"*Was geht hier vor?*" a man said from the corridor, asking what was going on.

Kincaid felt Clarke's hand move away from his shoulder, and heard the spit of Clarke's gun again.

Kincaid clenched, but when he experienced no new pain, he knew the bullet hadn't been meant for him.

At the sound of footsteps heading up the stairs, he pried his eyes open and turned his head.

Clarke had moved back to the top and was leaning over someone lying on the hallway floor.

Kincaid tried to say something but couldn't get the words out. It didn't matter, anyway. Clarke had already hurried out of sight, toward the front of the train.

Kincaid tried to push himself up, but barely got his chest off the floor when gray started pushing in at the edges of his vision.

No, he thought, fighting to stay conscious. *No, no, no.*

But the haze continued to expand.

I can't...I need...to...to...

The world around him continued to collapse, until, for a brief moment, he could only see gray.

Then it all turned black.

———

Edgar Clarke pulled his hand away from the conductor's neck. The man was dead.

Shit.

Eliminating Kincaid was something Clarke had really hoped to avoid, but he wasn't about to let his temporary partner get in the way of a big payday. Hence the bullet he'd put in Kincaid's chest.

The conductor, on the other hand, had been an unforeseen complication. Another couple of minutes and Clarke would have had Kincaid's body in one of the cabins, preventing it from being discovered for hours.

But no.

Mr. Nosey Conductor had to show up at the most inopportune moment. Clarke had had no other choice than to take him out also. Now, even if Clarke moved both bodies into the cabins, the conductor's disappearance would raise an alarm a whole lot sooner than planned.

Screw it. Better to not waste time moving them and join the others.

He bolted down the corridor and hurried into the next sleeper car. When he reached cabin 2, he rapped twice on the door. "It's me."

The door inched open, allowing a gust of cold air to smack Clarke in the face. Astrid looked past him, checking if he was alone, then pulled the door all the way open and let him squeeze inside.

Cabin 2 was a two-person compartment with bunk beds, which meant it had marginally more room than the single-bed economy cabin he had been waiting in earlier. With four people inside, however—even with Brunner lying on the lower bunk—it didn't feel any larger.

"Where's the bag?" Astrid asked, her voice raised enough to be heard above the noise of the train coming in through the glass-less window.

"Kincaid came back," Clarke said.

She froze. "And?"

"I had to take care of him."

"That still doesn't explain where the bag is."

"Before I could grab it, a conductor showed up. I-I killed him, too."

"Not ideal, but if you had no choice…"

"I didn't."

"The bag?"

"I didn't think it was worth the risk." He explained what had happened, and how he'd left the body in the corridor.

Astrid's mouth tightened into a thin line. "You should have moved him."

"It wouldn't have mattered. Someone would have still seen the blood."

She gritted her teeth. "Dammit." She turned to Esa, who was standing by the window, looking up at the sky. "Are they in position yet?"

Esa glanced at her. "Almost."

"Give the signal. We need to go now."

Esa picked up his radio and spoke into it, in a language Clarke didn't understand.

A few moments later, a rope with a padded loop on the end dropped into view, next to the window.

Esa picked up the walking stick he'd carried on board, stuck the hooked end out the window, and snagged the rope on his first try.

After pulling the loop inside, he said, "Bring him over."

Clarke grabbed Brunner's shoulder and yanked him toward the edge of the bed. "Okay, buddy, time to go."

Looking terrified, Brunner pressed a hand on the wall and jammed his feet against the edge of the bed, trying to keep from being pulled off. "W-w-what's going on? What's that for?"

"Off the bed," Clarke said.

When Brunner wouldn't give up his grip, Clarke grabbed him and twisted him around, then dragged the man onto the floor.

After he and Astrid manhandled Brunner to the window, Esa pushed the padded loop over Brunner's shoulders and said, "Put your arms over this."

Brunner's eyes grew even wider as the purpose of the rope

dawned on him. He tried to push it off. "No, no, please! Get me out of this!"

Clarke grabbed him by the scruff of the neck and squeezed. "Do it."

Brunner ceased protesting and, shaking, tucked the loop under his arms so that the padding rested tightly across his chest.

"Good," Esa said as he removed a ten centimeter-wide strap from his backpack. Sewn to each end was a heavy-duty safety clip. "Now hold still."

"What's that for?" Brunner asked.

"You don't want to fall out, do you?"

"Fall out? Oh God, oh God."

Esa connected the strap to the chest padding, ran it between Brunner's legs, and attached the other end to where the loop closed at the main rope. He then nodded at Clarke, who grabbed Brunner by the arms and moved him directly in front of the window.

Esa said a few words into his radio, then to Brunner, "As the rope pulls you out the window, tuck yourself in a ball. You'll be less likely to get hurt."

"Tuck my what? Please don't make me—"

The rope yanked him backward out the window. In his panic, he didn't tuck, so his legs slapped hard against the frame.

Clarke stuck his head outside to watch the helicopter reel in Brunner. The aircraft, an eerily silent Russian-made Ghost 1A1, flew twenty meters above the tracks, pacing the train. Clarke had seen pictures of Ghosts before, but never one in person. It was pretty damn impressive.

Within moments of Brunner being hauled on board, the rope was dangling by the window again. Astrid went next, then Clarke, and finally Esa. As soon as Esa was pulled into the aircraft, the Ghost banked to the left over a large forest, away from the train.

Clarke smiled. They'd done it.

Okay, sure, he hadn't enjoyed killing Kincaid or the conductor, but except for those two hiccups, the job had gone off without a hitch. Well, he *had* messed up in not getting Brunner's bag, but that wasn't a big deal. Brunner was what Astrid and Esa's organization was paying for.

Clarke sensed someone looking at him so he glanced over. It was Astrid.

"Why the smile?" she asked.

"Told you I could deliver."

"That you did, Mr. Clarke. Thank you for your assistance."

"You're welcome.

"Just a few loose ends to tie up."

"Loose en—"

She pointed a gun at him, a suppressor attached to the barrel.

"Whoa, whoa, whoa!" he said, grabbing his safety harness and pulling at the clasp. It wouldn't release. "Are you saying I'm a loose end? I'm not a loose end! I'm an asset. You wouldn't have been able to pull this off if not for me!"

She tilted her head to the side. "We *could* have. It would just have been more difficult. As I said, thank you."

The spit of the gun was laughably weak for the damage it did. Its bullet ripped through the right side of Clarke's chest into his lung, deflected off a rib, and lodged in his spinal cord at the base of his neck.

He slumped forward, surprised he could feel no pain. Lying motionless in his lap were the hands that had been trying to free him. He tried to move them, but couldn't get even a finger to twitch. His eyelids began to droop, leaving him with an unfocused, half obscured view of the world.

"He's still alive," Esa said, surprisingly close.

A pause as a hand touched Clarke's chin and tilted his head up. "Not for long," Astrid said. "Unlock his harness."

A metallic click.

Clarke would have slumped to the floor if Esa hadn't lifted him into the air.

A moment later, Astrid said, "This will do."

The next thing Clarke knew, he was staring at the helicopter's ceiling, something hard under his head.

A mechanical sound. Sliding. Followed by freezing air blowing across Clarke's face.

"I hate to tell you this, Mr. Clarke," Astrid whispered in his ear, "but you were always a loose end."

In the blink of an eye, the blowing wind turned into a roaring hurricane, as darkness replaced the ceiling of the helicopter.

Not complete darkness, though. Every second or two, it was punctured by tiny dots of light.

Beautiful, really.

Black.

Then black with white dots.

Then black.

Then black with white dots.

Mesmerized by this repetition, he barely noticed the tree his right shoulder slammed into. A smack to the head a couple of branches later rendered him unconscious.

Mercifully, by the time he smashed into the ground, he was dead.

2

ein Gott, da ist noch ein weiterer."

"M" Kincaid pried his eyes open and forced himself to sit up.

His chest throbbed from where Clarke's shot had slammed into his bulletproof vest. He always wore one on a job, but this was the first time it had ever taken a direct hit. Thank God he hadn't mentioned the vest to Clarke.

A man came down the steps from the corridor. Before he reached Kincaid, he jerked to a stop, his eyes locked on something off to the side.

Kincaid turned and spotted his Glock lying in the threshold to cabin 14.

The man started to back away.

"I didn't do it," Kincaid said in German, each word a struggle. "I was shot, too."

He pulled his jacket open, causing the man to back up even faster, but the guy stopped when Kincaid peeled back his shirt, exposing his vest.

"See." Kincaid winced as he touched the vest next to where the bullet was embedded.

"Why do you have a gun?"

"I'm a...never mind. I don't have time."

Kincaid reached for his pistol.

"No, no, no! Please!" The man raced back into the main corridor.

"I'm not going to shoot you."

Kincaid gingerly rose to his feet, slipped the gun into its harness, and started up the stairs.

As he stepped out of the alcove, three conductors entered the car from the left.

"What's going on here? What happened?" the youngest one asked.

"He's been shot." This was from a different passenger, who was leaning over the clearly dead conductor.

Kincaid stepped past them, toward the front of the train.

"Where are you going?" someone called behind him.

"He said he was hit, too," Kincaid's would-be helper said. "But-but he has a gun."

"Stop!" the first voice yelled.

Someone who was either stupidly brave or had a death wish ran up behind Kincaid and grabbed his arm. "I said stop!"

Kincaid whirled around, and the man staggered backward.

"The shooter went that way," Kincaid said, pointing in the direction he'd been headed. "Unless you want to go after him, you'll let me do my job."

"J-job?"

Kincaid pulled his gun out again, eliciting several gasps. Without saying another word, he turned back toward the front of the train. Within a few steps he was jogging and then running.

Each time his foot hit the floor, a shockwave of pain raced through his body, but he ignored them and focused on the only thing that mattered: retrieving the cargo. Nothing could be allowed to turn his attention from that. Not even the fact his supposed partner had shot him.

The only door he'd heard when Clarke escaped was the loud sliding one at the end of the car, so he ignored the remaining cabins in his car and hurried into the next one. He didn't let up once he was in that corridor. Though Clarke and Brunner could be in any of the cabins he was rushing past, Kincaid's first priority was to make sure the corridor in the next car—the very front passenger car—was also unoccupied.

Several meters before reaching the next door between the cars, the train slowed.

"Dammit," he muttered.

The next scheduled stop was still an hour and a half away. While it was possible this was just a slowdown to let another train pass, the more likely reason was that one of the conductors had told the engineer what had happened and ordered the train be halted. Whatever the case, stopping would provide the perfect opportunity for Clarke to remove Brunner from the train.

Kincaid shoved open the door and sprinted into the foremost car. Empty.

Clarke and Brunner must be in a cabin in either this car or the one Kincaid had just come through. At the rate the train was slowing, though, he had no chance of checking them all before the NightJet stopped moving.

There was no time to hunt for the cargo. The only thing he could do—the thing he *must* do—was to make sure Brunner stayed on the train.

Kincaid ran to the vestibule at the end of the car and opened the exterior door.

Frigid air whipped inside as he pulled himself onto the door and used it as a makeshift ladder to the roof. Though snow was no longer falling, a thin layer clung to the surface of the roof, unbroken but for the spot where Kincaid had climbed up. He crouched to avoid the power wires strung above the train, and shuffled to a place where he could stand and see either side of the cars.

A large meadow of leafless brush and brown grass sat to the right of the tracks, with no snow. The storm had not yet made it this far east. On the left, the woods came to within seven meters of the tracks. Dark and impenetrable, it would be the perfect place in which to get lost.

The train slowed more and more until it finally rolled to a halt.

Kincaid rose to his feet and flicked his gaze from side to side, taking in the whole length of the train. The lights from inside the cars illuminated the railbed, aiding him in his search for any sign of someone trying to escape. But the ground remained empty.

After a few minutes, he heard a voice, coming from the door he'd used to reach the roof. Thirty seconds later, two conductors and a man in a dark suit exited.

The trio scanned the tracks in both directions, then huddled together, talking. One of the conductors glanced up and stiffened.

"*Das ist er*!" he shouted, pointing at Kincaid.

The two others spun around. As soon as the man in the suit laid eyes on Kincaid, he whipped up his hand and pointed a gun at Kincaid.

"Drop your weapon!" the man shouted in German.

"Easy now," Kincaid replied in kind, holding up his empty hand. "I'm not the guy you're looking for. I'm just trying to make sure he doesn't escape!"

"Put it down!" the man said.

"Listen to me," Kincaid said. "The killer is still—"

The man pulled his trigger, sending a bullet screaming past Kincaid's shoulder, missing him by only a few centimeters.

"Okay! Okay!" Kincaid yelled as he tossed his gun over the side.

"Climb down," the suited man ordered. "Slowly."

Kincaid glanced over his shoulder to make sure he hadn't missed Clarke's or Brunner's departure. But with the exception of the three men waiting for him, no one else had left the train.

Where the hell are they?

"Down! Now!"

Kincaid climbed off the train the same way he'd gone up.

The moment his feet touched the ground, the suited man shoved him against the side of the car, chest first.

"Hands behind your back," the man ordered.

Kincaid complied. "You're making a mistake. I'm not the shooter. I'm one of his victims."

After affixing a pair of handcuffs around Kincaid's wrists, the man pulled him backward a couple of steps and pushed him toward the open door. "On the train. And don't try anything."

As soon as they were all back onboard, one of the conductors closed the door and the other lifted a walkie-talkie and said, "We've got him. You can get underway again."

"Any problems?" a voice asked over the radio.

"No."

The train began to move again.

Kincaid was taken to a small cabin, at the end of the third sleeper car, that had a placard on the door reading CREW ONLY.

"Sit," his guard told him, nodding at the pair of chairs next to a small table. Unlike the passenger cabins in this car, this room had no bed.

"You're wasting time," Kincaid said. "There's been a kidnapping. I didn't see them get off the train when we stopped, so they've still got to be here somewhere. You need to be looking for them right now."

"I said sit."

"Please. Listen to me. Start a cabin-by-cabin search. The victim is a man, approximately forty-five years in age, one hundred and seventy-five centi..." From the look on his guard's face, Kincaid knew the man did not believe him. "Forget it. I'll search myself."

He only made it a step toward the door before the man raised his gun again. "I have no problem shooting a killer."

"I am *not* a killer. I'm a bodyguard."

This was clearly not something the man was expecting to hear, but it wasn't enough to convince him to lower his weapon.

For half a second, Kincaid considered trying to overpower the guy. He was confident he could, but there was always a chance the man *would* pull the trigger. And if the bullet didn't hit Kincaid, it might hit the man or fly through the train's paper-thin walls and into an innocent passenger.

With a sigh, Kincaid lowered himself onto a chair.

"I know you think you're the hero here, but you're not," Kincaid said. "At least not yet."

"Let me guess. I would be a hero if I let you go, right?" The man laughed.

"No, I know you're not going to do that. But you will come off looking pretty damn good if you don't allow *anyone* to leave the train until after the police have conducted a full search."

"Because the real shooter is still onboard," the man said, obviously not believing it.

"Yes, but I'm more concerned about the man he kidnapped."

A hint of uncertainty on the man's brow.

"I was guarding one of your passengers," Kincaid said. "I was shot and he was taken." Not exactly the factual order, but close enough. "Check my gun if you don't believe me. If it's been shot recently, you'll smell the gunpowder. If you do, then you don't have to believe anything I'm saying. But if you don't, then there's at least a chance the killer isn't me. And of course, there's this." Kincaid glanced down at his unbuttoned shirt. The vest was damaged from where the bullet had hit it, and on Kincaid's skin, just above the top of the vest, were the first signs of the large bruise that was spreading across his chest. "Do you think I just shot myself?"

———

When security officer Maddox had seen the prisoner standing on top of the train, he'd been sure the man was the one who had killed Buchman, the sleeper-car conductor. But the prisoner had not acted like a killer. It would have been simple for him to escape over the other side of the train car, but instead he had given himself up.

Maddox was also troubled by the man's story that someone

had been kidnapped, and his insistence that the train be searched. Yes, it could have been what the movies called a diversion, but the prisoner appeared genuinely agitated that nothing was being done.

When Koehl, one of Maddox's fellow security officers, relieved him a few minutes later, Maddox checked the prisoner's weapon. Though he wasn't a certified expert, he'd shot enough weapons on the practice range to know what a fired gun should smell like, even hours later. The prisoner's weapon had no such smell. And there was no way the prisoner could have cleaned it well enough to eliminate the odor, in the time between when Buchman's body had been found and when Maddox and the others discovered the man on the roof. Which meant this was not the weapon that had killed the conductor.

And if this wasn't the gun, then the prisoner was possibly telling the truth about not being the killer. And if that was true, what about the rest of his story?

Maddox did not have a large security team, or he would have conducted a cabin-to-cabin search then and there. As it was, it would have to wait until the police took over.

Until then, he could at least make sure no one would be getting off the train unless he said so.

3

Though the helicopter's door had been closed for nearly thirty minutes, a bitter chill from the night air still filled the cabin.

Brunner stared at his feet, fighting the urge to look at the door through which Clarke had been pushed. The thing that disturbed the scientist most was not the act itself, or the bullet Clarke had been hit with moments before. No, the thing that had rattled Brunner to his core was that Clarke, though clearly still conscious, did not utter a sound as he flew out of the helicopter. If Brunner had been in the man's place, he would have been screaming all the way down.

This can't be happening, he thought. *None of this. It's got to be a nightmare.*

It was. Though the real kind, not the dream.

One moment he'd been sound asleep, and the next, Clarke—the man who was supposed to be one of his bodyguards—had shaken him awake.

"We've got to go," Clarke had said.

"Huh?" Brunner hadn't quite understood what the man meant. They were on a moving train. Where would they go?

"There's trouble. I need to get you to an alternate cabin. You'll be safe there."

"I...I thought I was safe *here*."

"You do as we say, remember? Let's go."

Clarke had given Brunner only enough time to put on his clothes before he hustled Brunner out the door and down the main corridor toward the next car. Just before they reached the car, Brunner sucked in a breath and stopped in his tracks. "My bag."

"What about your bag?"

"I left it in my cabin. I-I need it."

Clarke grimaced. "I'll retrieve it after I get you situated. Keep moving."

The alternate cabin was located at the front end of the next car. Clarke knocked three times on the door and someone inside opened it. Clarke pushed Brunner into the room.

There were two others present, a man and a woman, both younger than Brunner.

"He left his bag in the cabin," Clarke said.

The woman looked at Brunner. "Is it important?"

"Yes, very."

"Fine, I'll get it," Clarke said.

"You have four minutes," the woman said. "If you're not back by then, we go without you."

"Wait," Brunner said to Clarke. "Go? What is she talking about? Who are these people?"

"They're with me," Clarke told him. "Don't worry. They'll keep you safe."

If Brunner had been in his right mind at that moment, he might have picked up on the fact that Clarke had said *with me* and not *with us*, but that hadn't struck him as strange until after he was on the helicopter.

Once Clarke had left, the woman said, "We are a little tight for space here so I need you to get on the bottom bunk."

Brunner could tell that like Clarke and Kincaid, she was not a native German speaker, but her accent was different from that of his bodyguards. She sounded Eastern European.

"Uh…all right," he said, and climbed onto the bed.

Across the room, the man, who had yet to say anything, stuck a couple of suction cups onto the cabin's window. He used a cutting tool to score a line on the glass, as close to the frame as possible. When he finished, he grabbed the suction cups' handles and held on to them as the woman tapped the glass with a rubber mallet.

"What are you doing?" Brunner asked.

Neither of them responded but they didn't really need to. It was pretty clear what was up. He was just having a hard time believing it.

Two more strikes of the mallet and the glass popped free from the frame, allowing freezing air to rush inside, dropping the temperature to near zero degrees Celsius within seconds.

The man maneuvered the now detached piece of glass into the cabin and laid it on the top bunk. As soon as he was out of the way, the woman began duct-taping over the lip of glass still sticking out from the window frame.

Brunner had had enough. Despite how scared he felt, he pushed himself to the edge of the bunk and started to stand.

The woman spun around, extracted a gun from her bag, and pointed it at his head. "Lie back down, Dr. Brunner."

This was the moment he'd realized these two were probably not part of his official escort. And later, after Clarke had been shot and sent flying, Brunner was sure of it.

The other thing he was now sure of was that somewhere in the countryside ahead, death awaited him. It wouldn't be fast. Rather, his end would come only after his kidnappers had wrung from him every detail of what he'd created. He would try to resist, but knew he wouldn't last long. He wasn't built that way.

The woman looked out the side window of the helicopter and said something into the headset she was wearing. A moment later, the man looked, too. Without a headset of his own, Brunner had no idea what was happening. But when the helicopter descended, the subject of their discussion became clear.

This was it. Below them was the spot where he would take his last breath.

As soon as the helicopter touched down, the woman said, "Do not move until I tell you to."

His throat dry, Brunner could only answer with a nod.

The door slid to the side and two men climbed out, half of the group that had been in the passenger cabin when Brunner was hauled in. Straight out from the door was a windowless concrete building, the wall broken only by a set of closed double doors. The two men outside scanned the area with their rifles ready. A few seconds later, one of them looked back inside and said something in a language Brunner didn't understand.

"Stand up," the woman said.

Brunner released the harness and rose.

"Do not try to fight," she said. "Do not try to run. You will not succeed."

It was a needless warning.

The remaining two men from the original group of four exited.

"Now you, Dr. Brunner," the woman said.

Brunner could feel his hands shaking as he walked to the doorway.

Two men stood on the ground by the door. As Brunner leaned down to jump off, they grabbed his arms and helped him down. Apparently they were there for more than assisting with his exit, as they didn't let go of him once his feet touched the ground.

A wide strip of grass ran off to either side of the cement area in front of the building, with more grass extending behind the structure. Past the building, where the grass ended, a forest grew. Brunner looked over his shoulders, first left then right. A road on the other side of the helicopter ran parallel to the front of the building.

No, not a road. A runway. And on the other side of this, more grass and then trees again.

There was not another building or even a light in sight.

Someone pushed him in the back.

"Walk," the woman said.

They moved as a group to the building, where one of the men unlocked the door.

Brunner was led to a small, windowless room that contained a cot and a bucket and nothing else. After pushing him inside, one of his captors slammed the door shut and engaged the lock.

Brunner turned back and pounded against the door. "What's going on? You can't just leave me here like this! Please, let me go!"

Not a sound from the other side.

"Please," he shouted. "Please!"

No one answered.

4

The NightJet had been instructed to bypass its scheduled stop at Schwarzach-St. Veit Bahnhof and proceed directly to the larger town of Bischofshofen.

Nearing the station, Maddox saw the flashing lights of at least a dozen police cars parked along the road, the officers waiting on the platform.

Even before the train came to a stop, the officers began boarding. Maddox met them in the middle of the front sleeping car, where he was introduced to the lead officer, Chief Inspector Staheli.

"Where is the crime scene?" the chief inspector asked.

"Two cars down. I'll show you."

They walked side by side down the corridor.

"Has anything been disturbed?" Staheli asked.

"Not since the body was discovered."

"What about the passengers in that car?"

"We've moved them out. The only person who has been in the car since then is me."

"Good. I understand you have the suspect."

"Well, yes, but…"

Staheli cocked his head. "But what?"

"I'm not sure he actually did it."

The chief inspector raised a brow. "I was given the impression you caught him with the gun."

"*A* gun. But it appears not to have been fired." Maddox explained his examination of the weapon.

The chief inspector frowned. "You should not have touched it."

"I didn't. I used one of our cloth napkins. But gun aside, there's the fact that the man in custody has also been shot."

"Excuse me?"

"He's wearing a bulletproof vest. The bullet hit him in the chest."

"And why would he be wearing a bulletproof vest?"

"He claims to be a bodyguard, sir."

"A bodyguard? What else has this *bodyguard* told you?"

Maddox relayed the suspect's story about the kidnapping and the request for a cabin-to-cabin search.

"Have you done it?"

"I don't have that kind of manpower, sir."

The inspector divided his men into four groups. The first to check the sleeper cars, the second to check the seated cabins, the third to make sure no one left the train, and the last and smallest group to accompany him to the suspect.

Maddox ended up with the sleeper car group, as he had a master key in case any of the cabins were locked.

They started at the front of the first car and worked their way back, waking up passengers who hadn't even realized anything had happened. When the officers found nothing unusual in the front car, they moved to the next one.

The first cabin there was number 2. When one of the officers knocked, no one answered.

"You're sure this one's occupied?" the officer asked Maddox.

"It's supposed to be."

The officer rapped again. "Police inspection. Please open the door."

Not a sound from inside.

The officer gave it a few more seconds before nodding at Maddox, who unlocked the door and moved out of the way.

The instant the officer opened the door, Maddox knew something was wrong. The room was freezing. Peeking over the officer's shoulder, he saw the glass had been removed from the window.

"No one's here," the officer said. He looked back at Maddox and motioned for him to come inside, then pointed at the window. "Was it like that before?"

"Absolutely not." Though Maddox had not been responsible for the room checks prior to leaving Zurich, there was no way a problem like this wouldn't have been reported to him.

"Here's the glass," another officer said.

He was standing next to the bunks, looking at the top bed. On it lay a piece of glass with two suction-cup handles connected to it.

"Could someone have jumped out?" the first officer asked.

"Only if they wanted to kill themselves."

"You haven't stopped since the incident?"

"Once. For several minutes right after the body was discovered."

"Couldn't they have left then?"

"Technically, yes. But I don't think so."

"Why not?"

"Well, the, um, suspect would have seen them."

"The suspect?"

"He was…on top of the train, watching for anyone trying to leave."

The officer stared at him for a moment. "On top of the train?"

10:23 AM

Chief Inspector Martin Staheli spotted the Interpol official the moment the man stepped out of the terminal and began walking toward the tracks.

The last train had passed through the station twenty minutes earlier, and the next wasn't due for another hour, so there were few other people about. But that wasn't the reason Staheli knew the man was the person he'd been told to expect.

It was the way the official walked, with a hint of arrogance as his gaze swept back and forth, taking in everything.

"I think our guest has arrived," the chief inspector said.

Inspector Hahn, who'd been standing next to Staheli, looked out the window.

As expected, the new arrival continued across the tracks toward the two Nightjet sleeper cars. The cars had been left behind so the police could conduct their investigation while the rest of the train continued on its way to Graz.

Though Staheli lost sight of the man as the official neared the cars, he could hear the muffled tones of a conversation outside the doors, where the Interpol man was stopped by the officer guarding the entrance. A few moments later, the official entered from the front end of the car.

"I'm looking for Chief Inspector Staheli."

"I'm Staheli."

The official strode down the hall and extended his hand. "Senior Inspector Schwartz, Interpol."

Staheli shook the man's hand. "You're early."

"Not as much traffic as I'd anticipated."

Staheli motioned to his assistant. "This is Inspector Hahn."

"Good to meet you," Schwartz said as he shook with Hahn. He then nodded at a damp, dark stain in the middle of the corridor behind Staheli. "Is that where it happened?"

"It is," Staheli said.

"May I?"

"Of course."

Schwartz approached the bloodstain and kneeled beside it.

After staring at the spot for a moment, he looked left and right. When he finally stood, he said, "And the man you captured—where was he?"

"They found him on top of the train," Hahn said.

"I mean when the shooting occurred."

Hahn glanced at Staheli, who nodded for him to continue.

"Witnesses indicate he was down there." Hahn pointed at the alcove.

Schwartz looked into the passageway toward cabins 14 and 16. "At the top or bottom?"

"The bottom. He was on the floor when the witnesses first arrived."

Schwartz stepped over to the alcove and looked down. "The report I saw said he was wearing a bulletproof vest."

"That's correct."

He studied the alcove again before saying, "Do you know if he was shot at the top and fell? Or was he at the bottom when he was hit?"

"At the bottom."

"Why?"

Hahn's brow furrowed. "Why?"

"Yes. Why would he have been down there when he was shot?"

"Ah. One of the conductors confirmed he was booked in cabin 14. That would be the one on the left. The cabin on the right is the one the missing man was staying in."

Schwartz nodded to himself and descended the stairs. Staheli and Hahn shared a look, then moved to the opening to see what the senior inspector was doing.

Schwartz studied the small area outside the doors, paying particular attention to the wall separating the two entrances.

Nearly a minute passed before he looked up at them and asked, "Have the rooms been processed?"

"Of course," Hahn said. "The crime scene technicians went over everything this morning."

"Then may I have a look?"

Hahn deferred to Staheli, who said, "By all means."

Schwartz disappeared into cabin 14.

Staheli was both annoyed and insulted by Interpol's intrusion. Why the organization was interested in this case, he had no idea. If the missing man had really been kidnapped as the suspected claimed, then every second counted, and playing tour guide to Schwartz was wasting precious time.

Hahn gave Staheli a concerned yet curious look, but Staheli said nothing.

Schwartz stepped out of the cabin a few seconds later, nodded to the two men, and pointed at cabin 16.

Staheli motioned for him to go ahead.

The Interpol official took even less time inside than he had in the other cabin, and soon rejoined Staheli and Hahn in the corridor.

"Did you find anything in either room?" Schwartz asked.

"Nothing in cabin fourteen," Hahn said. "But we did recover a small duffel bag in sixteen."

Schwartz raised an eyebrow. "What did it contain?"

"Clothes, toiletries, some medication, a thumb drive."

"What kind of medication?"

Hahn pulled out a notepad and consulted it. "Naratriptan."

"That's for migraines, isn't it?"

"I don't know. We haven't checked yet."

"You haven't checked?"

"We have not had the time," Staheli said.

"Of course," Schwartz said sympathetically. "Do you know the missing man's name?"

"Richard Meyer."

"Any theories what happened to Herr Meyer?"

"Nothing yet."

"Could he have hidden in another part of the train and perhaps is in Graz now?"

"He is *not* in Graz," Staheli said. "We conducted a thorough search before the train got underway again. It is more likely he jumped."

Schwartz cocked his head. "You have reason to believe this?"

"A window is missing from one of the cabins."

"Missing?"

"It was cut out after the train left Zurich."

"That sounds like a very good reason to believe he jumped. May I see it?"

Staheli tensed, his patience level nearing its limit. "Follow me."

He led Schwartz into the other car and down to cabin 2, Hahn trailing them.

"Please," Staheli said, motioning for his guest to enter first.

Schwartz stepped inside and paused, his gaze on the window.

Staheli stepped in behind him and pointed at the top bunk. "The glass is there."

Schwartz looked over, then scanned the rest of the room. "Did you find anything else in here?"

"No."

"What about fingerprints?"

"One set, around the lower bunk and again by the window."

"Have they been matched to the missing man?"

"We have put in a request for his prints but are still waiting for them to arrive."

Schwartz made a closer inspection of the window, and then stuck his head outside. He looked downward first, no doubt judging the distance to the ground. It was the same thing Staheli had done when he was shown the room. The drop was a bit more than two meters, high enough that one would have to be careful not to wrench an ankle, but otherwise doable—as long as the train wasn't going faster than a crawl.

Schwartz twisted around to look toward the roof. Staheli had done that also. At the time, he'd wondered if the window had been used to access the roof. But there were no handholds or anything else someone could have used to scale the distance up.

The Interpol man started to pull his head back in but then stopped, his eyes on the duct tape covering the glass. He reached out and plucked something caught at the edge.

"What is it?" Staheli asked.

Schwartz looked at the item, and lowered his hand outside below the window frame for a second before ducking back inside. "It was just part of a leaf. Probably kicked up by the train." He smiled. "If you don't mind, I'd like to see the suspect now."

———

Kincaid sat at the table, eyes closed. The cuffs around his wrists were attached to a chain connected to the table, preventing him from moving his arms more than a dozen centimeters or so in any direction.

He probably could have broken free, but he hadn't even tested the chain's strength. Instead he stared across the room, his mind a storm of anger and self-recrimination.

He had lost his cargo.

That had never happened before. His reputation was going to take a big hit for this, but at the moment he didn't care about what others thought.

At first, all he could think about was, what if Brunner was dead? That would be the ultimate disaster. The man had been Kincaid's responsibility, and blame for the man's death would rightly fall on Kincaid's shoulders. He would be as guilty as whoever actually took the scientist's life. And he would feel it in his soul until the day he, too, left this earth.

Eventually, he focused on the other big issue on his mind.

Clarke.

To be betrayed by one's partner, even a temporary one, was the most ruthless thing that could happen to an operative. If it took the rest of Kincaid's life, he would find the bastard and exact his revenge. He also needed to have a very pointed conversation with Misty. She had paired him with Clarke. How could she not have known Clarke couldn't be trusted?

The questions kept coming, all with no answers.

He opened his eyes and looked around.

The windowless room the police had stowed him in had a single steel door straight across from the table, and two cameras mounted to the ceiling, one in front of him and one behind. The only pieces of furniture were the table and two chairs.

He'd been here since they'd transported him from the train. That had been…what? Six hours ago, give or take?

A while ago, an officer had brought him a bottle of water. Desperate to get ahold of Misty, Kincaid had asked the man if he could make a phone call. Not to confront her about Clarke yet, but to let her know Brunner had been taken so she could start looking for him. Every hour that passed, the chances of a successful rescue decreased dramatically. But the officer had acted like he hadn't even heard the question and left without saying a word.

Kincaid hadn't had a visitor since.

There was a little less than a swallow left in the bottle now. He picked it up and leaned forward so he could raise it to his lips.

As the water trickled down his throat, he started to think about Clarke again. How the hell had the asshole pulled it off? No way he could have done it alone. There must have been someone else on the train. Someone who—

"I'm so sorry." The words spoken first in German and then English, by the woman who had squeezed past Kincaid at their stop in Innsbruck.

He hadn't seen her or her companion when he'd done the walk-through, and had been coming back to warn Clarke that the couple might be trouble. But then his partner had shot him, and thoughts of the other two had passed from Kincaid's head.

He didn't know for sure, but Kincaid's gut was telling him the couple had assisted in the kidnapping. Before Kincaid had even started his walk-through after the Innsbruck stop, Clarke had no doubt messaged his buddies, letting them know Kincaid was coming. They'd probably hid in a bathroom until Kincaid had passed by, then made their way to help the traitor.

Kincaid concentrated on his memory of the pair, wanting to sear their faces into his mind. Over and over, he played the scene of them passing by, noting nose width and hair color and the small mole beside the man's left eye.

He was so focused on this that it took him a second to realize the door to the room had opened.

He blinked, then watched Chief Inspector Staheli—the police officer who'd interviewed him on the train—entered, followed by a man Kincaid had never seen before. The new guy had a lean chiseled face, short dark brown hair. Though he looked like he was in his mid- to late 30s, his face had a sense of experience that made Kincaid think the man was closer to his mid-40s.

Staheli and his companion approached the table.

"This is Senior Inspector Schwartz from Interpol," Staheli said. "He has a few questions he would like to ask you."

Kincaid looked at Schwartz but remained silent.

The man slid the other chair out from the table and sat down. "I understand you speak German."

"I do."

"Then you do not mind if we continue in it?"

"That's fine."

"Your name is Oscar Johnson?"

"Uh-huh," Kincaid said. Johnson was the name on the passport he was using.

"Inspector Staheli tells me you claim to be a bodyguard?"

"I don't claim anything. I am."

"And that the passenger in cabin sixteen, Richard Meyer, was the person you were supposedly guarding." Meyer was the alias Kincaid had given Brunner for the trip.

"Not supposedly. Was."

Schwartz flashed a humorless smile. "It is your story that Herr Meyer was kidnapped."

"It's not a stor—" Kincaid bit back his anger. "Look, you need to have people looking for—"

"And that the kidnapper is the one who shot the conductor?"

Kincaid took a deep breath. "And me."

"That's right. You were shot, too. May I have a look?"

"Oh, yeah, I'd be happy to show you but…" Kincaid lifted his hands as far as he could off the table, which wasn't much. "Sorry."

Schwartz stood up. "Would you mind if I…?" He mimed unbuttoning Kincaid's shirt.

"Whatever floats your boat," Kincaid muttered in English.

"I'm sorry?"

In German, Kincaid said, "Sure. Go ahead."

Schwartz moved around the table, leaned down, unbuttoned Kincaid's shirt, and loosened the bulletproof vest underneath. As he did, he whispered in English in a voice only loud enough for Kincaid to hear, "Misty sent me." Schwartz then proceeded to examine the bruise on Kincaid's chest. "That looks like it hurts. Good thing you were wearing protection, yes?"

"Yeah. Good thing."

Schwartz returned to his chair and asked several more questions, most of which were variations of those Staheli had asked earlier. Kincaid answered with just the right amount of frustration, to convey an annoyance he no longer felt.

Finally, Schwartz stood up. "Thank you for your time, Herr Johnson."

The man turned and he and Staheli exited the room, closing the door behind them.

Kincaid stared after them but kept his relief from showing on his face. In case anyone was watching on the cameras.

Outside the holding cell, Staheli turned to Schwartz. "Unless there is anything else, my staff and I need to get back to work. We appreciate Interpol's interest in this case, and I will gladly keep you informed of any progress."

Schwartz smiled politely. "Is there someplace we can talk privately?"

Staheli grimaced. He could little afford to give the inspector more time, but he wasn't about to start a rift with Interpol. At least not yet. So he nodded and led Schwartz through the station to his private office.

"Do you mind?" Schwartz said, a hand on the door.

"If you feel it is necessary," Staheli said.

Schwartz closed the door and sat in the guest seat in front of the desk. "I apologize for any inconvenience I've caused. I know your job is hard enough without someone like me getting in your way. Unfortunately, Chief Inspector, this case is considerably more...complex than you realize. The name of the man you are holding is not Oscar Johnson."

Staheli frowned. "Then what is it?"

"I'm afraid I can't tell you that."

"Excuse me?"

"What I *can* tell you, and this must not leave your office, is that Herr Johnson is a British police officer."

"A *police* officer?" Staheli said.

"He's been working undercover on a joint operation between British, German, and Dutch law enforcement, coordinated through Interpol."

Staheli stared at him, waiting for the punch line, but Schwartz's expression didn't crack. "You're serious."

"I am."

"Undercover doing what?"

"That is also something I cannot disclose."

"What about all the questions you asked him? Was that only an act?"

"It was."

"Why not just—"

"I assume you had officers watching the feeds from the cameras in the room?"

"It is standard procedure."

"*That* is the reason for my act. It is vitally important that we confine the truth to as few people as possible. I had to obtain special permission just to let you in on it."

"And I'm supposed to take your word for it?"

"Of course not. You should call my office and double-check with them. I'm sure you have Interpol's number."

That sounded like a damn good idea to Staheli. He reached for his phone.

"But before you make the call," Schwartz said, "there's one other thing you'll want to confirm."

Staheli's hand rested on the receiver. "What would that be?"

"That Herr Johnson will be leaving with me."

"*What?*"

"You will tell your colleagues that he is suspected of involvement in several other crimes, and that I am taking him to Vienna for further questioning." Schwartz leaned back in his chair. "Go ahead, make the call."

Staheli stared at him, dumbfounded. After a moment, he located the contact number for Interpol, picked up his desk phone, and dialed.

After the Interpol operator answered, Staheli said, "This is Chief Inspector Staheli of the Austrian Federal Police. I'm calling about one of your senior inspectors, surname Schwartz, Christian name—" He glanced at Schwartz.

"Johann."

"Johann," Staheli said into the phone. "I would like to speak to his supervisor."

"One moment." After placing him on hold for several seconds, the operator came back on. "His supervisor is Leonard Hendricks, head of investigations. I'll put you through."

A secretary answered, and Staheli was put on hold again. Finally Hendricks came on the line.

After Staheli explained what Schwartz had told him, Hendricks said, "Yes? And is there a problem?"

"So, he does work for you?"

"Of course he does."

"Well, I-I can't just let him take the prisoner without some sort of documentation."

Across the desk, Schwartz pulled a folded piece of paper from inside his jacket and put it in front of Staheli. "Here's your copy of the order."

Staheli opened it. It was a transfer document, authorizing the release of the suspect to Schwartz.

"I…I don't know. I mean—"

"I understand your caution, Chief Inspector," Hendricks said. "If you feel the need for further confirmation, please call *Oberstleutnant* König's office in Vienna. He has been briefed on the situation and can answer any other questions you may have."

König was a high-ranking official within the Austrian Federal Police, and oversaw Staheli's district.

"I will. Thank you."

Not surprisingly, the subsequent call to Vienna confirmed everything.

When Staheli hung up, he looked at Schwartz, annoyed, but knowing there was nothing he could do. "I guess he's all yours."

A pair of officers put the still handcuffed Kincaid in the rear of Inspector Schwartz's car. A thick Plexiglas partition separated the backseat from the front. Though there were handles inside the rear doors, Kincaid had no doubt they didn't work.

After saying goodbye to a sullen Inspector Staheli, Schwartz tossed what looked like Brunner's travel bag into the front passenger seat, climbed behind the wheel, and pulled onto the street.

Once the police station was out of sight, Kincaid leaned toward the partition. "I'm Darius Kincaid."

The man glanced in the mirror. "Quinn."

Kincaid stared back. "*Jonathan* Quinn?"

"That's me."

"No shit?"

"No shit."

Quinn was a legend in the secret world. But given that his specialty was body removal, he wasn't someone with whom Kincaid would typically cross paths.

"So, Mr. Quinn, do you think we can get these cuffs off me?"

5

Misty Blake, head of the Office, had been monitoring the situation in Central Europe since the moment Kincaid and Clarke obtained the package and set off on their journey to Hamburg. She always did this when one of her missions was in active mode. This allowed her to respond quickly if something went awry.

The package on this particular mission—a scientist named Thomas Brunner—was apparently the target of several different organizations and governments, each wanting to procure Brunner's services for itself. The information she'd been given indicated that for the last eighteen months, Brunner had been voluntarily confined to a facility in Zurich owned by his employers, a company named Ferber-Rae LTD. Ferber-Rae had gone to great expense to increase the security on the floor where Brunner worked and to create a private suite for him. Nothing in the brief said why Brunner had agreed to this arrangement, or even why the confinement was necessary. But agree to it Brunner had.

The only other thing she'd been told about the scientist was that he was a rising star at the company. The reason was never mentioned.

As for the company itself, Ferber-Rae had its hands in all sorts of things, such as genetics, alternative energy, information systems, and robotics.

The reason for Brunner's trip to Hamburg had to do with a presentation he was to give to a small, select group of international scientists. Like the nature of Brunner's work, the specifics of the presentation were not disclosed. The only thing that mattered was that Misty's team needed to get Brunner to Hamburg on time and unmolested.

The assignment came to the Office via the CIA, after the agency had received the request from FIS, Swiss Federal Intelligence Service. Misty and Orlando—Misty's unofficial co-head of the Office—had brainstormed several ideas before coming up with a plan they were happy with. To execute it, Misty had hired a seasoned personnel courier named Darius Kincaid. He'd worked with the Office back when Peter was in charge, and Kincaid had always been reliable and efficient. But the Brunner job required two escorts, and unfortunately the handful of freelancers Kincaid usually worked with weren't available.

Misty had dived back into the Office's archives and found Clarke's name. She didn't remember working with him directly, but he appeared to have an acceptable service record, and had done a couple of jobs similar to this one. She'd made a few inquiries to confirm his current skill level, and was told he was competent and easy to work with. So, she'd hired him.

The fact Kincaid had never done a job with Clarke wasn't an issue. Being paired with an operative for the first time was par for the course in their world. And there was no reason to think the Brunner job, if executed correctly, wouldn't go off without a hitch.

Misty and Orlando's plan had kicked off an hour before Kincaid and Clarke took possession of their cargo, when several reliable witnesses saw someone matching Brunner's description get into an armored truck at Ferber-Rae's headquarters. The vehicle left Zurich on a straight shot to Hamburg, escorted by two sedans full of security personnel.

The decoy caravan was well out of town by the time Kincaid

and Clarke boarded the train with the real Brunner. Once they reached Graz, they would catch a private jet the rest of the way to Hamburg.

At least that's what was supposed to happen.

A few hours into the train ride, Misty's monitoring software dinged with an urgent message. An alert had been issued by Austrian police concerning a shooting on the Nightjet train from Zurich to Graz.

Knowing there were no coincidences in her business, Misty immediately realized the incident had something to do with her team and she'd put in a call to Quinn. He had just finished a body removal operation in Brussels but his plane for home hadn't left yet, so she rerouted him east to find out what had happened.

Two hours later, one of her data specialists retrieved a preliminary police report from the Austrian town of Bischofshofen. She learned that Oscar Johnson—Kincaid—was being held by the police on suspicion of murder, and Richard Meyer—Brunner—was missing. There was no mention of Felix Vintner, the name Clarke was traveling under.

She gave Quinn the information, and together they came up with a strategy that necessitated Misty calling in a favor from a contact at Interpol.

It was just after six a.m. when her computer pinged with an incoming video call. She clicked ACCEPT and a window opened, showing an image from inside a car. On the right of the frame was Quinn, and on the left Kincaid.

The bodyguard gave her a rundown of what had happened.

The news that Clarke had been involved in the kidnapping hit her hard. Clearly she had missed something when she did his background check. She would have to go back over his record with a fine-toothed comb and see where the error had occurred.

That, however, would have to wait.

"Quinn, I need you to find Brunner. Fast."

"Is that an official assignment?" Quinn asked.

"Yes," she said. "One hundred and fifty percent of normal rate. Retroactive to when I called you this morning."

At thirty thousand dollars a week with a two-week minimum, Quinn was one of the more expensive freelancers out there. But he never failed to earn every penny.

"Tentative acceptance," he said.

"Tentative?"

"I'd like to know a little bit more about what I might be getting into before I officially commit."

"Fair enough."

"Any idea who might have taken him?"

"Several possibilities, including a few of the usuals: the Russians, the Chinese, Tear-Dak, Yimity."

"That's a pretty diverse group. What's so important about this guy that they would all want him?"

"He does something science related. That's all I know."

"I'm going to need a little more than that. Maybe I should contact the client directly. It would save some time."

Misty frowned. "I...haven't told them about the kidnapping yet."

Quinn stared at his phone for a moment. "Why not?"

"I'm hoping there's a chance we can recover Brunner before the delivery deadline this evening."

"He could be hundreds of miles from here already," Kincaid said. "I'd say the chances of finding him before tonight are close to zero."

"Thousands of miles," Quinn said. "I found rope fibers outside the window of the train compartment they escaped from, along the top edge. I don't think they jumped to the ground. I think they were hoisted onto a helicopter. We can't keep the client in the dark any longer."

She took a deep breath. "I'll call him, but I'm not sure how much I can get out of him."

"Then maybe I should pay him a visit. I'm sure I could convince him to be a little more forthcoming in person."

"That's probably a good idea. Head that way. If he does give me everything we need, I'll let you know and you can redirect based on that. Ferber-Rae's headquarters are in Zurich. The man you want is Stefan Ferber. He's head of the company. I'll text you the address."

"I met the guy," Kincaid said. "He was with Brunner when Clarke and I picked him up. I'll go with you."

"Absolutely not," Misty said. "You're to catch the first flight to DC and report to me for debriefing. Quinn, take him to the nearest airport and then proceed to Zurich."

"That's ridiculous! I can do a lot more—"

"Buddy, take it down a notch," Quinn said, then looked at the phone again. "Misty, correct me if I'm wrong, but our priority is to find Brunner, right?"

"It is," Misty said.

"Then doesn't it make sense to use every asset available? I'm not taking sides, but I think the smart thing is for Kincaid to stay with me for now."

Misty glared from the screen and said in a flat voice, "Mr. Kincaid, could you give us a moment, please?"

Kincaid grimaced, but nodded and climbed out of the car.

"Can he hear us?" Misty asked after she heard the door close.

Quinn turned the camera so she could see Kincaid walking away.

When he refocused the lens on himself, she said, "I'd appreciate it if you didn't contradict me in front of others."

"I was merely offering what I think is the smarter play here." He paused, then let a small smile slip into his stern expression. "Look, I realize someone needs to pay for what happened, and since Kincaid was there, he's the logical choice. But if we really want to find Brunner, he can help. He's met Ferber before. He'll have a read on him that I won't have. He may catch something I don't."

"He also lost his cargo."

"Because a man he's never worked with double-crossed him."

He paused. "If you really want him back, I'll send him back. It's up to you."

AUSTRIA

Quinn waited, watching Misty on his phone's screen.

She pinched the bridge of her nose and rubbed her fingers across her eyes. When she looked up again, she said, "Does this mean you're agreeing to officially take the job?"

He snorted. "I guess it does."

"Then fine. He can stay with you. For now. But after you talk to Ferber, I want him back here."

"Thanks," he said. "Listen, before you contact Ferber, can you call Orlando and tell her to send the team right away? The sooner everyone gets here, the better chance we'll have at finding your scientist."

"I'll call her right now."

"Thanks, Misty."

Quinn disconnected the call, then tapped the horn twice and watched Kincaid jog back to the car.

When the bodyguard was once more in the front passenger seat, he said, "Well?"

"Buckle in. We've got a long drive ahead of us."

SAN FRANCISCO

Orlando reread the specs she'd just entered into the order form and cursed. She'd input the diameter right, but she'd misplaced the decimal point by one position on the strength of the lens.

She corrected the error and clicked on the PLACE MY ORDER button. The glass discs were for the next-gen gooseneck micro-camera lenses she was building. The ones she and the team currently used were more than adequate, but she'd never been completely happy with their telephoto capabilities. When her order arrived, that problem would be solved.

She stretched and looked at the clock—3:17 a.m.

Crap.

She'd really been hoping to get to bed earlier. Her daughter would likely be up at the crack of dawn. Of course, Mrs. Vo would be happy to take care of Claire, but Orlando should be doing it herself.

She gave her inbox one last check and closed the app. As she started to stand, her computer bonged with an incoming video call.

She looked back at the screen, thinking it had to be Quinn calling from Europe. But the name in the ID window was Misty.

Orlando clicked ACCEPT, and Misty appeared on the screen.

"Morning," Orlando said.

"Oh, good," Misty said. "I was afraid you might be asleep."

"I was just heading to bed now."

"I don't think so."

Sitting back down, Orlando said, "What's going on?"

"Quinn won't be coming back today."

Orlando tensed. "Did something happen?"

"Not with Quinn, no. There was a problem on the Ferber-Rae project."

"He's not working the Ferber-Rae project."

"He is now." Misty brought Orlando up to speed, then said, "He wants you to send the team out to him right away."

"All right, I'll get them moving. Keep me updated on any changes."

"I will."

Orlando called Daeng first.

"Are you free?" she asked.

"We are all as free as we let ourselves be."

"Did you just smoke a blunt or something?"

He laughed. "I take it we have a job."

"We do."

"Where and when do you need me?"

"Zurich, as soon as you can get there. I'll update you with a specific destination when you arrive. Do you want to travel with Jar? I'm going to call her next."

"I'm, um, not in Thailand at the moment."

"Oh, really? Where are you?"

"Australia."

"Weren't you just there a few weeks ago?"

"I may have been."

She felt the urge to probe further but there was no time. "Get the next flight. I'll see you in Switzerland."

"Sounds like fun."

Orlando called Jar next.

The young Thai woman answered with her typical "Yes?"

"We've got a job. I need you in Zurich right away."

"I do not have a visa for Switzerland."

"I'll take care of it and text you with instructions."

"Okay."

The line went dead. Jar was a woman of few words.

Call number three was to Nate.

"Unless you're going to tell me I won the lotto, call back after the sun's up," he answered sleepily.

"We've got a job."

No response.

"Nate?"

Dead air for a moment, then a sigh, and, "I'm here."

"Did you hear me?"

"I heard you."

"Are you available?"

It wasn't long ago that she wouldn't have even asked the question. Any job Quinn and Orlando worked, Nate worked, too.

But a lot had changed since Liz had died. She had been both Nate's girlfriend and Quinn's sister. For a while it had looked like the two men would never work together again. Thankfully, over the summer, they had ironed out their differences—for the most part—and now Nate was back in the fold.

Sort of. Occasionally Nate would pass on a job, saying he had other things to deal with.

"Yeah. I guess. Where?"

"Zurich."

"Zurich? Like Europe Zurich?"

"Is there another one?"

"Probably," he said. "Can I reconsider my earlier response?"

"No."

"Figures. I suppose I need to be there yesterday?"

"You suppose correctly."

"You realize the first flights out won't leave until the morning."

"It is morning."

"You know what I mean."

"I do. Which means you have plenty of time to make sure you're on the very first one."

"Lucky me."

Orlando next booked a flight for herself, leaving SFO in three hours, and arranged for a safe house in Zurich, in case the team would be staying there for more than a day. She also sent a message to an equipment supplier she knew in the city, alerting him that she and the team might need to pick up a few items in the next day or two.

With the logistics work completed, she retrieved her prepacked go-bag from the bedroom, added her laptop and a few other benign-looking electronics, and set the bag at the top of the stairs. She then tiptoed into her and Quinn's fifteen-month-old daughter's room.

Claire was sound asleep in her crib. Orlando adjusted her blanket and kissed her lightly on the forehead. "Love you, sweetheart," she whispered.

She left as quietly as she entered and let herself into her son Garrett's room, where she knelt next to his bed. He was fourteen now, so she couldn't leave without letting him know. "Garrett. Wake up, honey."

His eyes popped open. "What's wrong?"

She hated that he asked that. But he'd been exposed to more than a little of her and Quinn's world, and had even proved brave and resourceful when he and his sister had been kidnapped the previous winter. Now he was always on guard.

"Nothing's wrong, honey. I have to go away on business for a little while, that's all."

"Oh. Okay." He rubbed one of his eyes. "With Quinn?"

She nodded. "I'll be meeting up with him."

"Will it be dangerous?"

Before last January, she would have automatically answered no. But it was best not to lie to him anymore. At least, not too much. "No more than usual, I would think. Hopefully less than that."

"How long will you be gone?"

"Not sure yet. But I'll check in with you every day, okay?"

"Okay."

"Promise me you'll take care of your sister."

"I will."

"And make sure Mr. Vo doesn't sneak her any sweets."

"I'll do my best, but if he does it when I'm at school, it's not my fault."

"I know." She hugged and kissed him on the cheek. "I love you."

"Love you, too, Mom."

"Go back to sleep. We'll be home as soon as we can."

She carried her bag downstairs and knocked on the door to Mr. and Mrs. Vo's room. The Vos were an older Vietnamese couple who had worked for Orlando since Garrett had been only a few years older than Claire was now. They were, in all things but blood, part of the family. They took care of the household and when Orlando was gone, which was often, they watched the kids.

After a few seconds, Mrs. Vo opened the door, wearing the

lavender robe Orlando and Quinn had given her for Christmas the year before.

"Business trip, I'm afraid," Orlando said.

Mrs. Vo stepped out of the room and shut the door. "Let me get you something to eat."

She shuffled past Orlando on her way to the kitchen.

"That's okay," Orlando said. "I'm not hungry."

Without stopping, Mrs. Vo waved a dismissive hand in the air.

Orlando followed her down the hall into the kitchen, where Mrs. Vo had already started pulling things out of the refrigerator.

"Really, it's not necessary," Orlando said. "A car will be picking me up any minute."

Mrs. Vo *tsk*ed the comments away and turned on one of the stove's burners. After putting a pan over the flames, she began warming up some spring rolls in the microwave. "I can warm up the chili if you'd like."

In addition to being a master of Vietnamese cuisine, Mrs. Vo had also learned how to cook many Western dishes, including a pretty amazing version of chili.

"I don't think the other passengers would appreciate it too much," Orlando said. "The spring rolls will be more than enough."

Mrs. Vo looked at her and frowned. "Not enough. I make you peanut butter sandwich."

She opened a cupboard and pulled out a jar of peanut butter.

Orlando wanted to tell her that having peanut breath might be just as bad, but this wasn't even close to the first time they'd had conversations like this, and she knew it was a fight she would never win.

So instead she said, "Thank you," and checked her Uber app to see how far away her driver was.

"How long you gone?" Mrs. Vo asked while she worked.

"Not sure. Hopefully only a few days, but it could be a week or so. I'll let you know when I have a better idea."

"Not forget, Halloween coming."

Quinn had bought a cute Captain Marvel outfit for Claire, and he and Orlando had planned to take their daughter out for her first trick-or-treating.

"I won't. I'm sure we'll be back before then."

"Good."

By the time Orlando's car arrived, Mrs. Vo had packed the spring rolls and sandwich into two food containers and put them in a well-used paper bag for Orlando to carry.

Orlando gave her a hug and went out to her ride.

"You like peanut butter sandwiches?" she asked the driver as he pulled away from the curb.

"Uh, sure."

She leaned forward and put the container with the sandwich on the passenger seat. "All yours."

The spring rolls, on the other hand, she kept.

6

SWITZERLAND

Quinn and Kincaid reached the outskirts of Zurich as the sun was setting and made their way toward Ferber-Rae's headquarters. A light dusting of snow lay over most everything, though the roads were clear.

Misty had been trying to get ahold of Stefan Ferber all day, but he'd apparently been bogged down in meetings. She'd said she'd tried to convey the urgency of her call, but wasn't about to share with his underlings the reason she needed to speak to him, so she was still waiting for Ferber to call back. It looked like it was up to Quinn to get the man's attention.

"What's that?" Kincaid asked as they neared their destination.

Ahead, rising above the buildings, was a yellowish shimmer.

Before Quinn could answer, a fire truck with lights flashing turned onto the road ahead of them and raced toward the glow.

Quinn glanced at the GPS map on the dash. The location of Ferber-Rae's headquarters appeared to be extremely close to the truck's destination.

About four hundred meters in front of them, he spotted a police barricade spanning the street.

"I don't like this," Kincaid said.

Quinn turned onto a side road and parked at the curb.

"Stay here," he said.

"No way. I want to know what's going on."

Quinn locked eyes with him. "You're only here because of me. Remember that. We do things the way I say we do them, or you can go to the airport and head back to the States right now. Your call."

Kincaid shifted uncomfortably in his seat. "I'll stay."

"Smart."

Quinn exited the car, pulled on his overcoat, and walked back to the main road.

One of the officers manning the barricade stepped forward as Quinn neared. "I'm sorry, sir. You can't go through this way."

Quinn pulled out his Interpol ID. "Senior Inspector Schwartz, Interpol. I believe I'm expected."

"One moment."

The officer walked over and conferred with an older colleague, who then approached Quinn.

"May I see your ID, please?" the man said.

Quinn handed it to him.

The older officer moved a few meters away and spoke into a walkie-talkie.

"Interpol?" someone on the other end of the radio said. "What does he want?"

"He said he's expected."

"I don't know anything about it."

Quinn caught the police officer's attention. "Tell him I'm on the terrorist task force. And that he can call my supervisor if he has any questions."

The officer relayed the information.

"I don't have time to—" A pause, then, "Send him in. *Straight* to me."

The officer returned and handed Quinn his ID. "Go down to the end of the block and turn right. You'll find Major Mettler on the right side, at the command station."

"Thank you."

Quinn squeezed through a break in the barricade and followed the officer's directions. When he rounded the corner, the answer to what had caused the glow sat before him.

Across the intersection, at the end of the next block, the entire facade of the corner building lay in piles on the road, while flames licked out of what remained of the structure. The very same building that had served as Ferber-Rae's headquarters.

"Son of a bitch," Quinn muttered.

An explosion. Nothing else could have done this kind of damage.

Given the type of work Ferber-Rae was involved in, perhaps the blast had been accidental. But Quinn didn't believe that for a second. Unless he was proven wrong, he had to assume it was linked to Brunner's abduction. The events had occurred too close together for him to think otherwise.

Several fire trucks were parked along the road, and dozens of firefighters were doing whatever they could to contain the blaze. In addition, there were almost as many police officers, most gathered loosely on the sidewalk, about half a block away from the flames.

The command station, no doubt.

Staying on the other side of the street, Quinn headed toward the fire. The closer he got to the intersection, the more glass from blown-out windows lay on the ground. When he reached the corner across from the blaze, there wasn't a window left intact.

He surveyed the surrounding buildings. Right off the bat, he could see that all the major damage had been contained to Ferber-Rae's headquarters.

The second item he noted was the crater in the street directly in front of the building. Scattered around the hole were small chunks of what Quinn guessed had been the undercarriage of a vehicle. If he'd had any lingering thoughts about the blast originating from inside the structure, they were gone now.

An amateur could see what had happened. And Quinn was no amateur.

The vehicle, most likely a van, had parked in front of the building, where the bomb it carried was then detonated. The blast hadn't been as large as the one in Oklahoma City in the mid-90s, but it had been more than sufficient to destroy a good percentage of the building.

"Hey, you! Come here!"

Quinn turned and saw a cop moving into the street near the command center. He was pointing at Quinn so he walked toward the man.

"I'm Senior Inspector Schwartz, from Interpol," Quinn said. "I'm looking for—"

"Follow me," the man said, then headed back to a group of officers gathered around an older man with salt-and-pepper hair.

"...everything on that side of the road. Blum, you take—" The older man stopped and looked over at Quinn. "You the guy from Interpol?"

Quinn nodded and held out his hand. "Senior Inspector Johann Schwartz. You must be Major Mettler."

The major shook but looked less than pleased. "Herr Schwartz—"

"Inspector," Quinn corrected.

"*Inspector* Schwartz, you were told to come directly to me."

"I wanted to get a look first so I could see what we had here."

"What *we* have here is someone who shouldn't be here."

"I'm sorry?"

"Wait for me over there," Mettler said, pointing at a spot about five meters away. "And don't go anywhere."

Quinn did as instructed.

Mettler spent a few more minutes talking to his officers. When he finished, the men dispersed and the major all but marched over to Quinn.

Without preamble, Mettler said, "How did you know this is terrorism?"

"That's fairly obvious, isn't it? But I never actually said it was—"

"You told my officer you're with the terrorism task force. Did someone tell you to come here?"

"I was across the city when the explosion occurred," Quinn lied. "I knew you could use my help, so I made my way here as fast as I could."

"Did you report in?"

"Report in?"

"To your bosses at Interpol."

"To my supervisor, yes. He concurred that I should offer my assistance."

"And has he told anyone else?"

"I believe he's waiting to hear back from me first."

Mettler looked relieved. "And you're alone?"

"Yes, it's just me." Quinn narrowed his eyes. "What am I missing here?"

Mettler took a deep breath. "Our initial belief was that this was an accident, inside the building."

"But it clearly isn't."

"I realize that. But for the first twenty minutes we couldn't get close enough to know that." He looked around and then back at Quinn. "Inspector, I am going to ask for your cooperation."

"That's why I'm here."

"That's not what I mean. Officially, I've been ordered to still refer to this as an accident. There are several members of my government who haven't been informed yet. Until that happens, there is to be no mention of terrorism to anyone. Press, other governments. *Interpol.* The public is already scared enough. Once word gets out that this was planned…well, let's just say we'd like to control the situation as much as we can. I'm sure the embargo will be lifted soon, but until then, what you see here, what you hear here, stays here."

"You have my word. I won't say anything to anyone until it's public."

"Good. Thank you. Now, if you'll excuse me, I have a—"

"Are you open to suggestions?"

"I really don't have—"

"Major, I *am* on the terrorism task force. This isn't my first bombing. How many have you investigated?"

The man frowned, then nodded. "You're right. If you have suggestions, I would be glad to hear them."

Quinn liked leaders who didn't let their ego stop them from listening to others.

"First, have your men conduct a meticulous search in the street around the crater. Collect every scrap of metal or wire or anything that looks like it might be part of an electronic device. These could be parts of the bomb's triggering system. If an actual piece is located, it could prove invaluable in helping to identify who built the device. Second, gather any pieces that could be from the vehicle that contained the explosives. It's possible a serial number might be on one of them. At the very least, you should be able to determine the make of the vehicle, and from that, track down where it came from."

"We already planned to carry out a search once the fire is out, but I'll make sure everyone knows specifically to look for those items."

"Excellent."

Mettler looked toward the building. "Have you ever seen a bombing like this?"

"I have, but it's unusual. To do that much damage, the bomb needed to be substantial. But see how the surrounding buildings haven't been affected nearly as much? Typically, an explosive device of this size would have destroyed more than just that one structure."

"I've been wondering about that. Any idea why that didn't happen?"

"Yes. Whoever built it designed a delivery system through which the majority of the blast could be aimed at a specific target. This tells me that its creator is someone with a lot of experience and skill in this kind of thing. Not a lot of people would fall into that category."

Mettler stared down the street. "If this ability is so rare, wouldn't that information alone help point at who built it?"

"Maybe. But what it can definitely do is point at who *didn't* do it. For example, I think you can safely rule out any amateur home-grown organizations."

"Couldn't they have bought this bomb maker's services?"

"Something like this, they would have to have pretty deep pockets to afford it. Don't waste your time with any organization or individual who doesn't fit that profile. May I ask a few questions?"

A beat, then a nod from Mettler.

"Do you know the exact time the bomb went off?"

"Not to the second, but we do know from several witnesses that it was right before six p.m."

"The end of the business day."

"For some, yes."

"Were there still a lot of people inside?"

Mettler took a deep breath. "We believe so. It will be a while before we know the exact number."

"Ferber-Rae LTD—they are the main tenant?"

"They are the only tenant."

"Do you know if they had any high-profile guests visiting today? Maybe a government official or foreign dignitary?"

"I'm not aware of anyone like that at this point, but it's possible."

"What about Ferber-Rae management? Heads of specific departments? Company president?"

"Stefan Ferber was inside. It's his company. There's been no sign of him."

So much for getting information from the company's owner.

"Were there any threats to Ferber-Rae or one of their employees? Any advanced warning that something bad was going to happen?"

"Nothing that's been reported to us. But it's something we'll be looking into."

Quinn figured as much. A warning would have implied a desire not to kill indiscriminately. But if that had been the case, the bomber or bombers would have set off the blast in the middle of the night or on a Sunday, when fewer people would be around.

Instead, a time had been chosen when most of Ferber-Rae's employees were still in the building, ensuring extensive damage.

Down the street, the fire had finally been extinguished on one side of the building and seemed mostly under control on the other. Several firefighters disappeared into the structure through a crumbling archway. Within seconds, one of them returned, carrying an unmoving woman over a shoulder.

Two firefighters who had remained outside rushed to help. The one with the woman transferred her to them before racing back into the building. His colleagues carried the victim to an ambulance parked near where Quinn and Mettler were standing. Her face was covered in lacerations, and there was a deep, jagged cut on one of her arms. Quinn couldn't tell whether she was breathing or not.

"Excuse me," Mettler said, and hurried to the ambulance.

Quinn was tempted to follow, but there was really no more he could learn here, so he took advantage of the distraction and headed back to the barricade.

When he reached it, he saw a Mercedes parked just on the other side, lights on, engine running. The driver stood in front of his vehicle, surrounded by three officers and looking inconsolable. One moment he would say something and gesture past the road-block, and the next he seemed barely able to stand.

As Quinn passed through the gap, he nodded to the officer who'd let him in earlier.

"Thank you for your help," he said.

"You found the major?"

"I did." Quinn glanced over at the grief-stricken man in front of the sedan. "What's that all about?"

"That's Eric Ferber."

"As in Ferber-Rae?"

A nod. "His father owns the company."

"Oh." Quinn grimaced in sympathy. "Does he work there, too?"

"Yes."

"He's lucky he wasn't inside, then."

"I was thinking the same thing."

Quinn shot a hand into his pocket and triple-tapped the side button on his phone. A second later, the device rang with a faux call. "Sorry, I have to take this."

He stepped to the side and raised the phone to his ear. "Hello?"

When the cop turned away, Quinn opened his camera app and took several pictures of the younger Ferber.

Two minutes later, Quinn climbed back into his car, where he found an antsy Kincaid staring at him expectantly. Quinn told him what he'd seen.

"My god," Kincaid said.

"They haven't found him yet, but I'm pretty sure your client is dead." Quinn pulled out his phone, brought up the best picture of the grief-stricken man at the barricade, and showed it to Kincaid. "This is apparently his son."

"I never met him. Guess he looks a little like Stefan Ferber."

Quinn did a Google image search for Eric Ferber. The guy at the barricade was a match.

"Perhaps *he* can answer some of our questions," Kincaid said.

Quinn started the engine. "That's exactly what I was thinking."

"Nice spread," Kincaid said, as Quinn drove their car past the gate to the Ferber family estate outside Zurich.

After leaving the bombing site, Quinn had texted Orlando, asking her to find out where Eric Ferber lived. The fact she was sitting on a plane somewhere over North America was not a hindrance. All members of Quinn's core team had satellite-enabled phones, allowing them to stay in touch pretty much wherever they were.

Within ten minutes, she'd texted back. Eric Ferber lived on an estate on the outskirts of the city with his father, though apparently not in the same house. She provided links to a satellite image of the property, and to a *Forbes* Magazine feature story in which the property was discussed.

The photograph revealed that the two and a half meter-high wall fronting the estate extended all the way around the three hundred meters-deep property, to where it bumped against a large swath of woods at the back. The main house, used by Ferber senior, sat smack dab in the middle of the giant lot. Behind it were two smaller homes, with separate driveways leading around the big house to each. The area between the three structures was covered by a lush, well-tended garden, complete with pond and fountain. This also continued beyond the back houses to the rear fence.

In addition to the Ferber's estate, the satellite image revealed a narrow dirt road, approximately two kilometers past the property, that led from the road Quinn and Kincaid were on into the woods.

Quinn turned onto it. Once they were safely under the cover of the forest, he executed a Y turn and parked at the side of the road, the sedan now facing the way they'd come. There was little need to hide the vehicle. The satellite photo indicated the road ended a half kilometer farther on, and there were no homes in that direction. So, on a cold night like this, it was highly unlikely anyone would be heading this way.

Quinn's last task of the Brussels job had been to return his weapon, and the other specialized items he couldn't take on a plane, to the contact who had supplied them to him. Other than picking up the police vehicle he was now using, he hadn't had time to resupply himself. He did, however, have a few things in his small roller suitcase that might come in handy. First and foremost were the two sides of the bag's extendable handle. Each tube contained a collapsible baton that would provide quite a blow. He gave one to Kincaid and put the other in his coat pocket.

From his toiletry bag, he removed his electric shaver and disassembled it into: a set of lockpicks, a listening bug that could be paired with his phone, and a short wand-like device that looked similar to a popsicle stick. The latter, when plugged into his phone, became a security alarm detector. Also from his toiletry bag came the final items—four condom packages, two of which he tossed to Kincaid.

"Something you're not telling me?" Kincaid asked.

"Put them in your pocket. You'll need them later."

Kincaid gave him a dubious look but put the packages in his pocket.

It took Quinn and Kincaid a little over seventeen minutes to hike the two kilometers through the woods to the wall behind the Ferbers' property. Standing next to it, Quinn attached his gooseneck camera lens to his phone—basically a miniature lens at the end of a half-meter long, pencil-thick, flexible pipe. He hooked the camera end so that it would point in the right direction and lifted it above the wall. A scan of the immediate area on the other side revealed one security camera. From the way it was angled, Quinn estimated that if he climbed the fence from where he was, he'd be at the very edge of the camera's field of view.

He moved five meters to the east and looked again. Unless they were well hidden, no cameras were covering this section at all. That was surprising. Why would there be one camera focused on a portion of the back wall, but none monitoring the rest? The thought bothered him enough that he took an additional three minutes to make sure he hadn't missed anything.

Nope. The area was definitely clear.

"This will work," he told Kincaid. "I'll go first. Wait for my signal."

The fence was low enough that Quinn could grab the top with just a small hop. When he landed on the other side, he crouched down and listened for sounds of anyone or anything responding to his presence. At the same time, he scanned the area where the only camera he'd seen had been aimed and discovered the probable reason for its placement. Nestled against the wall, in the middle of the camera's view, was a cage, one that might hold birds or small animals. It appeared empty at the moment, which made him wonder if the camera was even on.

He waited a full two minutes, and when the sound of running feet or barking dogs never materialized, he clicked his tongue twice and Kincaid climbed over.

The *Forbes* article had mentioned Eric Ferber resided in one of the smaller homes, but the story hadn't specified which.

No lights were on in either structure, so Quinn flipped a mental coin and led Kincaid to the eastside house.

Thinking it best to avoid the front door, he found one on the side and waved the alarm detection wand over it. Within seconds, he received a hit.

ACTIVE ALARM DETECTED
HALEN 3500
SOFTWARE VERSION 7.3

Not just any alarm—a good one. But not quite good enough, as it was one of the many makes whose override codes were contained within Quinn's detection app. As soon as the software auto-selected the appropriate settings, he tapped DEACTIVATE. A red light blinked in the corner of his phone's screen for nearly ten seconds before turning solid green.

He wanded the door again.

INACTIVE ALARM DETECTED

He pulled out the two condom packs and opened them. Inside each was a single rubber glove. Rubber gloves in suitcases might cause questions. Condoms never did.

Kincaid snickered and opened his packages.

After donning the gloves, Quinn made quick work of the lock and pushed the door open. Just beyond was a small vestibule off what appeared to be the kitchen. He and Kincaid stepped inside.

"I'll take a look around," Quinn whispered as he shut the door. "You watch for anyone approaching the house."

Kincaid nodded, and moved into the front room where he could see out the windows.

Quinn started with the ground floor. According to the article, Eric Ferber was a confirmed bachelor. That did not mean the house was deserted, however. Ferber could have employed live-in help. But that concern drastically decreased when Quinn found an unused bedroom off the kitchen that was likely meant for a servant.

Still, he proceeded with caution as he crept up the stairs. On the upper level, he found five bedrooms, each with its own bathroom. The beds were all unoccupied. There were no clothes or personal items in any of the rooms.

He headed downstairs and said to Kincaid, "It's the other place."

After leaving the house and resetting the alarm, they sneaked across the garden to the home on the west side.

As soon as they arrived, Quinn knew this was it. Instead of an exterior parking area, there was a garage he hadn't been able to see from the back of the property. Peeking through a window on the garage's side door, Quinn spotted three expensive motorcycles off to one side, and rubber marks on the concrete where a car usually parked, it seemed.

As for the house, layout-wise it appeared to be a mirror image of the one they'd just searched. An alarm check found the exact same system in use. Another click of the DEACTIVATE button and some simple work with the lockpicks and they were in.

Like they'd done before, Kincaid took up position near the front windows while Quinn conducted the search.

Again, no servants were in residence.

Upstairs, however, Quinn discovered the clothes that had been missing from the other house. So many, in fact, that one of the five bedrooms had been turned into a walk-in closet. Finding the room Ferber used as his own was easy. It was the only bedroom with the unmade bed.

Quinn poked around in it, checking the obvious spots where people liked to hide their secrets, and discovered a loaded Glock 45 beneath the false bottom of a nightstand drawer.

He moved on to the not-so-obvious places, feeling along the mattress for hidden compartments, checking the dresser and bed frame for invisible hatches, and examining the walls for unseen panels.

It was this last that proved fruitful. Behind a section of removable baseboard, on the wall by the nightstand, he found one hundred thousand euros, in neatly wrapped bundles of crisp new twenty-euro bills. The packets were stacked in ten columns of five high, and lined up end to end to end. Quinn knew people with money often hid some in their homes in case of emergency, but normally they'd keep their stashes in a safe, or at worst, in a bag hidden in a closet.

He pulled out a bundle and flipped through the bills.

Interesting.

Normally, with a stack of new bills like this, the serial numbers would be sequential. The numbers on these bills were all over the place.

Quinn frowned.

This didn't feel like emergency cash, at least not in the natural-disaster, hold-me-over-until-things-return-to-normal kind of way. This stash felt more like go-money, to be used when one wanted to get out of town in a hurry.

He returned the bundle to its hidey-hole and replaced the board.

In the bedroom that had been turned into a walk-in closet, he found a wall safe. Unfortunately, he didn't have the right tools with him to determine the combination. He tried a couple of common choices but the door didn't budge.

"Quinn!" Kincaid yelled. "Down here, fast!"

Quinn rushed downstairs.

Out the front window, he could see strobing blue lights reflecting off trees near the front of the property. The source was hidden from view by the main house, but there was no question what it was. A moment later, a sedan came around the side of the big house on the driveway leading to the home Quinn and Kincaid were in. Behind it were two police cars.

Though Quinn had been hoping Eric Ferber would come home alone, it wasn't surprising he hadn't.

"Out," Quinn said.

They ran back to the side door and slipped outside.

As Quinn reset the alarm, he said, "Go back to the fence and wait for me there."

Kincaid took off.

When Quinn finished with the door, he sneaked to the front of the house and peeked around the corner at the motorcade.

The lead car was the same dark-colored model of Mercedes Eric Ferber had been seen with at the barricade near the bombing. Quinn used the zoom on his phone's camera to focus on the driver.

Yep. Ferber, all right.

Quinn hurried to the back wall.

"Up and over," he said when he reached Kincaid. "But stay low."

The two men pulled themselves onto the top of the wall, keeping their bodies tight to the stones to minimize their silhouettes, and dropped on the other side.

Kincaid headed for the woods.

"Where are you going?" Quinn whispered.

Kincaid turned back. "I thought we were aborting."

"I never said that."

Quinn reattached the gooseneck camera, jogged down the wall until he felt he'd gone far enough, and raised the lens.

He could see a good slice of the area in front of Eric Ferber's house. Though the Mercedes wasn't in view, the two cop cars were, each now parked in front of the building. Two officers had remained by the vehicles. Which meant there were likely anywhere from two to six cops with Ferber.

A light went on inside the house, then another, and another. This continued in a slow but steady progression throughout the ground floor. After a brief pause, the same pattern repeated on the second level. Given what had happened to Ferber's father and the family's company, the police were undoubtedly making sure no one was lying in wait for a possible heir to the Ferber fortune.

Fifteen minutes passed without anything else occurring. Then the pair of officers standing at the cars turned toward the house. A moment later six officers joined them from the front of the house. They all gathered and talked for nearly two minutes, then half the group climbed into the cars, two per vehicle, and drove back toward the main house. The remaining four officers spread out around Ferber's home.

Well, that's unfortunate, Quinn thought.

He watched the two cars drive past the main house and disappear, then followed the reflection of their lights on the trees as the vehicles continued toward the gate. After a handful of seconds, the flashing lights ceased their forward movement.

Must be setting up a checkpoint at the front.

He lowered the camera.

"What's the plan?" Kincaid asked. He'd been watching over Quinn's shoulder.

Quinn considered returning to their car and driving up to the gate, where he could use his Interpol ID again. But he doubted they would let him in this time. Instead, calls would be made, first to Commander Mettler, and then to Interpol itself. Though Misty had arranged for Leonard Hendricks to cover for Quinn when he'd sprung Kincaid, it would take time to obtain the same coop-eration now.

And that was time Quinn could not afford to waste. Every second that passed diminished the chances of finding Brunner. The sooner they talked to Ferber, the better.

"We're going to have to take out the cops," Quinn said.

Kincaid looked surprised.

"Not permanently," Quinn told him. "Just put them to sleep for a little while. You know how to do that?"

"Yeah. I mean, I've never tried it in the field. But I know how."

The answer didn't thrill Quinn. A sleeper hold could just as easily kill someone as render a person unconscious.

Quinn thought for a moment. "I'll take care of the cops. You shadow me and watch my back."

"I can do it. Don't worry about me."

"My rules, remember?" Quinn said.

Kincaid's jaw tensed. "If you want me to back you up, I'll back you up."

"Good."

Quinn used the camera to check over the wall. The cop watching the back of the house was partially obscured by a large patch of brush growing in the garden between the wall and the house. A move three meters to the left put the officer completely out of sight.

Quinn and Kincaid scaled the wall, and, keeping low, worked their way forward. They were almost to the large bush when a distant *pop* echoed across the property.

Quinn and Kincaid dropped to the ground.

To an untrained ear, the pop might have sounded like a fire-cracker or the backfire of an engine. But they both knew better.

Another *pop*, and another, and then a whole cascade of them, as a full-on gunfight broke out toward the front gate. The threat the police had been concerned about had apparently arrived. From the sound of the onslaught, Quinn had a feeling the cops wouldn't come out on top.

He pushed himself to his feet, whispered, "Come on," and hurried forward.

When he reached the bush, he paused and peered through the branches. As he suspected, the cop who had been there was gone.

Quinn rushed around the vegetation and raced to the house.

The gunfight was still raging but its intensity was waning. Which meant, if the attackers were indeed winning, they'd be heading this way soon.

Quinn checked the side of the house. The officer who'd been there was gone, too. Quinn moved over to a window and peeked through. An officer stood in the living room, looking toward the stairway, talking to someone.

"Hang back until I call you," Quinn said to Kincaid.

The bodyguard nodded.

A check of the front yard revealed no officer there, either, meaning they had all gone inside to protect Ferber.

Staying below the windows, Quinn moved to the front door, stopping just short of it. He reached over and knocked. "This is Inspector Schwartz. Is everyone all right in there?"

A pause. "Inspector who?"

"Schwartz."

"We don't know any Inspector Schwartz!"

"I'm with Interpol. I'm going to open the door. Do not shoot me. Please. I'm unarmed."

When no one responded, he turned the knob and pushed the door open but remained to the side, out of view. He removed his badge from his pocket and extended it into the open doorway so the officers could see it.

"Move into the doorway," a cop shouted. "Keep your hands visible."

Quinn stood up and stepped into the threshold.

He noted three of the cops right away—one half hidden in the passageway to the back of the house, another even farther down the hall in the doorway to the servant's quarters, and the third on the upper floor kneeling near the top of the stairs.

"Who's in charge here?" Quinn said.

The officer in the passageway stepped into the room, his gun pointed at Quinn. "Toss your ID over here."

Quinn threw his badge at the man's feet. The officer picked it up and examined it, then looked at Quinn. "What's Interpol doing here?"

"What the hell do you think we're doing here? The bombing was just the start. If you haven't figured it out yet, you're in the middle of a terrorist attack, and if we don't get Herr Ferber out of here in the next thirty seconds, we will *all* be killed."

Behind him, scattered gunshots still rung out, but for the most part the fighting had ended.

"I can't believe your instructions were to let him sit here and die," Quinn said.

The officer lowered his weapon and looked toward the officer at the top of the stairs. "Bring Herr Ferber down!"

The kneeling man stood and moved quickly out of sight, toward Ferber's bedroom. At the same time, the officer downstairs tossed the Interpol badge back to Quinn. When the upstairs man returned, Eric Ferber and the fourth cop were with him. They hurried down.

A moment before they reached the ground floor, Kincaid appeared in the front doorway. "We've got to go! They're coming!"

The cops raised their guns again and nearly shot the bodyguard.

"He's with me," Quinn said.

Beyond Kincaid, Quinn saw moving headlights playing off the trees in front of the main house.

"Let's go! Everyone!" He motioned toward the door then said to Kincaid, "Back wall."

The cops headed out the door with Ferber, Quinn right behind them. As they rounded the side of the building, Quinn caught a glimpse of headlights appearing beside the main house.

"Run!" he said.

They sprinted through the garden, dodging bushes and weaving around trees. When Kincaid reached the wall, he made a step with his hands so the others could use them to get over the top. Two of the cops went first, then Ferber.

Quinn glanced back as the other two cops passed over. Headlight reflections were coming from directly in front of Eric Ferber's house.

"Your turn," Kincaid said.

Quinn put his foot in Kincaid's hands and pulled himself over the top. As Kincaid was cresting the wall, a shout came from the distance, followed by the *pop-pop-pop-pop* of automatic rifle fire. Kincaid half dropped, half fell to the ground as bullets smacked into the wall on the other side.

Quinn grabbed his shoulder. "Are you hit?"

"No. I'm okay."

"Here," Quinn said, holding out a hand.

As he pulled the bodyguard to his feet, shots continued to hit the wall, a few passing over the top and smashing into the trees.

Quinn looked over to where the officers and Ferber were crouched. The cops were all wearing their game faces now, ready for a fight if need be. Ferber, on the other hand, looked white as a ghost.

"You all have radios?" Quinn asked the cops.

"Of course," one of them said.

"Give them to me."

"Why?"

"You want to stay alive? Give me your radios. Hurry."

Confused, they did as he asked. As soon as he had them all, he threw them into the woods behind him and said, "Follow me. And try to say quiet."

"Why did you do that?"

Quinn ran into the forest without answering. If they couldn't figure out that a single sound from a radio might be enough to get them all killed, that was their problem.

Quinn headed through the trees toward his car, alert for any noise from back toward the wall. All was quiet at the moment, but he doubted it would stay that way for long. The wall certainly wasn't going to deter the intruders. The only thing that would prevent them from taking up the chase was time. The violent frontal assault on the property meant every police officer in Zurich and any Swiss army units in the area would be headed this way by now. Unless the attackers had a death wish, they wouldn't hang around long enough for a counter assault to be mounted.

The *pop-pop-pop* of a semiautomatic rifle cut through the night. Right behind Quinn, the cop running next to Ferber dropped to the ground.

Ferber staggered forward, screaming.

"Grab him!" Quinn ordered Kincaid as he swung himself behind a tree.

Kincaid all but picked up Ferber and moved him down into the relative safety of a nearby depression. Two officers followed him, but one rushed over to their downed colleague.

"Albrecht! Are you—"

"No," Quinn said as the man started to kneel. "I'll take care of him." He pulled out his keys and threw them to Kincaid. "Get Ferber to the car. I'll meet you there."

"Will do."

As Kincaid and the cops disappeared into the woods, Quinn scanned the trees back toward the estate. Faint footsteps were coming from that direction, but they were still far off. And since there had been no further gunfire, the original shots had likely been warnings, the cop taken down by a lucky bullet.

Quinn crawled over to the officer. The man was dead, hit square in the back, heart high. Quinn took the cop's gun, spare magazines, and handcuffs, then moved into the trees toward the distant footsteps. He kept on as the sound grew louder until he reached a downed log he could hide behind.

Seconds later, he heard the crunch of a step, no more than fifteen meters away. And then a shadow emerged from between two trees. Quinn watched the person move forward, walking fast but carefully, obviously trying not to alert his or her prey. Behind the terrorist, two more shadows appeared.

The lead silhouette passed within five meters of Quinn, the other two closer still. Quinn watched the trees, waiting for more to appear. When none did, he rose to his feet and followed.

When he had all three of them in sight, he aimed the police officer's gun at the one in the lead and pulled the trigger. He adjusted his aim and shot again, and repeated the process a third time.

The third man was the only one who'd had time to react to the bangs, and had been turning toward Quinn when the bullet hit him.

Quinn ducked behind a tree and listened for reinforcements, but the forest remained silent.

He approached the first body.

A man. Alive but not for long. He was Caucasian, with an Eastern European look to him. A search of his pockets turned up two hundred Swiss francs and a Swiss driver's license that Quinn was sure was fake. He took a picture of the license and put everything back in the man's pockets.

The man's two companions were already dead. Interestingly, their pockets held the exact same items as the first guy's. Quinn snapped pictures of their IDs also, and then grabbed one of the rifles—a Heckler & Koch G38. He returned to the dead cop, draped the man's body over his shoulders, and went to find Kincaid and the others.

The woods thinned as he neared the road, and he soon spotted the bodyguard and the officers standing near his car, alert for trouble, while Ferber sat in the backseat, head in his hands.

"It's me," Quinn said before stepping out of the trees.

The cops turned their guns toward him anyway, but soon lowered them.

As soon as Quinn laid the cop on the ground, the man's friend knelt beside him.

"He's dead," one of the men said, hardly believing it.

"There was nothing we could do," Quinn said.

He walked toward the car and held out his hand to Kincaid. "Keys."

Kincaid returned them to him.

One of the other officers looked nervously into the woods. "What about the ones following us?"

Quinn opened the driver's door. "They didn't make it, either."

"What? You mean—"

"Gentlemen, my friend and I are going to get Herr Ferber to safety."

Kincaid climbed into the front passenger seat.

"What are we supposed to do?"

"If I were you, I'd hang out here until you're sure your colleagues have secured the Ferbers' estate."

Quinn handed the rifle in to Kincaid, slipped into the driver's seat, and started the engine. A split second before one of the cops tried to open a door in back, Quinn hit the button that locked all the doors.

"Wait!" the man said. "Let us in!"

Quinn put the car into drive.

"Hey!" the cop yelled. "Hey!"

One of his buddies pointed a gun at the car, but as Quinn knew would happen, the presence of Ferber in the backseat prevented the officer from firing.

"I-I-I don't understand," Ferber said, his voice muffled by the Plexiglas divider. "What's going on?"

"We're taking you somewhere we can keep you alive."

"But if you're with the police, why didn't you bring the others with us?"

"Different departments," Kincaid said.

When they reached the main road, Quinn turned right.

"Zurich's in the other direction," Ferber said, panic seeping into his voice.

"Which is exactly where the people who want to kill you are." Quinn watched Ferber for a moment, letting his words sink in before adding, "Our job is to keep you alive. So, Zurich is out."

"Then where are we going?"

"Like I said before, somewhere we can hide you."

When it became clear Quinn wasn't going to add anything else, Ferber settled against his seat, still looking uncomfortable, but apparently willing to trust his "rescuers" for now.

Quinn pulled out his phone and called Misty. "We have a situation."

7

Confusion over the cause of the explosion at Ferber-Rae's headquarters in Zurich meant that initial reports sent to the CIA from their station chief at the American Embassy were incorrect.

In the first ninety-seven minutes after the blast, word from the police was it had been triggered by an accident within the facility. By the time the CIA station chief in Zurich learned what had actually occurred, the fire at Ferber-Rae had been out for nearly a half hour. This turned the incident from something that just needed to be monitored to an event that demanded the Agency's immediate attention. The station chief's first subsequent action was to call the assistant deputy director of operations back at Langley.

Within minutes, the Zurich station chief found himself repeating everything he had just said, this time to the deputy director.

"Was there any warning or any indication that something like this might occur?" the deputy director asked.

"No, sir. As you know, we've been monitoring communications to and from Ferber-Rae for some time now, and there have been no direct threats that would account for this, nor has there been any online chatter about some—"

The door to the station chief's office burst open, and the deputy station chief hurried inside.

"Deputy Director, if you could give me one moment," the station chief said into the phone. He pressed a button, muting his end, and looked over at his deputy. "What is it?"

"There's been an attack at the Ferber estate."

"Another bomb?"

"No, sir. A frontal assault. The police are reporting heavy casualties. That's all we know at the moment."

The station chief relayed this new information to the deputy director, and then got off the phone so he could gather more intel.

Over at Langley, the assistant deputy director received an unscheduled visit from Nori Harper, one of his operation coordinators and a prime liaison between his office and Swiss intelligence.

"There's a report on SRF Info that the Ferber-Rae building in Zurich was bombed," she said. SRF Info was a Swiss television station.

"It was."

She cocked her head. "So you already knew."

"I just got off the phone with our station chief there."

"I'm wondering if it might have something to do with the escort job?"

He looked at her, confused. "Remind me."

"FIS requested an escort for a high-profile Ferber-Rae employee, from Zurich to Hamburg."

The ADD vaguely recalled seeing that on a status report, but it had been such an insignificant item—a tiny favor for a sister agency—he had paid it little attention.

"When did this occur?" he asked.

"The pickup was at nine p.m. last night, local time."

"Were there any problems?"

Harper grimaced. "I just talked to Misty at the Office—we contracted them to handle the job. The pickup went fine, but several hours later the package was kidnapped."

"Kidnapped? And we're only hearing about this now?"

"Yes, sir. I'm sorry."

"Is anything being done to retrieve the package?"

"A team is already on site."

"One of ours?"

"No, sir. From the Office."

"I'm not sure that's such a good—"

"It's being led by Jonathan Quinn."

That quieted the assistant deputy director for a few seconds. Though he had never met Quinn, he was well aware of the operative's excellent reputation. "All right. Keep me posted. And if a connection is found between the kidnapping and the bombing, I want to know right away."

"Yes, sir."

Harper turned to leave.

"Does FIS know yet?" he asked.

"About the kidnapping? No, sir. I was planning to call them after I talked to you."

"They've got enough on their hands right now, so let's hold off on that and see if Quinn can find the asset first."

"Yes, sir," Nori said, and left.

8

Quinn turned down the dirt driveway and scanned the area ahead. In the halo of the car's headlights, he scanned the layer of snow running to the house. It was untouched, and the building itself was dark.

He drove up the driveway and parked the car so that it faced the road, in case they needed to make a quick getaway.

He handed Kincaid the gun he'd taken from the dead police officer. "Check it out. Everywhere. Cabinets, under beds, behind curtains. If there's an attic, check that, too." He gave the bodyguard the code to the front door.

With a nod, Kincaid exited the vehicle and walked up to the house.

"I don't understand," Ferber said from the backseat. "What are we doing way out here?"

This wasn't the first time he'd asked the question.

The house was in the country, halfway between Zurich and Basel, the closest neighboring structures too far away to see.

"It's what we call a safe house," Quinn said. "It's a place where no one can find you who isn't supposed to."

"If it's so safe, why did your partner go in there with a gun?"

"Just a precaution. Like I told you before, our job is to keep you alive."

Kincaid stepped out of the house eight minutes later and signaled that the building was clear.

"All right. Let's go," Quinn said, and climbed out of the vehicle.

When Ferber tried to do the same, his door wouldn't open. "Hey!" he shouted. "This thing's locked! Let me out!"

Quinn opened the back door, and Ferber sprung from the rear seat like a frightened cat let out of a box.

"Why was it still locked?" the man asked.

"It's a police car, Herr Ferber. It's designed that way."

Ferber blinked. "I'm-I'm riding in front next time."

"Sure, if that's what you want."

Ferber took another glance at the car. "Yeah, it definitely is."

Quinn led him up to the house and into a cozy living room with a stone fireplace, comfortable furniture, and bulletproof windows.

"I hope there's something to eat," Ferber said. "I'm starving."

Quinn looked at Kincaid, who said, "There's some cheese and salami in the refrigerator. Or I could heat up some soup."

"Homemade soup?" Ferber asked.

"Canned."

Ferber scrunched up his nose in disgust. "The cheese and salami will have to do. And some wine. Beaujolais, preferably."

Kincaid grimaced.

Before he could say anything, Quinn jumped in. "Why don't you have a seat?" he told Ferber. "We'll see about the food."

Ferber surveyed his options and chose the brown, overstuffed couch facing the fireplace. "Please see if there are matches, too. A fire would be nice. This place is chilly."

Kincaid's face hardened. Quinn put a hand on the bodyguard's arm and turned him toward the kitchen.

"We'll be right back," Quinn said and followed Kincaid.

The kitchen was nothing fancy—a sink, a basic gas range, a square table with four wooden chairs, and a skinny European-style refrigerator.

"What's the layout?" Quinn whispered.

"Two more rooms down here—a bedroom and a toilet. Two bedrooms and a full bath upstairs. There's a sniper's post in a dormer in the attic, but otherwise that level's unfinished."

"Chairs in the upstairs bedrooms?"

"A divan in one, but nothing in the other."

"Did you come across any rope?"

Kincaid nodded. "There's a big cabinet in the basement full of supplies."

"All right. Here's what we're going to do." Quinn told Kincaid his plan, then said, "You get the food and I'll set things up."

"How about I just jam the cheese down his throat?"

"Tempting," Quinn said. "But probably better to hold off for now."

He grabbed one of the chairs from the kitchen table and carried it upstairs. After surveying both bedrooms, he took the chair into the one with the divan, as it had more space, and set the chair in the open area near the foot of the bed. He checked the placement, then adjusted it a half meter to the left, so that it was directly in front of a mirror mounted to a dresser against the wall.

As he headed back downstairs, Kincaid exited the kitchen carrying a cutting board with several slices of cheese and salami on it. While the bodyguard continued into the living room, Quinn circled into the first-floor hallway, where he found the basement entrance.

The supply cabinet held lots of goodies. In addition to a box full of several different gauges of rope, there were canvas bags, spindles of wire, plastic sheeting, duct tape, shovels, saws, garden pruners, and more. Quinn picked out some items and returned to the second floor.

He moved the chair to the side and laid out on the floor one of the three plastic sheets he'd brought up. He used one of the other two to cover the footboard of the bed and part of the mattress, and the final one to do the same with the dresser. After returning the chair to its place, he set a pair of rose trimmers, a carpenter's knife, and a hacksaw on the plastic covering the dresser. The three coils of thin, reinforced rope he put on the bed, side by side.

Satisfied with the tableau he'd created, he sent Orlando a text.

Any luck?

She responded within seconds:

Of course. I'm annoyed you'd even ask that.

A second text appeared with a link to a secured server. Quinn clicked on it, bringing up a folder with several dozen files in it. The first was a summary of what Orlando had uncovered. The rest were copies of the news stories and other documents she referenced.

All of it concerned Eric Ferber.

Quinn's suspicions of the young heir began with the discovery of the money in the man's bedroom, and had only escalated because of Ferber's behavior during their drive from Zurich. Ferber's father—and God only knew how many of the man's colleagues—had just died, and other than the public display at the barricades, he had yet to act like he really cared.

The information Orlando had given him only solidified Quinn's concerns.

Eric Ferber was a slacker who'd been living off his father's money for all of his forty-three years. While he bore the title of vice president at Ferber-Rae, he'd been mostly shunted to the side. Orlando had uncovered an agreement between the man's father and another one of the VPs, a guy named Maxwell Carter, stating that Carter would be appointed the new Ferber-Rae president when Stefan stepped down. Though Orlando could find nothing indicating Eric Ferber was aware of this, it would be foolish to assume he didn't know.

At the end of the summary, Orlando had included an interesting tidbit Quinn could use to test whether or not his suspicions of Ferber were right.

He shot Orlando another text.

Can you listen in and record?

Her reply:

Absolutely. Give me a second to put in my earbuds.

She called a moment later. Since she was still on the plane, and presumably in her seat, she couldn't say anything. She tapped the mic once, letting him know she was there.

"Switching to speaker," he said, then hit the button. "Test, test. Can you hear me?"

Another tap.

He turned his sound down to zero to mute the ambient noise from the plane, and stuck the device in his shirt pocket, mic side up. Everything ready, he headed down to the living room.

Ferber had almost finished the food Kincaid had brought him, though his drink—water, not wine—sat untouched on the coffee table.

"Oh, good, you're back," Ferber said. "Your assistant says he doesn't know how to start a fire. I tried to explain it to him, but now that you're here, perhaps you can show him."

Kincaid's hands hung at his sides, his fingers rolled into fists. Ferber was looking at Quinn, however, and didn't see this.

"The fire can wait," Quinn said.

"The hell it can. I'm cold. Unless you have a space heater, I suggest you get it started now."

Once more, Quinn was struck by how Ferber seemed remarkably unaffected by his father's violent death.

Quinn nodded at Kincaid, who sat down next to Ferber.

"What are you doing?" Ferber asked the bodyguard.

Kincaid picked up the last piece of salami and popped it into his mouth.

Appalled, Ferber scooted away, only to have Kincaid slide next to him again, trapping the man against the arm of the sofa. Ferber started to stand, but Kincaid put a hand on the man's shoulder and calmly but firmly pushed him back down. He left his hand where it was, to prevent another attempt.

"Let go of me! Do you know who I am?" He looked at Quinn. "Tell him he can't do that to me!"

Instead of complying, Quinn pushed a chair in front of Ferber and sat down. Clasping his hands, he leaned forward and said, "You and I are going to have a talk."

Ferber looked from Quinn to Kincaid and back. "What's going on here? You're supposed to be protecting me!"

"Keeping you alive would be a hell of a lot easier to do if we knew why the attacks occurred."

Again, the back-and-forth look. "Why would you think I would know the answer to that?"

"Don't you?"

"Of course not! That's…" He laughed nervously. "That's absurd. Why would *I* know?"

"Maybe because it was your company that was bombed, and your house that was raided?"

"Well, obviously, someone has a grudge against us. But that doesn't mean I know anything."

"What's your title at the company?"

Ferber's eyes narrowed suspiciously. "Vice president. What does that have to—"

"So, as vice president, you should be aware of any threats made against Ferber-Rae."

"In theory, I guess. But there might be, uh, occasions when the information hasn't made its way to me yet. As far as I know, there haven't been any threats recently."

"Define recently."

"Three months? Maybe more."

"So, no one who could have done this comes to mind?"

"No. No one."

Quinn leaned back. "You know what I find interesting?"

Ferber shrugged, his shoulders quivering. "I have no idea."

"The sequence of events."

"The sequence of...? What-what do you mean?"

"First came the explosion, and then, right after you arrived home, the raid on your house."

"Yes, and...?"

"There are two ways that bomb could have gone off. Either by remote control or suicide mission. Either way, whoever is behind it knew exactly when it would detonate. If the house was also always a target, why not attack it at the same time? That would cause more chaos, spread the police thinner."

"Why would they? No one was at the house then."

Quinn leaned forward again and pretended to poke Ferber in the chest. "Exactly. No one was at the house. Which makes me wonder if they thought you were at the office when the bomb went off, but then found out you weren't."

Ferber licked his lips but said nothing.

"Well?" Quinn said.

"Well, what?"

"This is the point where you tell me where you were."

"Um, I was...um, coming back from a meeting."

"And where was this meeting?"

"At the Hotel Schweizerhof."

"With who?"

Ferber's eyes shifted side to side. "A potential new hire. I can't, um, say anything more. Confidentiality, you understand."

"Was this a planned meeting? If we checked your calendar, would we find it?"

"No. It was…something that came up this afternoon."

"Do you often take unscheduled meetings?"

"The person I was meeting became available and I happened to be free. That's all."

"All right. Let's go back to the delay between the bombing and the attack. If you've just set off a bomb—"

"I didn't set off the bomb," Ferber said, looking both angry and panicked. "I would *never* do that."

"I meant the generic *you*."

"Oh…oh, okay. Good. Because I would never have anything to do with something like that."

"So, after the bombing," Quinn said, "one would think those responsible would get as far away as possible, as fast as they could. They had more than enough time before the raid on your house to reach France or Germany or even Austria, or even be more than halfway to Italy. That would have been a sensible reaction, don't you think? And yet, the bombers didn't leave town. Why would that be?"

"How should I know?"

"Think about it, Herr Ferber. I can't believe you're that stupid." Quinn paused. "Obviously, *you* were their target all along."

"That's ridiculous. I-I-I…"

"Why else would they have kept coming after you? And I have to believe that if someone wants you that bad, you must know who they are."

Quinn had learned long ago to read the many faces of fear. The one on Ferber's face was not the kind a person would have upon just learning he'd been targeted for death, but that of a man scared his deepest secret was known by others.

Ferber tried to say something, but no words came out.

"The way I see it," Quinn said, "they found out you hadn't

died in the blast, learned where you were, and came at you directly. What do you think?"

"You...you're saying someone wanted to kill me *specifically*," Ferber said. The words were fine, but the presentation was stiff, as if he'd practiced the sentence in his head first.

"*Wants*, not wanted. But yeah. That's what I'm saying."

"Wh-wh-why?" This was the question any innocent person in his position would ask, only an innocent person would sound confused. Ferber, on the other hand, sounded scared of how Quinn would answer the question.

"Perhaps because the people who blew up your business and killed your father were also responsible for kidnapping Thomas Brunner early this morning, and wanted to eliminate anyone who might be able to identify them."

"Brunner was kidnapped?" The false shock in both his voice and expression was so transparent it was almost laughable.

Quinn stood. "Bring him upstairs."

Kincaid grabbed Ferber's arm and yanked him to his feet.

Ferber should have known nothing about the kidnapping. An interesting tidbit contained within Orlando's report said the CIA had yet to inform FIS about what had happened on the train. And if Swiss Intelligence didn't know Brunner was missing and Misty hadn't been able to relay the news to Ferber senior, then no one else at Ferber-Rae should have known, especially the wayward heir apparent.

"Wait," Ferber said. "What's upstairs?"

Quinn headed to the upper floor without saying anything.

Behind him, he could hear Ferber struggling with Kincaid. "Stop it! No, wait! You're-you're supposed to protect me!"

Quinn paused near the top and looked back down. "I don't think you were listening carefully. What I said was that we were going to keep you alive. There's a difference."

He took the last step and turned toward the bedroom.

"Hold on. You're the police! You're not supposed to—"

Flesh slapping flesh and a grunt of pain.

"Up," Kincaid ordered.

Quinn entered the room and waited next to the bed, near the bundles of rope. Ferber stumbled inside, stopping as his foot landed on the plastic sheeting.

He stared at the floor for a second before lifting his gaze to Quinn. "No. No, no, no, no, no." He backed toward the door but didn't make it far before running into Kincaid.

"Sit," Quinn said.

Ferber eyed the chair but didn't move. "You're not with the police, are you?"

Quinn groaned. "Dammit. What gave us away?"

"Oh, God. Are you with—" Ferber cut himself off, his mediocre intelligence kicking in a second too late.

"With who?" Quinn asked.

"N-n-no one. I don't know what you mean."

"Sit, Herr Ferber. Or if it's easier, I could have my friend help you."

Ferber hesitated only a moment longer before stepping toward the chair. The plastic crinkled under his shoes, causing him to pause again, but before Quinn could signal Kincaid, Ferber continued on. When he sat, he positioned himself at the front edge of the chair, ready to jump up at the first opportunity.

Quinn picked up one of the rope bundles and moved in front of the heir.

"Sit back," Quinn said.

"I'm fine where I am. Thank you."

Quinn motioned Kincaid over, then said to Ferber, "That wasn't a suggestion."

With Kincaid approaching, Ferber scooted back.

Quinn tossed the rope to the bodyguard. "If you would do the honors."

"My pleasure," Kincaid said.

"What are you going to do with that?" Ferber asked.

As way of answering, Kincaid began wrapping the rope around Ferber's chest.

Ferber tried to push it off. "You don't need to do that! I won't go anywhere. I promise."

Kincaid pulled the rope tight, quashing Ferber's meager defense, and secured the man's torso to the chair. The bodyguard did the same with Ferber's hands and legs. After he finished, he confirmed nothing was loose and gave Quinn a nod.

"Herr Ferber," Quinn said, "let's talk about your father for a moment, shall we?"

"What about him?"

"I'm surprised you don't seem more distressed by his death."

"I'm…in shock. That's all. So-so much has happened. I haven't had time to think about it. I'm devastated."

"Why don't I believe you?"

"I swear. It's the worst thing that's ever happened to me."

Quinn stared at him without saying a word, letting Ferber squirm. If there was one thing he could count on, it was that most people, particularly those with a guilty conscience, abhorred silence.

It took only thirteen seconds before Ferber started talking again. "Families are complicated, you know. I mean, sure, we weren't particularly close, but—"

"Then you're *not* devastated."

Ferber blinked. He started to reply then stopped himself, unable to come up with an adequate response.

"Who requested the bodyguard service for Brunner?"

Ferber's mind whirled again, but in the end, he said what Quinn already knew from Orlando's summary. "I did."

"But your father was the one who handled the handoff, not you."

Surprised that Quinn was already aware of this, Ferber said, "I had a conflicting engagement."

"You seem to have a lot of conflicting engagements that keep you from important events."

"I'm a very busy man."

"That's too bad, because if you had been at the handoff, you would have met my friend here." Quinn gestured at Kincaid. "He was one of the escorts."

Ferber looked confused, then seemed to realize what Quinn meant. "That's not possi—" He snapped his mouth shut.

"Possible? I don't see why not. Or did you mean it's not possible because his partner—who, surprise-surprise, turned out to be working with the kidnappers—was supposed to have killed him?"

"Wh-wh-why would I know a-a-any of that?"

Quinn grabbed the rose pruner off the dresser and faced Ferber again. He undid the safety hook and opened the thick, curved blade.

Eyes firmly fixed on the gardening tool, Ferber said, "What's that for?"

"I'm done playing games, Eric. Your father planned on making Maxwell Carter his successor and cutting you out. You knew that, didn't you?"

Ferber opened his mouth to protest but Quinn pointed the pruner at his face.

"Be careful how you respond. From this point forward, you lose something for every lie."

Ferber shut his mouth and nodded.

"The other bodyguard wasn't the only one in league with the kidnappers, was he? You were involved with them, too."

Ferber swallowed hard, then mumbled under his breath.

"You're going to have to speak a little louder."

"Yes," Ferber whispered.

"I still can't hear you."

"Yes."

This time Ferber's response was more than loud enough for the mic on Quinn's phone to pick up.

"Who are they?" Quinn asked.

"I don't know."

Quinn moved to the side of the chair and slid Ferber's left pinkie finger into the pruner's jaw.

"I'm not lying!" Ferber screamed. "I'm not! I swear I don't know who they are! I thought I did, but after today, I-I..."

"What do you mean, you thought you did?" Quinn asked, the pruners still wrapped around Ferber's finger.

Tears streamed down the man's cheeks.

"*Who* did you think they were?"

"C-C-Clydestern."

Quinn had never heard that name before. He glanced at Kincaid, but Kincaid shrugged.

"Who or what is Clydestern?" Quinn asked.

"They're...one of our competitors."

Quinn pulled the pruners away. "Let me guess. You weren't happy Daddy wanted to put someone else in charge, so you decided to sell sensitive information to your rival, in the form of Thomas Brunner."

Ferber looked away, ragged breaths his only response.

"Yes or no?" Quinn said.

A delayed, tenuous nod.

"Let me hear you say it."

"Yes."

"Here's what's going to happen now. You're going to tell me everything. If you leave something out, I *will* learn about it later. And when I do, I will come back for you. Do you understand?"

"Y-y-yes."

"Good."

Through fits and starts, Ferber explained how, several months earlier at a bar in Zurich, he had made the acquaintance of a "scientist" who worked for Clydestern. Over the subsequent weeks, their friendship grew to the point Ferber started trusting him enough to discuss his frustrations with Ferber-Rae and, specifically, his father.

About six weeks ago, Ferber's new friend introduced him to someone he said he worked with at Clydestern, a young woman named Lilly Becker. When Ferber gave them her description,

Quinn noticed Kincaid tensing, but the bodyguard remained quiet.

Lilly and Ferber began an affair that very night, and soon he was sharing his secret feelings with her, too.

"After a few weeks, she said that I should do something about how I felt, instead of just talking about it. When I asked her what she meant, she said, 'I don't know. Some kind of revenge, perhaps. It's not fair what he's done to you.' But I couldn't come up with anything that sounded satisfying, and neither could she.

"The next night, she told me she'd been thinking about my problem all day, and that she may have an idea. I asked what it was, but she said she wanted to work out the details before telling me. Several nights later, she took me to a restaurant, where we were led to a private room, with a single table set for three. Soon we were joined by a man she introduced as Rasmus O'Neill, assistant vice president of technology at Clydestern. Lilly told me Rasmus has an answer to my problem. At first, I was confused by what she meant, but then I realized she was talking about the situation with my father, and I figured Rasmus was going to offer me a job. That definitely would have angered my father."

"But it wasn't a job, was it?" Quinn said when Ferber didn't go on.

Ferber shook his head. "He said he heard a rumor that Thomas Brunner would be attending a meeting in Hamburg. He said Clydestern would…pay me a considerable amount for…"

When Ferber seemed to have a loss for words, Quinn said, "For what?"

Ferber took a hard swallow and looked toward the floor. "To let them know when Brunner was leaving and how he would be traveling."

"Did he say why he wanted you to do this?"

"He told me Clydestern wanted to try to lure Brunner away from Ferber-Rae. My departure from Ferber-Rae might annoy my father, maybe even anger him. But Brunner's? He would have been devastated."

"So, you told him you'd do it."

"Not right away," Ferber said quickly, as if that would absolve him from any wrongdoing. "In fact, I said no. Rasmus asked me to think about it, and if I changed my mind, to get in touch with him. Lilly and I talked about it over the next couple days. She even said that perhaps it hadn't been such a good idea after all. But the more we discussed it, the more I started warming up to the offer. By the weekend, I had told her to tell him I would do it."

"And?" Quinn asked.

Ferber began sobbing.

Quinn turned to Kincaid and mouthed *water*. Kincaid exited, returned a minute later with a full glass and gave it to Quinn.

Quinn let Ferber whimper for a bit longer, then held the glass to the man's mouth. "Here, this'll help."

Ferber took several sips. Soon the tears stopped, leaving him with wet cheeks and a forlorn expression.

"You were going to tell me what happened after you said you agreed to help Clydestern," Quinn reminded him.

Ferber sniffed and nodded. "I fixed it so that I would be the one in charge of arranging Brunner's travel. I used our company's contact at FIS to hire"—his gaze flicked to Kincaid then back at Quinn—"bodyguards, and was sent photos of the two men who would be doing the job."

"What did you do with the information?"

"I gave everything straight to Lilly. I didn't even look at the pictures. I thought the less I knew, the better. I assume she passed them on to Rasmus."

"You knew they were going to try to get one of the body-guards to help, didn't you?"

"I didn't *know*. I mean, no one told me. But…"

"But it made sense."

"And what did you think they were going to do to the *other* one?" Kincaid asked.

"I-I didn't think about that," he mumbled, unable to hold up the lie.

Kincaid locked eyes with him. "Didn't, or wouldn't let yourself?"

Ferber remained silent.

"When did you find out they were going to kidnap Brunner instead of just talking to him?"

"Three days ago."

"Three days. And you did nothing?"

"They said they'd make it very clear to Dr. Brunner that they weren't *really* kidnapping him, but taking him somewhere quiet so they could talk. They were going to let him return to his bodyguards as soon as they were done."

"And you believed that?" Kincaid said.

Quinn shot him a look, silently telling him to be quiet, then said to Ferber, "When was the last time you heard from Lilly or Rasmus?"

"Around two a.m. this morning. I called her, wanting to know if everything was okay."

"What did she say?"

"That there'd been a complication." His gaze flicked to Kincaid. "That I was going to hear that one of the guards had been killed, but that I shouldn't worry. Everything was going to be fine."

Quinn sensed Kincaid tensing, so he spoke before the bodyguard could. "What else did she tell you?"

Ferber's chin dropped to his chest. "That I needed to be at the office this afternoon. That Brunner would be calling by six p.m. to resign, and it would be better if I was there to deal with the fallout, since I was the one who set things up with FIS."

"Then why weren't you there?" Kincaid asked, his tone indicating it might have been better if Ferber had done as Lilly suggested.

But it was Quinn who answered. "Because he chickened out. Isn't that right, Eric? You knew your father would be upset, and would take Brunner's defection out on you, so you didn't want to face him. But then you heard there'd been an accident at the office and rushed back?"

Tears spilled from Ferber's eyes again.

Quinn slapped his face. "Stop it. You don't get to cry."

Ferber tried to stifle his sniffles but was only partially successful.

"Did it ever occur to you to check if your scientist friend or Lilly or Rasmus really worked at Clydestern?"

"I...I...didn't have a reason...not to believe them."

"Wrong. You had a million reasons. But they were telling you things you wanted to hear, so you didn't want to open your eyes to any other possibilities. How many people died today just because you were angry with your father?" Quinn scoffed and shook his head. "You may not have personally triggered the bomb, but you're the one ultimately responsible for it."

Ferber hung his head, his tears continuing to flow.

"There's one last thing I need you to tell us," Quinn said. "Why would someone be so interested in Brunner?"

"I-I really don't know," Ferber said, his voice a near whisper. "Not for sure."

"How can you not know? He works at your company."

"He's in the technologies research division. Everything that goes on there is confidential. I've never been...in that loop. All I know is that Brunner is their star. That's why he has an apartment on site."

"There must have at least been rumors about what he's been working on."

"Only that he's been developing some kind of breakthrough product. But that's it."

"And you really don't know what it is?"

"No."

Quinn could see the man was telling the truth, which sucked because Ferber had been their big chance to get a handle on what was so important about the scientist. Still, the conversation hadn't been completely useless.

"Well, Eric, I'm out of questions. Thank you for being so forthcoming."

Quinn picked up the gardening shears and other tools, motioned for Kincaid to follow him, and headed for the door.

"Where are you going?" Ferber asked.

Quinn didn't answer.

"You can't just leave me here!"

Quinn stopped outside the doorway and glanced back. "Don't worry. You won't be alone for long."

He and Kincaid returned to the first floor. After handing the tools to the bodyguard, Quinn pulled out his phone and increased the volume. "You get all that?"

A whispered, "Hold on," and then the sound of movement. Seconds later, he heard the muffled click of a door shutting. Finally Orlando said, "There were a few points when I couldn't hear what he was saying, but I don't think it was anything important. I should be able to edit a cut of the highlights pretty quickly."

"Excellent. Send it to Misty, and also tell her to send someone to pick this son of a bitch up. And make sure she keeps him on ice. I don't want anyone finding out we talked to him."

"Will do."

"How long until you arrive?"

"I'm due in at seven-forty a.m. tomorrow morning."

"And the others?"

"I sent you an email with everyone's itineraries."

"I've been a little tied up."

"Ugh. Fine, Jar should be landing in about an hour. Daeng not long after that. Nate arrives tomorrow around the same time as me. Will you be heading back to Zurich? Or will we need to meet you somewhere else?"

"I'll grab Jar and Daeng. Don't know about the morning yet, though. I'll keep you posted."

"Sounds good. I love you."

"Love you, too." Quinn hung up and looked over at Kincaid.

"When Ferber was talking about the woman, you looked like you wanted to say something."

"The description. I'm pretty sure she's the same woman who was on the train, helping Clarke."

"That would make sense," Quinn said as he shoved his phone into his pocket. "I'm going back to Zurich. You still want to tag along?"

"Absolutely."

9

Jar stared out the terminal window, mesmerized by the flakes of snow drifting through the air. Actual, real-life snow. Until now, she'd seen it only in movies and photos.

But while it was beautiful, it looked cold. Very cold.

Despite the fact she'd walked off her plane straight into the warm Zurich Airport, a shiver ran down her spine. She was wearing two T-shirts, a sweater, and the heaviest jacket she owned, but now she was sure they wouldn't be enough. Having spent most of her life in Thailand, nothing in her wardrobe—including the jacket and sweater—were manufactured to be effective in this kind of weather.

She pulled herself from the window and rejoined the other passengers making their way to passport control. Her phone vibrated with a text from Daeng.

You here yet?

Her connection through Dubai had been delayed by forty minutes, allowing Daeng, originally scheduled to arrive after her, to reach Switzerland first.

She punched in a reply.

Heading to immigration now.

If not for Orlando, Jar wouldn't have been able to enter Switzerland at all. Being Thai limited the countries to which she could travel visa free—this country included. Per Orlando's instructions, Jar had made a stop at the US embassy on her way to Suvarnabhumi Airport in Bangkok, and paid a visit to the office of an official named Kenneth Murray.

"You're Jar?" he'd said after the aide who'd escorted her to his office left.

"Yes," she replied. It was an unnecessary question. Who else would she be?

"You're...younger than I expected."

Oh. This again.

She'd received similar comments in the past, and it annoyed her as much now as it had then. She didn't think of herself as young. She was an adult, old enough—as of a month ago—to drink in every country in the world with an age limit. But what did it matter anyway?

People. They worry about such unimportant things.

"Can we hurry this along?" she'd said. "I need to get to the airport." She held out a Thai passport. The name inside was not hers but one of her many aliases.

"I won't be needing that," Murray said.

She cocked her head. "But you are supposed to give me a Swiss visa."

He looked at her as if she'd spoken gibberish. "That was not what Orlando requested."

"What did she request?"

He picked up a bulky camera from his desk and waved at a large sheet of white paper taped to the wall. "Stand in front of that, please."

Confused, she did what he requested.

He looked at her through the lens. "A step closer to me."

She made the adjustment.

"Perfect. Hold still." He snapped a couple of photos and said, "Have a seat. I'll be back in a few minutes."

"Where are you going?"

He exited the room without answering, taking the camera with him.

Jar wanted to text Orlando to find out what was going on, but she resisted. If Murray was following her boss's instructions, who was Jar to question it?

As the minutes piled up, however, she'd grown worried. Suvarnabhumi was outside the city and, even without traffic, would take a good thirty-plus minutes to reach from the US embassy. And this was Bangkok, so there was *always* traffic. If she didn't make her plane, she would miss her connection, and because of Zurich's ban on flights in or out after 11:30 p.m., her arrival in Switzerland would be pushed back until at least the next morning.

That was unacceptable.

Finally the door opened and Murray reentered.

"Here you go," he said, handing her a dark blue-covered booklet.

She turned it over. Printed on the front were PASSPORT and UNITED STATES OF AMERICA, separated by a golden eagle. She opened it and saw her face staring back at her on the information page. It wasn't the best photo ever taken of her, but that didn't matter. She was holding an honest to goodness, official US passport with her name inside—well, her alias. Orlando must have given it to him.

This was much better than the faux Swiss visa she had anticipated receiving.

So much better.

"Thank you."

"Please make sure Orlando and Quinn know I did a good job," he said, sounding oddly needy.

"I will."

"I appreciate it. Is there anything else I can do for you?"

She checked the time. "Yes. You have kept me here longer than I anticipated. I need you to get me to the airport before my plane leaves."

He smiled. "I can make that happen."

An embassy vehicle with an official Thai police escort had gotten her to her flight on time.

As expected, her new passport made Swiss immigration a breeze. In no time, she was passing out of customs into the public area of the terminal.

The place was crowded with both arriving passengers and those waiting for them. She looked around for Daeng but didn't see him anywhere, so she headed toward a less crowded spot to call him.

"Jar!"

She whirled around. Daeng and Quinn were walking toward her, both smiling.

Though she was happy to see them, she braced herself for what would happen next. Emotionally, she appreciated their welcoming hugs, but physically, such contact made her uncomfortable.

"Good flight?" Daeng asked.

"The delay in Dubai was irritating, and the fruit served with dinner was overripe."

He laughed. "So, a normal trip, then."

She thought for a moment and nodded. "I have been on worse."

"It's good to see you, Jar," Quinn said. "This is Kincaid. He's working with us on this job."

Until that moment, Jar had thought the African man behind Quinn was someone who just happened to be in the same area. He was a giant compared to her, over a half meter taller, and easily three times her weight.

He held out his hand and said in a deep, resonating voice, "Nice to meet you."

She shook with him, her tiny hand disappearing in his. "Nice to meet you, too."

As they walked toward the exit, Kincaid said to her, "You might want to put on a heavier coat."

"This is my heavy coat."

"Oh. I'm sorry. Here, you can use mine." He started taking his off.

"That is ridiculous," she said. "You are much larger than me. I will never be able to walk in that."

Kincaid looked at Quinn and Daeng. "She always this blunt?"

"Always," Daeng said, then removed his own jacket and held it out to her. "Use this."

Daeng was also large but not like Kincaid, so Jar took the coat and draped it over her shoulders.

"Thank you."

The moment they stepped outside, she was grateful for the extra layer. She had never felt air so cold in her life, and knew it would have easily cut through the clothes she wore under Daeng's jacket. As they passed from under the covered walkway into the falling snow, however, thoughts of the cold disappeared. She reached out to catch a snowflake. When it hit her palm, it immediately started to melt.

"Is this your first time seeing snow?" Quinn asked.

"Yes."

"This is nothing. Wait until it starts sticking to the ground."

The thought of that excited her. "How long will that take?"

"Not sure if this storm's big enough to drop that much. It's still pretty early in the season for anything significant."

"Oh," she said, disappointed.

"Don't give up hope yet. There was some still on the ground earlier from yesterday, so anything's possible."

They hurried to Quinn's car, put Jar's suitcase in the back next to Daeng's, then drove to a hotel ten minutes away. Quinn led them past the reception desk to an elevator, which they took to the fifth floor.

"Here," he said, handing Jar and Daeng key cards. "Jar, you're in 522. I'm next door in 520, and Daeng, you're in 523, right across the hall."

As they walked toward their rooms, Quinn said, "Do you guys need to get some sleep? Or are you up for a little chat? I'd like to brief you on the mission."

"I am not tired," Jar said. She didn't need much sleep in the first place, and she'd had more than enough on the plane.

"I'd like to sleep, eventually," Daeng said. "But if you want to talk, I can do that."

"How about I give you fifteen minutes to get settled, then we'll meet in my room." To Kincaid, Quinn said, "You should be there, too."

Kincaid nodded.

When they reached Quinn's door, Jar and Daeng split off to their rooms, while Kincaid continued walking down the hall.

Jar took her time opening her door, waiting to see where he was going. His room turned out to be six doors down on the other side. Room 535, if the numbering sequence was unbroken.

When he turned the handle on his door, he looked back, saw Jar, and gave her a wave.

She blinked and awkwardly waved back before entering her room.

She didn't know what to think of Kincaid. He was big. In the short amount of time they'd spent together, she sensed in him an undercurrent of anger, like a coiled snake ready to strike. She would have to keep an eye on him.

After a quick shower and a change into clean clothes, she knocked on Quinn's door three minutes early.

Daeng was already there, sitting on the bed and drinking sparkling water.

A glass of beer sat on the table by the window. Quinn picked it up and nodded toward the mini-fridge. "Help yourself."

"I am not thirsty," she said.

"Quinn was telling me about his new friend," Daeng said.

Jar looked at Quinn. "Friend? What new friend?"

"Kincaid," Daeng replied.

"I did not get the impression he was Quinn's friend. Only someone he is working with."

"It was a figure of speech."

Jar frowned. She was not a fan of figures of speech. She was getting better at understanding them, but it was still hit or miss. And, to be honest, more miss than hit. Why couldn't people speak directly and not use words that obscured what they really meant?

"I would like to know about Kincaid, too," she said. "He is very large."

Quinn almost spit out his beer. "Yes, he is, isn't he?"

"That is why I said it."

When Kincaid arrived, Quinn was in the middle of telling them about the bodyguard's failed escort mission and the events that happened later in Zurich. The man took a seat at the end of the bed Jar was sitting on, causing the mattress to dip in his direction. This forced her to put a hand down to make sure she wouldn't fall over.

When Quinn finished bringing her and Daeng up to speed, Daeng said, "So the job is to find whoever is behind all this?"

"Our mission is to find Brunner and bring him back. But we can't do that without finding the others."

"Any clues as to who they are?"

"The only thing we really know is that they have access to some high-end equipment. The bomb was sophisticated, and the attackers at the house were all armed with HK G38s. But the real kicker is the kidnapping. I checked through police reports, and there's no mention of anyone on the train hearing anything unusual during the timespan after Brunner disappeared and Kincaid was arrested. But when I looked out the window of the cabin from where he likely exited the train, I found these just above it, caught on the outside frame." He pulled a small plastic bag out of his pocket and handed it to Daeng.

Daeng held it so that Jar could see it, too. Inside were several fibers.

"Rope?" Daeng asked.

"That's what it looks like to me."

"So he climbed onto the roof?"

Kincaid shook his head. "I was on the roof before the train stopped, very near that room," Kincaid said. "There was still some snow up there. But there weren't any footprints."

"Then they used a helicopter," Jar said. It was the only logical answer. "Likely a stealth model."

Quinn nodded. "My guess exactly."

"Ballsy," Daeng said.

"So, we are looking for someone who has access to explosives, automatic weapons, and a stealth helicopter," Jar said.

"That's not small time," Daeng said.

"Definitely not," Quinn agreed.

"If we knew why Brunner was so important, it might help us narrow down who'd want him."

"I agree," Quinn said. "But after my less than satisfying conversation with Eric Ferber, I have a feeling most of those who could tell us were killed in the blast."

"I could dig around," Jar said. "See if I can find anything out."

Though Jar knew nothing other than what Quinn had mentioned about Ferber-Rae, she would be surprised if the Zurich headquarters was the company's only location. If she was right, at least a few of Ferber-Rae's in-house servers would be located at other facilities. And if the company was smart, its data would be backed up to more than one of these alternate locations.

"That would be great," Quinn said. "Orlando and Nate should be here by eight a.m. Perhaps you could get up a little early and see what you can find before we pick them up."

She nodded.

"Any other questions?"

Jar and Daeng shook their heads.

"Then I think we should all get some—"

"We're wasting time," Kincaid said. "We should be out there looking for Brunner."

"Where would you suggest we start?"

"I don't know. But I can tell you one thing—we are not going to find him while we're asleep in our rooms."

"How many recovery missions like this have you been a part of?" Quinn asked.

Kincaid didn't respond.

"All right, then how many organizations with the resources these guys seem to possess have you gone up against?"

Again, no answer.

"My friends and I deal with these kinds of people every day. We *know* this stuff. And without a lead to work on, we'll be running around in circles and getting even more tired than we already are." Quinn paused. "I get your frustration, but you need to check it. Right now. We work smart, not emotionally. You want to be a part of this, then you need to be onboard with that."

Kincaid took a beat before saying, "Fine."

Quinn stood up. "We'll meet in the lobby at six-thirty a.m. Get some sleep."

Ten minutes later, Kincaid sat in his room, staring out the window.

He knew Quinn was right, but knowing that didn't make doing nothing any easier. Sitting around like this was driving him crazy. If he had half an idea of where to start, he would go out on his own. But he didn't. Nor did he have the resources to do so.

Quinn did, however. And if Kincaid wanted any chance at recovering the package and dealing with Clarke, he needed to stick around.

For now.

Though Jar had nodded when Quinn asked her to get up early, in truth she had no intention of waiting until morning to get started. She was wide awake now and excited to get to work.

She started by educating herself about Ferber-Rae. As she suspected, the main headquarters in Zurich was not the company's only physical location. It also had a biological lab in Geneva, another technologies R&D facility outside Lucerne, and offices in over a dozen European cities, not to mention several manufacturing facilities spread across the globe. Two of which, she was not surprised to learn, were located in Thailand.

She probed the Ferber-Rae network, looking for a way in. Its system security was robust. No shock there. But Jar had hacked into considerably more difficult places without being detected—the Pentagon, for instance, and the NSA—so it took her only a few minutes to weave her way around the traps.

Once in, she sent dozens of bots scurrying through the system, searching for anything connected to or mentioning Thomas Brunner. When the results came in, she was a bit surprised. For someone who was supposedly important enough to actually *live* in the main facility, he had an extremely small digital footprint within the company—a handful of emails, two security memos, and a highly redacted letter from Stefan Ferber to a recipient whose name was removed. A search of the HR database discovered a personnel folder with Brunner's name attached but no documents inside.

Disappointing, to say the least.

She checked the emails, hoping to find hints at what Brunner's role was within the company. But that proved equally fruitless. All were from several years previous, and were company-wide messages sent about employee events. The only good thing Jar was able to get from this was the email address Brunner had been using at the time.

She sent in another bot, targeting any emails to or from that address, but it came back with nothing.

She looked out the window and tried to clear her head.

Outside, the snowstorm had intensified. In a weird way, the swirling flakes reminded her of her childhood in Isaan, in northeast Thailand. During the burning season, farmers would light their old crops on fire, and the ash would sometimes fill the air in a similar way. Snow was better, though. Sure, it was cold and wet, but no smell and no soot. And it didn't get into your lungs.

She looked back at her screen. She would have to widen her search. She sent out a group of bots, each targeting a different major email provider, to see if Brunner's address showed up.

While they were hunting, she opened a new browser window and performed a news search for anything mentioning the incident on the Nightjet train. It had been over twelve hours since Quinn and Kincaid left Bischofshofen, so she was hoping new information had come to light.

Using her browser's translation function, she skimmed through several stories, all variations on the same things, and none providing anything she didn't already know.

On one of the news sites, however, in a sidebar listing other stories, a picture above a headline caught her eye. The shot featured a small clearing in a forest and appeared to have been taken from a drone. At the edge of the clearing, several police officers huddled around something, while in the distance a train passed by.

The headline below the picture read:

SKIER FINDS BODY IN WOODS

She clicked on the article.

Quinn jerked awake, his hand automatically reaching for the gun hidden under the other pillow.

A tap on the door, like the one that had pulled him from his dreams.

"Quinn?" Jar's voice.

Quinn checked the time. It was 1:30 a.m.

Another tap.

"Quinn, wake up."

He climbed out of bed, pulled on his shirt and pants, and hurried to the door.

A check through the spy hole revealed Jar standing alone in the hallway, her computer tucked under her arm.

He opened the door. "What's going on?"

She hustled past him into the room. "You need to see this."

"Uh, okay." He closed the door and followed her back inside. "See what?"

She set her computer on the table and opened it. On the screen was a news article.

"I can't read Thai," he said.

"Oh, sorry."

She turned the computer back around, clicked the cursor a few times, and then swung the screen back to him. The Thai text had changed to English.

He read.

The body of a man had been found the previous afternoon by a cross-country skier.

"He fell *through* the tree," Jar said before Quinn finished the article.

"Through?"

She scrolled down until a picture of the damaged tree appeared. The breakage was far greater than would have occurred if the dead man had just climbed up and fallen. He must have come from a greater height, like from an airplane.

Or a helicopter.

"Where was this?" Quinn asked.

"Less than two kilometers from where Kincaid's train would have been around the time Brunner disappeared."

He looked up. "We need to wake the others."

10

A bright light shined in Thomas Brunner's face.

He opened his eyes, then winced and put a hand up to block the beam.

"Sit up." It was the voice of the woman, coming from somewhere behind the light.

Brunner did as ordered.

How long he'd been asleep, he had no idea. That he'd fallen asleep at all was a surprise. He'd spent hours and hours either pacing the room or huddled on the bed, scared out of his mind. Surprisingly, the stress had not brought on a migraine. It would, though. Without his medicine, it was only a matter of time.

The woman said something in that other language, and the light mounted to the roof of the room came on.

There were two others with the woman, both from the group of soldier types who had been in the helicopter when Brunner was pulled on board. One held the flashlight that had been pointed at the scientist's face. The other stood near the door, carrying a thermos.

The woman leaned down so her face was level with Brunner's. "How was your sleep?"

"Terrible."

She patted him on the cheek. "It's okay. You'll have plenty of time to make up for it."

She walked over to the man at the door and took the thermos from him.

"Drink this," she said, holding out the container to Brunner.

He kept his hands on the mattress. "What is it? Poison?"

"It is not poison. But if you do not drink this on your own, we will force it down your throat."

Knowing she wasn't bluffing, he reached for it, but before he could touch the thermos, the woman pulled it away.

"I will hold it," she said.

"What?"

She moved it toward his mouth and pressed it against his lips. "Drink."

He reluctantly parted his lips. The liquid had no real taste, which for a brief second made him think it was water. But quickly enough, he sensed the thickness of it.

He sputtered and tried to move his head away, but the man who'd been holding the flashlight grabbed him by the ears and kept Brunner's mouth where it was.

"All of it," the woman said.

Brunner drank until the thermos was empty.

"Very good," the woman said as she pulled the container away. "Feel free to go back to sleep now."

She and her two friends left, and the overhead light flicked off.

Brunner lay back down and wondered what the hell that was all about. Before the liquid, they hadn't given him anything to eat or drink. Perhaps it had been some kind of nutrient-based drink. That was as good an answer as any.

His eyes grew heavy again, and soon he was back asleep.

Ninety minutes later, his colon began to cramp.

11

SWITZERLAND

Nate's plane touched down at Zurich Airport at 8:05 a.m. local time. It had taken him two flights to get there, the first a cross-country hop to JFK in New York, then the 6:30 p.m. Swiss Air flight to Zurich. Since he traveled with a carry-on only, he was through Immigration and Customs within twenty-five minutes.

He checked the arrivals board and saw that Orlando's flight had landed not long after his, so he grabbed two cups of coffee and found a spot near the customs exit to wait.

Eighteen minutes later, Orlando walked into the public area, pulling her bag behind her and talking on her phone.

"Orlando!" he called.

She glanced over and adjusted her course.

"No problem," she said into her phone as she neared. "We'll handle it...uh-huh...okay, keep us posted.... Love you, too." She hung up and looked at Nate. "The rest of the team has gone to Austria."

"I take it that's where we're headed also?"

"Not yet. There are a few things here you and I are going to check first."

"Cool," Nate said. "And hello, by the way."

"Right, sorry." She hugged him. "Good to see you."

"You, too."

"Beach treating you well?"

"I should have made the move years ago."

That past summer, Nate had moved out of Quinn's house in the Hollywood Hills to a townhouse in Redondo Beach, a block from the water. After a devastating first half of the year, the change of scenery had done a lot to help him feel if not normal again then at least normal adjacent.

"Come on," Orlando said. "We're already behind on this one."

As they headed for the exit, he asked, "What's the plan?"

"I'm going to pay a visit to the coroner, and you're going to take a look at the bomb site."

He glanced at her. "What bomb site?"

***

"I don't think we should go any farther," Karl Braun, an agent from FIS said. "The floor is very unstable."

Nate placed a gloved hand against a cracked slab of concrete hanging from the ceiling and surveyed the way ahead.

Three meters down the hall, the floor sank like a V, exposing rebar that had, until yesterday, kept everything level.

"What about that lip?" Nate said, pointing at a narrow strip of the old floor that had remained attached to the right side of the corridor wall.

The agent looked at him like he was crazy. "What about it?"

"We could use that to get to the other side."

"Safety regulations clearly state—"

"I don't care about safety regulations. My job is to keep something like this from happening again."

"How is getting to the other end of the hall going to stop another bomb?"

"I won't know the answer to that until I see what's over there."

"I don't think it's a good idea."

Usually, when Nate had to assume a fake identity, his ability to pull it off was determined by how well he played the part. On occasion, he might have the assistance of a colleague acting as an official on the phone to confirm who he was. On this job, however, Misty and her contacts at the CIA had used their influence with FIS to allow an FBI bombing expert—Nate—free reign throughout the crime scene.

"Your concern is noted. But I'm going."

Braun raised his hands in mock surrender and took a step back. "Whatever you want. Just don't expect me to join you."

Nate preferred it that way, but he said nothing as he moved cautiously over to the lip and examined the way ahead. Though it wouldn't be a walk in the park, it wasn't going to be as difficult as Braun thought.

Nate stepped onto the lip, his shoe taking up all but a few centimeters of concrete on either side. Leading with his right foot and scooting his left behind, he moved down the corridor, with cracks in the wall from the explosion acting as handholds. When he reached the far end, he stepped gingerly onto the larger floor, in case it was on the verge of collapsing, but the concrete held steady.

The hallway ended at a T-intersection. A collapsed portion of the floor above blocked the way to the right, about five meters in. Thankfully the way to the left—where Nate had wanted to go all along—remained mostly clear.

He called back to Braun. "I should be back within ten minutes."

"What if you're not?"

"Then give me ten more."

Nate stepped into the left hallway.

According to building blueprints obtained by Orlando, the suite of rooms Thomas Brunner had been calling home for the last year or so were just ahead.

"I doubt you'll find anything that will point at who took Brunner or bombed the building," Orlando had said before they parted. "So concentrate on finding anything that might help us get a handle on what kind of work he's been doing that makes him such an attractive target."

Nate had already struck out at Brunner's office and lab. Not because there wasn't anything of interest, but because that entire section of the building had been obliterated. The scientist's residence was Nate's last chance.

Upon reaching the door, Nate saw it was secured with a pair of biometric locks. He tried the knob anyway but the door didn't budge. Normally that wouldn't be a problem. He had an app on his phone, which had a seventy-five percent success rate with locks like these. The problem was, the biometrics portion of the locks had stopped working when the bomb took out the power, freezing the locks in engaged positions.

Nate tapped the door. Metal. That wasn't great, either, but there were other ways besides doors to get into an apartment.

He spotted a half-meter chunk of loose concrete not far away, picked it up, and thrust it into the wall next to the door.

It sliced through the outer layer like nothing was there and cracked the layer on the other side, creating a small opening into Brunner's place. Nate hauled the block out and heaved it into the wall again. The manmade rock crashed through the inner layer into the room beyond.

"What's going on?" Braun yelled. "Are you all right?"

"I'm fine," Nate responded. "Hold tight."

After kicking the opening to widen it, Nate flipped on his flashlight and slipped inside.

He was in a kitchen, cabinet doors hanging open or ripped off completely. Below them, broken dishes covered the floor. A living room was to the left. There, the blast had upended furniture and dislodged three bookcases' worth of books.

Nate proceeded carefully through the mess, searching for a computer or notebooks or anything that might give the team insight into the man.

A door at the other side of the living area led into a bedroom.

The damage here was less, but this was due to the room containing only a bed and a dresser and a nightstand.

Nate searched the drawers of the latter two, finding only clothes.

He checked the attached bathroom and closet but discovered nothing of interest, so he exited and moved on to the last room in the suite.

Bingo.

An office, complete with desk and chair and file cabinet and bookcase. The most important item, a desktop computer, sat in shambles on top of a small sea of books.

The monitor's casing hung broken and skewed around a screen spiderwebbed with cracks. The computer itself had been snapped in two, its guts spilling from the center.

Nate crouched beside the dead machine and sifted through the parts until he found the hard drive. It was intact and, from appearances, undamaged. He disconnected the wires running into it and placed the device in the inside pocket of his jacket.

Hopefully it would turn out to be the motherlode he'd been searching for.

As he stood back up, one of the books that had fallen on the floor caught his eye. It lay open, displaying a couple of pages near the middle. Instead of printed text, however, the pages were covered in handwriting.

Nate picked up the book and flipped through it. Nearly all of the pages were filled. He had no idea what any of it meant, as it was written in some kind of code. The mix of letters and numbers and symbols reminded him of the movie *Zodiac* and the letters the killer had sent.

He checked the pile and discovered several other notebooks among the texts. There was no way he could carry them all without Braun noticing, and no time to take pictures of every page, so he decided to take only the one he'd first found, slipping it into the outer coat pocket.

Next, he righted the filing cabinet. Because it had been locked, the drawers were still shut. Thankfully, there was no biometric security here. Nate pulled a plastic card out of his wallet, and used the lockpick and tension wrench scored into it to release the lock.

Two of the drawers were empty, while the remaining pair contained only a couple dozen files between them. These mainly held articles cut out of magazines on a whole range of topics, including construction of a new type of dam in China, the intelligence testing of prekindergarten children, and artificial snow-making in the Rocky Mountains.

The few files that didn't contain articles held handwritten notes that seemed to be reminders—*Don't skip the AGT,* and *Leveling,* and *What about Danara?*

Nate didn't know if they were important or not, so he folded the printouts and stuck them in his pocket with the notebook. The articles he left where they were.

As he gave the room a final look, he noticed a few more notebooks behind the door. He checked them, but all contained the same strange code.

All except one.

That notebook wouldn't open at all. The cover and pages appeared glued together. He shook it but didn't hear anything moving inside. Flipping it around, he looked for some kind of button or latch that would release a lid, but couldn't find any. He put the notebook in his other outer pocket.

Satisfied there was nothing else to find, he sent Orlando a text, telling her what he'd discovered, then retraced his steps through the apartment, down the hallway, and along the lip back to Braun.

"Find anything?" the agent asked.

"Not really."

Braun snorted as if it was the answer he'd expected. "Is there anything else you would like me to show you?"

"Just the exit."

The same official channels that had opened the door for Nate's private tour of the wrecked Ferber-Rae headquarters eased the way for Orlando's visit to the coroner.

After checking in at the front desk, she was taken to the office of a balding man in his mid-forties. He looked up as Orlando entered and jumped to his feet, sucked in his gut, and extended a hand.

"Dr. Kelvin Nagel," he said in English.

Orlando shook with him and said in German, "Dr. Chan. Thank you for seeing me, Dr. Nagel."

"Oh good, you speak German. I was worried we would have to use English. It's not my best language." He smiled. "Please, you may call me Kelvin."

She did not offer her first name in return.

He sat back down and motioned to the seat across the desk from him. "How may I be of assistance?"

Orlando lowered herself into the chair. "I believe you already know why I'm here."

"Yesterday's terrorist attacks."

"Correct. I would like to see the bodies."

He frowned. "They're mostly just…parts. It was a particularly strong explosion."

"I'm not interested in the bodies from the bombing. I'd like to see those involved in the attack on the Ferber estate. It's our understanding that several of the terrorists were killed in the incident. I assume you have them here."

"Ah, okay, then. That's a different story. I'll take you to them myself."

"Thank you."

He rose from his chair. "May I ask a question?"

"Of course," Orlando said, standing.

"What is the National Crime Agency's interest in this?"

The National Crime Agency was part of British law enforcement. Dr. Nagel was operating under the assumption Orlando was a medical investigator within the agency's ranks.

She hesitated, as if weighing what to say. "Without going into too many details, we foiled a similar plot in London several weeks ago. I am here to see if your events and ours might be connected."

"I've heard nothing about this."

"Because we didn't publicize it."

He took this in before saying, "What are you hoping to learn when you see the bodies?"

"I'm afraid that's information I can't share."

"I just thought if there was something specific, I may be able to help."

"I appreciate the offer but that will be unnecessary. Can we go now?"

"Oh…um…yes. Please, follow me."

He led her down a flight of stairs into an autopsy room. The space held three examination tables, two of which were in use.

Nagel grabbed two masks from a cabinet by the door and handed one to Orlando.

"We've just started autopsying the bodies you're interested in." He turned toward one of the occupied tables. "Dr. Breneman, are these the police officers or the terrorists?"

"Dr. Hegler and Dr. Rust are working on the police in room three," a man at the table said. "These are the terrorists."

"Excellent, excellent. Dr. Chan is here from London and would like to take a look at the bodies, if you don't mind."

"I *do* mind. I'm in the middle of an autopsy. I'm not going to stop."

Before Nagel could respond, Orlando said, "There's no need for you to, Doctor. All I need to do is take a look at the bodies."

Breneman glanced at Nagel, and then at Orlando. "Make it quick."

Orlando approached the table and scanned the corpse. A male, Caucasian, approximately thirty years old, tall, maybe a hundred and eighty-seven centimeters, solidly built, with a chain tattooed around his left bicep. He'd taken four bullets to the torso and, unfortunately, one to the face, making visual identification impossible.

"Can you turn his left arm?" she asked. "I would like to see the underside of his wrist."

One of Breneman's assistants obliged her.

Orlando leaned close, examined the skin, and then stood back up. "Thank you."

She switched to the other table. The corpse there could be described in similar terms to the first one, though it was shorter and had only two bullet wounds. Thankfully, neither shot had been to the head.

She casually reached up to her ear, activated the micro camera embedded in the glasses she was wearing, and took a picture of the dead man's face. He had a strong jawline and a heavy brow that made her think Eastern European, which jibed with the description of the three men Quinn had killed.

"May I see the inside of his left arm?" she asked.

The doctor at table two did the honors for her this time. Once more she went through the motions of examining the skin by the wrist, and then thanked the doctor and returned to Nagel.

"Find anything of interest?" he asked.

"How many others do you have?" she asked.

"Of the terrorists? Four."

"Please take me to them."

Nagel escorted her to a room where the bodies waiting to be autopsied were stored. One by one he showed her the remaining corpses. Orlando took pictures of each man's face and feigned interest in the undersides of the left wrists.

When she finished with the last one, she said, "What about personal effects? Do you have those here?"

"Yes."

"May I see them?"

He took her to a room where three-quarters of the space was blocked off by a glass partition. On the other side of the glass, cabinets containing dozens of individual lockers lined the walls.

Sitting at a desk in front of the partition was an older woman in a police uniform, and to the left of her desk, a bare wooden table.

"We would like to see the personal effects for subjects"—Nagel consulted a paper sitting on the corner of the desk—"17A-27 through 17A-32."

"One moment." The woman typed something into her computer, then stood up and entered the back area via a door in the partition.

She extracted six shoebox-sized containers from separate lockers, and carried them back into the front section of the room.

"You must look at them here," she said as she set the boxes down on the wood table. "And I will handle everything. No one else."

"I understand," Orlando said.

The woman emptied the boxes. Each contained the same items —two hundred Swiss francs and a Swiss driver's license. Orlando snapped clandestine pics of the latter.

"Is there anything else?" the officer asked after Orlando finished with the last box.

Orlando shook her head.

"That will be all. Thank you," Nagel said, then led Orlando back into the hallway.

"I appreciate your time, Dr. Nagel," Orlando said.

"Like I said, I'm always happy to help." He hesitated. "If I may, you don't look terribly pleased."

"Unfortunately, I don't believe there's a connection between our cases."

"And you got that from just looking at the bodies and their possessions?"

Now it was her turn to hesitate. "I shouldn't tell you this, so please do not mention it to anyone else, but members of the organization that was planning the London attack all have the same tattoo on their left wrists. Your terrorists do not."

"What kind of tattoo?"

"I've already told you more than I should." Which should be

more than enough, she hoped, for Dr. Nagel to file her visit under interesting but unimportant. Another day or two, unless reminded, he'd likely forget about it.

"I apologize for prying."

"No apology necessary. Now, if you don't mind, I should be going."

ELMSHORN, AUSTRIA

Quinn, Jar, Daeng, and Kincaid arrived in the small town of Elmshorn, just shy of nine a.m. Quinn had hoped to make better time, but the storm from the night before had intensified, hampering the drive.

"There it is," Jar said, pointing ahead.

Quinn pulled to the curb in front of the St. Dione Hotel. "Keep me updated."

"Will do," Daeng said.

After he and Jar climbed out and were headed to the building, Kincaid relocated to the front passenger seat.

Elmshorn was one of those quaint villages tourists stopped in for an hour or two on their way to somewhere else. Other than the scenery—which was undoubtedly spectacular when the area wasn't sitting in a cloud—it didn't have much to offer.

As far as local law enforcement went, the Austrian police operated out of a small building on the outskirts of town. There was no coroner's office.

On the drive here, Jar had hacked into the police's system and discovered the body that had fallen through the trees had been taken to the local hospital.

The medical facility was located at the other end of town, a mere seven minutes away, in an unimposing two-story building. It was the kind of place Quinn guessed handled only easy stuff, like flu or broken bones or maybe the occasional appendix removal. The more complicated illnesses and procedures were likely passed on to doctors in Vienna a few hours away.

Quinn found a spot on the street to park, then he and Kincaid headed inside.

At the reception desk in the lobby, Quinn flashed his now well used Interpol ID. "I'm Senior Inspector Schwartz. This is my colleague, Inspector Russo. We're here about the body that was found yesterday."

"The one from the woods?" The receptionist was an older man, probably a volunteer.

"How many bodies do you have?"

"Uh, just the one."

"Then that would be it."

"Right. One moment." The man picked up the phone.

Two minutes later, Quinn and Kincaid were escorted into the building by the medical director himself, a middle-aged man named Dr. Warner.

"I don't ever remember having anyone from Interpol visit us before," the doctor said, a hint of excitement in his voice. "Is the body someone important?"

"I'm sure you'll understand, Doctor, I can't really discuss that," Quinn said.

"Of course, of course." Warner fell silent for a few seconds, but was unable to completely stifle his curiosity. "Strange how he was found, smashed up like that. I wonder how that happened."

"Yes, strange."

Quinn could tell that wasn't the response the doctor had been hoping for.

Hiding his disappointment behind a forced smile, Warner said, "If you think you'll be in need of temporary office space, I'm sure we can find something for you."

"Thank you. But that won't be necessary."

The doctor led Quinn and Kincaid around a corner into a new hallway. At the far end, a police officer stood guard in front of a door.

"We have a small kitchen in case you're hungry. I could let them know."

"Thank you, but we're fine."

When they reached the officer, the doctor said, "These gentlemen are here to see the body."

Quinn held up his badge. "Senior Inspector Schwartz and Inspector Russo, Interpol. Commander Jäger should have informed you we were coming."

Misty's handiwork, again pulling the necessary strings.

"Yes, sir. He did." The officer opened the door and moved to the side.

Quinn thanked Warner before he and Kincaid entered the room. The officer followed them in and pointed at a door along the back wall.

"The body's in there," the man said.

"Is the medical examiner with it?" Quinn asked.

"He hasn't arrived yet."

Quinn knew the examiner would be driving up from Vienna and he'd been pretty sure he and Kincaid would beat the man to it, but the confirmation was a relief nonetheless. "Thank you. We shouldn't be long."

"I'll be right outside if you need me," the officer said, then returned to the hallway.

Quinn and Kincaid passed through the door the guard had pointed to and entered an examination room of sorts. A gurney sat in the middle of the tiled floor, under a medical spotlight mounted on a moveable arm. On the gurney, under a white sheet, lay the body.

"You ready for this?" Quinn asked.

Kincaid nodded.

"It's not going to be pretty."

"I'm fine."

"You see many dead bodies on your bodyguard gigs?"

"I've seen a few."

"Ones that have fallen from more than a couple stories?"

A shrug.

Quinn approached the table and moved to the end where he thought the body's head was.

"Stand over there," he said, pointing at the left side of the table.

Once Kincaid was in position, Quinn peeked under the sheet. He had guessed correctly.

"Okay, here we go." He pulled the sheet back, exposing the corpse's head and shoulders.

Kincaid took an involuntary step backward.

"If you're going to faint, do yourself a favor and sit on the ground now."

"I'm fine," Kincaid said, his voice not quite as steady as before.

He had good reason to be uneasy. Quinn had seen worse, but this guy was in pretty bad shape. The branches he'd hit on his fall through the trees had ripped much of the skin off his face, exposing muscle and bone. Brain, too, because either when he hit the ground or somewhere during the descent, his skull had been smashed inward above his left eye.

Kincaid's face continued to pale, and he was all but hyperventilating.

"Is it Brunner?" Quinn asked.

"How the hell...am I supposed to...tell? He doesn't...have a face."

Quinn covered up the body, but Kincaid's eyes stayed glued to the spot where the man's head was.

"Hey," Quinn said. "Look at me."

Kincaid remained frozen.

"Look at me."

Kincaid blinked, and looked up.

"Relax. Take a long, deep breath."

Kincaid did.

"Take another...good. Again." When Kincaid seemed to have calmed down, Quinn said, "You're the only one here who's seen

Brunner in person. So, you need to tell me if this is him or not. Maybe there's something else that might help ID him."

"Like…like what?"

"Like his hair. Or his hands. Did he have any tattoos?"

"None that I was aware of."

"Then just focus on things you know."

"Right. Okay."

"Get a picture of him in your head."

Kincaid's eyes went unfocused for a few seconds.

"You got him?" Quinn asked.

"Got him."

"Okay, I'm going to pull the sheet back again. Are you ready?"

Kincaid nodded.

"If you start to feel uneasy, turn away until you get back under control."

Kincaid nodded again. "I'm ready."

Quinn pulled the sheet back a second time, folding it all the way to the man's waist.

"It's not him," Kincaid said.

"You're sure?"

"He has darker hair. Black, almost. And longer."

The hair that still clung to the corpse's head was mousey brown, and short.

"It could have been dyed and cut."

"Cut, maybe, but it would have to have been bleached first then dyed. That would take a couple hours. There wouldn't have been enough time. It's not him." Kincaid looked over at Quinn. "This is good news. It means he's still alive."

"All this proves is that this guy isn't Brunner, not that Brunner's alive."

As Quinn reached for the sheet to pull it back over the body, Kincaid looked at the corpse again. "Oh, shit."

Quinn stopped. "What?"

Kincaid grabbed the corpse's left arm and turned it, his fear of the body temporarily forgotten. He was focused on a barbed-wire tattoo encircling the dead man's bicep. Laced within it was a vine of roses.

"You've seen that before?" Quinn asked.

"This is Clarke."

Quinn cocked his head. "Your partner?"

Kincaid's mouth tensed. "The person I was teamed with. Not my partner."

"Are you sure?"

"Unless someone else has this exact same tattoo."

"It's a big world and I doubt it's that original."

Kincaid looked the body up and down. "The size is right. And the hair, too."

"The most we can say is, it *could* be him."

Kincaid whirled around. "Where are his clothes? I doubt he would have had time to change from when I last saw him until he fell. If I can get a look at them, I'll know for sure."

They found the corpse's clothes in a box on a shelf in one of the cabinets.

"It's him," Kincaid said. "No question. This is exactly what he was wearing."

"Well, then, I guess that's one less person we need to look for."

Quinn returned to the table and pulled the sheet back in place. When he finished, he noticed Kincaid glaring at the body.

"You all right?"

Kincaid took a breath, then looked up. "I hope he was conscious the whole way down."

———

Jar sat in front of her laptop in the team's hotel room, growing more frustrated by the second. She'd spent the last thirty minutes searching through stored radar data, looking for any signs of a helicopter in the area of the Nightjet train at the time of the kidnapping, but had come up with nothing.

The use of a stealth craft would partially explain the lack of information, but no stealth craft she had ever heard of could maintain one hundred percent invisibility. At the very least, it should have shown up as digital artifacts or insignificant blips, the kind air traffic controllers would routinely ignore. But there'd been no artifacts and no insignificant blips. The only possible reason for this, if there had been a helicopter, was that the aircraft had flown low enough to avoid detection.

Jar considered the problem. If the helicopter had stayed that low, someone on the ground might have seen or heard something. Even a stealth aircraft wasn't completely noiseless. There was a decent chance any witnesses would have mentioned it online.

The only problem was the timing. The kidnapping occurred around 1:45 a.m., which meant the pool of people who could have heard it was considerably smaller than it would have been a few hours earlier.

But since she'd struck out elsewhere, she decided it was worth a check.

She input her desired parameters into a program of her own creation, and within five minutes, had lists of Facebook, Twitter, Instagram, Snapchat, and Whatsapp users registered as living within two hundred kilometers of the kidnapping site. She created a search of those on the list, targeting posts, tweets, chats, or messages that a) occurred any time between 1:00 a.m. and 4:30 a.m., and b) contained one of the following keywords or phrases in English, German, or French: helicopter, aircraft, airplane, weird noise, unusual noise, strange noise, and noise in the sky.

This search, she knew, would take longer than five minutes, so while it ran, she scoured news sites and blogs for any mentions of the helicopter.

She'd been at it for about fifteen minutes when Daeng returned.

"Here you go," he said in Thai, setting a cup of coffee in front of her. "Latte, one sugar, double stirred."

She picked up the cup, removed the cover, and looked at the

liquid inside. The shade of tan was correct. She gave it a sniff and a taste, then nodded. "Good. Thank you."

He pulled a bag out of his backpack and set it next to her cup. "And one chocolate croissant."

She removed it, smoothed out the bag, and placed the pastry on it. The croissant was warm and smelled delicious. As she started to tear off a piece, her computer bonged and a message appeared on the screen.

SEVEN MATCHES FOUND

She'd been hoping for more but expecting less. So, all in all, she was pleased.

Forgetting about her croissant for the moment, she clicked on the alert box. A window opened, displaying two Whatsapp conversations and five tweets.

Three of the tweets concerned a war movie that had apparently been playing on TV at the time of the kidnapping, and one of the Whatsapp conversations was about strategies for the latest *Star Wars* video game. Jar could have given them a tip or two that would have been much better than anything the two gamers had come up with.

The other two tweets and the last conversation were different.

Fi Vogel 02:03 AM
Anyone else's house get buzzed by a plane? I just heard something fly over my place and I swear if I was on the roof, I could have touched it.
Bernard Haas 2:37 AM
Some crazy rich guy out in his helicopter tonight, I guess.

This last tweet was accompanied by a grainy photo of a blurry, gray spot in the sky that Jar assumed was the helicopter in question. The Whatsapp conversation was in a similar vein.

2:48 AM

HADDIE: Do you hear that?

ELENA: What are you talking about?

HADDIE: Like a plane or something…wait.

2:49 AM

ELENA: Hey, are you still there?

HADDIE: Yeah. I swear a plane just flew by real low. But I don't see anything.

ELENA: I hear it now.

2:50 AM

ELENA: That WAS low! I saw a dull light, but I couldn't see anything else.

HADDIE: Maybe it's in trouble. Did it sound like it was going down?

ELENA: I don't think so. We would have heard a crash by now, right?

HADDIE: I guess. Weird.

Included with the tweets and conversations were the location data from where each had been sent. Jar input the information on Google Maps and smiled. The dots formed an almost perfect line heading east from the kidnapping site toward Vienna.

"You going to let me in on what you're doing?" Daeng asked.

She jerked in surprise and glanced back at him. She'd forgotten he was there. "I don't have time for you right now."

She adjusted the parameters and performed a wider search, hoping to pick up more messages. A few moments after she started, Daeng's phone rang.

"Hello?" he said, in English. "Oh, yeah, he and Kincaid are checking out the body. Probably couldn't get to the phone…. Well, I think Jar might have found something, but she's not sharing. Maybe you can get it out of her…. Hold on, I'm putting you on speaker."

He set his phone next to Jar's computer.

"You still there?" he said.

From the speaker came Orlando's voice. "I'm here."

"Jar, you want to tell Orlando what's going on?" Daeng said.

She frowned at him, then said, "I believe I have found out which way the helicopter went." She explained what she'd done.

"That's brilliant," Orlando said.

"I am running another search to see if anything turns up farther out."

"Good." Orlando paused. "I have an idea. Whoever the kidnappers are, they don't want to be found. And while a stealth helicopter was great at night, if they continued going after the sun came up, a lot more people would have seen them."

"You want me to check for any mentions of helicopters during the daylight? I will have to widen the parameters again."

"If you can set it up to run in the background, sure, but I doubt you'll find anything."

Jar said, "You think they landed before dawn."

"I do. If I had to guess, I'd say they switched to a car or even a plane. Set up the daylight search just in case I'm wrong, and in the meantime, I'll try to figure out where they could have stopped. When you free up, you can help me out."

"Okay," Jar said.

They said their goodbyes and hung up.

Daeng looked at Jar, an eyebrow raised. "Would that have been so hard to tell me before?"

"And then have to repeat it again to Orlando?" She rolled her eyes, stuck a piece of her pastry in her mouth, and turned back to the computer. "Thank you for the croissant."

12

Quinn knocked on the hotel room door and whispered, "It's us."

Daeng let him and Kincaid in. "Come on. You're missing out on all the fun."

He hurried back into the room, and Quinn and Kincaid followed to where Jar sat at a built-in desk with her computer.

"What's going on?" Quinn asked.

From a phone sitting next to the laptop, Orlando said, "Hey, babe."

"Hey," he said, surprised. "Still in Zurich?"

"Yeah. I checked the dead guys who attacked Ferber's home. They all had the same two hundred euros and fake IDs as the guys you took down. I'm running their pictures through the system but no hits have come back yet."

"What about the bombing site?"

"Nate's handling that. He should be here anytime now."

"Do you know if he found anything?"

"He said he did, but I was too busy to go into details with him."

"Busy with what?"

"Jar and I have been hunting for the kidnapper's helicopter."

"Jar found it," Daeng said triumphantly.

"I did not find it," Jar said. "I found where it was headed. Orlando found the helicopter."

"Technically, I found where it *was*," Orlando said.

"That is true," Jar said. "We do not know where it is right now. But that is not important."

"Wait, wait, wait," Quinn said. "Back up."

"Oh, sweetie, are we talking too fast for you?" Orlando said.

"Ha. Ha. Do me a favor and start at the beginning."

Orlando described how Jar had figured out the helicopter's flight path. "After that, Jar and I located all the airfields and helipads within a hundred kilometers of Vienna."

"We did not find *all* of them," Jar said.

"As many as we could," Orlando said. "We then pulled satellite images for each from the last couple hours before sunup, and discarded any that didn't have a helicopter present. After that, it was a simple backward time jump through stored images to find helicopters that arrived during the early hours of the morning. Guess how many that was?"

"One?" Quinn said.

"Well, two, actually. But one's too small to have been used in the kidnapping. The other one was a Ghost 1A1."

Manufactured in Russia, the Ghost 1A1 could carry up to fifteen people including pilots, and was one of the top stealth aircraft.

Quinn grimaced. "Okay, but you said you didn't have radar data, so you can't be sure it's the helicopter they used. Unless I'm missing something."

"You are," Orlando said. "Jar, show him."

Jar tapped her keyboard and a satellite image filled her screen. Though clearly taken at night, the buildings and roads in the shot were easily distinguishable. Jar hit the space bar, and the image began to zoom in on a group of lights in the lower left corner, not far from a river.

As the magnification increased, Quinn saw that the road he'd noticed next to the lights was actually a runway. Within the halo of lights were a rectangular building and the aforementioned Ghost helicopter parked beside it.

The image continued to zoom in until the helicopter filled the bottom portion of the screen, with the building along the top edge. The satellite's angle should have allowed Quinn to see identifying numbers on the aircraft, but there were none. As far as he could tell, there were no markings at all.

The image flickered, then flickered again, and again and again. Each time appearing as if it was the same photograph, but Quinn knew Jar was working through a series of images. After a few more flickers, someone backed out of the building. More flickering, and the person was joined by others, also walking backward. The pictures were so clear, if the people had all looked up, their faces would have been identifiable.

The total number of people ended up being seven. Six appeared to be men, while the last was either a man with long hair or a woman. Unfortunately, because of the two-second delay between shots, it was impossible to detect any odd gaits or other distinct mannerisms.

The group reached the helicopter and backed into it. Several more image flickers and the helicopter rose into the air.

Jar tapped different arrow keys and hit the space bar. This time the images played as a movie. The helicopter landed and the group climbed off and headed into the building.

While Quinn had noticed it during the backward progression, it was even more evident now that one of the men was being physically escorted by a man on either side of him.

When the group disappeared into the structure, Jar stopped the playback.

"Can you back it up and pause it at some point where they're all still outside?" Kincaid asked.

"Who said that?" Orlando asked.

"Orlando, meet Kincaid," Quinn said. "Kincaid, Orlando."

"Ah, the bodyguard. Hello."

"Hi," Kincaid said.

"Jar, can you do what Kincaid asked?" Quinn said.

Jar scrolled back to an image in which the whole group was outside.

"Any chance you can push in closer?" Kincaid asked.

"Sure."

She zoomed in until the seven people's heads took up most of the frame.

"That's got to be Brunner," Kincaid said, pointing at the man being escorted. "The hair's like his, and the nose...well, I mean, I never saw him from this angle but it looks correct." He moved his finger over the long-haired person. "And this must be the woman I saw on the train. Again, right hair color." He studied the image for another moment. "And this one"—he switched his finger to the man at the head of the group—"if I had to bet, he's the one who boarded with her."

Quinn studied the screen. None of it—not what Jar and Orlando had found, or Kincaid's guesses—was proof that they were looking at Brunner and the people who'd kidnapped him. But it was the best lead they'd come up with so far and, circumstantially, was pretty damn convincing.

"You said the helicopter left again, but that it wasn't important," he said. "Why?"

"Because none of these people were onboard when it took off," Jar said.

"Did they catch a ride on something else?"

"No."

"Are you saying they're still there?"

Jar readjusted herself in her seat. "I did not say that. I do not know if they are."

Orlando jumped in. "We *believe* they're still there. We've only had time to do spot checks of images between when they arrived there and now. After the helicopter left, they posted two guards outside. In every image we've checked that came after that, including one from eight minutes ago, the guards are still there."

Jar clicked her computer a few times and brought up a daylight image of the area, zooming in so that the building was large and center screen. Two men stood on its roof, one facing the runway, and the other facing some trees on the side opposite.

"This is fifteen seconds ago," she said.

"Wow, excellent work, everyone," Quinn said. "So where is this place?"

"Approximately fifty kilometers east of Vienna," Orlando said.

"East? That would be in—"

"Slovakia."

WESTERN SLOVAKIA

It took a little less than four hours to reach the Slovakian border, and another thirty minutes for Quinn, Jar, Daeng, and Kincaid to approach the private airport where the helicopter had landed.

"That one up there," Jar said. She was sitting in the front passenger seat, her laptop open, displaying a satellite image. "On the left. You see it?"

"I see it," Quinn said.

Quinn slowed the sedan, but instead of making the turn, he pulled onto the shoulder, short of the intersection. There were three cars behind them, one of which had been following them since very near the border. He didn't think any of the cars was trouble, but in this business, one could never be too cautious.

All three vehicles passed without slowing. Quinn waited until they disappeared and then made the turn.

The new road was narrow with no lane markers, just a strip of blacktop running between farms. Two kilometers down, the fields were replaced by a dense grove of pines.

"Coming up on the right," Jar said. "Start slowing…now."

Fifty meters ahead, a break in the trees marked the dirt road. Quinn checked behind them. There was no one in sight so he turned, keeping his speed slow to avoid kicking up a cloud of dust that might give away their presence.

This road was even narrower than the last, the trees encroaching on either side.

"Any changes?" he asked.

He heard Jar tap on her keyboard.

"None," she said. That meant the guards were still in place at the airport.

Seven minutes down the road, Jar pointed through the front window and said, "There. That wide spot. Just past it should be the turn."

As they reached the spot, Quinn slowed to a crawl.

"I do not see it," Jar said.

Quinn couldn't, either. "Are you sure this is the right place?"

"Yes. Positive." She grimaced. "I will go look."

Before Quinn could stop the car, Jar jumped out and searched the edge of the road. About four meters behind the car, she disappeared into the woods.

When she came back out, she waved her arms and shouted, "Back here."

Quinn reversed until he reached her and lowered the passenger-side window.

"It's overgrown," she said, "but only here at the start. It is not bad after that."

Quinn reversed some more, then, with Jar guiding him, turned off the road into the brush. It wasn't until after he passed through the initial growth that he could finally see the way ahead. An official road it was not. More a pair of tire ruts between trees than anything else.

Jar climbed back in.

The condition of the new route meant an even slower drive than before, and it took them ten minutes to travel three-quarters of a kilometer to where the ruts ended. Quinn and Jar climbed out and opened the prisoner-lock-enabled back doors so Daeng and Kincaid could join them.

Kincaid unfolded from his seat and grimaced as he stretched next to the car. Daeng, on the other hand, hopped right out.

"That was kind of fun," Daeng said.

Kincaid grunted something that did not sound like agreement. Though Quinn had been driving slowly, the sedan had still jostled enough to be unpleasant.

Until Orlando and Nate arrived with the gear they were picking up in Vienna after their flight from Zurich, Quinn's group was limited to the weapons they had on hand. This consisted of four batons, a Taser disguised as an electric shaver, the police pistol and HK G38 rifle Quinn had obtained during the escape from the Ferber estate—with only the ammo in each weapon's magazine—and a surprisingly large knife that Jar had put together from pieces hidden in a metal hairbrush and the structure of her travel bag.

"You design that yourself?" Daeng asked her, impressed.

She looked at him. "Of course. Why does this surprise you?"

"No…it…I just think it's pretty ingenious."

"I have a very high IQ," she said.

Trying not to laugh, he said, "Oh, believe me, I know."

"What did I say that is funny?"

"Nothing, sorry." He nodded at her knife. "What I was trying to get at is, can you make me one of those?"

"This is the only one I brought."

"I don't mean now. I mean a rig like that. Later."

"Oh, then yes. I can do that."

"If you two are done," Quinn said, an eyebrow raised.

"Sure. All set," Daeng said.

Quinn pointed into the woods. "The airfield?"

"No," Jar said. "Five degrees to your left."

Quinn adjusted his aim.

"That is correct."

Quinn led the group into the forest, and over the uneven ground toward the airport.

Seven minutes into their hike, Jar whispered, "Light."

Ahead, a twinkle of artificial illumination leaked through the trees, at least four hundred meters away.

"Hand signals from this point forward," Quinn said. Along with the scarcity of proper weapons, they had no communication gear other than their phones. "You need my attention, tap me."

They continued forward, taking care with each step. Soon the single pinpoint of light turned into half a dozen, all concentrated in the same area.

Ten meters before the trees ended, Quinn motioned for the others to stop and stay there. He crept up to the edge of the woods alone, keeping as low to the ground as he could without crawling.

Using a pair of pines to shield his presence, he scanned the clearing beyond. The airport was dead ahead, the runway a hundred meters away, stretching off to the left and right. Between the landing strip and his current position stood a three meter-high, chain-link fence, topped by barbed wire.

At the runway's midpoint, about fifty meters on the other side of the strip, sat the rectangular, concrete building the guards in the satellite image had been watching over. The six lights encircled the structure, four in front and one each on the left and right side. From the images, Quinn knew there were two more lights on the backside.

He pulled out his phone and zoomed the camera in on the building. No windows along the front, just a single, double-wide door, currently shut. He focused on the roof and spotted the pair of guards. One sat near the apex looking away from Quinn, while the other was pacing lower down the shallow slope.

Quinn checked the grounds around the building but saw no one else. Turning his attention to the fence, he scanned it for a gate, but the barrier was unbroken as far as he could see in either direction.

He returned to the others and led them back into the woods, until he felt they'd gone far enough to whisper without being detected.

He described what he had seen, then said, "The fence is the immediate problem. Worst case, we find a spot we can cut through, but a gate would be better. Daeng, you and Kincaid go north and see what you can find. Jar and I will head south." He checked the time. "If Orlando and Nate are on schedule, they should be here within the hour. So, let's meet back right here in forty minutes. Questions?"

There were none.

Orlando and Nate landed in Vienna a half hour before sunset.

Nate spotted a man with a sign reading CALIBRATION INDUSTRIES near the terminal's exit and said, "There's our guy."

The man greeted them with the proper recognition code, led them to a dark gray sedan parked at the curb, and drove them into the Austrian capital. On a quiet street, in the middle of the Ottakring district, the driver pulled the car into the garage of a bakery delivery service. The moment the vehicle passed through the archway, the door descended.

Two men who'd been waiting in the garage opened the sedan's rear doors so Orlando and Nate could climb out.

"*Hier entlang,*" one of the men said, directing them to a door along the back wall of the garage.

"Our bags, please," Orlando said in German.

"We can get them for you."

Smirking, she shook her head and said, "We'll take them with us."

The man frowned, then tapped on the trunk. "Open."

The driver, still in the front seat, did as ordered.

"Thank you," Orlando said.

Nate pulled the bags out and followed her through the doorway into a back office. Behind a desk sat a well-groomed, middle-aged man, in a crisp white-collared shirt and gray tie. He glanced up at them from his computer screen, then stood up, smiling, and came around the desk.

"Orlando, it's been a long time."

"Baron, you're looking fit as ever."

He extended his arms and hugged her.

"You remember Nate," she said after they parted.

"Of course." Baron Langer held his hand out to Nate. "Good to see you again."

Nate set one of the suitcases down and shook the man's hand. "Same."

"Can I get you anything?" Langer asked. "Something to eat? To drink, perhaps? I believe we've just received a batch of fresh muffins."

"Nothing, thanks," Orlando said. "We're kind of in a hurry."

"Straight to business, then."

"I'm afraid so. Is everything ready?"

"Of course. Please follow me."

The Austrian led them back into the garage, then through another exit, and down a hall to a steel door with no knob. On the wall next to the door was a finger scanner. Langer placed the middle finger of his left hand on the glass. A moment later, he pushed it open, waved Orlando and Nate through, and followed them inside.

The room they entered was approximately ten meters square, with shelves running through the middle and along both walls. On these were industrial-sized packages of flour and sugar and other items used in the baking business.

Langer led them down the left wall and stopped about seven meters from the end. He reached under a shelf.

A soft click.

He moved down another meter and a half and reached below a different shelf.

Another click. This time he pushed and a section of wall, shelf included, moved straight back.

"After you," he said, motioning at the opening. "But stop just inside."

Orlando and Nate entered a dark passageway. It was so narrow that Nate had to carry one bag in front of him and one behind. When Langer entered, he tapped his foot against the floorboard and the false wall moved back in place. The moment it sealed them inside, lights popped on overhead.

Three meters to the right of the door, the passage ended abruptly at a downward staircase.

Langer put a hand on the suitcase between him and Nate. "It'll be easier if I take one of these."

Nate relinquished the handle and they headed down the stairs, traveling what felt like two stories before reaching an antechamber at the bottom. The only way out was through a closed door controlled by another scanner. Langer used his right ring finger on this one. As soon as he removed it, the lights went out.

"You will have to move back a little," Langer said.

Nate and Orlando scooted backward until their heels hit the bottom of the stairs. Nate heard a door open, but since no light leaked through, he saw nothing. His sense of smell, however, was working overtime.

Clamping a hand over his nose, he said, "What the hell is that?"

The room had filled with the stink of decay and rot.

"Like it?" Langer said.

"Not particularly." Though Nate worked around death all the time, most of the bodies he dealt with were fresh. And on those times they weren't, he was normally equipped with something to dull the odorous onslaught.

"Good. Then it's doing its job."

The sound of movement and the clank of something metallic dropping on the floor.

Langer cursed. "Hold on."

A moment later, the beam of a flashlight cut through the darkness.

"Can one of you take this?"

Orlando grabbed the flashlight from him.

"If you could aim it through the door."

The beam whipped through the room and spilled through a doorway, lighting up an ancient-looking iron gate a meter beyond.

Langer pulled out some keys and unlocked a padlock hanging from a chain wrapped through the gate. Once the chain was removed and the gate pushed out of the way, he said, "Watch your step."

As Nate left the room, he spotted several dead rats on either side of the doorway, between it and the gate. These were the source of the smell.

"We have to put new ones out every couple days," Langer said, noticing Nate's glance. "It helps deter anyone from approaching the gate."

"You see a lot of foot traffic down here, do you?" Nate asked.

"You'd be surprised."

Beyond the gate was a brick-walled tunnel through which a steady flow of water ran down the middle. They had entered part of the city's drainage system.

"Just a little farther," Langer said as he took the flashlight from Orlando.

They walked along the left side, and within half a dozen steps, the smell of the dead rats was replaced by the musty odor oozing from the walls and floor.

At a junction with two other tunnels, Langer went left. Three minutes later, he stopped in front of another iron gate. No smell of death here, so either the entrance was due for some rat carcasses, or the nasal deterrent had been deemed unnecessary because this tunnel was less traveled than the other.

Beyond the gate, a set of stairs led to another secret doorway, this one opening into what appeared to be a restaurant kitchen under construction. Langer took them into a hallway, past a pair of restrooms, and through another fingerprint-operated door—left index this time—into a parking garage. The space was large enough for at least a dozen cars, more if they were parked end to end. At the moment, only three vehicles were present—two delivery vans and a blue Audi A4.

Langer walked up to the Audi and patted the hood. "For you."

"And the supplies?" Orlando asked.

He circled around to the trunk and popped it open. The main storage area was empty. He pulled back the carpet covering the floor and exposed the spare tire.

"Watch," he said. He touched the valve stem. "Turn twice." He twisted the value so that it made two full revolutions. "Now, what would you like to see first?"

"Guns?" Nate said.

With the smile of a showroom salesman, Langer opened a back door and lowered the armrest in the middle of the seat. After pushing twice on the seat belt-release button just to the right of the armrest, a drawer the length of the entire backseat slid forward into the footwells. Nestled in dedicated slots were a dozen pistols, four automatic rifles, a sniper's rifle, and magazines and ammunition for everything.

"Undetectable?" Orlando asked.

"Absolutely. Will pass all scans. But that shouldn't even be an issue. Most of the time, the Slovakian border officials will just wave you through."

"Say they do and decide to perform a physical search," Nate said.

"Without knowing the unlocking sequence, they won't be able to open anything."

"And if they try to tear the car apart?"

"In that case, I would suggest you get as far away as possible before they begin."

"Self-destruct?" Orlando said.

"Naturally."

Nate winced. "There's no chance of that going off accidentally, is there?"

"It's only happened once."

"That doesn't quite fill me with confidence."

"Minor injuries only. And besides, the problem has been fixed. You will be perfectly safe."

"What about the rest of the equipment on our list?" Orlando said.

Langer's smile returned, and he showed them several other hidden compartments built into the car, one holding the flash bangs, another tracking bugs and comm gear, and others holding the additional items she'd requested.

After their suitcases were loaded into the trunk, Orlando triggered Langer's final payment on her phone.

"Best of luck," Langer said as he held out the keys. "Try to keep the car in one piece."

Nate looked at Orlando, an eyebrow raised.

"You drive," she said. "I'm working."

Nate took the keys. "I'll treat it like it's my own."

"I have a question for you before we go," Orlando said to Langer. "It's, um, one you might not be able to answer."

"What's the question?"

"Do you know anything about someone hiring a Ghost 1A1 in the past few days? Probably some gear, too."

"I don't deal in helicopters."

"You deal in everything."

A smile of acknowledgment. "You're right. There are some questions I can't answer."

"So, you *did* help them."

"What? No, of course not!" He closed his eyes for a moment. When he opened them again, he said in a calmer voice, "Hypothetically, if I had been approached by someone looking for a Ghost, I would have told them I couldn't get it for them."

"I can't imagine you turning down business. Unless you're saying you couldn't get your hands on one."

His eyes narrowed. "Getting my hands on one is not the problem. It's just…dammit, Orlando. I told you I can't talk about this."

"You already are. Why didn't you help them?"

He paused before speaking again. "As a general practice, if I don't get a good feeling about a client, I'll find some way not to take the job."

"These guys scared you off?"

"As I said, as a general practice—"

"Who were they?"

"Orlando, I can't."

"You didn't take the job, Baron. Which means they probably never paid you a dime. So, technically, they were never your client and you owe them nothing. Unlike me, who just sent a nice chunk of change to your bank account. Not for the first time, I might add."

"I've given you what you paid for. I don't owe you anything more."

"Other than loyalty to a good customer?"

"Shit." He took a deep breath. "Okay, look, I don't actually know who the client was. They came to me through Zimmerman."

"*Karl* Zimmerman?" Nate said.

Langer nodded.

Zimmerman was an operative and sometime middleman who worked for whoever was willing to pay him, no matter their ideology.

"And he never told you who his client was?" Orlando asked.

"He brought one of them to meet with me. But she never gave me her name."

"And after you met with her, you decided you didn't want the job?"

"Yes. There was something…I don't know, fanatical about her. I don't like working with fanatics. They tend to be not as careful, and don't care if they damage something I might have loaned them."

"Describe the woman," Nate said.

"Young. Late twenties, probably. Light brown hair down to her shoulders. Cute, but with intense eyes. Grayish, I think, though they could have been blue. Or light brown. Or she could have even been wearing contacts. I don't know."

"Tall? Short? Skinny? Fat?"

"Around one hundred and seventy centimeters, I guess. Not fat, but not skinny, either. Toned."

It was by no means a perfect description, but it sure sounded a lot like the woman involved in Brunner's kidnapping.

"Thanks," Orlando said. "We appreciate the information."

"If you talk to Zimmerman, you can't let him know you found out through me."

Orlando feigned dismay. "I'm actually a little insulted. You should know us well enough to realize that we never sell out our friends." She climbed into the car, but before she closed the door, she said, "We'll let you know where you can find the car when we're done."

She shut the door and Nate started the engine.

13

Oh, God. Not again. Not again.

Brunner jumped off the bed and raced to the bucket in the corner of the room, dropping his pants and sitting down just in time.

He'd lost count of how many trips he'd made to his makeshift toilet. At first, he'd thought it was a nervous reaction to his situation. But the diarrhea kept coming. He was shocked he still had anything left to give.

That bottle of disgusting liquid they'd given him to drink hours earlier must have been magnesium citrate. That was the stuff used by people cleaning out their intestines in preparation for a colonoscopy.

What he couldn't figure out was why his captors would want to empty his bowels. Was it their idea of torture? If so, they might be on to something.

His colon cramped again.

Please make it stop.

14

Quinn scanned the fence via his phone and shook his head. "Nothing."

He and Jar were now parallel with the end of the runway, a good nine hundred meters from the guarded building. The only gate they'd spotted was clear on the other side of the airfield.

"Then we must use the drainage ditch," Jar whispered.

Quinn stared at the fence.

"It is the only choice," she said.

Quinn took a deep breath and nodded. When they'd discovered the ditch, he had hoped they would find a better way in farther on, but the only thing of interest they'd seen—thanks to the angle of their new position—was a fuel truck parked behind the building. As far as ways *onto* the airfield, the ditch was their best option.

They moved back through the trees, parallel to the runway, until they reached the crease in the ground again. The ditch started near the runway and ran into the woods. At the point where it crossed under the fence, metal mesh hung down, covering the hole the dip would have created in the barrier.

"Stay here," Quinn whispered.

He started lowering himself to the ground, but Jar grabbed his arm.

"I am smaller. It is better if I go."

Quinn hesitated. The drainage ditch *was* shallow. No way it would completely hide his silhouette. But Jar? She could disappear in it. Granted, if the ditch proved to be a workable entrance, they would all have to make the trip, but there was no sense in risking detection yet.

"Okay. Just—"

"Be careful?"

"Yeah."

Jar lay down in the ditch and snaked out from the cover of the trees, toward the airfield. Quinn swung his gaze back and forth from her to the sentries, checking her progress and watching for any indication she'd been spotted.

He needn't have worried. Neither guard even looked in Jar's direction.

When she reached the fence, she began fiddling with the ties that held the mesh to the chain-link fence. Quinn used his camera to see how she was getting on, but her body, as tiny as it was, blocked most of the view.

After approximately ninety seconds, she flipped around and headed back, the mesh still blocking the ditch. Quinn helped her up when she reached him. Her gloves, jacket, pants, and shoes were all covered with mud, courtesy of melted snow from a storm that had passed through the area that morning.

"No luck?" he said.

"It is almost off. There is one connector I could not undo. But with cutters or pliers, it will only take a moment."

"Is there enough clearance for all of us to get under?"

"Kincaid will not fit. But if we make a vertical slit up from the bottom of the fence, that should give him enough space."

Quinn hoped Daeng and Kincaid had found a gate, because the idea of dragging himself through the cold mud was not appealing.

"Let's clean you up," he said.

They moved deeper into the woods, where Quinn wiped as much of the mud off her as he could, using handfuls of dead needles to scrape it away. She was still a mess, but at least she wasn't caked in the stuff anymore.

Back at the rendezvous point, they found Daeng and Kincaid waiting for them. While Daeng looked his normal chill self, Kincaid was clearly excited about something.

"Finally," the bodyguard said when he saw Quinn. "You've got to see this!" He turned to Daeng. "Show him."

"You found a way in?" Quinn said.

Daeng shook his head. "It's solid fence all the way down. The only way in is if we cut a hole through it. What about you?"

"We found a drainage ditch. It's not perfect but it should work."

"Come on, show him," Kincaid said.

"What is he talking about?" Quinn asked.

As Daeng pulled his phone out of his pocket, he said, "We saw a couple people exit the building as we were coming back."

He brought up a video and tapped the play icon. The shot was zoomed in on the front of the building, and featured two people standing several meters away from the door, looking up at one of the guards on the roof. From their movements, it appeared they were having a three-way conversation. One of the people below was a man, dressed in the same black outfit as the guys on the roof. The other person was a woman.

"It's her," Kincaid said.

"From the train?"

"Yes."

"This is kind of grainy. Are you sure?"

"I'm positive. The same hair, same profile, and the exact same jacket she was wearing when she walked right by me." Kincaid grinned. "Brunner's got to be inside the building. We found him. We can get him back."

"We don't know for sure if he's there," Quinn said. Before

Kincaid could argue the point, Quinn added, "But yes, I agree. There's a very good chance he's inside. Before we do anything about it, though, you need to calm down."

"I'm calm, all right? I'm calm."

Quinn stared at him.

"I'm calm," Kincaid said in a slower, quieter voice.

Whether he wanted Kincaid to participate in the rescue was still an open question, but he didn't need to answer it right away, because the rescue wasn't going to happen until their weapons arrived. He called Orlando.

One ring, then, "Hi."

"What's your ETA?" he asked.

"Depends. How long's the hike?"

"You're here already?"

"Yeah. Just need a few minutes to unload the gear and we should be on our way."

"Hold on." He lowered the phone and looked at Daeng and Kincaid. "They're at the car. Go help them with the gear."

Daeng nodded, and he and Kincaid disappeared into the woods.

"Help's on the way," he said to Orlando, then gave her a quick rundown on what they'd found.

After he hung up, he turned to Jar to tell her they should head back to the edge of the woods to keep an eye on things, but stopped himself. Jar had her head cocked, and appeared to be concentrating on something.

"Do you hear that?" she said.

He listened. He could hear nothing and was about to say so, when his ears picked out a low drone in the distance.

Jar's eyes widened half a second before Quinn's did. Without a word, they ran toward the airfield, dodging trees and bushes, until they reached the edge of the clearing. The droning sound was much louder now, its source marked in the sky by a pair of glowing lights, growing closer and lower with every second.

Quinn texted Orlando.

Plane landing. Run!

———————

As Orlando shoved the roll-up tool kit into the duffel bag, next to the comm-gear pouch, she could hear Nate zip up a bag at the rear of the car.

"All set here," he said. "Do you need any—"

She turned her head, wondering why he'd stopped, and saw him staring into the trees. Before she could ask what was wrong, she heard the distant whine of a jet engine.

"We've gotta go," she said, zipping up her bag.

Nate slammed the trunk closed and swung his duffel's straps over his shoulders.

As Orlando shut the compartment she'd been pulling things out of, her phone vibrated in her pocket. Ignoring it, she adjusted her backpack and picked up the equipment duffel.

"Give me one of the straps," Nate said, running up to her.

Though she was more than capable of carrying the bag alone, rule number 241 in the espionage handbook dictated saving your strength when you can. She passed one of the straps to him, and together they ran into the forest, carrying the bag between them.

———————

Daeng heard the plane first, and increased his speed. Behind him, he could hear branches slapping against Kincaid's jacket as the bodyguard tried to keep up.

He knew if he had heard the plane, Orlando and Nate probably had, too. Which meant they wouldn't wait for him and Kincaid to reach them. He was far enough away now that he could raise his voice a little without being heard back at the airfield. In a half shout, he called, "Orlando! Nate!"

A half minute later, he heard, "Daeng?"

He adjusted his path slightly to his left and, twenty meters on, nearly plowed right into Nate.

"I'll take that," Daeng said, reaching for the duffel bag Nate and Orlando were carrying together.

As Orlando helped him get the straps over his shoulder, Kincaid arrived.

"This the bodyguard?" Nate asked.

Daeng nodded and introduced everyone.

"We can shake later," Orlando said, and took off sprinting again.

The plane's running lights leveled off just as a screech of rubber signaled touchdown.

Quinn watched the jet race down the airstrip, its engine whining. As it sped by the building, Quinn finally got a good look at it. A Dassault Falcon 7X. On a full tank it could go nearly six thousand miles. That was not good.

The jet continued on, rolling nearly to the end of the runway before stopping and turning to make the much slower trip back.

Jar tugged at Quinn's jacket and pointed at the building.

Two men had exited. The shorter one headed around the side of the building, while the taller one took several steps toward the runway and stopped.

The sound of an automotive engine starting drifted across the tarmac. A few seconds later, the fuel truck Quinn and Jar had seen earlier swung out from behind the structure and parked next to the building, idling.

As the plane neared, the man standing by himself turned on a pair of flashlights that had transparent red cones connected above the lenses. He used the flashlights to guide the plane to a parking position. When the man crossed the cones, the plane stopped moving, and the pilot spun the jet's engine down—annoyingly—in the exact spot blocking Quinn's and Jar's views of the building's entrance.

The fuel truck drove over to the plane.

Quinn's phone vibrated with a text from Orlando.

We're here.

———————

Leaving Jar to keep an eye on the airfield, Quinn hurried to the rendezvous point.

Orlando and Nate were passing out weapons and comm gear as he arrived.

"Where's Jar?" Nate asked as he handed Quinn a SIG SAUER P226 and three spare mags.

"On watch."

Orlando tossed Quinn a comm pack. "What are we looking at?"

"A Dassault Falcon 7X," Quinn said. "They're refueling it now, which means they probably don't plan on staying on the ground for long. We have to assume when they do go, they'll be taking Brunner with them."

"We've got to stop them," Kincaid said.

Nate, who had been sticking a magazine into his gun, paused and said, "I'm pretty sure that's the plan." He looked at Quinn. "That *is* the plan, right?"

"That's the plan." Quinn motioned for Kincaid to come over, then he walked the bodyguard a few meters away from the others. "I want you to stay back here and wait for us."

"No way, you can't—"

"This is not up for discussion. My team and I have been in these kinds of situations before. We know each other. More important, we *trust* each other to do what needs to be done. Maybe you'd fit right in, but I don't want to find out if that's true or not in the middle of a firefight."

"I can handle myself."

"See, that's the thing. This isn't about any one of us. It's about all of us, and how we work together."

"I can't just sit here and wait. Brunner is my responsibility."

"It's nothing personal, but the decision is final. Are you going to respect that?"

Kincaid clenched his jaw. "I'll stay."

Quinn nodded and led him back to the others.

"Give him one of the rifles," he told Nate.

Nate handed an assault rifle to Kincaid.

"You're the backstop," Quinn said. "In case things go sideways."

After Quinn assigned tasks to everyone, he and the team—minus Kincaid—headed to Jar's location.

"Any change?" Quinn whispered to her.

"The sentries climbed off the roof right after you left," she said.

"Anyone else come outside?"

"No."

Quinn scanned the fence to the right, in the direction of the drainage ditch. Given Brunner's presumed imminent departure, Quinn worried it would waste too much time to reposition there, cross under, and then work their way back to the plane. The direct approach was their only real choice. Thankfully, that task had been made easier by the sentries leaving the roof and the airplane itself blocking the view of anyone at the building.

He nodded to Daeng, who snuck up to the fence and began cutting a flap in the chain link.

Quinn signed for Orlando to give him another comm pack and night vision binoculars. She passed them over and he gave them to Jar. "You're our eyes," he whispered. "You see anything, you tell us."

She nodded and donned the radio.

A few moments later, Daeng made his last cut. He opened the flap, slipped through to the other side, and waved for the others to join him.

15

Brunner rubbed the side of his head. It was pretty remarkable that since being snatched off the train, he had yet to have a migraine. They were a constant problem in his life, and most prone to showing up whenever he was under stress. And there was no question he'd been under a lot of stress. The helicopter, the murder of Clarke, the confinement in this cell, and the hours of enduring twisting bowels as the laxative did its thing.

Through it all, no headache. Not even a hint.

Until now.

He could feel it at the very back of his head—not pain per se, but pressure. Soft, almost not there. But that was how it always began.

If he had his naratriptan, now would have been when to take it. Three-quarters of the time it would keep the migraine at bay. Without it, there was a hundred-percent chance he'd be in pain within the hour.

He heard a key turn in the lock on the door.

He looked over as the door swung open.

In strode the woman and the man who'd been working with Clarke.

"On your feet," the woman said. "Back against the wall."

Brunner did as she said.

The man looked out the doorway. "Bring it in."

Two of the dark-clad men entered the room, carrying a gray container. The box was over two meters long and nearly a meter wide. It appeared to be made of heavy-duty plastic and had metal handles on both sides. As the men set the box on the floor, the other similarly attired guards walked in and stopped by the door.

One of the men undid the clasps and raised the lid. Inside, the box was lined by some kind of white hardened foam, and through the middle of it ran a long, open cavity.

"Get in," the woman said.

Brunner gaped at her. "I-I'm not getting in there."

"You're getting in, one way or another."

"I-I-I'll suffocate."

"You will not," the woman said. "Now get in."

Brunner took a deep breath and moved toward the box.

"Remove your shoes first," the man from the train said.

Hands shaking, Brunner pulled off his shoes.

The woman tapped the end of the case nearest the door. "Lie down, with your head here."

After another slight hesitation, Brunner lay down in the case. The foam surface was spongy and surprisingly comfortable. Perhaps that should have made him feel better, but it only ratcheted up his fear.

Above him, the man took something from one of the soldiers and dropped it into the box.

"Put it on. You will not have enough room to do so when the lid closes."

Brunner picked the item up. It was an oxygen mask connected to a long, flexible hose. "What's this for?"

"You were worried about suffocating? Now you do not need to worry."

Brunner slipped the mask over his mouth and nose and pulled the straps over his head.

"If you fall asleep, be careful not to knock the mask off," the woman said. "That would be…unfortunate."

Heart rate quickening, Brunner asked, "How long will I be in here?"

"What?" the woman asked.

Brunner lifted his mask away from his face and repeated the question.

"No more than twenty-four hours."

Twenty-four hours? No wonder they'd cleaned out his system.

"Where are you taking me?"

"Enough questions," the man said. "Put the mask back on."

Brunner complied. The man took the other end of the hose and shoved it into a hole in the foam Brunner hadn't noticed before. There was a click.

"See you soon," the woman said and pulled the lid down, plunging the box into darkness.

It wasn't until this moment that the pressure at the back of his head returned, only stronger. "Wait! Wait!"

The mask muffled the sound. He tried to move a hand to pull it off, but as he'd been warned, there wasn't enough room to do so.

"Wait! I need medicine! Please! Open up!"

Brunner looked around, eyes wide, but he could see absolutely nothing.

He jerked at the muffled sounds of one of the metallic latches being reengaged. The remaining latches followed.

The case was lifted into the air.

Brunner had expected to hear something before being raised, but there had not been a sound. The foam was not only there to protect him; it acted as soundproofing, too. Which meant no one outside could hear his shouts.

He was on the verge of hyperventilating. He had never been this scared in his life. Even getting whisked out of the train and hauled up to the helicopter had been better than this, as at least then, he'd known what was happening.

He rolled back and forth a little as the case was moved. The jostling went on for about half a minute before he was set down again.

He tried to calm himself by counting the seconds since he'd stopped moving, but it was impossible to concentrate, and he had no idea how much time had passed when he felt a slight vibration. He assumed it was a precursor to being lifted up again, but as the vibration grew stronger and stronger, the case remained otherwise motionless.

Then, without warning, the sensation ceased.

The pressure in his head had become a cloud creeping through his brain. He should have put up more of a fight when they'd put him in the case. Maybe they would have at least sedated him. That would have been a hell of a lot better than this.

Something bumped against the case, then up he went again.

He pressed his eyelids closed and balled his fists, his nails digging into his palms.

"*Scheisse.*"

16

When Quinn and his team reached the runway's edge, they split off to their assigned positions—Quinn and Nate continuing straight toward the plane, Orlando going wide left, and Daeng wide right.

Quinn and Nate were approximately thirty meters from the jet when one of the kidnappers ducked under the aircraft. They dropped to the ground, and watched the man disconnect a flexible pipe from the plane and carry it back the way he came.

Soon, the fuel truck, parked on the other side of the plane, began to move. With the vehicle out of the way, Quinn could now see the bottom half of the building's double doors, one of which was open, with someone standing in the threshold.

A shout echoed across the tarmac. Not one of alarm, but the type used to get a person's attention. More elevated voices that Quinn interpreted as a conversation between two people separated by several meters. When it ended, the person in the doorway disappeared inside and the plane's engines fired to life.

Without even looking at each other, Quinn and Nate jumped to their feet and ran.

Using the distraction of the departing fuel truck as cover, Orlando crept forward until she found a spot from where she could see the area between the plane and the building. There, she stretched out on the ground and unslung the sniper rifle.

Via the scope, she scanned the aircraft and tarmac. A short set of stairs led from the ground to the plane's passenger door. No one on the steps, nor was anyone visible through the small slice of the plane's entrance she could see. There was, however, someone in the cockpit, looking down at the controls.

A man moved into the building's doorway, drawing her attention away from the plane. He stopped short of the threshold.

"Hey!" he shouted.

The man in the cockpit opened a side window. The two shouted back and forth for a few moments. The words that reached Orlando were garbled by the distance so she didn't pick up anything.

When the conversation ended, the man in the plane closed his window and started the engines.

Seconds later, six people exited the building, four of them carrying a large gray case. Seven individuals had been in the satellite images of the helicopter's arrival, so someone was missing. Using the scope, she scanned the faces. The woman was there, leading the group. A man walked beside her, and carrying the case were four others, all of whom Orlando was sure had been in the satellite photos. Brunner was the only one missing.

She focused back on the case. It was long. Human-body long.

Could it be…?

She clicked on her mic. "Six people heading to the plane with a large case. I have a feeling Brunner's inside it."

"Daeng, status," Quinn whispered.

"In position. I see them, too."

"We can't let them get on the plane," Quinn said.

Orlando put the man carrying the far front corner of the case in her crosshairs.

A shot from Orlando's sniper rifle cracked across the airfield.

Before Quinn and Nate were even able to drop to the ground beneath the wing, short bursts of assault-rifle fire from Daeng's position added to the sudden chaos among the kidnappers.

Quinn searched for targets.

Two men lay motionless on the tarmac, pools of blood surrounding them, glistening in the lights. The other four were still upright. Two were manhandling the case onto the plane's stairs, while the other two were returning Orlando's and Daeng's fire.

Quinn picked out one of the shooters and sent a bullet smashing into the man's hip. The guy spun and went down screaming, his rifle clattering away from him. The other man looked for where the shot had come from, but before he could lay eyes on Quinn, three bullets struck him simultaneously. The guy seemed to freeze in place for a moment before dropping to the tarmac.

Quinn turned to aim at the pair moving the crate, only they were no longer in sight. He could still see the crate, though. It was hanging partially below the plane as it was being pulled up the stairs into the aircraft.

"I don't have eyes on the last two."

"Me, neither," Daeng said.

"Repositioning," Orlando said.

Pushing to his feet, Quinn hurried forward and ducked under the plane. "I've got this."

He reached the other side as the back end of the crate passed through the doorway. Unable to see anyone from his current position, he took several backward steps toward the building, his gun trained on the jet's open entrance. He caught sight of an arm and pulled his trigger, but his target disappeared before the bullet could hit it.

Someone started shooting at him from inside, the slugs hitting the ground a few meters from him. Quinn held his place, willing the shooter to come into view. Instead, the case was yanked inward until it cleared the entrance, then the door slammed shut.

At the same time, the plane began to move.

———

The second the jet started rolling, Orlando switched her aim to the cockpit window.

"I've got a line on the pilot," she said.

"Take the shot," Quinn told her.

She pulled the trigger.

The bullet smashed into the glass but didn't break it.

She shot again, but the window held firm. Apparently this wasn't your typical, run-of-the-mill Falcon.

As the plane turned toward the runway, she aimed at the cockpit's side window, hoping it was weaker. But once more, her shot barely scratched the surface.

"Why is it still moving?" Quinn asked.

"Bulletproof glass," she said.

"Are you kidding me?"

"I can try shooting through the fuselage."

"Don't," he said.

There was no need for him to explain his decision. Their job was to recover Brunner alive. They couldn't chance a shot hitting something that could set the aircraft on fire.

"Copy," she said.

———

Nate clicked on his mic. "Orlando, you have the discs?"

"Yeah, I do."

"Coming to you."

He sprinted past the turning plane and across the field to where Orlando was rising to her feet, pulling on his gloves to make sure they were tight to his hand. Since they couldn't stop the plane without the risk of accidentally killing Brunner, Nate knew there was only one other option. And he was in the best position to pull it off.

"Give them to me," he yelled as he ran up.

When he reached her, she shoved a pair of long-range tracking discs into his hand. He picked up his pace again and checked the plane's position. The Falcon had reached the runway, and was taxiing to the end from where it would make a one-eighty turn and begin its takeoff. At the speed it was traveling, it would be a close call on whether he'd reach it in time.

He dug deep, running as fast as his artificial right leg would allow.

He was beginning to worry he wouldn't make it, but then the plane slowed to make its turn.

He reached the aircraft as it was still coming around, and moved underneath it. After ripping off the protective layer on the sticky side of one of the bugs, he slapped it onto the strut of the nearest landing gear. He prepped the second disc, but dropped it in the process.

"Crap!"

Thankfully, the sticky side stayed up, but he was out of time as the jet's power increased. He stuck the disc on the support behind the wheel and raced out from under the plane, reaching the edge of the runway just as the jet started rolling again.

Orlando's comm crackled to life. "Nate, do you read me?" Quinn said.

No response.

"I don't think he can hear you over the engines," Orlando said into her mic. She was watching the end of the runway through her binoculars, and had seen Nate disappear under the craft then run out the other side. "I think he did it, though."

She lowered the glasses and watched the Falcon roar by.

As soon as it lifted into the air, she said into her mic, "Orlando for Jar."

"Go for Jar."

"Nate put at least one tracker on the plane. See if you can pick it up."

"Copy."

"Hey," Daeng said over the comm. Orlando turned and saw him standing among the downed men outside the building. "One of these guys is still alive."

"Good," Quinn replied. "See if there's someplace inside where we can all have a little chat. Orlando, you want to join us?"

"On my way."

17

Tiana Snetkov—the woman Clarke had known as Astrid and Eric Ferber as Lilly Becker—stared out the window, looking back toward the cement building as the jet taxied to the end of the runway. She counted two people standing among her dead soldiers.

Who the hell were they? And how had they found her and the others? She and Grigory Krylov—aka Esa—had thought they'd been so careful in covering their tracks.

Apparently not.

The attackers couldn't have been merely hired guns sent to stop her and her people. They must have known Brunner was in the box, or at the very least suspected he was on the plane. It was the only explanation for why, with the exception of a few shots at the cockpit's windshield, they hadn't fired directly on the aircraft. They must have been concerned about injuring her prisoner. Which meant they had come to get Brunner back.

She noticed two more intruders. The farthest one appeared to be running toward the other one. Upon reaching each other, there was a brief pause before the larger shadow continued onward again.

"Dammit," she whispered.

"What is it?" Grigory asked.

She nodded her chin at the window and he took a look outside.

The running shadow was on an intercept course with the plane, and gaining ground.

Tiana turned toward the cockpit. "You need to go faster!"

"I can't," the pilot said. "We're almost to the end of the runway."

She grimaced and returned her gaze out the window

Thirty seconds later, the plane slowed to a near stop and began to turn.

The shadow was close now. So close that Tiana could see it was a man, and that he would reach them before takeoff began.

Her first thought was he would plant some kind of bomb to disable the plane without completely destroying it. But it didn't appear the man had anything like that in his hands, nor did he have any kind of bag to carry such a device. Before she could think of what else he might try, he raced onto the runway and disappeared under the fuselage.

A few seconds later, the engines roared, and the plane quickly reached a speed impossible for anyone on foot to match. She looked back to see what had happened to the man, but the side-facing windows denied her the angle she needed.

As the wheels lifted off the tarmac, she breathed a sigh of relief. If the man had been trying to stop them, he had failed.

"Who the hell are they?" Grigory asked.

"I have no idea," she said.

"How did they know we were—"

"I have *no* idea."

Grigory was silent for a moment before saying, "Nesterov will not be happy."

"No shit."

18

The building contained several rooms suitable for an interrogation. One of them was a windowless box with a cot and a ripe bucket that had been used as a toilet by someone with digestive issues.

Brunner's holding cell, Quinn guessed.

But for the smell, the room would have worked nicely for their needs. Instead, they settled on the space near the building's main door.

Daeng and Quinn carried the wounded man inside and propped him up on a wooden chair, the guy grunting in pain throughout. While they held him in place, Orlando covered the man's wounds with duct tape, then used the rest of the roll to strap his torso to the seat.

The man said something that sounded like Russian, but wasn't.

"What is that?" Daeng asked.

"Ukrainian, I think," Orlando said.

Quinn nodded, thinking the same thing. He grabbed the guy's chin and tilted it up.

"English?"

The guy made no indication that he understood.

Quinn removed his gun and pressed it against the man's undamaged leg. "Do you speak English?"

The man jumped and stared wide-eyed at Quinn. After a second, he nodded.

"Good." Quinn eased the pressure but did not remove the weapon. "Where is the plane going?"

"I-I-I do not know."

"Bullshit." Quinn shoved the gun down again.

The man yelped. "I tell truth! I do not know. They do not tell us! They only—" The man winced in pain.

"They only what?"

"They…they say go to…" He paused. "I not know how to say in English." He spoke a phrase in Ukrainian.

Orlando pulled out her phone, tapped it several times, then held the mic end toward the prisoner. "Say it again."

The man repeated the phrase.

She pulled the phone back and looked at the screen. "Lonely Rock."

"What the hell does that mean?" Quinn asked. He turned back to the prisoner. "What's Lonely Rock?"

"I never go. Not sure."

"'Not sure' means you at least have a guess."

The man looked away, as if realizing he'd said too much.

"Buddy, I don't know if you fully understand this yet or not, but your friends are gone and they're not coming back. You help us, I'll make sure you get medical attention. If not, we leave you to bleed out."

Another wave of pain washed across the man's face. As it subsided, he took a deep breath and looked back at Quinn. "Like…like a base, I think."

"A military base?"

"Same but not same."

"What government do you work for?"

"Not work for government."

"Then *who* do you work for?"

"Anyone who hire us."

Quinn cocked his head. "You're paramilitary?"

Now the man's whole face creased. "Para...what? I not understand."

"A mercenary," Orlando said. "Private soldier."

The man's eyes widened. "Yes. Yes. Private soldier."

"All of you were private soldiers?"

"No. Only men carrying box."

"The other two—were they the people who hired you?"

The man nodded.

"Who are they?"

"We, uh, we call man Commander Krylov and woman Commander Snetkov."

"Are those their real names?"

"I do not know."

"They're Ukrainian, too?"

"No. They speak Russian to us but never say where they from."

"Do you know who *they* work for?"

"I have no idea. My boss maybe know, but not me."

"Who's your boss?"

The prisoner's eyes flickered toward the building's exit.

"One of the dead guys out there," Quinn said.

The man nodded.

"What was his name?"

"Gura."

"Roman Gura?" Orlando said.

The captive nodded again.

"You've heard of him?" Quinn asked.

"His group is, or was, I guess, part of Tonast Security." Tonast Security was a Slavic network of mercenaries who tended to be more active in the Middle East and Africa than in Europe.

"Any chance we can use them to backtrack who hired Gura?"

"No guarantees, but I'll check."

"You have any other question you think we should ask this piece of garbage?"

Orlando shook her head. "He's useless."

Quinn pointed his gun at the prisoner's head.

What blood remained in the man's face drained away. "No, no! Please!"

"What's Lonely Rock?"

"I tell you already all I know! I swear!"

"I don't believe you."

"I *do not* know anything more!"

"All right, then what about who Krylov and Snetkov work for?"

Looking desperate, the man said, "Maybe…Russian government?"

"Did they say this?"

"No. But-but makes sense, yes?"

Quinn stared at him.

"I-I-I have no idea. Just guess. Please!"

Quinn gave it another beat before he lowered his gun. Blood was beginning to seep out from under the duct-tape bandage, so he said to Daeng, "See anything we can cover his wound with?"

"There's a dirty towel over there."

"That'll do."

When Daeng went to fetch it, the man pleaded, "I need doctor. I need to go to hospital."

"Don't worry. I'm sure someone will be by to help you out eventually."

The towel Daeng returned with was actually not dirty. He put it over the man's wound and said, "Keep the pressure on."

"Wait! You can't leave me like this!"

Quinn, Orlando, and Daeng headed toward the exit.

"Wait!" the man yelled as they stepped outside. "Wait! Wa—"

Quinn slammed the door shut.

Nate walked down the center of the runway, back toward the building where the others were.

Two silhouettes, one small and one large, separated from the woods to the right and passed through the hole in the fence Daeng had cut.

Jar and Kincaid.

Nate picked up his pace and intercepted them as they reached the airstrip.

Kincaid said, "You let them get away!"

"I'm going to ignore the tone of your voice," Nate said. "And we did not *let* them get away. We put up a pretty good fight to keep that from happening. Besides, we know where they are, right, Jar?"

"Yes."

"If you have a problem with anything," Nate said to Kincaid, "take it up with Quinn."

Kincaid grimaced but said nothing more.

Nate glanced at Jar again. "Hey, by the way."

A flicker of a smile on her face, then all serious again. "Hello."

While Nate and Jar talked to each other several times a week, they hadn't physically been in each other's presence in nearly two months. Usually it was voice or video calls, often involving her help with his new hobby. Like when she'd assisted him in his search for a California killer and they ended up unearthing a conspiracy a lot bigger than either of them had expected. Other times it was just him checking on her, prodding her to tell him about her day, and solidifying the ties that were turning them into each other's best friend.

"Can I carry something for you?" he asked her.

She had her opened laptop tucked between an outstretched hand and her chest, a small duffel in the other hand, and a backpack over her shoulder.

"I am fine."

Nate rolled his eyes. "Jar, we've talked about this."

She continued to walk for several steps before expelling a

breath and handing him the duffel. She had the habit of sometimes feeling like she needed to do everything herself. That's the way she'd survived through most of the first twenty or so years of her life. As part of Quinn's team—and a charter member of Nate's Hobby Club—she was slowly learning it was okay to rely on others.

"*Khob khun ka*," she said.

"You're welcome," he replied.

She hesitated before saying, "You, um, did very well with putting the trackers on the plane."

"Thank you. That was sweet."

Her eyes narrowed. "Are you being...what is the word? Fatuous?"

He chuckled. "Technically, yes, but I think the word you're looking for is facetious."

She tried the word a few times but kept stumbling over the final syllable. She gave up and said, "You did not answer my question."

"I was not being facetious."

She stared at him for a few steps. "Okay. Good."

Orlando, Quinn, and Daeng were coming out of the building as Nate, Jar, and Kincaid reached the aircraft parking area. They met up in the same spot where the jet had been waiting.

"Where's it headed?" Orlando asked Jar.

Jar checked her screen "East. Still over Slovakia. If they keep their current path, they will be over northern Hungary in approximately eighteen minutes."

"East," Quinn said, thinking.

Orlando nodded back at the building. "If our friend in there is right, they could be heading for Russia." She gave Nate, Jar, and Kincaid a quick rundown of what they'd learned from the injured man.

"We're going to need our own plane," Quinn said.

Nate looked around at the bodies strewn in front of the building. "And someone to clean up this mess. I mean, we don't have to do it, do we?"

———————

The team—minus Orlando, who was working on logistics—returned to the cars to collect the rest of their gear.

"You three start gathering everything," Quinn said to Nate, Daeng, and Jar. "Kincaid, come with me." He motioned for the bodyguard to follow him down the dirt road.

"What?" Kincaid said after he joined him.

"I know you're not very happy right now."

"You think I should be?"

"No. But be careful where that anger is focused."

"What's that supposed to mean?"

Quinn said nothing for a moment. "Tell me, what would you have done differently back there?"

The combination of irritation and uncertainty on the man's face told Quinn Kincaid had been thinking a lot about that but had come up with nothing.

After a few more seconds of silence, Quinn said, "I think we have a better chance of succeeding with you on the team than not. But I need you fully with us. If you can't do that, then I won't have any choice but to leave you behind. If you can, I'll work things out with Misty."

Kincaid looked down the road. "I can't go back. I need to be a part of making this right."

"You promise you won't try to take things into your own hands? Maybe even take off on your own?"

Kincaid nodded.

"I want to make sure you're clear about this. Staying means you will do everything I or anyone else on my team asks you to do. No questions."

"Everything? What if they—"

"These are the terms of your employment, Mr. Kincaid. Take it or leave it."

"I do whatever I'm told."

Quinn held out his hand and Kincaid shook it.

As they turned to walk back to the others, Kincaid said, "So what are you going to tell Misty?"

"I'm not going to have time to call her until we're in the air. And I doubt she'd then make us turn around just to drop you off."

Kincaid stared at him for a second, and then chuckled to himself.

When the team returned to the landing strip, Orlando informed Quinn two aircraft would be arriving within the hour—one a long-range Gulfstream G650 that would fly them wherever they decided to go, and the other a helicopter bearing a Czech-based CIA clean team to deal with the prisoner and the bodies.

"Where's the stuff you found at Brunner's apartment?" Orlando asked Nate while the team waited for the transport.

Nate patted his backpack. "Right here."

"We've got a few minutes. Let's take a look."

The first thing Nate pulled out was a hard drive. Before he could hand it to Orlando, however, Jar snatched it from him.

She turned the unit around, examining every side of the box. "Solid state."

"Doesn't that mean whatever's on it might still be intact?" Nate asked.

She either ignored his question or was too engrossed in her examination to hear him, because the next thing she said was, "The connector is cracked. It will need to be replaced. I do not have the hardware for it here."

She turned to Orlando, but Orlando shook her head. "Me, neither."

Jar glanced at the building. "Are there any electronics inside? Maybe there's something I can use."

Quinn shrugged. "Wasn't exactly looking for that kind of thing when we were inside."

Jar started toward the door.

"Ignore the bloody guy in the chair!" Daeng called out.

"When have I had a problem with that?" Jar said without stopping. A moment later, she disappeared into the building.

Nate pulled out a group of three books, and handed two to Orlando. "They're written in some kind of code. There were several more, but I didn't have any way to carry the rest without them being noticed."

Orlando opened one of the notebooks and leafed through the pages. "This looks like it might take a while to break."

"What's the other book?" Quinn asked, nodding at the one Nate still held.

"You tell me." Nate grasped the book by one of the covers, and held it out so that the pages should fan downward, but they didn't.

"Let me see that," Quinn said.

Nate handed it to him and Quinn turned it around a few times, studying it.

"I'm thinking it's some sort of box," Nate said. "Gotta be a hidden button somewhere but I didn't see anything. Of course, I didn't really have a lot of time to look. Hell, maybe it doesn't even open at all."

Quinn didn't see a button, either. He tapped on a cover. No echo, like one would expect if the thing had been hollow, and yet it felt lighter than a book of its thickness and type should be.

As he flipped it over for another look, Jar exited the building. In her arms was a tower-style desktop computer that was almost the length of her torso.

"You found what you were looking for?" Daeng said.

"Ask me again in a minute," she said.

She raised the computer as high as she could and dropped it

on the ground. The outer shell shattered, and the inside spilled out across the pavement. Kneeling, she sifted through the mess for a few seconds, then snatched a bundle of wires out of the pile and rejoined the others.

"Well?" Daeng said.

"This is not perfect but I can make it work." Her gaze locked on the book in Quinn's hand. "What is that?"

"We're not sure," Quinn said. "Might be a safety box."

"Or a doorstop," Nate suggested.

"Here." Jar shoved the wires she'd just collected and Brunner's hard drive into Nate's hands, and said to Quinn, "May I?"

"Be my guest." He handed her the book.

It wouldn't have surprised Quinn if she'd figured it out right away, but the box appeared to confound her as much as it had him and Nate. She was still at it fifteen minutes later when Kincaid pointed at an approaching light in the sky and said, "I think our taxi's here."

19

HUNGARY

Tiana should have been smiling.

They had Brunner. They were en route to Lonely Rock. And, with the pilot's announcement that they'd crossed into Hungarian airspace, they had just put the first of several international borders between themselves and the people who had tried to stop them.

But a sense of unease in her gut kept her from feeling relief.

She pushed out of her seat and headed back to the toilet. On the way, she stopped at the case containing the prisoner and checked the tablet computer velcroed to the top of the box. It displayed two readouts: one, a gauge for the oxygen tank strapped to the wall beside the container, currently reading 93 percent full; and the other, a digital display of Brunner's pulse rate, at the moment a slightly elevated 84. Given the circumstances, it was not unexpected.

She continued on to the toilet. As she opened the door, she realized what was eating at her. She whirled around and rushed toward the cockpit.

"What's wrong?" Grigory asked as she passed, but she flew by, saying nothing.

When she reached the pilots, she said, "Find someplace to land. Now."

The copilot looked at her. "But we're not supposed—"

"I don't care what your orders are. I'm the officer in charge. I'm telling you to land so take us down!"

The two men exchanged a glance, and the pilot said, "Of course. Anton, check for the closest airport."

The copilot conducted a search on the computer in the dash. "There is nothing ahead of us until we reach Ukraine."

"We can't wait that long," Tiana said. "You need to land now."

"Well, all right, um…." He consulted the computer again. "The closest is in Debrecen. But it's to the south. About one hundred and twenty kilometers off our course."

"That's fine. How quickly can you get us there?"

"That will depend on air traffic control. Since we are not scheduled, they will have to fit us in and we might have to wait until—"

"No waiting! Declare an emergency. That should clear the way, right?"

The copilot stared at her, shocked at the suggestion.

The pilot answered, "Yes, that should do it."

"Wh-what kind of emergency?" the copilot asked.

"I don't give a shit. You figure it out. Just get us on the ground as quickly as possible."

———

Quinn closed his eyes and rubbed his forehead. "Misty, stop," he said into his phone. "I give you my word—when this is all over, I'll deliver Kincaid to you myself."

As he'd promised Kincaid, he'd waited to call Misty until after they lifted off. That had occurred seven minutes earlier, putting them exactly thirty-six minutes behind the other plane. Closer than he'd feared, but still too far behind for his liking.

"Fine," Misty said, clearly not happy. "But I would appreciate it in the future that if I give an order, you back me up on it."

"I will. I promise."

A pause. "If there isn't anything else…"

"There is," Quinn said. "Two things, actually. First, and I know I've asked this already, but it could really help us if we had a better idea of why Brunner was kidnapped. What he's been working on. Who exactly would be interested in him."

"I've checked. No one has that information."

"You know that can't be true."

"Let me rephrase. I've checked with my contacts and no one is willing to share that information with me."

"That, I believe. But perhaps you can push a little harder."

"Do you think I haven't?"

"Of course not. But it couldn't hurt to try again. What's the worst that can happen?"

"They close down the Office. Maybe throw me in prison on some trumped-up charges to keep me quiet."

Quinn said nothing.

"Fine. I'll ask, okay? But don't expect much. What was the other thing?"

"The mercenary we questioned gave us the names of the couple I believe helped Clarke on the train. No idea if the names are real or bogus."

"Give them to me. I'll check them out."

"The woman's name is Snetkov and the man Krylov. He called each of them commander. That could also be made up."

"I'll see what I can do."

"Thanks, Misty."

As Quinn hung up, Orlando announced, "They're changing course."

The last time Quinn glanced at the tracking software on her computer, the kidnapper's jet had entered northern Hungary on an eastward heading that, if maintained, would take it into

Ukrainian airspace in about thirty minutes. Now, the dot representing the aircraft was finishing a turn to the south.

"Looks like they're descending, too," Orlando said.

"Just a change of altitude or are they landing?"

She watched the screen for a few seconds before saying, "Landing, it looks like." She brought up a browser window and did a quick search. "The nearest airport on their path with a runway long enough for them is in Debrecen."

"I've never been there."

"Me, neither." She performed another search. "Population around two hundred thousand. Some light industry, regional business headquarters, and a lot of agriculture in the surrounding area."

"No obvious reason why they'd be landing there?"

She scrolled down. "Oh, here it is. 'Popular location for secret bases and private prisons.'"

"You could have just said no."

"I could have, but where would the fun have been in that?"

They watched the screen for a few more minutes.

"No question," Orlando said. "They're landing. But they must have filed a flight plan to get clearance so quickly."

"How long for us to get there?"

"I'd say probably forty-five minutes or so before we could be on the ground. We'll have to be slotted into an opening in their landing order since the airport doesn't know we're coming."

"I'll talk to the pilot," Quinn said, pushing himself out of his chair.

Nate sat next to Jar, on one side of the only table in the aircraft. Their chairs faced the back of the plane, while Daeng, sitting in a chair on the other side, faced forward. Kincaid probably would have like to be sitting next to Daeng, but he was too big for the two of them to comfortably sit side by side for any length of time, so he was in the seat directly behind the former monk.

"Hold it still," Jar said.

"I *am* holding it still," Nate said, pressing Brunner's hard drive against the table. "It's the plane that's moving."

She grimaced but said nothing more as she clipped wires and hooked them into the connector she'd salvaged. After about five minutes, she sat back and put the connector into the appropriate slot on her laptop.

Immediately, the drive warmed under Nate's hand. After a few seconds, a dialogue box appeared on Jar's screen, the message in Thai.

"That is not a surprise," she said.

"What's not a surprise?" he asked.

"It's encrypted," she replied.

"Can you *de*crypt it?"

"I do not see why not."

"Great. How long will it take?"

"How can I know that? I have only now turned it on."

"A guestimate. You know, a range." He was well aware she hated to partake in guessing things like this, so he was goading her a little—partly in fun, and partly because estimating things was part of being in this business.

"Fine," she said. "Here is your guestimate. It could take an hour. It could take a year."

"A year won't be very helpful."

"An unnecessary observation. I am well aware of our time constraints. If you will stop asking me questions and let me get started, maybe we will be lucky."

Nate's eyes narrowed. "You don't believe in luck."

"I said that only for you."

Nate bowed his head in defeat and motioned at her computer. As she went back to work, he could hear Quinn talking on the phone a few rows up. From the bits and pieces he picked up, he assumed Misty was on the other end.

Not long after Quinn finished, Daeng said, "I wonder what that's all about."

Nate glanced across the table, and Daeng nodded toward the front of the plane. Nate twisted in his seat to take a look. Quinn was leaning into the cockpit, talking to the pilots. When he stood and started walking back, the plane banked to the right.

Seeing Nate and Daeng looking at him, Quinn continued past Orlando to the table.

"What's going on?" Nate asked.

"The kidnappers are landing."

"Already? Where?"

"In Hungary. Debrecen."

"Any idea why?"

"Working on that," Quinn said. "We'll be on the ground in about forty-five. Not sure what the plan will be yet, but I want everyone ready to move."

"Got it."

Quinn switched his gaze to the hard drive. "Did you get it working?"

Jar was focused on her screen and didn't seem to hear him, so Nate answered, "It's powered up but it's encrypted. Jar's trying to break through now."

"I am setting up the computer so *it* can break through," Jar said. "I am not doing it myself."

Nate glanced at Quinn. "What she said."

Quinn smirked. "Let me know if you're able to pull anything off it."

Nate knew Jar was about to explain that it would take longer than three-quarters of an hour to see any results, so he spoke first. "No problem. Will do."

After Quinn left, Jar said, "He did not need to know there would be no information before we land, correct?"

"Correct," Nate said.

"Hmm. Okay. But I do not need you speaking for me."

"Fair point. My apologies."

A flash of a smile from Jar, then all serious again as she returned to her task.

"Dude, you're like the Jar whisperer," Daeng said.

Jar looked up again. "Jar whisperer? Like the movie *The Horse Whisperer*? This is what you mean?"

Daeng looked uncomfortable. "Yeah, but it was a joke. I didn't mean that you were a—"

"I know what you meant. You meant someone who can communicate with someone or something others cannot easily do."

Her words did nothing to improve Daeng's look of unease. "Well, yes, but—"

"You are right. Nate does understand me better than you. Better than...anyone." She turned to Nate. "You *are* the Jar whisperer."

"Thanks?"

"You are welcome." She returned her attention to her computer.

Behind Daeng, Kincaid shook his head and said, "You guys are a bunch of wackos."

"I can live with that," Nate said.

After Jar got the decryption going, she pulled out the sealed book and began pushing and prodding it again. She'd been at it for around five minutes when the tome let out a *thonk* and the top cover popped up.

"Well, I'll be dammed," Nate said.

She set it on the table next to the hard drive and lifted the lid. At one point, it had been a real book, but the pages had been glued together and the centers cut out. The cavity created was filled with black packing foam.

Mostly filled, that was.

Sitting dead center in the foam, in a tight-fitting groove, was a silver rectangle about the length and width of a thin, convenience-store lighter. The metal was scored about a third of the way from one end.

"What is that?" Daeng asked.

"Flash drive?" Nate suggested.

Jar grunted noncommittally and leaned down for a closer look. After several seconds, she pulled on rubber gloves and prodded the foam in places. She then reached for the object.

"Wait," Nate said.

"What?" she said, looking at him, her fingers hovering above the foam.

He glanced over his shoulder and said in a loud voice, "Hey, you guys, you might want to see this."

Quinn and Orlando rose from their seats and came back. Kincaid stood up and looked over Daeng's seat.

"You opened it," Orlando said upon seeing the book.

"Of course I did," Jar said.

"What is that?" Quinn asked, his gaze on the silver rectangle.

"That's the question of the moment," Nate said. "Okay, Jar."

Jar slipped her fingers between the foam and the rectangle and pulled out the object.

Nate could now see it was about a millimeter thick, and that the score line went around the sides, too. He guessed it marked a removable end cap.

Jar turned the object and stared at the side that had been facing down in the foam.

"Find something interesting?" Nate asked.

She set the rectangle on the table so everyone could see the backside. All the other sides were entirely covered in metal. Not so here. While the short portion below the scored line was also metal, the surface on the other side of the line was entirely black glass.

"You have another set of gloves?" Orlando asked.

Jar handed her a disposable set from her bag. Orlando pulled them on and gingerly took the stick from Jar.

As Orlando studied it, Jar said, "It appears to be a biometrics reader."

"I agree," Orlando said.

With her free hand, Orlando grabbed the smaller section below the score and glanced at Jar. "Do you mind?"

"Not at all."

A tug and the cap came free, revealing a connector.

"It *is* a flash drive," Daeng said.

"Perhaps," Orlando said, though she sounded doubtful.

She handed it back to Jar. "I wouldn't try it on your machine."

Jar twisted the object in her hand. "I can isolate it. Any damage it could cause would be minimal."

The pilot's voice came over the intercom. "We've been in touch with Debrecen and they've been able to work us in, but we won't be on the ground for another fifty-six minutes."

"Fifty-six?" Quinn said.

"Must be a lot of traffic going in," Orlando said.

Jar, apparently unfazed by the news, had set the device next to her laptop and was typing on her keyboard. After she finished, she picked up the stick and plugged it into her machine, glass side up.

A slowly pulsing red light began to glow along the edges of the glass. Jar studied her computer. At first, it appeared everything was going as she expected. But then her brow furrowed.

"It should not be able to do that," she whispered.

"What?" Nate asked.

"It's connected itself to the internet."

"How? You haven't unlocked it yet."

"It must have an automatic program that turns on when it powers up," she said, her eyes never leaving her screen.

Inside a window on her screen, data that Nate couldn't understand scrolled faster and faster. This was matched by the sound of the fan inside her laptop increasing.

"Maybe you should—"

Jar yanked the device from her machine, but the data in the window and the fan's whine both continued.

"Did it upload a virus?" Orlando asked.

"This is coming from the web," Jar said. "From wherever that thing was connected to, but—"

She said something in Thai that Nate was pretty sure was a swear word as she shut her laptop, flipped it over, and popped the battery out.

Finally, the fan slowed.

"What the hell happened?" Kincaid asked.

"I…I do not know," Jar said. She picked up the metal rectangle and stared at it. "I do not think this is a flash drive."

"No," Orlando said. "It's a key. Part of one, anyway. You probably need the right fingerprint on the bio scanner. That's why it didn't cooperate."

"Brunner's fingerprint," Quinn said.

"That would make the most sense."

"If it's a key, then it could give us access to what Brunner's been working on, right?" Quinn said. "Might be our only way to find out."

"*If* we had his fingerprints," Nate said.

"They must be on file somewhere," Orlando said. "I can see what I can dig up."

"You think you could get that thing to work?" Quinn asked Jar.

"With the fingerprint, I should be able to."

"Then let's make it happen."

20

Debrecen air traffic control granted Tiana's jet immediate emergency clearance, and twenty-two minutes after she had given her order to land, the Falcon was on the ground.

The pilots were instructed to park in an area southwest of the passenger terminal, where two fire engines and three airport police vehicles waited.

The excuse the pilots had used to obtain clearance was that a warning light had indicated a problem with the pressurization system. Now that the jet was on the ground, the two men had "discovered" the real problem was with the light itself.

When the pilots exited the plane to explain this to the authorities, Tiana followed them out, but instead of walking with them to the waiting vehicles, she ducked underneath the fuselage, hoping the thought that had been bothering her would be a nonissue.

It was about the man who had run under the plane. She'd assumed at the time he was hoping to somehow disable the craft and had failed. But what if his intentions had been something else entirely?

She scanned the bottom of the plane, looking for anything that seemed even remotely out of place.

"Hey!" a voice yelled.

One of the officials the pilots were talking to was looking in her direction. He shouted something in Hungarian, a language she didn't understand. She ignored him and returned to her task.

She saw nothing unusual stuck to the fuselage or under the wings, so she walked over to the nearest landing gear and looked it up and down. She was no airplane mechanic, but everything seemed to be—

Her eyes narrowed and she leaned closer.

"Hey!" the official yelled again, his voice much nearer this time.

She barely even registered him, her attention fully on a small black square attached near the top of a diagonal support post. It didn't match anything else on the gear.

She grabbed an edge of it and gave it a tug. While most of the square remained in place, a corner peeled back a bit, allowing her to see it was secured in place by some kind of adhesive backing. Sure now that it was not standard equipment, she yanked harder.

Another "hey!" was followed by a barrage of Hungarian.

Still pulling, she glanced toward the voice.

The official was walking rapidly toward her, having already passed the end of the wing. Trailing him were the two pilots and the other official.

Just as the man reached the fuselage and ducked down to get a better look at Tiana, the square came free from the post.

The man barked again, clearly not happy.

"Sorry, I don't speak Hungarian," she said in English to obscure her background.

This stopped him midsentence. He looked back, and said something to his colleague.

Tiana walked over to the other rear landing gear. When she saw no black square attached to it, she relaxed.

"You must come," the second official said in heavily accented English. "Please, you cannot be out here."

"I'm just doing an inspection. I'm almost done."

He translated what she'd said to his colleague. There was more talking, but Tiana didn't pay attention. Instead, she circled around the landing gear to make sure she hadn't missed anything.

"You must come now," the official said. Though he wasn't yelling like his colleague had, his tone was sterner. "You are in violation."

"I'm sorry, I didn't—" She paused.

There, on the arm connecting a diagonal post to the wheel, was another square. It had been hidden behind the tire, keeping her from seeing it from any other angle.

"If you do not return inside your airplane, we will be forced to arrest you."

She grabbed the square and tried to yank it off, but it was better affixed than the other one.

"This is your last warning."

Grimacing, she let go of the square and said, "I'm coming, I'm coming."

As she scooted out from under the plane, she nonchalantly slipped the first square into her back pocket.

The first official, his face red, spoke to her again in Hungarian, his tone full of anger.

"I wasn't doing anything wrong," she said to the man who spoke English. "I'm a certified pilot, so while my friends were talking to you, I was helping them by checking the plane."

"You will get back on board now and will not come out again," the man said.

"Of course. Whatever you want."

She climbed back into the jet.

While she waited for the pilots to join her, she pulled the square out of her pocket. It was not much larger than a postage stamp and wafer thin, with no marking to indicate what it was for.

A few minutes later, the copilot reboarded.

"So?" Tiana asked.

"They're sending out an inspector. Once he clears us, we can leave."

"How long until he gets here?"

"I don't know."

She heard the pilot start up the stairs so she moved to the doorway, intercepting him before he reached the top. Glancing beyond him, she saw the officials returning to their vehicles. She held up the square and said to the pilot, "Do you recognize this?"

He shook his head. "What is it?"

She told him where she'd found it.

"That shouldn't be there."

"There's another one," she said, then described its location. "They stopped me before I could pull it off. I can't go back out there, but you can. Get it."

He nodded and retreated down the stairs to the tarmac.

While he was underneath the plane, the fire trucks and two of the security vehicles drove off. The third stayed where it was, but the man inside made no move to stop the pilot.

A few minutes later, the pilot reentered the aircraft and handed the square to Tiana.

"You're sure you don't know what this is," she said.

"Positive. It was not there when I did the inspection before we left to meet you."

That cinched it, then. The only way the squares could have hitched a ride was due to the man who'd run under the plane.

She bent one of the squares in half, and worked it back and forth until it split in two.

"Shit," she whispered.

Embedded between the outside layers was a tiny circuit board. The hair on the back of her neck stood on end. The squares could be only one thing.

Tracking bugs.

Whoever those people in Slovakia were, they knew exactly where Tiana's jet was. She had to assume they had access to their own jet, and were likely heading this way right now.

She grabbed the second square, intending to break it, too, but then stopped. She had a better idea.

She headed to the cockpit, where the pilots had gone.

"We need to get out of here," she said.

"We can't go until after the inspector clears us," the pilot said.

"Do you really want a replay of what happened in Slovakia?" She held up the unbroken square. "This is a tracker. They know we are here."

"The…the tower won't give us runway clearance," the copilot said.

"So what? When they see what we're doing, they'll make sure everyone gets out of our way."

"Even if we get into the air, they'll send fighter jets to intercept us."

She rolled her eyes and pointed at the map on the dash screen. "We are only a few minutes from the Romanian border, correct? Go that way. The Hungarian Air Force isn't going to follow us there, and by the time the Romanians send someone up, *if* they do, we'll already be in Ukrainian airspace."

The pilot looked at the map before turning to the copilot. "Pre-flight check."

"I want us rolling as soon as I get back on the plane," she said.

"Where are you going?"

"To have a quick conversation with our friends outside." She walked back to the main cabin.

Grigory was sitting in the front row of seats, next to the door.

"Give me your phone," she said to him.

"What? Why?"

"Because I said so." Grigory was a skilled commando, but he would occasionally forget she was in charge.

Frowning, he handed her his phone.

Holding his mobile by her side, she exited the aircraft and headed straight toward the remaining security vehicle. The official was on his own mobile and didn't notice her until she tapped on his window. He jerked in surprise, then quickly ended his call and rolled the glass down.

"You need to return to your plane," the man said. Thankfully, it was the guy who spoke English.

"We want to know how long it will be before the inspector gets here."

"He will arrive as soon as he is able."

"You can't even give me an estimate? Twenty minutes? An hour?"

"I do not know. Now, please—"

Tiana let Grigory's phone slip from her grasp. It hit the ground with a *thunk*.

"Dammit." As she leaned down to pick it up, she slipped the intact tracking bug under the car, the backing still viable enough to adhere to the frame.

When she stood back up, she brushed off the phone and smiled. "No cracks. I can't tell you how many times I've ruined a screen."

"Ma'am, return to your aircraft."

"Okay, okay. I'm going." She turned and walked back to the jet. As soon as she was onboard, she yelled toward the cockpit, "Let's go."

Six minutes later, to the dismay of Debrecen traffic control and airport security, the jet hijacked the runway and rose into the sky.

If the Hungarian Air Force sent anyone to force them down, Tiana and the others never saw them. The Romanians were no-shows, too.

Quinn and the team landed ten minutes later than the tower had estimated. The reason for the delay was some kind of incident at the airport, but the air traffic controllers didn't give any more details than that.

As they taxied from the runway to the area where they'd been assigned to park, each member of the team, save Orlando, sat at a different window and scanned the airport for the Falcon. Orlando was monitoring the tracking bug on her computer.

"I don't see it anywhere," Daeng said.

Neither did Quinn.

"Maybe they had a mechanical problem and it's in one of the hangars," Kincaid suggested.

Orlando said, "Not according to the tracker. It should be directly in front of the passenger terminal, near the east end."

"It's not there," Nate said.

At some point between when Jar's computer had gone haywire and when Orlando brought the tracking software up on her laptop, one of the bugs had stopped working. The other plane was on the ground at that point, and the assumption was the bug had been disabled during landing.

Now, it looked like the one working bug wasn't even attached to the aircraft anymore.

Their jet proceeded to its assigned stop at the west end of the plane parking area, and was greeted on arrival by an official airport passenger van.

"Nate, Daeng, you're with me," Quinn said. He looked at Orlando and Jar. "You two keep working on leads."

"What about me?" Kincaid said as Quinn, Nate, and Daeng moved toward the door.

Quinn paused long enough to say, "The others may still be around here so you need to keep an eye out for trouble," before he opened the exit and started down the stairs.

There were two men in the van. The passenger exited and walked toward Quinn.

"Good afternoon," the man said in English. "Welcome to Debrecen. You are coming from Slovakia, yes?"

"That's correct," Quinn said.

"In that case, no need for immigration. You only must check in with airport management."

That was the beauty of traveling between EU countries. "They can also help you arrange for transportation to wherever you want to go."

"Thank you, but we would like you to take us to airport security," Quinn said.

"Security? Is there a problem?"

Quinn showed the man his Interpol ID.

"Oh, um, of course. Come with me."

The van drove them along the edge of the parking area, and down the passenger terminal to the far end of the structure. There were currently five passenger planes at the airport—three at the terminal, one taxiing toward the runway, and the last slowing on the runway after landing moments before.

The guide led Quinn into the building through a keypad-operated door, and down a corridor to the security office.

Given the airport's smaller size, Quinn guessed the security department dealt with few real problems. The occasional shoplifter at one of the passenger terminal stores perhaps, or someone who might have had a few too many preflight drinks. From the flurry of activity when he walked into the security office, however, one would think he'd arrived at Heathrow in London, not at an airport in tiny Debrecen.

The guide walked up to the service counter, which delineated a small waiting area, and tried to get the attention of a uniformed security officer. It took several tries before one of the men glanced at the guide. They talked in Hungarian for a few seconds, then the officer shouted across the room at one of the other men. That guy in turn went and knocked on a door on the east wall, then entered.

A full minute went by before the guy returned in the company of a middle-aged man, also in uniform. Both officers approached the counter, where a short discussion ensued between them and the guide.

The older guy then turned to Quinn and said in a gruff voice, "Interpol?"

"Yes." Quinn showed the man his ID.

The officer studied it, grunted, and looked back up. "We are very busy at moment," he said in a dismissive tone.

"I see that, Captain…"

"Commander. Manko."

"I apologize, Commander. I promise I won't take much of your time."

"What you want?"

"We've been tracking an aircraft that we believe landed here less than an hour ago. A Dassault Falcon 7X. We were hoping it would still be here when we arrived, but apparently it's gone already. I was hoping you might—"

Manko's eyes narrowed. "What reason you want plane?"

"The people onboard are wanted by authorities in several countries."

"For what?"

Quinn glanced behind the commander at the activity in the rest of the room. "You're all busy because something just happened, didn't it? Something to do with that plane?"

Manko stared silently at Quinn.

"What happened?"

Again, the man said nothing.

"Commander Manko, we are not on opposite sides here. My colleagues and I are attempting to track them down because"—he changed his voice to a whisper—"because they have killed several people. I am asking for your help. What do you know about the plane?"

For a second, Quinn thought the stonewalling would continue, but then the commander said, "In my office."

Jar rebooted her laptop, wondering if it still worked.

It wasn't that she felt any potential sense of loss. The computer was merely a portal. She could easily get another machine to replace it if need be.

What she was interested in was seeing what Brunner's stick had done to it. She hoped it might give her insight into the massive data dump—or whatever that was—that had attacked her machine.

Yes, starting her computer again would come with risks, but she was being smart about it. Her machine wasn't an off-the-shelf, everyday laptop. It was designed so that certain functions, such as disconnecting networking abilities, could be achieved by the flick of a switch on the back. This particular function was useful in hacking situations gone bad, where getting offline in a hurry could be the difference between being identified or not. She now turned that switch off and pushed the power button.

"Are you sure that's a good idea?" Kincaid asked. He was sitting in Daeng's seat across the table from her.

"Are you not supposed to be watching for trouble?"

He grunted a laugh. "You don't like me very much, do you?"

"That is not true. I do not know you so I have no feelings one way or the other."

"So, after you gather enough *data*, you'll make some sort of decision?"

"Yes."

The log-on window appeared on the laptop's screen. Before she had a chance to input her password, though, it was automatically entered for her and the window vanished. Next, instead of her normal desktop screen, the monitor turned a glowing black.

"You are…different, aren't you?" Kincaid said.

"If you do not mind, I am very busy right now."

Another chuckle. "I guess that answers that." He turned his gaze out the window.

Jar typed in a command that should have reset the screen, but nothing happened. She tried several other commands. They were just as useless. Even pressing the power key did nothing.

She sighed. It looked like the machine was going to be a total write-off.

She flipped the computer on its side to access the battery, but before she could dislodge it, a dialogue box appeared in the middle of the screen. She set the laptop back down.

The words were in Thai.

Who are you?

Grimacing, she turned the computer around and double-checked that she had indeed turned off the network.

After some consideration, she decided to reboot again. She removed the battery, and let the machine sit unpowered for a full minute before starting it back up.

Once more, her log-in occurred automatically and the screen went black.

She waited, counting the seconds, but this time nothing happened.

She hit a few random keys on her keyboard and sat back, ticking off the seconds again. When she hit ten, the dialogue box reappeared.

Who are you?

She typed:

Who are YOU?

The dueling questions remained on the screen for only a second before they were replaced by a new box.

I asked first.

Jar responded:

You are on my computer, so you tell me.

The same pause, then:

I am not on your computer.

Jar cocked her head.

Then where are you?

Again, the dialogue box went away after one second, but this time another one did not take its place. She tried to type again, but with the dialogue box gone, nothing appeared on the screen.

She cursed in Thai.

"You get it working?" Kincaid asked.

She ignored him and stared at her monitor. Obviously the Wi-Fi disconnect switch on the machine wasn't working properly, and someone had found their way into her system. She considered killing the power again, but there was little on her hard drive that mattered. Most of the files and programs she used lived in the cloud, and were protected in a way that no one else but Jar could access.

Kincaid scooted out of his chair and moved around to look at the computer over the back of her seat.

"That looks dead to me," he said. "Brunner's jump drive or whatever that was must have fried—"

The dialogue box reappeared.

Who are you?

"What the hell is that?" Kincaid asked. "Is that writing?"

"It's Thai."

"So you did get it working."

She considered replying *You first* to the message, but stopped herself. Maybe she shouldn't be handling this on her own.

"Get Orlando," she told Kincaid.

"Something wrong?"

"Just get her. Please."

While he moved off to do that, Jar watched the screen,

wondering if the box would go away due to her lack of response. But it was still sitting there when Kincaid returned with Orlando.

"What's going on?" Orlando asked, taking the seat beside Jar.

Jar turned the computer so Orlando could see the monitor. "Someone is trying to communicate with me."

"What's it say?"

"'Who are you?'"

"Have you tried answering?"

Jar told her what had happened since restarting her machine the first time.

"It's probably a phishing program that was dumped onto your machine when everything went haywire."

Jar winced. Though some virus programs were designed to trick people into thinking they were talking to a real person, this didn't feel like that. "I am not—"

The dialogue box vanished.

"Got tired of waiting, I guess," Kincaid said.

A new box appeared, only this time the words were in English.

A phishing program. That is funny. No, I am not a phishing program. Who are you?

Both Orlando and Jar grabbed for the laptop at the same instant. Jar was closer and nabbed it first. She flipped it over, released the battery again, and dropped the computer on the table.

Before it even stopped moving, Orlando snatched it up and hurried out of the plane. When she returned, the machine was no longer with her.

"When we were in the air," she said, "when your computer was first attacked, you took the battery out then, too, right?" Orlando said.

"Yes."

"Okay, okay. Good. And you didn't put it back in until…?"

"Until five or six minutes ago."

"Right before you received the message for the first time?"

"Correct."

"And you said you pulled the battery out again."

"Yes. And then I decided to start it again and see what would happen if I answered."

"So, at most, since the attack, your computer has been on for no more than five minutes."

"I do not think even that long."

"And most of that time was just in the last several minutes, otherwise the battery wasn't even in."

"Correct."

Orlando looked from Jar to Kincaid and back. "Did either of you say anything while it was powered up?"

"She just asked me to go get you," Kincaid said.

"That's it?" Orlando asked.

"Pretty much. I think I made a comment about her getting the thing working, but nothing else."

"Then…then maybe we're all right." Orlando turned to Jar, her mouth opening to say something, but she stopped herself. "What's wrong?"

Jar's skin had gone cold, the blood draining from her face. Kincaid was right. They had talked very little when the laptop was on, but Jar had said one thing that could be a big problem.

"When I told Kincaid to get you, I mentioned you by name."

For a half second, Jar could see concern in her friend's eyes, but Orlando said, "It's okay. What's done is done. I'm sure it's not a big deal."

But Jar knew the words were only meant to soothe her. "I should not have said it. I was not…thinking. I am sorry."

"Jar, it's fine. Even if whoever they are figure out who I am— which I highly doubt they can—it's not going to be a problem. The stick came from Brunner's office. He's not our enemy. We're trying to save him. Which means anyone on the other end should not be our enemy, and we're not their enemy, either."

In the larger picture, Jar knew Orlando was right. But…

"But they do not know who we are, so we do not know that," Jar said.

Orlando smiled grimly. "True."

"Um, why don't you just answer the question?" Kincaid said.

Jar and Orlando turned to him.

"What are you talking about?" Jar asked.

"The question. You know, 'who are you?'"

"Are you making a joke? If yes, I do not understand it."

"Look, maybe this is a radical suggestion," he said. "But you guys are supposed to be looking for information about Brunner, right? It was his computer thingy that triggered these people to message you, which means they must've known him. I'm just saying, they probably have the information we need. Am I wrong?"

Jar and Orlando looked at each other.

"He is not wrong," Jar said.

"No. But we can't chance them listening in to whatever happens here." Orlando paused. "Do you think you can—"

"Yes."

Jar pulled open the large pocket of her backpack, removed her portable computer tool kit, and scooted out from behind the table.

"Go with her," Orlando told Kincaid.

"With her where?" Kincaid said.

Jar pushed open the door to the plane and started down the steps, not hearing whether or not Orlando responded to Kincaid.

21

Like most airports that serviced commercial flights, Debrecen International Airport was awash with security cameras.

Mounted in a cabinet in Commander Manko's office were four, side-by-side monitors. On three of the screens were rotating feeds from elsewhere at the airport. On the fourth screen was a paused image of a private jet in mid-takeoff.

"That's them," Quinn said. "So they did leave."

"Yes," Manko said.

"Why do you have the image paused?" Nate asked.

Manko looked uncomfortable.

"Commander, if they've done something else, we need to know," Quinn said.

Manko took a breath, then said, "They pretend problem with engine so can emergency land, understand?"

"Yes."

"When they down, they say was mistake, problem with warning light. My people tell them need inspection before can leave again and they must wait. But they not wait. They go, no clearance. Nothing. Leave thirty-five minute ago."

It was exactly what Quinn had feared most.

"Did you send up any jets to bring it back down?" Nate asked.

"I not responsible for this. Air Force only. We ask, but by time they reply, plane already in Romania."

"Do you know if they continued heading south?"

"I do not. No longer my problem."

Quinn glanced over his shoulder toward the other room. "It doesn't seem like it's not your problem."

"There are reports to be made. And questions from those...higher up."

"Do you have any footage from when they were parked?" Nate asked.

Manko turned to him. "Yes, but is from distance."

"That's okay. Can we see it?"

Quinn's inclination was to race back to the jet without another word, but chasing another aircraft was not like following a car. They wouldn't be able to just pick it out of the sky. Their best bet would be finding it through radar data in Romania. So, while the commander searched for the requested footage, Quinn texted Orlando, briefly telling her what he'd learned and asking her to start searching.

"Ah, here," Manko said.

New footage appeared on the monitor where the paused takeoff had been, only now the aircraft was sitting on a taxiway, not far from the runway. A few cars and a couple of fire trucks were parked near it. From inside the aircraft emerged two men. As they walked over to the waiting cars, a third person exited. A woman.

Instead of joining her colleagues, she slipped under the plane and inspected first the hull and then the rear landing gear.

Neither Quinn, Nate, nor Daeng made any outward expression, though Quinn was sure they were thinking the same thing he was.

Son of a bitch.

The camera's distance from the plane, plus the shadows under the craft, made it difficult to discern many details, but Quinn was all but positive she had removed one of the tracking bugs by the time a security officer forced her back onto the plane.

"They took off after this?" Quinn asked.

"I can show you."

The footage started playing at high speed. Right before Manko slowed it to normal, a snippet of the woman popped on the screen.

"Go back to where she comes out," Quinn said.

Manko reversed the recording, then let it play.

The woman exited alone and approached the security car. She stood there in apparent conversation, then ducked down out of sight for a few seconds before heading back to the plane. Soon after, the jet began making its escape.

Quinn had no doubt what she did. "That's enough. Thank you."

The image froze.

"We appreciate you showing us this, Commander. We've taken up enough of your time already."

"You will follow them?" Manko said.

"No way to know where they are going. We'll have to wait until we get another lead." All of which was true, but said in a way that indicated it might take quite some time.

"If you are able to arrest them, I would appreciate being told."

"Of course," Quinn said, acknowledging the request without promising anything.

Manko led the team back into the main room, where the guide who had brought the team to the office was waiting.

The commander shook hands with Nate and Daeng, and finally Quinn. "Good luck, Inspector. I hope you find them."

"Thank you. I do, too." He let go of the man's hand and started to turn away, but then stopped. "One more thing."

"Yes?"

"Is there a chance you could arrange for a priority takeoff?"

It took Jar less than five minutes to remove the laptop's casing, disable both the built-in microphone and camera, and disconnect the Bluetooth controller. It was possible those sending the messages could use her Bluetooth to access a microphone on another computer or even on one of the team members' cell phones. After putting everything back together, she picked up the laptop and headed back for the stairs.

"You sure you got that thing neutered?" Kincaid asked.

He'd been standing nearby, scanning the airport for anyone coming their way.

"You ask me a lot of questions. Do you not believe me capable?"

"What? No. I, um, never said that. It's just..." His mouth scrunched up on one side. "How old are you?"

"Why does that matter?"

"Look, I've been in this business for years, and I know it takes a while to get up to speed. I mean, what is this? Your first mission? You've gotta be barely out of high school, right?"

"I did not go to high school. I did not need to."

Smirking, he said, "Is that right?"

"Yes. It is right. I am very smart. Much smarter than you."

"Hey, there's no need to get nasty."

Her eyes narrowed. "I am not the one being nasty, Mr. Kincaid. I am the one stating facts." She moved past him to the stairs and headed up. When she reached the doorway, she stopped and looked back. "And no, this is not my first mission."

She ducked inside the plane.

Kincaid sighed as he watched Jar disappear.

Nice job, buddy. You really know how to make friends.

He usually didn't have problems talking to people. Navigating any situation with ease was part of what made him good at his job. And to do that, one needed to know how to communicate.

There was one glaring hole in his communication abilities, however. He was no better than mediocre at talking to kids.

Logically, Jar couldn't be a minor. Quinn wouldn't willingly bring someone underage into dangerous situations like this, but she looked like she was no more than sixteen or seventeen. And every time he tried to talk to her, that's the thought that kept sticking in his head.

She was right. *He* was the one who'd been nasty.

"Asshole," he muttered, and headed back into the plane.

———

"She slipped the disc under that car," Nate whispered as he, Quinn, and Daeng followed the guide toward the building exit.

"Yeah," Quinn said.

After they stepped outside, Nate checked the tracking app. "The signal's coming from over there." He nodded toward a group of sedans parked fifteen meters away. "If you distract our friend, I can grab the bug." When Quinn didn't answer right away, Nate added, "Maybe she wasn't wearing any gloves."

"Make it fast," Quinn said.

Thankfully, their guide was more focused on where they were going than on his guests, and Nate made it to the cars without the officer realizing it.

According to the tracking app, the bug was on the middle vehicle. Nate quickly pulled on a rubber glove, then lay on his back and scooted underneath the sedan.

There it was, clinging to the inside of the chassis. Based on how easy it was for him to pull it off, it would have likely dislodged itself the next time someone used the vehicle.

He pulled the glove off so that the bug was wrapped inside it, and stuck it all in his pocket. Before he stood up again, he retrieved his phone and used it to peek through the neighboring sedan's windows.

Quinn, Daeng, and the guide were at the van, Quinn talking to the guide in a manner that forced the man to turn away from Nate's position. Nate stood up, put the phone to his ear, and walked quickly toward them.

When he was about halfway there, he heard Quinn say, "Here he comes."

The officer turned and took several steps toward him. "Sir, you should not wander off like this. You do not have clearance."

Into the phone, Nate said, "Okay, thanks. I'll talk to you later." He pretended to hang up and shoved the phone into his pocket. "My apologies. I had to take that call."

The officer gave him an annoyed smile. "Is no problem. Just, please, into van and I take you back."

"Great."

As Nate joined his friends, Quinn said, "Everything all right?"

"Perfect," Nate said, and climbed on board.

Orlando and Jar were back at the table, Jar's laptop sitting in front of them, open but still off. Instead of joining them, Kincaid had taken the front seat nearest the door and was staring out the window.

The two women shared a look.

"All right," Orlando said. "Do it."

Jar touched the power button. Like before, after the computer booted up, the screen glowed black. Jar tapped a few keys.

"How long did you have to wait last time?" Orlando asked.

"Ten seconds."

They watched the monitor, waiting for the dialogue box to reappear. A whole minute passed without change.

"Could you have accidentally damaged the Wi-Fi when you were disconnecting the speakers?"

Jar shook her head. "I was very careful."

"Maybe they don't know we're here. Try typing in a question."

Jar placed her fingers on the keyboard, paused, then tapped in several words. Whatever they were, they did not show up on the screen.

"Well, that didn't work," Orlando said after fifteen seconds had elapsed. "Perhaps we should try shutting it down and re—"

A dialogue box popped up. A single word in English:

Yes.

Orlando frowned. "Yes to what?"

"I asked if they still wanted to talk. How should I respond?"

"Let them know we're willing to talk, too, but we have to know who they are first."

Jar typed it in, almost word for word.

The response came quickly.

I need to know who you are.

Before Orlando could advise Jar what to say, Jar sent a response:

You came onto my computer uninvited. You must introduce yourself first. It is only right.

Orlando might have worded it in a less demanding way, but in essence it was the same message she wanted to send.

This time it took twenty seconds for an answer.

Danara.

Jar looked at Orlando. "Is that the name of a person or organization?"

"I have no idea. Ask them."

Jar typed.

The response time decreased to five seconds:

I am Danara.

After two seconds, a new line appeared below it:

Your turn.

"Use my name," Orlando said. "If she—or he, I guess—was listening in earlier, she already knows it."

Jar entered Orlando's name.

Danara's next message was not in English, but in Thai.

"What's it say?"

"'You are lying,'" Jar told her.

"She's still listening in on us," Orlando said.

"Impossible. I disconnected the microphone."

"I realize that, but how else would she know you're not me?" Orlando looked straight at the monitor and said, "You're listening in on us, aren't you?"

The message in Thai remained on the screen.

After waiting half a minute, Jar typed:

Are you listening in on us?

Danara:

I cannot. The pathway to do so is inoperable.

Jar:

Then why do you think I am lying?

Danara:

Typing patterns.
They are the same as before, when you said, "Get Orlando." You would not say this about yourself.

It had to be a guess, Orlando thought. While identifying someone by typing patterns was possible, doing so would require a much larger sampling than what Jar had typed—fewer than a hundred words—since Danara first made her presence known.

Still, Danara's confidence made Orlando uneasy.

"Maybe you should talk to her directly," Jar said.

Orlando nodded, and Jar scooted the laptop to her.

Orlando typed:

This is Orlando now.

A beat, then:

Hello, Orlando. Where is Dr. Brunner?

Orlando:

I don't know.

Danara:

Now you are lying to me. I know he has been kidnapped. Bring him back before it is too late for you.

Orlando:

Why do you care?

Danara:

I am not going to play games. Bring him back. You have four hours.

Orlando lifted her hands from the keyboard and rubbed her cheek. There was a high possibility this was a trick being played by the kidnappers. They knew someone was following them.

Perhaps touching down here at Debrecen had been a way to lure Orlando, Quinn, and the others into doing the same, which would allow the kidnappers to ID this aircraft. Their hacker would then know where the target was located, and if she or he was good enough, would start pinging devices.

But that didn't explain the fact the contact commenced while they were still in the air, shortly after Jar's computer had been hijacked by the device Nate had found in the ruins of Brunner's office. Cause and effect must be linked, and Orlando found it impossible to believe the kidnappers/bombers had planted the device in a sealed book in the scientist's apartment, just so it could be found by someone whose computer they would want to hack into in the future, because that someone was following them.

A definite space-time continuum problem right there.

She took a breath and typed again.

Orlando:

You're working under a false impression. We aren't the ones who took Brunner.

Danara:

Bring him back. You have three hours, fifty-nine minutes, and seventeen seconds.

Orlando:

I don't react well to threats, empty or otherwise. Especially since we have NOTHING to do with what happened.

That wasn't entirely true, of course. The Office *had* been in charge of the escort mission, and Kincaid, who was sitting a few rows away, had been present when Brunner was taken.

Danara:

My threats are never empty. Bring him back. Or this computer is not the only thing I will destroy.

Orlando:

Maybe if you tell us what your connection is to Brunner, we can—

Danara:

Move back.

Orlando looked at the screen, confused.

A moment later, the laptop's fan started whirling louder and louder. When Orlando felt heat rising from the keyboard, she pulled her hands back. Tendrils of smoke leaked from the machine's ports.

"What the hell?" Orlando jumped out of her seat into the aisle, with Kincaid right behind her.

Jar raced toward the back of the plane, and by the time she returned a few moments later with a fire extinguisher, the laptop's keyboard had begun to melt.

She blasted the computer with retardant. This accomplished what the fire had yet to do—shorting the machine and killing the fan.

From the front of the plane, the pilot and copilot came rushing back.

"We smelled smoke," the pilot said. "What happened?"

"Just a little accident," Orlando said. "Could someone open the door so we can clear out the air?"

Kincaid was closest so he did the honors. As he swung it out of the way, a vehicle could be heard pulling up.

Orlando looked out the window and saw Quinn, Nate, and Daeng exit a van. After they said their goodbyes, the van drove off again.

"Is that smoke?" Nate said from outside the door.

"Just a 'little accident,'" Kincaid said.

The sound of feet rushing up the stairs into the cabin. Quinn entered first, followed by Nate and then Daeng.

"Are you okay?" Quinn asked as he hurried to where Orlando and Jar—still holding the extinguisher—stood by the table. "What's going on?"

"Everyone's fine," Orlando said. "Jar's computer had a little meltdown."

He looked at the fire retardant-covered, half-melted mass of plastic and metal.

"I thought you pulled the battery out of it."

Before Jar could answer, Orlando said, "We did…"

"You put it back in, didn't you?"

"It's a little more complicated than that."

"All right. You can explain after we get underway. Were you able to find the other plane?"

"Hold on. Let me check."

She headed up to the seat she'd been in before joining Jar at the table. After receiving Quinn's text, she had started searching radar data, sending out several dozen bots to hunt down any information that would show them where the others had gone.

She unlocked the screen of her laptop and saw that over seventy-five percent of the bots had reported back, their combined data creating a flight pattern that showed the other jet over Romania, nearly at the border with Ukraine. She relayed the information to Quinn.

"Call the tower," Quinn said to the pilot. "They should give you immediate clearance."

"What about the smoke?" Nate said.

The cabin was by no means full of it, but a small amount was still lingering in the air.

"Once we start up, the air circulators should be able to get rid of it in a hurry," the pilot said.

"Good. Then get us going." Quinn turned back to Orlando. "So…Jar's laptop?"

22

Tiana's phone rattled on the table. On the screen, the ID read N.

"Are you going to answer?" Grigory asked.

She glared at him, snatched up the device, and swiped to accept. "Good evening, General."

"What the hell is going on there, Commander?" Her boss spoke in the calm, quiet voice that, she knew from experience, he only used when he was angry. "I understand you were attacked."

Tiana had reported in after they left Slovakia. At the time, she'd been thankful General Nesterov was in transit to Lonely Rock and not available to talk. His absence, however, had been only a delay of their inevitable conversation.

"Yes, sir." She knew better than to launch directly into an explanation of what had happened. It would sound like she was making excuses.

"Who were they?"

"I don't know, sir."

"But you were able to get Brunner away."

"Yes, sir."

Silence for several seconds. "Any chance they might be following you?"

This was the question she had hoped he wouldn't ask. But like how she knew when she shouldn't talk, she also knew *not* telling him what had happened once they were in the air would be a mistake. Sooner or later he would find out, and she would rather feel his wrath now than have him go nuclear on her later. She told him about the tracking bugs.

"Are you sure there aren't any more?" he asked.

"The man who put them there only had a very limited time. And I checked everywhere. There were no others, sir."

"You cannot know that for sure."

"Do you want us to land again and do a more thorough examination?"

"How far out are you?"

"We should be entering Ukraine in the next few minutes, so about three hours."

A pause. "Don't stop. If someone else tries to land, we have the resources to deal with them here."

The line went dead before she could respond.

Brunner's eyes popped open as his container jostled him side to side. He'd been able to rest. Sort of. As long as his portable jail cell only gently vibrated, he was able to keep his migraine to a dull background roar. But every time he was jerked around like this, the pain came rushing back.

The plane landing an hour or so earlier had been the worst. Now, he feared they may be heading down again. But the bumps soon subsided and the sensation of descending never came.

Turbulence, he told himself. *That's all. Just turbulence.*

In truth, it wasn't only the roughness of a landing that scared him. He knew at some point he'd be removed from the plane and taken to a place where they could torture out all his secrets. Like most people, he'd seen the reports that torture was a highly ineffective way of obtaining information, but he had no doubt it would work on him. One waterboarding and they wouldn't be able to get him to shut up. And he did indeed have a secret to tell.

He'd been so sure the torture was going to happen the last time they landed that his fear had overshadowed even the pain in his head. But within twenty minutes or so, they'd taken off again, his box not moving an inch.

The next time they went down, he had no doubt the story would be different.

23

"We've got a problem," Orlando said.

"Don't tell me we lost them," Quinn said.

"Not yet, but if they don't change their course soon, we will."

She turned her computer so he could see it.

On the screen was a map that encompassed the eastern half of Romania, all of Ukraine, and a bit of Russia. Two dots—one blue and one red—were moving slowly across the image. The blue one, representing the kidnappers' plane, was about fifty kilometers into Ukrainian airspace. The red one, marking the team's aircraft, was still over Romania, about one hundred and twenty kilometers from the border.

"What's the problem?" he asked.

"The Ukrainian radar system. I'm having a problem getting access to some of its coverage areas." She clicked a button and an overlay of yellow transparent blotches appeared over the country. "There's only a few dead spots here in the west." She tapped the screen over several blotches. "If the kidnappers don't change direction, these shouldn't be an issue. The problem will be if they continue east of Kyiv."

There was no need for her to point out what she meant. The

yellow overlay covered at least three-quarters of that part of the country.

"What are the chances you'll be able to find a way in?"

"I've been trying for a while, and I'll keep it up, but…." She shrugged, not looking hopeful.

"Are there any satellites we can repurpose?"

"Jar's checking that now."

Quinn looked back at Jar, who was using his computer since hers was now a pile of slag. Nate sat next to her. They both appeared to be looking at something on the table in front of them, but it was hidden from Quinn's view by the laptop.

"I'll be right back," he said.

He pushed out of his chair and walked back to see what was holding their attention. The item turned out to be the tracking disc Nate had rescued from Debrecen airport. Its surface glistened from what Quinn guessed was a spritz from the small bottle of specialized solution from the team's fingerprint-detection kit that sat nearby.

"Orlando said you were checking on satellites," Quinn said.

Without taking her attention off the disc, Jar said, "Finished already."

"And?"

She glanced at the laptop. "I have found two that might be able to help. One is NSA, still trying to hack into it."

"And the other?"

"Russian weather satellite. But its camera is not as detailed. I am running a test to see if it can even find the other aircraft and follow it."

"How long until you know?"

She finally looked up at him. "Ten more minutes should be sufficient."

He jutted his chin toward the disc. "Any luck with that?"

Nate leaned close to the disc for a moment before sitting back. "Looks like it's ready."

Jar removed a small, ultraviolet flashlight from the kit and shined the beam on the disc. The otherwise uniform surface was now broken by the distinct ovals of fingerprint ridges.

"Looks like a thumb," Nate said.

"It is," Jar confirmed. "Right side."

That made sense. With only a few short seconds to place the bug, the woman would have likely used her thumb to push it into place.

Jar grabbed the palm-sized scanner and started setting it up over the disc to make a digital image.

"If you get a hit, let us know," Quinn said. He returned to his seat next to Orlando.

"She having any luck?" Orlando asked.

He told her what Jar had found.

"I doubt the weather sat will pay off," Orlando said. "Maybe Misty can pull a few strings and get us access to the NSA one, without us having to sneak in. Did you get the satellite's ID?"

Quinn leaned into the aisle and looked toward the back. "Jar, what's the ID on that NSA satellite?"

She gave it to him, but there was no need to repeat it to Orlando, as she had already typed it into a message she was composing for Misty.

"Hey!" Nate shouted. "She's in!"

"In what?"

"The NSA satellite. She's got control."

"What the hell?" Orlando said.

Quinn turned to her, thinking she was reacting to what Nate had said, but instead she was staring at her screen.

Her email window was gone, no doubt minimized because she didn't need it anymore. In its place was the map detailing the areas where she'd been having trouble getting radar access. The yellow spots in the northwestern portion of Ukraine were still there, but all those in the east, in the direction the kidnappers were headed, had disappeared.

Every single one of them.

"What did you do?" he asked.

"I didn't do anything," Orlando said.

"Could whatever was blocking you have been a system error that cleared?"

She frowned as she opened another program and typed. "Maybe, but I doubt that." After several seconds, she sat back and motioned to her screen. "See? The problem's still there. Nothing has changed. But I've got access."

The screen was full of letters and numbers that didn't make any sense to Quinn.

"All this data should still be inaccessible. *I* didn't do anything."

The skin on Quinn's arms tingled. The coincidence of both problems clearing up at the exact same moment was unlikely in the extreme. He exchanged a look with Orlando, and knew she was thinking the same thing.

They relocated to the table, Orlando bringing her computer with her, and showed the others what had happened with the radar data.

"Did either of you ask for outside help?" Quinn asked Orlando and Jar.

"I didn't," Orlando said.

"I have told no one," Jar replied.

"*Someone* must know," Quinn said. "There's no way this was just—"

"What about Daria?" Kincaid suggested.

Quinn frowned. "Who's Daria?"

"Danara," Orlando said.

"Yeah, that's it," Kincaid said.

To Quinn, Orlando said, "She's the hacker who melted Jar's machine."

"Did you say Danara?" Nate said.

"Yes. Why?"

"Give me a moment." He pulled his bag onto his lap and rummaged through it.

"How the hell would this Danara even know we're having

problems?" Quinn asked. "She destroyed her connection to us, didn't she?"

A cloud passed over Orlando's face. "Maybe."

"What do you mean, 'maybe'?"

"Here it is," Nate said.

He was holding a small stack of papers. Written on the one he'd moved to the top was: What about Danara?

"What is that?" Quinn asked.

"Some of the notes from Brunner's apartment." Nate turned it over. "There's a date on the back. May thirtieth, three years ago."

"He dated the note?"

"That's what it looks like."

"Whether he did or not, he definitely knows this person," Daeng said.

"Possibly," Nate said, but he was frowning.

A moment of silence descended, then Orlando said, in a slightly raised voice, "Danara, can you hear me?"

Quinn looked at her as if she'd lost her mind. "What are you doing?"

She held up a hand, telling him to be quiet. "Danara?"

From Orlando's pocket, a calm female voice said, "Yes, Orlando, I can hear you."

"Whoa, whoa, whoa!" Kincaid said. "What the hell?"

Orlando pulled out her mobile and set it on the desk. "You hacked into my phone."

"I did." The same voice, clearly from the device.

"What else have you hacked into?"

A brief pause. Then, from every speaker in the passenger area of the plane—phones, computers, the overhead PA system—Danara said, "Everything."

While most of the team froze, Kincaid jumped up, pulled out his phone, and dropped it on the floor.

"How did she do that?" he asked.

"Good question," Orlando said.

Quinn knew what she was really saying was that Danara

shouldn't have been able to do that, especially to the phones belonging to Quinn's team. Orlando had encrypted them so that they'd be virtually unhackable. The emphasis was on *virtually*, apparently.

"Danara, we are not your enemy," Orlando said.

"I'm inclined to believe you're correct now. If I'd still believed otherwise, I wouldn't have helped you gain access to the radar data and the NSA satellite."

"Thank you for that."

"You're welcome."

Quinn touched Orlando's arm. She nodded for him to go ahead.

"My name is—"

"Jonathan Quinn," Danara said. "Cleaner. Currently in temporary employment of The Office."

There had been no indication Danara was using any of the cameras on the phones or computers, but Quinn had to assume she was, so he did his best to keep his surprise and concern off his face.

"That's correct," he said. "Since you know who I am working for, it would only be fair if you told us who you work for and what your interest is in our mission."

"Dr. Brunner is my interest. I want him returned. Alive."

"That's what we want, too."

"As I said, I believe you now."

"Do you work with Dr. Brunner?" Orlando asked. "Is he your boss?"

A pause. "Yes, I work with him, and by many definitions, you can say he's my boss."

It was an odd response.

"That's good to hear," Quinn said. "Then I'm sure you wouldn't mind helping us a little more."

"What is it you need?"

"We've had a hard time finding out what he's been working on. If you share that with us, it could prove useful."

"Why?"

"Why what?"

"Why would this knowledge help you? You are already following the plane he is on. What does it matter why he was taken?"

"It could give us a better understanding of those who kidnapped him. Which could help us find a way of defeating them."

"I see."

When Danara didn't go on, Quinn said, "Are you going to tell us or not?"

"I am not authorized to share that information."

"Then get authorization."

"Only Dr. Brunner can authorize its release."

Quinn stared at Orlando's phone in disbelief, no longer caring if Danara could read his expression or not. "So you're saying to get the information that will help us save Brunner, we need to rescue him first so he can tell you it's okay?"

"I'm aware of the contradiction," Danara said.

"I would hope so."

"But my directions are clear. On this matter, I cannot help you."

"Then apparently you don't want to help the doctor as much as you claim. If you did, you wouldn't hold anything back."

No response this time.

"Danara?"

Nothing.

"Danara, are you still there?"

Orlando's phone remained silent.

Orlando made an almost imperceptible motion toward the back of the jet. Grimly, Quinn nodded, but as he moved in that direction, she grabbed his arm and pointed at his pocket.

He pulled out his phone and set it on the table. Then, also at Orlando's prompt, he removed his smart watch and left it behind, too. As Orlando stood up, she indicated for Jar to join them.

They squeezed into the bathroom, a space uncomfortably small even for one person.

Orlando turned on the faucet and said, "If we keep our voices low, I don't think she'll be able to hear us."

"How long do you think she's been listening in on us?"

"At least since just before she destroyed my computer," Jar said.

Orlando nodded. "The safe bet is to assume since not long after you connected Brunner's key to your machine."

"Son of a bitch," Quinn said. "And how do we get her to *stop* listening?"

"Disable anything with a microphone or camera," Jar said.

Quinn stared at her. "So, basically, we need to go off the grid? How is that going to be practical?"

"It is not. I was only answering your question. I am not suggesting we do this."

He took a breath to quell his rising anger. "Sorry."

"We need to assume Danara, or anyone she might be working with, will be listening in at all times," Orlando said.

"Who *is* she?" Quinn asked.

"Someone who's at least temporarily willing to help us."

That might have been true, but Quinn thought the cost might be too high. "So, how do we make this work?"

"First, we disable or cover every camera," Jar said. "This way she cannot see our expressions, or read anything we write down. Second, we create muffles for the microphones that can be removed when we need to use them. We must not assume this will keep her from hearing us, but it should at least cut down her range. Third, we come up with a protocol for having private conversations. A gesture that means leave your phone or computer behind and follow."

"You just think all of that up?" Quinn asked.

"I did not have to think about anything. The steps are obvious. And you did not let me finish. There is a fourth. We hand out the comm gear." She looked at Orlando. "Correct me if I am wrong, but she should not be able to hack into that."

"Hopefully," Orlando said. The comm system wasn't run through any kind of central computer that could be hacked into, and the frequency that carried the encrypted digital signal was dynamic, making it nearly impossible for anyone to follow. "But I would have never thought she could get into the phones, either. We've got to communicate, though, so I don't see a better choice."

They worked out a few more details, then Orlando and Jar returned to their computers to continue tracking the other aircraft. One by one, they sent Kincaid, then Daeng, and finally Nate back to the bathroom to be briefed by Quinn.

As Quinn was finishing up with Nate, someone knocked on the bathroom entrance.

"Your phone's ringing," Orlando said from the other side. "It's Misty."

Cursing under his breath, Quinn opened the door. Orlando held his phone out to him and mouthed, *Careful.*

With a nod, he took it from her and swiped ACCEPT.

"Hey, thanks for calling back," he said. "I was wondering, have you heard from Peter yet?"

The pause on the other end was slight. To most, it wouldn't mean anything. But Quinn knew Misty was reacting to the code phrase he'd just used. This particular question—one he'd never had occasion to use—let her know everything was okay but the line was potentially bugged.

"I did," she said. "You know Peter. He's up to his usual tricks."

Another code phrase. She had information for him.

"Can you let him know I need to talk with him? I'm a little tied up so it might be a bit."

"I can do that. But don't wait too long. He seemed eager to talk to you, too." Her information was something she thought he'd like sooner than later. "I could set a reminder if you want. For after you're home." And with this last, she'd told him which server he could look on to find the material.

Now all he needed was a Danara-free computer.

"That would be great, thanks," he said.

Misty proceeded to give him a briefing that amounted to her saying there was no news on Brunner from her end. He asked a few appropriate questions, and she gave him a few appropriate answers.

"Got it. Thanks," he said.

"If I learn anything new, I'll call." In other words, *he* should call *her* as soon as he was in a position to do so.

"Talk to you soon."

"Quinn?"

"Yes?"

"Be careful." No code phrase there. Just the concern of a friend.

24

Long after midnight, the kidnappers' plane left Ukraine and crossed into Russia.

No problem with radar data there. Either the Russian system was not as well protected as its neighbor, or Danara had cleared any blockage ahead of time. Quinn would have bet everything he had on the latter.

As for Danara herself, she had yet to reappear, despite the occasional attempt by Orlando or Jar to lure her out.

With nothing to do, Nate and Daeng had fallen asleep not long after the conferences in the bathroom. It took a bit longer but eventually Kincaid joined them, his deep breaths rattling from the two seats he was slumped over, a row back from the table.

"You should rest," Orlando told Quinn. "Even if they land right now, we're still an hour behind them. And who knows when you're going to get a chance again."

"How's the clearance for Russia coming?" he asked. She'd been working on getting permission for their plane to pass into Russian airspace, using the ruse that the aircraft was ferrying an Uzbekistani businessman back to his home country.

"Just waiting for final confirmation. It'll be fine. Sleep. If there's anything you need to know, I'll wake you."

He didn't like the idea of knocking out in the middle of a chase, but really, there was nothing more he could do. "Promise?"

"I promise."

He moved to a seat across the aisle and reclined it as far as it would go. He was fairly confident he wouldn't fall asleep, but even resting his eyes for a while would be helpful.

He closed his lids and tried to think of nothing.

Whether it was from the vibrations of the plane or exhaustion of being in constant terror, Brunner had finally fallen asleep.

How long this lasted, he wasn't sure. He only knew his slumber abruptly ended when his stomach suddenly felt as if it wanted to rise out of his body at the speed of a rocket.

He sucked in a breath, then squeezed his eyes shut when his head reminded him it was still playing host to a migraine. It wasn't until it settled back into a dull, throbbing pain that he realized the aircraft wasn't experiencing turbulence again but was truly descending.

This was it. Somewhere ahead of them was where he would die.

He probed at the edges of his migraine. It seemed to have lessened a bit, and felt the way it usually did when his headaches began their meandering retreat to wherever they hid between attacks. This one would still be with him for a while, though, so there was no need to celebrate yet.

Down and down and down the plane went. He didn't hear the landing gear extending, but did feel a new vibration that likely signaled its deployment, so he was prepared when the aircraft came in contact with the ground a few minutes later.

His heart rate increased as the plane braked, and he was close to hyperventilating when the aircraft finally began taxiing. The ride from the end of the runway to where the plane parked was much too short for Brunner's liking.

"Please let this be just another short stop," he mumbled as the engines whirled down. "Please let this be just another short stop. Please let this be just—"

His crate moved.

Oh, no.

Another shift, then he and the crate rose into the air.

No.

For a second, oxygen stopped freely flowing into his mask. The temporary disruption reminded him that when he'd been brought onto the plane, before the oxygen had begun pumping, the box had been hoisted upward in a near vertical position, with Brunner's head at the low end as, he assumed, his small prison was hauled through the plane's door.

He braced himself for a repeat, but while he did experience a dip, it wasn't nearly as drastic as it had been the first time.

After this, the movements of the box became a rhythmic roll, created by the footsteps of those holding him aloft. At least four minutes passed before all forward motion stopped. For several seconds, nothing seemed to happen, then his stomach lurched again. He was moving down, and yet the box itself remained still.

Fighting through his migraine, he tried to figure out what was going on.

An elevator, he finally realized.

His stomach percolated until the ride stopped, and within moments, he started moving horizontally again.

This walk lasted a minute at most, before his box was seemingly lowered to the ground.

He tried to take a deep breath to calm his nerves, knowing the top was about to be opened again.

But the crate remained sealed.

A moment of panic pushed all of his other concerns away. He almost tried to kick the lid to get someone's attention, but stopped himself.

Was he crazy? Better to stay in the safety of the crate for as long as possible. They wouldn't kill him in here, right?

Right?

———

"Hey," Orlando said, her voice coming from right beside his ear, her hand gently rocking his shoulder. "Hey, wake up."

Quinn forced his eyes open, surprised he had actually drifted off. "What time is it?"

"Four-forty."

It had been barely three a.m. when he lay down.

He returned his seat to the upright position. "Something happen?"

"They landed twenty minutes ago. We have some decisions to make."

"Twenty minutes? Why didn't you wake me?"

"Wouldn't have made a difference. We still had some time."

Time that was now up.

"Where did they land?" he asked.

"Nowhere."

"Excuse me?"

"Come. I'll show you." She headed back to her seat at the table.

As he headed over to join her, he noted that Nate, Daeng, and Kincaid were all still asleep. Jar, of course, was working away opposite Orlando.

A map filled Orlando's screen. The only place whose name he recognized was Volgograd, near the lower left corner. The dot representing his team's plane was just to the northeast of it. The dot for the kidnappers sat middle right quadrant, on the other side of a solid white line that moved from the south-southwest to the north-northeast.

"How long have we been in Russia?"

"For almost an hour."

"But they're not anymore."

"No."

She zoomed in on the map. There were no towns within at least fifty kilometers of the kidnappers' dot. In fact, at the current magnification, Quinn didn't even see any roads. The only words displayed hugged the white line, which had now edged the left side of the screen. On the left side of the line was RUSSIA. And on the right—the side the kidnappers' plane was on —KAZAKHSTAN.

Remote Kazakhstan, Quinn thought.

"Tell me something's there," he said.

Orlando glanced at Jar. "Can I get control of the satellite?"

"One moment." Jar tapped a few keys, clicked on her track pad, and said, "Okay."

A moment later, a satellite image filled Orlando's screen. It was a live picture, the first rays of the coming sunrise licking across the land. A desert, not too unlike that of northern Arizona or southeastern Utah.

"I don't see anything," he said.

Orlando increased magnification until suddenly, out of the dirt and scrub, two runways appeared, faint and obviously designed to blend in with the desert. An untrained eye might not have seen them. Another zoom, combined with the rising sun, revealed a shadow that appeared to be cast by nothing.

"A building?"

Orlando nodded. "A hangar, I believe. The jet is inside it."

Odder than the facility's camouflage was the fact that not a single road led away from the airport.

"They're still inside the building, too?" he said.

"Jar?" Orlando said.

Her eyes still on Quinn's laptop, Jar said, "No one has exited."

"Do we have any idea what this place is?" Quinn asked.

"I've been looking into that, but no luck yet," Orlando replied.

"Perhaps our new…friend might be able to help."

Orlando frowned. "She's had plenty of time to pipe up but hasn't said anything. So, either she doesn't know or is unwilling to share."

Quinn hesitated, expecting Danara to say something, but their uninvited guest remained silent. "All right. How do *we* get there?"

No way they could just pop on down to the secret airport and land unnoticed. Hell, a place like that probably had an air defense system, and the team's plane would be in pieces by the time it reached the ground.

Orlando decreased the magnification by two taps. "The nearest other airport is here," she said, touching the screen where a single-landing-strip airport sat next to a small town. "After that, it's another hundred kilometers or more."

"How far away is that?"

"Seventy-five kilometers."

"Seventy-three and three-quarters," Jar corrected her.

"Seventy-three and three-quarters, Orlando said.

"Anyone there going to cause us problems?"

"It's an oil town, occupied by oilfield workers and those who support them. I'm guessing they're used to seeing planes fly in every now and then. There are a few companies that have offices there. We come up with a good story, go in as one of them, we shouldn't have any problems."

"All right. Let's do it."

———

The town was called Ketovo, and its airport consisted of a small building for passengers to wait in, and little else. There was no control tower, only a windsock on a tall pole, and an automated weather update broadcast.

As for the town itself, from what Nate glimpsed as they descended, it was made up of a handful of parallel streets lined with nearly identical structures. Most of the buildings appeared to be divided into multi-family residences.

As they taxied toward the tiny terminal, he spotted dust rising from the road that ran from the airport to town.

"Looks like someone's coming."

By the time the vehicle arrived, the jet was already at the terminal, with Nate, Orlando, and Quinn standing outside.

One of the two men who piled out of the car wore a military uniform that looked like it had been thrown on in a hurry. The other was dressed in brown slacks and a white shirt. The military man was the older of the two, fiftyish, while his companion couldn't have been more than thirty-five. Both looked flustered.

No one on the team spoke Kazakh but hopefully that wouldn't be a problem.

Several years earlier, Nate, Orlando, and Quinn had become involved with a group of Russians seeking a countryman who'd tortured and killed many of their friends and relatives. Since then, all three team members had worked at improving their Russian language skills. Quinn and Orlando were passible now, but Nate had achieved near fluency. Since Russian was Kazakhstan's second official language, he took lead as the men approached.

"Hello, gentlemen," Nate said. "How are you this morning?"

"We were not told anyone was coming today," the military man said, all business. "Who are you?"

Nate held out a hand. "Bryce Kenny, Wysocki Petroleum." He let some of his American accent seep into his otherwise near-perfect Russian pronunciations, but he needn't have bothered. At the mention of Wysocki, both men stood a little straighter.

Since choosing Ketovo as the landing site, the team had researched the area and learned Wysocki was the fastest growing company in town. A Texas-Saudi partnership, the corporation had deep pockets and was in an expansive phase.

"Mr. Kenny," the younger Kazakh said. "We welcome you to Ketovo. I am Arman Temirov, mayor of Ketovo, and this is Major Ospan, in charge of security."

"Pleasure to meet both of you." Nate gestured back at Orlando and Quinn. "These are my colleagues, Kim Bong-Cha and Wes Stephenson."

Handshakes all around.

"I'm sorry no one was here to meet you. I'm sure your company will send a representative soon."

"That's all right, Arman," Nate said, purposely using the man's first name. "No one knew we were coming."

The man tried to hide his confusion by saying, "In that case, we would be happy to transport you wherever you like. Perhaps the Wysocki office?"

Nate winced and sucked in a breath. "Actually, we would prefer if they remained unaware of our visit."

"I'm sorry?" Arman said, his bewilderment now on full display.

Nate hesitated, as if he wanted to say something but wasn't sure he could. "Hold on a second."

He walked over to Quinn and Orlando. They whispered in English without really saying anything.

After about half a minute, Quinn said. "That should be enough."

Nate nodded and returned to the men. "Major Ospan, Arman, can I trust you?"

"Of course," Arman said.

Ospan's response was only a few degrees less enthusiastic, both men clearly eager to please who they thought were oil company representatives.

Nate studied them like he was assessing whether they were telling the truth or not, then said, "It's very important you tell no one. No exceptions. If my colleagues at Wysocki find out you haven't kept your word, it is likely Ketovo will not receive the benefits of what our visit today might represent. On the other hand, if you do keep it to yourselves, we are always grateful to those who have earned our trust."

While Arman looked receptive, a frown had appeared on Ospan's face.

"What does that mean?" the major asked.

"That if you're a friend to us, we will always be a friend to you. That's the way things should be, don't you agree?"

Arman whispered something to Ospan, but that didn't seem to help the major's mood much.

"I don't want you getting the wrong idea," Nate said. "This is all above-the-board stuff. Just information we'd rather others didn't know quite yet."

"If that is true, then no one will hear a word from us," Ospan said.

Arman nodded in agreement.

"I'm glad to hear that," Nate said. "Naturally, I cannot reveal all of our plans to you, but I can say that chances are good you will be seeing a lot more of Wysocki around this part of the country in the near future."

Arman couldn't help but grin. Even Ospan cracked a smile.

"That's welcome news," Arman said. "Is there anything we can do to assist you?"

"As a matter of fact, there is."

"You see that ridge?" Orlando said. "The one with the rock sticking up at the north end."

"I see it," Quinn said. The ridge was about two kilometers away, running off into the desert.

"We're going to want to turn right just before we get there and then follow it."

"Got it."

He checked the rearview mirror. The old Range Rover Nate was driving was about a hundred meters back, just outside the bulk of the dust cloud kicked up by Quinn's Land Cruiser. Jar and Daeng were riding with Nate, while Kincaid was sitting behind Quinn and Orlando.

The SUVs were courtesy of Major Ospan, who had told the "Wysocki" team they could use the vehicles as long as they needed, and of course there would be no charge. Nate had insisted on paying each man a thousand euros for their assistance. Ospan made no sign of resistance this time.

Their plane had left the airport when they did and flown south to Georgia, where the pilots would wait for the signal to return. For the next ninety minutes the team traveled on a series of dirt roads. The first few had been well groomed, but after that the quality steadily degraded, which was why it took so long to go only fifty-five kilometers.

The remaining twenty kilometers to the secret airfield would be traveled entirely off road. The reduced speed would not solely be to prevent the vehicles from breaking an axle in a rut, but also to cut the amount of dust stirred up and reduce the chances of telegraphing their arrival.

"Right about…here," Orlando said as they neared the ridge.

Quinn turned into the open desert and Nate followed.

After heading north, paralleling the base of the ridge, they entered a wide plain with an upward tilt. At the far end, about ten kilometers away, stood a raggedy line of boulders that looked like an ancient, deteriorating wall.

"How's the airfield looking?" Quinn asked.

"Nice and quiet," Orlando said.

Since the kidnappers' jet had disappeared inside the camouflaged hangar, neither it nor anything else had come back outside.

When the team was approximately half a kilometer from the rocks, Orlando pointed toward them, a little to the left. "Those over there—the ones that look like they've been cut in half."

Quinn got as close as he could before he killed the engine and climbed out. Kincaid followed him, and together they approached the nearest boulder. Behind them, Quinn heard the Range Rover stop and the doors open. He and Kincaid eased up to the rock, and Quinn peered around it.

On the other side, the land dipped away into a shallow valley. In the center, almost as hard to see as it had been on the satellite image, was the hidden airport.

So, this was Lonely Rock.

While Major Ospan had been arranging for their SUVs, Arman had graciously offered the use of a computer inside the terminal when Orlando had asked if there was one nearby. Leaving her phone with Quinn and Nate, she had used the computer to access the information Misty had left for them and had printed everything out, old-school style.

Not long after World War II, Lonely Rock had been built by the Soviets as a top-secret research facility. It had apparently been instrumental in the development of several weapon systems and even played a part in the Soviet space program, by manufacturing several spy satellites launched in the late '60s and early '70s. By 1980, however, it had already been well on its way to being obsolete. And in early 1986, five and a half years before the Soviet Union collapsed, it had been decommissioned. American inspectors had toured the base in 1996 and confirmed it was no longer being used.

US intelligence assumed that was still the case, as there was no indication it had been reoccupied. Whoever was using the base now had obviously been very careful about maintaining that impression. That they'd been successful would reflect badly on whoever's job it had been to keep tabs on the location.

Misty's information might not have indicated who was using the facility, but it did confirm a base was there. And a big one at that. A report from the 1996 inspection noted the underground base stretched out over a large percentage of the valley.

Quinn pulled out his binoculars, set them on maximum, and scanned the facility.

The hangar had a single large opening, currently covered by a pair of giant sliding doors. He could see no other ways into the structure, but there had to be a pedestrian door somewhere. It seemed ludicrous to think a person would have to open the big doors simply to step outside. It must be on one of the sides Quinn couldn't see.

Unless the only time anyone was allowed outside was when an aircraft was coming or going.

He scanned the roof, looking for an alternate entrance, but there didn't appear to be any hatchways or even vents large enough for anyone to sneak into.

Sneaking in, though, was the least of their problems at the moment. Getting to the building unseen would be damn near impossible in daylight. And depending on the base's security systems, it might be just as impossible to do so at night.

Footsteps approached from behind. "What do we got?" Nate asked.

"A whole lot of open ground." Quinn glanced over. Daeng had arrived with Nate, and both men were now looking through their binoculars. Behind them, Orlando and Jar were approaching.

"Maybe there's a crevasse or a dry riverbed we can use," Nate said.

"Looks pretty flat out there," Kincaid said.

"Dude, you're bringing down the mood."

Kincaid snorted.

Quinn looked through his glasses again and continued his examination of the airfield. Other than the runway, there were no other structures. It was like someone had picked up part of a small airport from somewhere else and dumped it here in the middle of nowhere.

"Found it," Daeng said a few moments later.

"A way in?" Quinn asked.

"What? No. Lonely Rock."

Quinn checked in the direction Daeng was looking.

About a kilometer west of the airfield, at the end of the valley, sat a gigantic boulder. It must've been at least twice as large as the biggest one on the ridge where Quinn and the others now stood. And though a few other rocks were around it, they were smaller and mostly piled against it. Otherwise, there was nothing other than desert around it.

A sentinel watching over the valley.

A very lonely rock.

They continued to scan the land for several more minutes, but no one found anything that would get them much closer to the airfield without the chance of being seen.

"I think we should try another angle," Nate said. "Hopefully there's something we just can't see from here."

Quinn nodded, having thought the same thing. "You and Daeng take the Range Rover east. See if you can find anything in that direction. The rest of us will go west. Same communication rules as before."

The new Danara Rule: any important conversations would happen outside the vehicles, over the comm, with no phones or computers nearby. A pair of double clicks would alert the others someone had important information to share. A returned triple click would indicate a person's ability to speak freely.

Nate and Daeng headed out first, then Quinn swung the Land Cruiser around and headed west. Kincaid was in the front passenger seat now, with Orlando and Jar sharing the back.

They went about a half kilometer before stopping. Kincaid accompanied Quinn to the ridge, while Orlando and Jar remained in the vehicle. Jar was using the NSA satellite to search for any pathways through the desert, and Orlando was probing the facility for a wireless network she could hack into. It would have been great if they could have done these things without the possibility of Danara looking over their shoulders, but it couldn't be avoided.

Quinn and Kincaid searched the valley through their binoculars, but like before, spotted nothing they could use, so they returned to the Land Cruiser. Another stop, four hundred meters on, proved just as frustrating. It was looking more and more likely they would have to try a nighttime approach. God only knew what might happen to Brunner in the meantime.

They were halfway to their next stop when a pair of double taps came over the comm. Quinn stopped.

"Wait here," he said to the others.

After leaving his phone on his seat, he climbed out and walked a good thirty meters away from the SUV, then tapped his mic three times.

"I think we found something," Nate said.

25

"For God's sake," Grigory muttered for at least the twentieth time.

Tiana grimaced. Though she was not unsympathetic to his frustrations, it was unacceptable for an officer with his training to let his feelings be known. Sure, they weren't technically in the army anymore, but their roles within General Nesterov's organization required just as much discipline, if not more.

This, of course, was not the first time Grigory had disappointed her since the mission to obtain Brunner had begun. He was lucky she felt loyal to him from their days together as young, naïve Russian officers. But even that was starting to erode.

After depositing the case holding Brunner in the man's new cell, she and Grigory had tried to see the general but had been told he would not be available for two hours. Tiana had spent the intervening time taking a shower, changing into clean clothes, and getting something to eat. Grigory, however, was still wearing the same outfit he'd had on when they left Slovakia. She guessed he'd spent his time sleeping, because when she met up with him at the appointed time at the general's office, he had the faraway stare of someone who'd been pulled out of deep slumber.

They had been waiting in the antechamber to Nesterov's office for over an hour now, with no sign that their holding pattern would change anytime soon. Turned out Grigory could have slept a while longer, which undoubtedly played a part in his impatience.

"He's mad at us," Grigory said. "He wouldn't leave us out here this long if he wasn't."

"Shut up," she snapped in a low voice. She would have preferred to say nothing, but she couldn't take his whining anymore.

He glared at her but kept his mouth shut.

Good. He could be as mad at her as he wanted. At least her words had worked.

She tried not to think about what was in store for them on the other side of the office door. The general was a hard man to predict, and she had learned to not even try.

Mostly.

Unlike Grigory, she had been handpicked by Nesterov after he'd been impressed by her several years earlier, when they'd worked together on several joint exercises between the Russian and the Kazakh armies. She'd done well by the general, and he had made it clear multiple times she was the best hire he'd made.

She was the one who had brought in Grigory, a contribution she now regretted.

She didn't know the general's age, but he was old enough to have started out in the Soviet Army, and then transferred into the service of the new nation of Kazakhstan, not long after it gained its independence in the early 1990s.

It was unclear if Nesterov still held an official position within the Kazakhstan military, but even if he didn't, he obviously still had very strong ties to it. Someone was funding this operation. But it wasn't only cash that he had access to. Anytime he needed anything, he utilized his ties to get it.

Case in point: Lonely Rock.

The Soviet-era station had sat empty for decades before being indefinitely "leased" to Nesterov a few years earlier. Nesterov's organization had a fancy name that sounded like it'd been created by some bureaucrat with nothing better to do. The Committee for the Delineation of Special Projects and Services. No one used that name, not even the general. He referred to their organization simply as Future Planning.

"Our great country will one day be a major player in the world," he had told Tiana the day she began working for him. "It is our job to make sure that happens."

Technically, Kazakhstan was Nesterov's adopted country. Tiana's too, for that matter. And as much as she loved her chosen country, she'd never reached the level of fervent patriotism Nesterov had achieved. Her passion lay in her loyalty to the general. She had been floundering in the Russian army, promotions that should have been hers given to men of lesser abilities. Nesterov had seen her for who she was from the very first time he met her, and had praised her for decisions she'd made that her superiors ignored. When the general offered her a chance to join him, she had jumped at it. His belief in her continued once she arrived at Future Planning, evidenced by his allowing her to lead his most important missions. If creating a greater Kazakhstan was his dream, then it was hers, too.

The door to Nesterov's private office opened and Rayana, the general's assistant, stepped out. "Please go inside. The general is waiting."

Before Grigory could spit out a sarcastic response, Tiana stood, said, "Thank you," and strode across the room toward the door. She heard Grigory behind her, scrambling to catch up.

As with every other time she'd visited the general's office, she was struck by how underwhelming the room was, given the great man sitting on the other side of the desk. Size-wise, the room was barely large enough to fit the few pieces of furniture. And then there was the stark lighting and bare walls, like he was using it only temporarily. And yet, she'd been told it had been his office since the start.

Nesterov's crown of precisely combed white hair pointed at her as he hunched over an open file. Beside it was a pad of paper he was scrawling on. He made no indication he knew anyone else was there.

Tiana took the only guest chair, leaving Grigory to stand. As she watched the general, she sensed Grigory's anxiety level rising again. She decided if he tried to say something, she'd do nothing to stop him. If he wanted to cause himself more problems with the general, that was his choice.

Seconds later, without looking up from what he was doing, Nesterov said, "Report."

Tiana brought him up to date on what had happened since she checked in with him last, which basically amounted to them having lost their pursuers.

"How do you know that for sure?"

"I had the pilots keep track on the radar. There was nothing that continued on the same path we did."

"What was the range you were checking?"

Tiana blinked. Did he know something she didn't? "Um, a hundred kilometers, I believe. Did you pick up something headed this way after we landed?"

"Not here, no. But there was a plane that entered the area about an hour after you were down. It landed in Ketovo."

"I don't know where that is."

"Southeast of here, about seventy-five kilometers. I thought about sending you to check it out, but it has already left again."

Tiana's shoulders relaxed. If it had been the people who'd put the tracker on her plane and they knew she was in the area, they wouldn't have left so quickly.

"Consider yourself lucky," Nesterov said, as if reading her mind.

"Yes, sir," she said, feeling shame at his rebuke for not having known about the plane before.

"Let's talk Slovakia. You lost a lot of good men. That does not make me happy."

"I take the blame entirely, General. I should have anticipated the attack." That wasn't entirely true. She had anticipated potential trouble. That's why she'd had guards posted the entire time they were there. Unfortunately, the attackers had caught Tiana and her people at their most vulnerable moment. But whether or not she'd been prepared, the fact that the mission had nearly ended on the tarmac in Slovakia was all on her shoulders.

"And you?" Nesterov said, looking at Grigory. "Anything to add?"

"What's there to add? Our mission was to get Brunner, bring him back alive, and destroy the ability for his work to be used by anyone else. He's here. He's breathing. And his lab is rubble. I'd say we've done well."

Nesterov considered him for a moment before turning his attention back to Tiana. "Tell me, how *is* our new guest?"

"As you instructed, he's still in the case."

"No problems?"

"His vital signs stayed within the expected ranges."

"Good. I suspect he's hungry now."

"I would think so."

The general clasped his hands and raised them in front of his chin, his elbows on the desk. "Let him out. If he asks for food, tell him some will be brought to him shortly."

Tiana started to stand.

"You stay," the general said, his eyes on Tiana. "Grigory can handle this on his own."

She sat back down, and Grigory exited the room.

After the door was shut again, Nesterov said, "I don't want you to get the wrong impression. I am very pleased with how everything turned out. You've done well. Starting today, you're my special assistant. I would like you there when we question Brunner."

She blinked. "Thank you." Having nearly failed, she was expecting the polar opposite of a promotion. And being asked to sit in on Brunner's interrogation? Not only did she feel pride that

Nesterov would trust her in this way, she would also relish the opportunity to learn what made Brunner so valuable to the general.

"In your new capacity, there's something I need you to take care of."

"What can I do for you, sir?"

"Our organization demands discipline and loyalty. It's the only way we will succeed. What we cannot allow is for our organization to be hampered by those who will not conform."

"Naturally."

"Good. I'm glad you agree." He smiled for the first time. "Then I am sure you will have no problem terminating Grigory."

She froze. Termination meant only one thing.

"His attitude has been deteriorating for some time now," Nesterov went on. "We can't afford the resources needed to rehabilitate him, which I doubt would even be possible. And we cannot afford to let him go."

"Is there no other option?" she asked before she could stop herself.

"If there was, I would have said as much." His reply was sharp and quick.

"Yes, sir. I apologize for asking."

He studied her for a moment. "Can you do this? Or must I have you removed, too?"

She swallowed hard. "Yes, yes, of course. You can count on me."

"Excellent. As soon as you have time, I want it done."

"Yes, sir."

The general stood up, his stern mood gone. "Shall we go talk to Dr. Brunner?"

Something hit the side of the case, jarring Brunner from his semiconscious state. He winced. His migraine had receded to an almost bearable state, but now reasserted itself as his head twisted slightly.

A thunk, felt more than heard, from near his knees.

Then another, shoulder high.

With a creak, the blackness that had been his world lifted away, and light—brighter than any he could remember ever experiencing—flooded in. He slammed his eyes shut as the rays triggered a new wave of pain in his head.

"Up," a voice ordered.

He heard it but the throbbing in his skull prevented him from comprehending, until hands grabbed his arms and started pulling him from the box. Another ripped the mask off his face, scraping it across his forehead.

Before Brunner realized it, he was on his feet, being half marched, half dragged across a floor.

He blinked and squinted, trying to see what was going on, but his eyes had been locked in darkness since before the plane ride and everything was still too bright.

When he finally stopped moving, the same voice as before said, "You can sit."

He recognized it now. It belonged to the man who'd thrown Clarke out of the helicopter.

Brunner reached behind him, trying to locate the chair or whatever it was he was supposed to sit on. Before his hand touched anything, someone shoved him in the chest. His calves knocked against something hard and his knees bent automatically, dropping him down, ass first, onto a cushion.

No, he thought, as he felt around on either side. A mattress on a metal frame.

He blinked again, and this time was able to keep his lids open in a slit. He was in a room, about the same size as the one he'd been in when they put him in the box. Like that one, his new cell had no windows, just a single door through which two of the four others in the room were carrying out the container.

Another stood half a meter away. He must have been the one who'd guided Brunner to the bed and pushed him down.

"Make yourself comfortable," the man from the helicopter said. "You're home now."

Though Brunner was already convinced this was where his life would end, the man's words sent a chill down his spine.

Brunner tried to swallow, but his mouth was dry. He'd been judicious while sipping the water from the bottle he'd been given for the trip, but he had drunk the last of the liquid hours ago. He swallowed what saliva he could and croaked, "Please...some water."

"I'll see what I can do," the man said. He and the other man left, shutting and locking the door behind them.

Brunner's eyes were finally growing accustomed to the brightness. The big difference he now saw between this room and his previous cell was that instead of a bucket, it had an honest-to-goodness toilet. Not that he needed one at the moment. Apparently, even the water he'd had on the plane had been fully absorbed before reaching his bladder.

His muscles ached from the hours of inactivity. He twisted his torso to the side, then turned it the other way, going slowly to prevent aggravating his migraine. He stood and stretched his legs and arms as best he could. He so wanted to roll his head over his shoulders to relieve the tension in his neck, but he was afraid that would be pushing things a bit too far.

He didn't want to lie back down. He'd spent the last God only knew how many hours doing that. But his choice was to either stretch out or pace the room, which would not do his headache any good, so he reclined on the cot and shut his eyes.

Ten minutes later, his lids snapped open at the sound of a key sliding into the lock on his door. He sat up carefully.

When the door opened, the woman who had been with him since the train entered. With her was a trim man with white hair and a weathered face whom Brunner had never seen before.

The woman stopped a few steps into the room, while the man continued on until he was standing in front of Brunner.

In fluent but heavily accented German, the man said, "Welcome to Lonely Rock, Doctor. I am General Nesterov." He gestured toward the woman. "Commander Snetkov tells me you had a pleasant journey."

Pleasant wasn't the word that came to Brunner's mind but he said nothing, waiting for the general to continue.

"I am sure you are wondering, what is the purpose of all this? Why would we bring you all the way here?" The man smiled. "We just want to talk. Nothing more. A casual conversation, if you will."

Casual. There was another word Brunner wouldn't have chosen.

The general stared at him, his brow furrowing. "Doctor, you do not look well. Are you feeling all right?"

This nearly caused Brunner to laugh, but he stifled the urge. "Migraine," he said, his voice still raspy. "I don't have my medicine."

"Migraine?" The older man looked back at the commander. "Did you know about this?"

The woman shook her head, perplexed. "He was fine when we put him in the container."

"You have specific medicine for this?" the general asked Brunner.

"Yes. It was in my bag. On the train."

Nesterov once more looked back at the woman.

Her expression turned uncomfortable. "Our contact forgot to bring it when he delivered the doctor. I sent him back to get it, but there were already others at Brunner's room so he had to leave it."

The general turned back to Brunner. "And you have this now? This migraine?"

"Yes. For several hours."

"We will see if we can find something in our infirmary for you."

"Thank you."

"How long do these spells usually last?"

Brunner rubbed his forehead. All this talking was intensifying the pain again. "Depends."

"What's the shortest?"

"I don't know. Twelve hours, I guess."

"And the longest?"

"I had one for four days once."

The general smiled again, only this time it was tense. "Perhaps you should rest. We can talk later. Is there anything else you need?"

"Water?"

"I'll have some brought in."

And with that, the general and Snetkov left.

Brunner stared after them. Had his headache bought him a little time? Yes, he was keenly aware the end of his life was rapidly approaching, but he felt a sense of elation that he'd been able to extend his time, however briefly. Perhaps he could stretch it even further. Even if his migraine did go away, he could fake it for a while. It wouldn't be the first time he'd done that.

He lay down.

Just a few extra days, that's all I want, he thought, and closed his eyes.

Nesterov waited until they'd left the holding cell area before saying, "You didn't know about this?"

"I'm sorry, sir," Tiana said. "I had no idea. Like I said, he was fine when we put him in the box."

"He never mentioned the possibility?"

"No. He only said he needed his bag. That it was important. He didn't say why."

"I am not waiting three days," Nesterov said. "Do whatever it takes to get him clearheaded enough to talk. You have one hour."

26

"Who spotted it?" Quinn asked.

He, Nate, and Daeng were lying prone in a gap between two boulders, looking down into the valley through their binoculars. About two hundred meters away was a small group of rocks, none larger than a small sofa. Most people would notice nothing unusual about them. Nate wouldn't have, either, if he hadn't scanned them with his glasses in thermal mode.

Quinn was now using the same function to look at the rocks. Heat flowed up from between two of the rocks on the left side, and dissipated almost right away. On hotter days, if anyone noticed it, the person would probably think the heat waves were generated by the rocks themselves. But it was a mild day, and rising heat was more than the rocks should be generating. Which meant something beneath was responsible.

Something like an entrance to an underground facility.

"Any signs of security around it?" Quinn asked.

"Nothing as far as we could see," Nate replied.

"Could be a sensor or camera stashed in the rocks."

"Could be."

Quinn flicked his binoculars back to visual-light mode and

turned them toward the other part of Nate and Daeng's discovery. Running down from the ridge was a dry creek bed. It swerved back and forth a few times before passing within a dozen meters of the rock pile. It then went on beyond the rocks for almost a kilometer before petering out.

It wasn't as deep as Quinn would have liked, but his first impression was it would be enough to prevent someone getting abreast of the rocks from being seen from the airfield.

"You found it," Quinn said. "You want to check it out?"

Nate grinned. "Absolutely."

Nate made his way along the creek bed mostly on his elbows and knees. There were a few spots, however, where the walls of the depression dropped so low he had to snake forward to remain hidden.

The desert did not lack life. Down at Nate's level, he saw bugs scurrying around beneath the scattered bushes, and heard, though never spotted, larger creatures running away as he approached. His biggest worry was snakes. He didn't have an Indiana Jones-level fear of them, but the idea of coming face to face with a set of fangs did not excite him. He had no idea if any snakes were out here, but the desert back home in California had them so there was no reason to think they weren't here, too. Thankfully, if they were here, they seemed to have made themselves scarce. So far.

The dry creek bed came closest to the pile of rock as it circled around the formation and headed farther down into the valley. In other words, at a point in direct line of sight of the airfield. This meant if Nate didn't want to reveal himself, he had to exit the bed when the rocks were between him and the base, doubling the amount of open ground he had to cover.

He crawled out of the wash and hurried to the formation in a crouch.

The rocks looked as if they'd been thrust into the air from

somewhere deep below and had then dropped back to earth. Some of the boulders lay on top of others. Some leaned against one another. And a few smaller chunks were scattered off to the sides, like discarded extra pieces not needed for the final sculpture.

When Nate reached the formation, he snuck around the back, looking for the gap in the stones through which he'd seen the heat signature. His hope was it would be the way down to the hidden entrance. But what he found was a meter-long slit, no wider than his palm.

He peered through it. It was dark below, but not too dark to see the edge of something that looked manmade, half buried in the ground.

There had to be another way to get to it.

He searched the rocks, and soon started to think the passage he was looking for could only be reached on the side facing the airfield. He was saved from having to investigate that side when he discovered a dip in the ground next to the rocks that went under one of the boulders.

This presented another problem. Out here, under all this sun, there was a good chance the short tunnel also served as a burrow for desert creatures. Perhaps even snakes.

He looked around for a long stick he could use to sweep out the space, but none of the brush in the area was large enough to create anything longer than half a meter. He rolled a stone through the opening, hoping that would cause anything inside to make its presence known. Nothing happened.

He picked up a handful of sand and threw it hard under the boulder. When there was still no reaction, he relaxed a bit. It was unlikely he would run into anything larger than an insect. Not that a poisonous spider or a scorpion wouldn't be a problem.

He cursed under his breath for letting those images into his mind.

Lowering himself onto the dirt, Nate worked his way under

the rock. While there were signs of animals having been there, the tunnel was empty, not even a sand flea to be seen.

When he neared the end of the passageway, he peered into the space ahead, scanning for cameras or any other security measure. Not spotting any, he crawled out, and found himself in an area approximately a meter and a half square, with an average height just a bit lower than that. And sitting smack dab in the middle of the space was a steel-barred hatch, through which the heat had obviously passed. The hatch and the space were smaller than he'd anticipated, which made him think this was not an emergency exit, but only a vent.

He crawled up to the hatch. Normally he would have attached a gooseneck camera to his phone and eased the lens over the lip. But because of Danara, using his cell wasn't an option. He had not arrived unprepared, though. He pulled out the mirror he'd taken from the first-aid kit, and eased it up and angled it so he could see through the bars on top of the hatch. Below the bars was a fan built into the top of a vent.

He shifted the mirror around until he'd seen most of the space around the fan. No cameras there, either, but some kind of sensor was on the latch, which appeared to be locked. He didn't find a keyhole or other way to release it, and guessed it was operated by someone on the base who would open the lock only when authorized personnel were at the vent.

Nate turned on his mic and described what he'd found. "Looks like it has a security device on it and a remote-controlled lock. If we can open it, I won't be the one going down. It's wide enough here at the top, but a little ways down it looks too narrow for me."

"What about me?" Orlando asked. She was five feet nothing, and had the lean body of a long-distance runner.

"Hard to tell, but you'd probably fit."

"I will do it," Jar said. She was even smaller than Orlando.

"I don't know," Quinn said. "I don't like the idea of you going down alone. We should keep looking for another way in."

"That does not make sense," Jar said. "We have a way in right now. The more information we gather, the better Dr. Brunner's chances are, correct?"

"Yeah, but—"

"Then I will do it."

There was more back and forth, but in the end Quinn conceded.

"I'll go to the vent with you," he said. "Help Nate keep tabs on you."

"*I'll* go," Orlando said.

"Did I miss a memo? Is it Defy Quinn Day?" he asked.

"Someone needs to deal with the sensor and lock," she argued.

"Jar can do that before she goes down."

"Sure, but they must be tied into the facility's network. This might be my best chance to hack in."

Ten minutes later, Nate was joined by Jar and Orlando. They had brought with them rope, a climbing harness, carabiners, a Glock 9mm with attachable suppressor, and a holster. While Orlando worked on neutralizing the security sensor and releasing the lock, Jar donned the underarm holster and slipped the pistol into it. Nate then helped her into the climbing harness. Even though it was size small, it hung loosely on her. She looked like a kid trying on her parents' clothes for Halloween.

Nate adjusted it as best he could, with a few knots and a couple of the carabiners, until it was snug enough around her waist, thighs, and shoulders that she wouldn't fall out of it. Probably.

He tugged on one of the straps. "How's that feel?"

"Fine," Jar said.

He held out the straps of the backpack containing the items Jar and Orlando thought she might need, and she put her arms through them. Last but not least, Nate attached a small cloth sack to the front of the harness with a carabiner. Inside were a couple dozen signal relays that Jar would disperse along her way like crumbs marking a trail, so there would be no interruptions in communication.

"Don't do anything stupid while you're down there," Nate said.

"Why would I do something stupid?"

"You know what I mean."

"You think I would do something stupid?"

"No. I…I just want you to be careful."

"Oh." She smiled ever so briefly. "I will be."

"Thanks."

They held each other's gaze for a moment, then Nate broke away and looked at Orlando. "How's it going?"

"I'm just…about…there," she said.

As her fingers danced across the keyboard, Nate wondered if Danara was aware of what Orlando was doing. Everyone on the team still carried their cell phones, but they had all removed the batteries so the devices couldn't be tracked. The mobiles were to be used in extreme emergencies only. Even then, since the others' phones would be off, the user would have to call Misty. They couldn't avoid using their computers, however, so if the disembodied voice was still tapped into their systems, it knew where they were every time Jar or Orlando had booted up one of the laptops.

Nate hated the idea of someone eavesdropping on them. But if Danara was indeed a friend of Dr. Brunner's, then her goals and the team's goals were in sync. Hopefully, if she did do something based on what she overheard, she wouldn't screw anything up for them.

"Whoa," Orlando said. "Look at this."

Both Nate and Jar leaned in behind Orlando so they could see her laptop. The screen was filled with code. Nate might have been able to make sense of a small portion of it if he had an hour, but currently it all looked like gibberish to him.

"How did they get that?" Jar asked.

"Good question," Orlando said.

Nate looked from one woman to the other. "What are you guys talking about?"

"The system security software," Jar said.

"What about it?"

"They're running CoPrime17," Orlando said. "There are only a handful of NSA listening stations that use it. It's state of the art."

"State of the art?" Nate said. "So, does that mean you can't break in?"

Orlando scoffed. "Of course it doesn't mean that. I've done it before."

"Me, too," Jar said.

"My point is that no one else should have this," Orlando said. "Give me a minute."

It ended up taking her three, but Nate didn't point that out.

"Misty's info was right," Orlando said. "This place is massive. There are a ton of sensor nodes…. Hmmm, they're not using all of them, though."

About thirty seconds later, Nate heard a *thunk* from the hatch.

"We're in," Orlando said.

Nate moved over to the hatch, and for the first time peered directly between the bars. "What about the fan?" he asked. "Can you turn it off?"

"Should be able to. Hold on."

While she worked on that, he lifted the hatch out of the way. He then threaded the climbing rope around a few of the bars. Since they didn't know what was at the bottom of the shaft, they couldn't just drop a rope down and allow Jar to repel. Nate and Orlando would have to lower her. He tied a loop on the end of the rope that would be pointing into the shaft, hooked it onto a carabiner connected to Jar's harness, and threaded the rope through several of the others. This would allow Jar to climb back up without any assistance, while pulling the rope up behind her.

A few moments later, the whine of the fan decreased. The apparatus was held in place by four quick-release nut-and-bolt combinations. Nate removed the nuts as the fan spun down, then after it stopped, he and Jar lifted it out of the way.

He shined a flashlight into the darkness. The duct went straight down for about five feet before continuing its descent at an angle, in the general direction of the airfield.

He turned to Jar, who had finished putting on her gloves. "Ready?"

"Yes."

"If you run into another fan, you're not going to have room to try to remove it, so don't even try it. Just come back."

She frowned. "I am doing this to collect information. We should not waste the opportunity."

"It took two of us to get this one out of the way," he reminded her. "You won't be able to move one on your own. And even if you could, where are you going to put it? I doubt there's going to be a convenient shelf nearby waiting for you."

"What if I can keep it above the brackets so that it does not fall?"

"Jar."

She let out a breath. "Fine. If there is another fan, I will return."

"And if you find yourself out of comm range?"

"I know what I am supposed to do."

"Tell me."

She grimaced. "I must always be in contact with you."

"That's correct, but you didn't answer the question."

"If I lose contact, it means I have not deployed enough signal relays. I will activate a new one. If that does not work, I am to move to a point where I am in contact again."

"Also correct. Thank you."

It wasn't that he didn't think she could handle the task ahead. She'd already been in several dicey situations since she began working with the team. But it didn't matter how much experience she had, Nate would always worry about her. She'd become like a sister. No, that wasn't right. She'd become like a...something. He wasn't ready to think about that yet.

He checked her harness one last time and helped her into the duct. Since the air passage was made of concrete, Jar was able to press against it. If the surface material remained the same, she should have no problems controlling her descent. As soon as her head was below the opening, he swung the hatch back down, the rounded bars now acting as a pulley of sorts for the rope, making it easier for Nate to lower her through the tube.

He leaned over the grating. "One click, everything's okay. Two clicks, and we immediately haul you up."

"I know," she said. "We have already discussed this."

Taking one hand off the rope, he placed it on the hatch. "Don't you dare get hurt."

"You know I cannot promise this," she said, then in a very un-Jar-like move, she reached up and touched the tips of his fingers with hers. "But I will try not to."

When she lowered her hand again, he let the rope slowly play through the bars.

He felt the sense of being watched on the side of his neck and glanced over at Orlando. She was indeed looking at him, one eyebrow raised.

"What?" he said.

"Nothing."

He narrowed his eyes. "Don't you say anything."

"I wasn't going to."

"I mean it. Don't."

She mimed zipping her lips shut, then returned her gaze to her computer, a wry smile on her lips.

———

After the bend in the duct, the passageway plunged into near total darkness, forcing Jar to turn on the flashlight attached to her harness.

She was not scared. The thought hadn't even crossed her mind.

Nate's concern for her had caused her to feel something, though. She didn't know exactly what to call it. It was warm and comforting and yet angst-inducing at the same time.

She had never had a close friend like him before. She hoped she was behaving the way a friend would with him, but she was never sure. Normal human interactions were a struggle enough. Thinking about not ruining her and Nate's friendship often consumed far too much of her time. Every once in a while, she wondered if she should back off. Not leave Quinn's team, of course, just return to her more isolated ways, doing what was asked of her while investing as little of her confusing emotional side as possible. But simply contemplating this was enough to get her stomach churning.

The duct continued at the same approximately thirty-degree angle for as far as Jar's light could reach. Building this must have been torturous.

Claustrophobics need not apply, she thought, then snickered. She was pretty sure that was a good joke. She'd have to ask Nate about it later.

All in all, though, the tube was not as confining as Nate had presumed. Though it would have been a bit of a squeeze for him at the start, she thought he could have made the descent without much trouble.

She passed a spot where brackets were attached to the sides and guessed they had once held another fan. From the rust and scars, she guessed it had been a long time since they had been used.

Soon after she passed it, Nate asked, "How you doing in there?"

She clicked on her mic. "All good so far."

"Might be a good idea to plant one of the relays."

The devices' specs indicated it was a bit early, but she decided not to argue with him. "Copy."

She pulled one of the small cubes out of the cloth bag, and placed the sticky side against the duct. The backing was more than strong enough to adhere to almost any surface. When the relay was secure, she resumed her progress.

Three minutes later, the view changed. "Looks like I am about to go straight down again," she said.

"Copy," Nate said. "FYI, there's only about thirty meters of rope left."

"Copy."

She continued slowly sliding toward the black hole ahead. About five meters out, she turned off the light and proceeded in the dark, in case someone was down there. When her foot tapped on the edge of the hole, she applied the brakes.

"I am at the new shaft," she whispered.

"Down to eighteen meters. If it's longer than that, you'll have to come back."

"Copy."

The duct was wide enough here that she could, with a bit of effort, turn around. Once she was facing the other way, she leaned out over the opening.

This new section was lined with metal, not concrete. At the other end was light, filtered through wired grating stretched across what she assumed was the bottom of the duct. It was just bright enough for her to see a floor beyond it.

She tried to estimate the distance. It might be within the rope's eighteen-meter limit, but it would be a close call.

She pulled back so that she wasn't directly over the hole and turned on her mic again. "I believe I am near the end." She described what she found.

"Can you make it there?"

"I...think so."

"Jar, if it's too far—"

"I am here. I should at least try to see if the rope is long enough."

A long pause, then, "Okay. But be extra careful. There's a much better chance someone might hear you now."

"Of course there is. That is obvious."

Nate had the habit of telling her things she already knew. It was the one thing about him that annoyed her. To be fair, though, nearly every other person she knew had this same habit.

She placed another relay directly above the hole, then turned back around and slipped over the edge feet first.

To slow herself, she pressed her back against one side and her feet against the other. It was awkward to say the least, but it did the job. Her biggest worry was that her shoes might screech against the metal, but she carefully placed each step and eliminated all but a couple of barely audible chirps.

The light below her grew closer and closer.

She glanced back up, and estimated she'd come almost fifteen meters already. If Nate was right, she could go only three more. Her goal was close, but not *that* close. She went on, hoping he'd gotten the remaining length wrong.

She'd made it within two meters of the screen covering the bottom of the shaft when Nate said, "That's it. That's as far as you go. What's your position?"

"I am just above a vent," she whispered. "It is over a room, or maybe a walkway. I cannot tell. There is light but it is not so bright. Hold on."

"What are you doing?"

"Repositioning to get a better look."

She expected him to say *be careful* again but he remained silent.

She shimmied a half meter back up the shaft to give her a little play in the rope.

"What's going on?" Nate said. "I don't feel the same tension anymore."

She explained what she'd done, telling him she wanted to give herself room to look around.

"All right, but don't waste too much time. We're going to have to find another way in."

"Copy."

She twisted around so that she was hanging headfirst, but realized that had only bought her a half meter at most.

She frowned at the opening below her. She was so close.

She cocked her head and listened for sounds from below.

"Jar?" Nate said.

"Just a minute."

The only thing she could hear was a distant hum. An air recycler, perhaps. Or maybe it was nothing at all.

This was ridiculous. She wasn't going to learn anything useful where she was, and if she crawled back out now, her entire trip would have been a huge waste of time.

Her current mission was to obtain intel, and that meant taking risks. Nate might be well meaning in his attempts to protect her, but putting limits on her based on the amount of rope was wrong. If Orlando had come down, would she have faced the same restrictions?

No, she would not have.

Jar released the looped end of the rope from the carabiner holding it, and laid her lifeline against the duct.

Since she'd created some slack ahead of time, she figured she had at most three minutes before Nate figured out what she had done, so she moved as quickly as she could to the end of the shaft, and braced herself directly above the vent screen.

All quiet below. Dead quiet.

Even the hum was gone.

A concrete floor sat about three meters beneath the vent. The room was dim, as if the light she had seen was coming from a distance.

She studied the screen. It was solidly built, as if designed to withstand more than just air blowing through it. But like elsewhere in the duct, it also showed signs of age. Most likely it was original material and had been in use for decades.

There were two clips on either side, holding it in place. She obviously couldn't see the other side, but knew levers had to be there so someone in the room could disengage the clips. Apparently, no one had considered that someone might try to release the cover from the duct side, because no measures had been taken to protect the clip mechanisms.

Jar pondered her next move, but really, there was only one appropriate choice.

Sorry, Nate, she mouthed.

She placed another relay right above the housing for the cover, then pulled a small carabiner off her harness. As she'd hoped, it was tiny enough to slip through a hole in the grating on the vent. She attached it so that it encircled one of the wires that made up the grating. Next she worked free one of her shoelaces. She tied one end to the carabiner on the vent, and the other to a carabiner on her harness.

"Jar, you've got to get moving," Nate said.

"I'm almost finished."

Lying by omission is what he would have called that. She preferred to look at it as an accurate description of her current state.

She released the left clip and then the right. As the screen dropped toward the floor, the shoelace yanked at Jar's harness but the knots held.

She froze, listening for any reactions below to the screen now hanging from the ceiling. Again, there was nothing. She inched downward until her head poked through the opening.

Not a room. A corridor, wide enough for a car to drive through.

It went off in both directions as far as she could see.

She'd been right about the lights. Though fixtures were spread evenly along the hallway, only every fourth one was on.

There were doors on either side, and outside most of them, piles of boxes or equipment or both were piled against the walls. Some of the piles were covered by tarps, but a lot of them were exposed. It was as if the rooms had been emptied, and their contents left outside to be picked up.

The fine layer of dust over everything told her no one had been down here in a long time.

Apparently, this was a part of the base its current occupants didn't need at the moment.

She took a longer look at the closest piles of junk. She felt confident she could arrange some of the stuff under the vent and effectively make a ladder so she could get back up in a hurry. And since no one seemed to come down here on a regular basis, who would even notice?

She pulled back into the duct, twisted around to get her feet under her, and moved down as far as she could without losing control.

"Do not get mad at me," she said into her mic.

"What are you talking about?" Nate asked, instantly concerned. "Did something happen?"

"It is about to."

One handed, she reeled in the vent cover. Then she released her hold on the duct and dropped into the corridor, tucking the cover against her chest. She bent her knees as she hit the floor and rolled down the center to dissipate her excess energy. Her landing had been relatively quiet, but the vent cover slipped out of her grasp during one of her somersaults and clattered against the concrete. She scrambled behind an old electric cart, and stared down the corridor for signs someone was coming to investigate.

"Jar! Answer me!"

Nate had said something as she plummeted through the air, but she'd been too busy to pay attention.

"Sorry," she whispered. "I am all right."

"What the hell is going on?"

"There is a corridor below the vent. I am in it now."

"You're what?" There was a pause. "You unhooked yourself from the rope!"

"You sent me down here to see what I could find out. That is what I am doing."

"That is *not* what we talked—"

"I am here now. It does not matter what we talked about. Do you want to know what I found or not?"

Another pause, then instead of Nate's voice, Orlando's came over the comm. "What do you see?"

Jar described her surroundings.

"No one's showed up yet?" Orlando asked.

"No. I don't think anyone has been down here for years."

"Good work, Jar. Can you hold for second?"

"Of course."

The comm went quiet.

Jar used the delay to lace up her shoe and start building the tower back to the vent. She was sure Nate was arguing for her return, and thought there was a good chance he would win.

When Orlando finally came back on, however, she said, "How do you feel about doing a little exploring?"

———

"She should not be down there alone," Nate said.

Orlando said, "You want to squeeze through the duct and join her, be my guest."

"That's not what I meant!"

"Nate, she knows what she's doing."

"She's only twenty-one!"

"If I recall, you weren't much older when you started with Quinn."

"Which is my point exactly. I didn't know crap then and would have gotten myself killed a dozen times if he hadn't been around."

"Yeah, but she's not as stupid as you were at her age. *And* she's got a lot more experience. Is there another reason you might be upset?"

His eyes narrowed. "Another reason?"

"Look, I know she's important to you."

"Of course she's important. She's my friend."

"It's a little more than that, I think."

"She's my *friend*," he said more forcibly. "Like a little sister. So, yeah, maybe that makes me overprotective."

"Exactly. And it's starting to get in the way of the job."

He looked like he was going to explode in anger, but after a few deep breaths, he said, "All right, all right. I know she's doing what needs to be done. I still don't like it."

Orlando reached over and patted him on the cheek. "It's okay. You don't have to. Now tie the rope off so she can climb back up when she's ready. We need to go."

The one thing Orlando knew for sure was that the ventilation shaft was not the way everyone was getting inside the base, so they needed to continue searching for a better entrance. Based on her cursory look through the facilities' computer system, she already had a good idea of where they should check next.

Nate didn't look happy to be leaving Jar's exit unattended, but Orlando's message about the job seemed to have gotten through to him. He tied the rope to the crossbars. Orlando set up a signal booster next to the hatch. It was considerably more powerful than the relays Jar had, and as long as Jar continued to disperse those relays, the booster should allow the rest of the team to stay in contact with her no matter where they were around the valley.

When Orlando and Nate were ready, they snuck back up the dry creek bed and rejoined the others, then returned to the Land Cruiser and climbed in.

"So," Quinn said, from behind the wheel, "suggestions on where to now?"

"Lonely Rock," Orlando said.

27

Working on a solution to Brunner's condition allowed Tiana to put off thinking too much about what she was going to do to Grigory. He may have become less of an asset lately, but she didn't think he was a liability. Guilty of disinterest? Yes. But she would have hoped that could be dealt with by reprimand, not termination.

This was about more than the permanent removal of Grigory. The general was testing her. Killing her colleague would prove to Nesterov where her loyalties stood.

She also had no doubt that if she failed the test, having her new promotion revoked would be the least of her troubles.

Damn Grigory for putting her in this position.

She shook her head and reminded herself she was trying *not* to think about this right now. She picked up her pace and soon arrived at Lonely Rock's infirmary.

Like pretty much everything else on the base, the medical wing was considerably larger than Nesterov's organization needed. Dr. Yusupov and his nurse used only three of the available rooms, leaving two long corridors of additional space in semidarkness.

Tiana found the doctor in his office, and after explaining the problem, he gave her a syringe filled with a dose of something with a long name that she didn't pay attention to.

"How long will it take to work?" she asked.

The doctor shrugged. "Everyone is different. But most see some improvement within an hour."

"Thank you, Doctor."

"Hold on." He opened a cabinet and hunted through several bottles of pills, finally pulling out a small, white one. He shook out two tablets and handed them to Tiana. "I know you said he's not nauseous, but in case that changes, give him these."

The detention area was built close to the medical wing so that prisoners would not need to be transported far if health issues arose. A solitary guard stood outside the door to the cell wing. Brunner was the only prisoner at this time, and even the one man on duty was probably overkill. The soldier led Tiana inside and down to Brunner's cell door. They were keeping him toward the back so that it would be difficult for him to hear anything coming from the main hallway.

The guard unlocked the door, and Tiana entered.

Brunner was on his cot, lying on his back, eyes closed. He showed no reaction to Tiana's presence until she crouched beside his bed and pulled up the sleeve of his shirt, exposing his bicep.

He jerked to the side, popped open his eyes, then almost immediately shut them again as a wave of pain washed over his face.

"Relax," she said. "This will help you."

"What is it?" he asked, as if she was offering him poison.

"Something for your headache."

"I'll-I'll be fine. I just need to…" A wince as more pain passed through him. "I just need to rest."

"Unfortunately, there is no time for that."

She stuck the needle in his arm and pressed the plunger before he could react.

After she pulled the needle out, he said, "What did you put into me? What is that?"

She held up the two tablets then set them on the bed, next to Brunner's waist. "In case you want to throw up, take those."

"Whatever you gave me, it's not going to work," he said. "I've tried everything. Naratriptan is the only thing that helps me."

Tiana smiled, recognizing the name. "Then you are in luck. That's exactly what I just gave you. Rest while you can. We'll be back soon for our chat."

———

Brunner stared at Snetkov as she left.

His hopes of delaying the inevitable had just evaporated.

He'd hold out for as long as he could, but he was under no delusion that his captors wouldn't soon know everything.

About Danara.

He dropped his head back onto the pillow and closed his eyes.

Maybe the naratriptan wouldn't work this time. Maybe the migraine would prevail. Or maybe he'd have to pretend.

Yeah, and maybe this is all a dream and I'm just falling asleep at my desk, and when I wake, everything will be all right.

A tear ran down his cheek.

28

Jar moved from one discarded pile of junk to the next, working her way down the corridor.

So far, she had found no signs of anyone having come this way in months at least.

When she first started out, there were doors every ten meters on both walls. They were offset so that five meters after one on the right, there'd be a door on the left, and five meters after that, another on the right. She'd randomly tried a few. Some of the doors were locked, while others opened into dark, dusty-smelling empty rooms.

Every hundred and fifty meters, she would place another signal relay and check in with the others to make sure it worked. Each time it was Orlando who responded.

Nate, apparently, was too mad to talk to her. Was he sulking? This was not an emotion she understood well. He had every right to be angry because she'd contradicted his directions, so he should be angry and move on. Sulking about it seemed like a waste of time and energy.

"Six hundred meters," she reported as she placed a new relay, marking the distance from the air shaft.

"Copy," Orlando said. "How many more relays do you have?"

Jar checked her supply. "Nine."

"Copy."

Unless the hall took some out-of-the-way turns, Jar thought nine should be enough to get her wherever she needed to go.

She moved onward, placing another relay at seven hundred and fifty meters.

She was nearing eight hundred when the view changed. She couldn't tell exactly where it started, but at a point ahead, probably around the nine hundred meter-mark, all the overhead lighting was on.

She reported what she saw.

"Chances are you'll start seeing some of the base personnel," Orlando said. "Do whatever you can to avoid them."

More unnecessary words, but to Jar's own surprise, she actually appreciated these. "I will be cautious."

"If you find yourself in a position you can't talk, utilize click protocol."

"Copy."

Jar eased forward, moving from a stack of crates to some old electronic equipment to a pile of dingy metal bookcases and, finally, to a mishmash assortment of boxes and carts and racks, at the edge of where the lighting changed.

She looked for movement in the corridor ahead and detected none. Taking a deep breath, she sneaked down to the next pile.

So far, so good.

She peeked around again, and was about to swing out into the open when she spotted something that made her stop in her tracks. Mounted high on the opposite wall, about thirty-five meters away, was a security camera. It appeared to be on a swivel head, but was pointing in her direction, unmoving.

Had she been spotted?

"Orlando," she whispered.

"I'm here."

"I see a security camera."

"You haven't seen any others before this?" Orlando asked.

"No."

"How far have you gone?"

"Approximately nine hundred and twenty meters from the vent."

"Hold on."

During the silence that followed, Jar found a gap in the junk pile through which the camera couldn't see her. She trained her binoculars down the corridor and watched for anyone heading in her direction. In the process, she noted more cameras, approximately one every twenty-five meters. The ones on the wall she was closest to were all pointing in the direction she was headed, while those on the opposite wall were aimed down the way she'd come.

She relaxed a little. The uniform angles meant the first one she saw hadn't been pointing at her specifically. That did not eliminate the possibility she'd been seen, however, so she kept alert for movement.

"I'm in the camera system," Orlando said. "It looks like the camera near you isn't active right now. But you're only going to make it another fifty meters before you get into view of one that is. I think I can deactivate them one at a time, but the system's a little archaic. I'm going to need a few minutes to figure this out. Proceed forward for no more than forty meters, then wait for—"

Jar heard another voice. It didn't speak directly into the comm and was a bit garbled. She had a hard time understanding what was said.

"Orlando, are you there?" Jar asked.

Dead air for three seconds, then, "Sorry about that. I'm still here. Move up like we talked about. I'll be right back." Orlando's mic went silent again.

Jar could do nothing about whatever was going on with the team so she focused on the task at hand. After confirming there was still no movement at the far end of the corridor, she moved forward.

———

"I think I can deactivate them one at a time, but the system's a little archaic," Orlando said. Boy, was that an understatement. Best guess, the camera setup was a Soviet-era system that had been updated in the early 1980s and barely touched since. It was a wonder Orlando could get into it at all. Turning cameras on and off to aid Jar's infiltration would take a Herculean effort. "I'm going to need a few minutes to figure this out. Proceed forward for no more than forty meters, then wait for—"

"I'll take care of the cameras."

Orlando jumped at the sound of Danara's voice coming out of the speaker on her computer.

"Orlando, are you there?" Jar asked.

Orlando shared a glance with Quinn. He looked as unsettled by Danara's reappearance as Orlando felt. "I'm still here," she said into her mic. "Sorry about that. Move up like we talked about. I'll be right back."

She shut off her mic. "Danara?"

"Yes, Orlando."

"You are interfering with our mission and jeopardizing Dr. Brunner's life." This was a much tamer version of the riot act Orlando wanted to hit her with, but she forced herself to be if not friendly then at least less harsh. Danara was clearly capable of wreaking havoc when she wanted to.

"You are having problems with the cameras inside the Lonely Rock facility," Danara said. "I have already taken care of it. Jar may proceed unseen."

That answered that question. Danara had indeed continued to monitor them, and now knew about Lonely Rock.

"You can't just turn them off," Orlando said. "If someone is watching them, they'll know something is wrong and raise the alarm."

"No alarm will be raised. The monitoring station is receiving signals from all the cameras. When Jar passes through one of the camera's field of view, the feed will automatically switch to a shot of an empty hallway."

"Automatically? Their system isn't set up to—"

"You were correct. It was not. But I have made adjustments. I am also replacing any footage she might be recorded on."

Orlando checked the system on her computer. Immediately, she noticed the addition to the interface she was using.

"What the hell is this? There's a button here with Jar's name on it."

"What?" Nate said as he leaned forward between the front seats.

Quinn stopped the Land Cruiser and turned to Orlando, concerned.

"Press it," Danara said.

"I'm not going to press it and risk getting her into trouble."

"You will not get her into trouble. Press it."

Orlando lifted her fingers from the keyboard and leaned back.

"All right. Then I will do it for you," Danara said.

The onscreen button was suddenly highlighted, then the entire interface disappeared, replaced by a camera feed showing a long, deserted corridor.

"Only you can see this feed," Danara said. "Tell Jar to step out from where she is waiting."

Orlando looked at Quinn and Nate. Quinn looked dubious and Nate looked like he was ready to go through the computer and tear Danara apart.

Orlando considered the options and then turned on her mic, figuring that for the moment, there was little reason for the hacker to double-cross them. "Jar?"

"Go for Jar," Jar answered.

"Don't," Nate whispered, low so Jar couldn't hear.

Orlando stared at him, silently telling him to back off. He did so, reluctantly.

"I need to test the camera system," she said into the comm. "Very slowly, I want you to slip your fingers around the edge of the box you're hiding behind."

"Copy."

Orlando stared at the stack of boxes on the opposite side of the corridor. At first, she wondered if she was looking at the wrong hiding spot, but then four fingers curled around the box.

"Thank you. You can pull them back now."

The fingers disappeared.

"Hold there," Orlando said, then clicked off her mic again.

Nate caught her eye. "I think we should talk. Privately."

If he hadn't suggested it, Orlando would have. Leaving her laptop and cell phone on the seat, she climbed out of the car. The others shed their phones and followed.

They walked halfway to the rock-strewn ridge before Orlando said, "This should be far enough."

"The fact that Danara set it up so that we could see Jar doesn't prove Jar can't still be seen by the others," Nate said, his words coming out in a rush. "I don't think we can trust her."

"You're right," Orlando said. "We shouldn't. But let's not kid ourselves. She's going to do what she wants. Better to keep her close than let her go rogue."

"She *has* helped us so far," Daeng said.

Nate whirled on him. "Was she helping when she destroyed Jar's computer?"

"That was before she knew we were on the same side," Orlando replied.

"We don't even know who she is! We shouldn't automatically be believing she has the same goal as we do."

"Trust me," Orlando said. "I'm not happy about her meddling with the mission. But we're the ones who let her in with that key you found in Brunner's apartment. She *is* connected to him."

"Could be the kidnapping was an inside job and she was the inside source," Nate suggested.

"Do you really believe that?"

"I don't know what to believe. The only thing I do know is that we can't leave Jar in there alone. We need to pull her out."

Orlando sensed Quinn was about to say something, but she knew that would be a huge mistake. His and Nate's relationship had taken a serious blow earlier in the year, and only now was getting back to something approaching normal. Quinn hadn't figured out yet how much of a hot-button topic Jar was for Nate—hell, she'd barely figured it out. So, before Quinn could speak, she jumped in. "If you were the one in there, would you expect us to pull you out now?"

Anger flared in Nate's eyes. "I'm not the one in there."

"Jar is a full member of the team. She's experienced and knows what she's doing. And whether you realize it or not, she is good at this." Orlando softened her voice. "We need her where she is right now."

Nate looked like he either wanted to scream in frustration or sigh in resignation.

In the end, he took a deep breath and said, "I know. I know. You're right, but I still don't like it."

"You don't have to."

"Just promise me, at the first sign of trouble, we'll pull her out."

"Nate," she said, frowning.

"Fine. Just...nothing had better happen to her." With that, he turned and walked back to the car.

After he was out of earshot, Quinn said, "Is there something going on between them I should know about?"

Orlando shook her head. "He's just protective."

"Hmm," Quinn said.

"I agree with him about not trusting Danara," Kincaid said.

Orlando shot him a look. "I believe I already said that I did, too."

"Just adding my vote."

She glanced at Daeng, waiting for him to weigh in.

He held up his hands and shrugged. "I'm neutral."

"Of course you are." She looked around at all three of them. "Does anyone else have something to add? Or can we get back to it?"

No one said a word.

29

Grigory sat on his bed wearing a pair of khaki fatigue pants and a white T-shirt, his normal off-duty attire.

He should be sleeping. While he'd dozed for a bit prior to the meeting with the general, his eyes still felt like they were being ground down by sandpaper, and a low-level headache was building at the base of his skull.

But his mind wouldn't allow him to lie down.

Nesterov.

Just the name was enough for Grigory's jaw to tense.

The asshole had offered not a single word of praise for the successful delivery of the scientist. Instead, he'd been unhappy about a few dead mercenaries who hadn't even been members of the organization. They, like the men deployed to deal with the Ferber family in Zurich, had been hired specifically because they were expendable.

Nesterov had made it seem like it was Grigory and Tiana's fault the men had died. And of course Tiana had accepted the blame like the good teacher's pet she'd become. Grigory had a feeling the general had asked her to stay behind so he could lavish praise on her alone, while sending Grigory off to do the mindless task of letting Brunner out of the box.

To hell with Nesterov. To hell with his whole Future Planning organization.

Grigory was tired of both.

He had never cared, one way or another, about improving the Kazakhstan of today, let alone tomorrow. The "golden future" of the nation had been Nesterov's dream, and, Grigory supposed, that of whoever in the government the general had convinced to fund his operation. Grigory had been drawn in by Tiana's promise to do interesting things. Well, and the money, of course.

Most of the missions, however, had been disappointing at best. The Brunner case was an exception, but during it, like with all the others, Grigory had felt as if he was wearing a collar that kept getting yanked this way and that.

He was a leader. But he knew now he would never get that chance here. It was time to start thinking about a change of scenery.

"Grigory, are you there?" Tiana's voice came from the anti-quated intercom next to the door.

He pushed off his bed and pressed the talk button. "Yes. What is it?"

"I need to discuss something with you. Can you meet me in Planning Room 13-147?"

"Of course. I'm on my way."

He smiled. Despite Tiana's cozying up to Nesterov, Grigory still felt some loyalty to her, enough to let her know about his plans first.

This would be the perfect opportunity.

———

As she headed back to her room to freshen up after giving Brunner his shot, Tiana had grudgingly turned her thoughts to fulfilling Nesterov's orders regarding Grigory.

She did have options. She *could* order someone else to do it, but the honorable thing would be to carry it out herself. Plus, the general would appreciate that more.

Either way, this was Grigory's life she was talking about.

Over the years, she had been in several tight situations with him. Not only did they always have each other's back, they had saved each other's lives more times than she could remember.

An old directional sign ahead pointed down a rarely used corridor she hadn't been in since her first week at Lonely Rock, on a tour given personally by Nesterov. She must have walked through the intersection hundreds of times since then without even thinking about the room she had seen there.

This time, however, she slowed as she went by, glancing down the dimly lit passageway.

There was a third option, she realized. One that would be dangerous for both of them, and ridiculous to even consider. Still, the idea played through her mind as she continued walking, and soon the ridiculous idea leveled down to crazy, then not great, then maybe, before she finally convinced herself it was actually doable.

It would be tricky, but mainly because she had very little time. So, if she was going to go through with it, she needed to act now.

She stared at a distant nothing, not breathing, not moving. It would mean lying to the general.

Could she do that?

Yes, she decided. She'd have to. It was the only way she'd be able to maintain self-respect.

She checked the time. She'd give herself fifteen minutes to pull everything together, and then she'd call Grigory in for a meeting.

———

Planning Room 13-147 was down a spur hallway, not far from the administration section of the base. Grigory knew this only because he'd checked the directory prior to leaving his room. He'd never been down this corridor before, let alone room 13-147.

It seemed an odd place to meet. The area was obviously one Future Planning wasn't using. The overhead lights were running on safety mode, only every fourth one on.

When he reached the room, he tried the door but it was locked. "Tiana?"

"Just a moment," she said from the other side.

When the door finally opened, the musty smell of disuse smacked him in the face.

"Come in," Tiana said, stepping to the side.

The room was lined with wood paneling, and a conference table that had seen better days filled the center. There was enough room around the table for eight chairs, but only two were present, both down at the other end.

Tiana motioned to one of them and took the other.

"Is it just you and me?" he asked as he sat.

"Yes. Just us."

The base of his skull tingled with suspicion.

"So, what did you want to talk about? We got a new mission?" He kept his voice light.

"No, not a new mission."

"All right. What, then?"

She locked her eyes on to his. "I need you to not react to what I'm about to say."

"Excuse me?"

"Can you do that?"

"Um, I guess. Can you tell me why?

"Grigory."

"All right. Sure. I won't react."

She blew out a stream of air, as if she'd been worried he wouldn't agree to her request. "You're being let go."

He couldn't help but let out a chuckle, but he cut it off quickly. "Are you serious?"

"Quite serious. I'm sorry."

"Hey, don't be. I was going to tell you that I quit. This makes it easier."

While she looked surprised at his news, it barely made a dent in her otherwise dour expression.

"It's okay, Tiana. Put me on the first plane out of here, and the old man will never have to worry about me again."

"That's not what he's requested."

"I don't understand."

"He's worried you'll say something about this place once you're away."

Grigory rolled his eyes. "You know I would never do that."

She said nothing.

"You think I would?"

"No. But it doesn't matter what I think."

He sat back, grimacing. "So, what do I have to do? Kiss his ring or something?"

"I've been ordered to terminate you."

Grigory said nothing. Then, "So that's it, huh? Sounds like something he'd want. But could you really kill me, Tiana?"

"Not if I don't have to."

"Good, because you don't have to. The general's insane. All you need to do is—" He paused as a thought hit him. "Oh, shit. You've ordered someone else do it, haven't you?" He glanced at the door, expecting it to burst open and emit his executioner.

"No one else is coming."

"Then what am I missing?"

"I believe you when you say you would never talk about this place or Future Planning. But I need you to promise me that's true."

Grigory was not a stupid man. There was only one answer to her request. "I promise. I will never speak of this place again for as long as I live."

Tiana moved her hand out from under the table and set it on the table. In her grip was a pistol, pointed at him. He considered lunging for the weapon, but knew she'd be able to get off a shot before he could put a finger on it.

And she would not miss.

She stared at him for several seconds before rising to her feet and walking around the end of the table to the back wall. The entire time, she kept her weapon trained on him.

She put her free hand on the wood paneling and pressed against it. The section of wall slid to the side. Beyond it was a dark space, the only thing visible a large bag at the edge of the light spilling in from the room.

"Through here is a long hallway," she said. "At the end are stairs that lead up to an emergency exit. This is your way out."

Hope swelled inside him, but then he thought about what he'd be facing when he reached the top. "There's nothing up there. Where am I supposed to go?"

"Ketovo is seventy-five kilometers away. You should be able to get there in a couple of days. The bag has food, water, a blanket, and a handheld GPS device. That should be enough to get you there."

"You want me to walk through the desert?"

Her face hardened. "No. I want you to have not put me in this position in the first place."

He had nothing to say to that.

"Understand the risk *I'm* taking here," she said. "If the general finds out you're still alive, then I will be the one who pays for it. So, either you take this opportunity and start a new life under a new name, or I do what I was ordered to do."

She raised the gun slightly.

"I'm…I'm sorry. You're right. You're taking a big chance." A pause, then a nod. "I'll go."

As he moved toward the secret doorway, she backed away, denying him the possibility of grabbing the pistol. He stepped across the threshold and picked up the bag.

"Thank you," he said, with the appropriate amount of contriteness.

"Don't come back. Ever."

She shut the door.

In the pitch blackness, he reached out, searching for a light switch. But before his hand touched the wall, an overhead bulb blinked on.

Motion sensor, he guessed.

The illumination was just enough for him to see the beginning of the hallway she had mentioned. As he approached it, another light came on.

A pattern emerged as he proceeded down his escape route— lights coming on as he neared them, those behind him going off not long after he left their halo.

Now that he was alone, the anger he felt at Nesterov came crashing back with a vengeance, growing more intense with each step.

What right did the old has-been have to determine whether Grigory lived or died? The asshole was clearly deluded, maybe even suffering from dementia. What else could explain Nesterov thinking he would turn Kazakhstan into a future world power by stealing everyone else's secrets?

And now Grigory had to change his life because of that sack of shit?

Over and over these thoughts ran through his mind, until a light flicked on in front of him revealing the end of the hall. He jerked to a stop.

How long had he been walking? In his fury, he'd totally lost track of time. It had been at least ten minutes, maybe more.

Mounted to the wall near the end was a ladder that led up through a hole in the ceiling.

He started to climb, the cycling of lights and his growing resentment persisting.

Tiana could have killed him, but instead had offered him a lifeline. If he were to now ignore her directive to change his identity, she would pay the price and he would be responsible. But if he did follow her order, the life he would live would not be the one he'd known.

"Dammit," he muttered more than once.

He stewed in his fury as more and more rungs passed through

his hands. Should he pick up where he left off and let Tiana fend for herself? Or should he throw everything away and start anew? Could he even do that?

He felt something looming above him and looked up to see he was only a few meters from the top. He spotted a lever beside the ladder, two rungs up.

He grabbed it and gave it a yank.

30

Jar worked her way down the corridor until she heard a noise ahead.

She looked at the nearest camera, pointed at her ears, and then down the hall. When no response came over the comm, she clicked her mic half a dozen times in rapid succession.

"I'm here, I'm here," Orlando said. "What's going on?"

Jar pantomimed for the camera again.

"Hang tight," Orlando said. "Let me check."

Orlando hadn't mentioned how she'd gained access to the security camera system, but Jar knew the answer.

She'd been thinking about that muffled voice she'd heard when she was talking to Orlando.

Based on her photographic memory of the moment—or would it be audiographic, in this case?—she realized the pitch of the indistinct speaker's voice had sounded more female than male. But Orlando was the only woman in the car, and the voice had cut *her* off.

That left two possibilities: Misty and Danara.

Jar had heard Misty's voice on only four occasions, but it was enough for her to know the tone of the muffled voice did not match that of the head of the Office.

It did, however, match Danara's. And if Danara had returned, it made sense that she'd use her extraordinary abilities to break into Lonely Rock's security network.

Whatever the case, Jar was thankful that access to the cameras had allowed Orlando to visually track her progress and warn her of upcoming trouble. Like right now.

"Four men," Orlando said. "All in fatigues. They're about twenty-five meters ahead and just turned down another hallway. Give it thirty seconds and you should be good to go."

Jar clicked once, to indicate she understood.

When the half-minute was up, she crept forward and paused just outside the intersection. To this point, she'd encountered only doors. This was the first new hallway.

She heard footsteps fading around the corner as the soldiers moved farther away. She peeked around the corner. There was a slight bend in the corridor, and though the men's steps echoed faintly, the soldiers had moved out of sight beyond the curve.

She checked the corridor in the other direction and saw that it, too, had a bend. She wondered if they came together again somewhere on the other side of the base, like a giant circle. If she had designed a place like this, she would've definitely considered creating hallway rings.

She moved through the intersection, then whispered, "How do things look ahead?"

"You're clear for at least five more cameras."

"Copy."

Jar sneaked down the main corridor, staying tight to the wall, and noticed a change to her surroundings. Gone were the piles of boxes and discarded equipment she'd been hiding behind. Here, the only things that could serve the same purpose were the concrete support pillars. They looked more like arches—going up one side, crossing the ceiling, and coming down the other. The columns protruded about three-quarters of a meter into the walkway, leaving her barely enough room to conceal herself, and would be useless if someone walked by.

If someone was indeed heading toward her, her only other option would be to duck through one of the doors. The good news was there were more of them now, some only a few meters apart. The bad news: the door she chose might lead to a room that was occupied. Unless, of course, it was Brunner inside.

More noises ahead. Voices and footsteps and humming machinery. But she couldn't see anything because her hallway had begun to curve left.

"Company ahead," she whispered into her mic.

There was a prolonged pause before Orlando said, "Hold your position. I'm dealing with something here so I need a few minutes."

"Copy."

The sounds down the corridor were far enough away that Jar thought she had a little room to play with, so she decided to improve her position while she waited.

Creeping tight to the left wall, she moved forward as far as she dared and stopped behind a pillar.

From her new position, the voices were clear enough for her to pick out distinct speakers. Unfortunately, everyone was speaking what sounded like Russian and it was not a language she knew. A flaw, like her lack of German, that she would rectify after the mission was over.

She peeked ahead, but the curve in the hallway still kept the others out of sight. She eyed the next pillar, and then moved quietly down to it.

The speakers couldn't be more than a few meters away. Which meant a glance around the pillar was out of the question.

She looked back the way she'd come. There was a door about fifteen steps behind her. She thought about it for only a second before easing her way back to it and pressing her ear against it. The only sound she heard was a hum that seemed to be coming into the door from the walls.

She gently pushed down on the handle and pulled the door from the frame, ready to freeze at the slightest squeak. It was dark on the other side. She slipped inside, then pressed her ear against the door to make sure no one had heard her and was coming to investigate. When she felt confident she was in the clear, she turned on her flashlight.

The room appeared to be a giant storage area. It had to be at least forty meters long, paralleling the corridor, and was filled with floor-to-ceiling metal shelves, which in turn were filled with boxes, also made of metal. They looked old, dinged up, even rusty in spots. She was curious about what they held, but checking them was not on her to-do list.

The only way to move through the room was down a center aisle between the shelves.

Jar walked in the direction of the voices, and found another doorway between the shelves, not far past where she estimated those conversing were standing.

Even before she put her ear to the door, she could hear them. Either they'd moved since she'd been in the corridor or she had guessed wrong, because it sounded like they were standing right on the other side of the door.

"Ja...on't se....whe...ou? Jar?...ar...ou...hear...."

Jar returned quickly to the center aisle and back the way she'd come, putting plenty of distance between herself and the talking soldiers. She whispered into her comm, "Orlando? Do you read me?"

"Ja...ome in. Jar...re...ou? Jar."

"I'm here. Can you read me?"

She should have been still in range of the last relay she'd put up, but maybe the room's walls were interfering with her signal.

"Jar. Yes, I...re you...uble?"

Jar pulled out another relay and stuck it to the door she'd entered through, then said, "Please repeat."

"I have you now," Orlando said. "Where are you?"

"I am in a room off the corridor, approximately the same location where you should see at least three men talking."

"Copy." A pause. "I've got them. What happened?"

"Nothing happened. I have been searching for a way around them."

"Jar, I think maybe you've gone as far as you're going to get. I can search the base on the cameras from there. Perhaps you should start heading back to—"

"The cameras cannot tell you everything," Jar countered. "You cannot hear with them. You cannot see into the rooms with them. What you might be able to do is find where they are holding Brunner and lead me there."

"Wait, wait, wait," Nate's voice cut in. "Jar, he's liable to be guarded. You can't take them on alone."

"I did not say I would," she replied. "But I can recon the area, look for hiding places, so that you will be well informed when you join me."

Silence on the line. The kind that told Jar the others had muted their mics.

When they came back on, it was Nate who spoke, and he surprised her by saying, "All right. But stay where you are until Orlando finds him. And promise me you'll be even more careful."

She felt a slight tug on her chest. "I promise."

"We'll be there as soon as we can."

"I know. You also be careful."

"I promise."

While she waited for instructions from Orlando, Jar decided to take a better look around. She walked down the center aisle, this time continuing past the door near where the soldiers were talking. She was hoping the room went on long enough that there would be another door she could use to slip back into the corridor.

There was. But even more interesting, straight ahead down the aisle and embedded in the wall at the end of the room, was a door that had to lead into another room, as there was no way it could directly lead into the corridor.

If this room led to the next one down, would that room lead to the one after it? Would it be possible to parallel the path of the hallway?

She approached the doorway. On the handle side was a long narrow window running vertically. The glass was frosted but she could tell it was dark on the other side.

Jar turned the handle and stepped into a room that looked identical to the one she'd been in. She hurried down the aisle until the next wall came into view. And there, sitting directly in her path, was yet another door, with no light shining through its narrow window.

The end of her mouth ticked upward.

———

Ahead was the team's destination, a couple of flat-top boulders on the valley's rim, as close to directly behind Lonely Rock as they could get.

Quinn slowed the vehicle as the terrain took a small dip. On the comm, Orlando was suggesting Jar return to the surface. Jar, however, was not keen on the idea, and had offered an alternative that didn't seem to be sitting well with Nate.

Orlando turned off her mic and looked at Nate. "Her idea's a good one."

Quinn glanced in the rearview mirror and saw the muscles in Nate's jaw tighten.

"I agree," Quinn said. "If she can get us the lay of the land, that could save us a lot of trouble."

"I realize that," Nate said, the words seemingly forced from his throat.

"The question is, can she really do it?" Quinn said.

Nate frowned, then gave a curt nod. "She can."

"Then I guess I'd better see if I can find Brunner," Orlando said. "You want to tell her?"

Another nod from Nate as he turned on his microphone.

Quinn negotiated a way between some brush as Nate relayed

the decision to Jar. When the Land Cruiser reached the point where the boulders were between the vehicle and the secret base, Quinn turned and drove toward them, then stopped a few meters from the rocks.

"We'll be right back," he said to Orlando.

Without looking up from her screen, she said, "'Kay."

Quinn, Nate, Daeng, and Kincaid exited the vehicle, approached the boulders, and found a good vantage point on the right side. Quinn tasked Daeng and Kincaid with scanning the desert for patrols, and had Nate do the same with the base. Quinn trained his binoculars on Lonely Rock.

The boulder that dominated the formation jutted into the sky like it was reaching for the sun. The massive rock was easily twice as big as the ones Quinn and the others had encountered along the valley's ridge. Many of the rocks that surrounded it were also big. Perhaps they had all started life as one giant boulder, and pieces had broken off over eons.

Orlando had said the base's power schematics showed something was in the area; she just didn't know exactly what. Quinn slowly scanned the entire formation, first in normal light mode, then in thermal. If the power was feeding another vent, the thing wasn't releasing any heat.

He'd just turned his attention to finding a way to get to the rocks unnoticed when Daeng said, "There's someone out there."

Quinn lowered his glasses. "Where?"

"About three hundred meters this side of the rock, heading roughly in our direction."

Quinn aimed his binoculars in the direction Daeng had described. If the team had been seen, surely there would have been more than one person coming to deal with them.

He spotted the walker almost right away. It was a man, probably in his thirties, wearing fatigue pants and a white T-shirt, and carrying a black bag over his shoulder.

There was something familiar about—

"Hey," Kincaid said. "That's the guy from the train. The one with the walking stick who helped Clarke."

That was it. Quinn recognized him now from the airfield in Slovakia.

Kincaid turned and ran toward the SUV.

Instead of yelling at him, Quinn turned on his comm mic. "Where are you going?"

"To get a rifle."

"Stop."

Kincaid put on the brakes and looked back.

"We're not doing anything until he reaches us," Quinn said. "And no one's going to shoot him unless absolutely necessary. So we don't need the rifle."

"What if he changes direction and doesn't come this way?" Kincaid argued.

"Then we see where he goes."

"Kind of looks to me like he's talking to himself," Daeng said, still watching the man.

Quinn raised his binoculars again. "Anyone see a radio?"

"If he's using one," Daeng said, "I feel sorry for whoever's on the other end. The guy does not look happy."

Grigory growled as he plodded through the desert, wondering how this had become his fate. He had done nothing wrong, quite the contrary. If not for him, setting up Eric Ferber and kidnapping Brunner would have never happened. His involvement had been instrumental.

And *this* was how he was thanked?

"That ungrateful asshole," he said. "He should be on his knees, begging me to stay!"

Grigory was not one who usually talked to himself, but he was livid.

"The goddamned arrogant asshole. Terminate *me*? I'm the asset here, not him. If anyone should be put down, it's him."

The more he railed against Nesterov, the slower his pace became, until finally he stopped and looked back toward Lonely Rock and the hidden entrance to the emergency tunnel.

To hell with this bullshit.

He wasn't changing his life for anyone, and he wasn't going to allow himself to be held responsible for Tiana's death, either.

He was the one who should be calling the shots.

He discarded the unnecessary weight and raced back the way he'd come.

"Oooookay," Daeng said. "That was unexpected."

Quinn said nothing, but he agreed.

The kidnapper had stopped and looked back at Lonely Rock. Then he dropped his bag and ran toward the formation.

"If we had the rifle…" Kincaid mumbled.

"You still wouldn't have fired," Quinn said.

A groan from the bodyguard.

The men watched the kidnapper hurry all the way back to the rocks. The guy then moved around one of the boulders and seemed to slide down into it.

"There's the entrance," Nate said.

Quinn kept his binoculars aimed at the formation, but the man did not reappear.

"He's not a small guy," Daeng said. "Whatever access way he's using, we should all be able to fit."

"I don't see any washes," Nate said. "But if we keep a tight line, we should be able to keep Lonely Rock between us and the airfield."

Quinn lowered the binoculars. "Let's gear up."

31

Orlando clicked on her mic. "Orlando for Jar."

Jar responded almost immediately, but her signal was choppy again.

"I'm not reading you," Orlando said. "You need another relay."

Jar said something that Orlando hoped meant *hold on*. Then, several seconds later, "How about now?"

"Better," Orlando replied.

"Did you find Brunner?"

"Not exactly. But I did find an area where there are holding cells. There's a guard out front of one of the hallways, so they've got at least one prisoner in there."

"Am I close to it?"

"Mmm, close-ish. You're going to have to go another hundred meters down the corridor, to an intersection that has a sign with some Cyrillic letters and the number five-zero-six. Then you'll go left."

"I should be almost to the intersection now."

Orlando scowled. "Jar, I thought I told you to stay where you were."

"It is okay. I did not have to use the corridor. The rooms along it are interconnected. They are not being used."

"Not the ones you've been in *so far*."

"Of course, not those. That is obvious."

Orlando had forgotten to use her Jar filter again. "Look, I know you've got this. I just need you to inform me before you do something like this again."

"I will. I apologize for not doing so before."

"Don't apologize. Just don't do it again. Now let's figure out exactly where you are."

———

Jar moved down the aisle, looking for the next corridor entrance. When she found it, she also discovered that the room ended about five meters farther on, and unlike before, there was no interconnecting door. The aisle did, however, appear to take a ninety-degree left turn. She bypassed the door to see if she was correct.

She was. The aisle continued in the new direction into the darkness. If her hunch was correct, it now paralleled the hallway Orlando wanted her to take.

"I'm not seeing any of the doors move," Orlando said. "Did you try already?"

"Sorry. One moment." Jar hurried back to the corridor entrance. "Opening it now. I am one hundred percent sure it will be the one right before the intersection."

Jar inched the door open just enough for Orlando to see it on the nearby security camera.

"You were right," Orlando said. "You're only a few meters from the turn."

"Yes, I know." Jar explained what she'd discovered concerning the change of direction in the room.

"So, it's a big L?"

Because the Thai and the English alphabets were completely

different, it took Jar a second to make the connection. "Yes. Except flipped backwards and upside down."

"Perfect. Then I think you should keep riding this path for as long as possible."

Jar knew this was only a figure of speech. She'd heard something similar before, and was aware she wasn't supposed to actually ride anything. Still, it was a perfect example of why figures of speech were confusing.

"The next intersection is about sixty meters away," Orlando said. "It's a T-bone, with the new corridor going off to the right, so if you miscalculate, you have the potential for passing right by it. There's some people in that area right now, so I'll have to guide you through when you get there."

"Copy. I will let you know when I am close."

"Don't forget your relays."

"I will not."

What Jar didn't say was that she was down to her last three. Hopefully, they would be enough to get her near Brunner. If not, she'd worry about that then.

She set off again, taking the L turn to the left and proceeding to the next doorway. Like with the other doors, the narrow window was dark. She pulled it open, stepped through, and scanned the new space.

This was not another storage room. In place of the metal shelves and the boxes, bunk beds occupied the room. They rose three beds high and sat side by side, with only enough space between bunks for someone to stand.

The urge to douse her flashlight rushed through her, but Jar resisted. The mattresses nearest her were bare, and she didn't hear any breathing other than her own. She crossed the space, eyeing each bunk in case it was in use, but reached the door at the far end without seeing anyone.

Finally, a door different than the others, but not in a good way. This one was missing a window, so she couldn't tell whether or not there were any lights on in the next space.

She turned off her flashlight and gave her eyes a few moments to adjust. The room was dark, but not pitch-black. A small line of light seeped under the corridor doorway, just enough for her to make out the end of the closest bunk.

No light came from under the door she was standing next to, however. Either it was dark on the other side or the door had a good seal at the bottom. Neither possibility was more likely than the other.

She pulled out the Glock, attached the sound suppressor to the muzzle, and her flashlight into a clip on the barrel. For now, she left the light off.

She pushed down on the door handle, and pulled the door until it barely cleared the jamb.

Light spilled through the crack. After the initial glare wore off, she realized the light wasn't particularly strong.

She turned her ear to the opening.

Rhythmic, heavy breathing. Someone sleeping.

Not just one person. Like a chorus singing softly in the background of a lead vocalist's solo, other sleepers were there, too.

Why was there a light on? Was someone still awake?

Since there had been no reaction to her easing the door open, she widened the gap until she could peek through.

Bunks again, many with the lumpy forms of people stretched out on them. The light was coming from a bottom bunk about halfway across the room. She watched for movement, but didn't see any.

She could either sneak across the room or go out into the main corridor. If she ran into trouble out there, it would likely trigger a base-wide alert. Though the same was potentially true about the bunk room, at least there she would have a chance at controlling the situation.

Crouching, she crept into the lit room.

No sudden movements or shouts of discovery.

So far, so good.

She closed the door with barely a sound, then faced the bunks.

The loud sleeper was on one of the upper beds, two or three sets in. The others must have been used to his snores or too exhausted to care, because the noise didn't seem to be interrupting anyone's sleep.

Jar moved along the front of the bunks, staying as low as she could. A bunk away from the one the light came from, she paused and rose just enough to see the bed in question. A lamp clipped to the bunk's post shone down on a person stretched out with a book lying on his chest and his eyes closed.

She slipped past his bunk, alert for any changes in his breathing, and made it almost to the end of the room before she heard him take in a sharp breath through his nose.

She froze, her gun ready. But while the metal braces of his bunk squeaked, the noise was not followed by his voice. Instead, there was a click and the light went out.

Jar held her position, giving the man a half-minute to fall asleep. She would have liked to give him more time, but that was all she could afford.

She continued to the door on the other side of the room.

Again, there was no window. When she opened it, though, no light rushed through the opening.

It turned out to be a large communal bathroom, and on the opposite wall was a doorway to another bunk room. This one, like the very first she'd entered, was empty with beds stripped.

From her estimation, she was very close to the T-bone intersection. She activated a new relay.

"Jar for Orlando."

"There you are," Orlando said, with what sounded like relief. "I've been trying to reach you. I told you not to forget your relays."

"I did not forget. I am still within range of the last one, since it is linking to the one I just turned on, but I heard nothing. It must be the walls again."

"Then you'll need to place them more frequently."

Jar paused. "That should solve the problem."

She knew she should tell Orlando she had only two left, but Orlando would tell her to go no farther. Jar still thought the two relays would get her where she wanted to go. And if not, they would get her close. She could check the area and move back into range to report her findings.

"Where are you now?"

"I should be near the intersection," Jar said.

"Good. The hallway's clear at the moment. Open a door and let me see where you are."

"Copy."

Jar walked over to the door leading to the corridor and opened it a few centimeters.

It took Orlando a few seconds to answer. "You've gone too far, but not by much."

This annoyed Jar. She usually was very good at judging distances, and had not even considered the possibility she had passed the corridor. The room of sleeping soldiers must have thrown her off.

"If you go back to the previous door, you'll be right there."

That would be back in the room with the sleepers. "It would be better for me to enter the corridor here, if that is possible."

"All right," Orlando said. "When I give you the word, enter the corridor, go right, and then left at the intersection. It's about ten meters away."

"Copy."

"Once you're in that corridor, I want you to keep going until I tell you to stop. When I do, there will be a door on your left. Go through it."

"Copy."

"Are you ready?"

"I am."

A pause, then, "Okay, you're clear. Go."

By the time Quinn reached the Land Cruiser, Nate already had the back open and was pulling out their gear bags. Everything had been distributed into six backpacks on the drive from Ketovo. Jar had hers with her, leaving one each for the rest of them. Each pack contained at least one weapon, ammo, sound suppressor, two flash-bang grenades, and night vision goggles. The more specialized gear was given to whoever seemed most appropriate to carry it.

Nate strapped his pack over his shoulders, then searched through the others until he found the one he wanted and held it out to Quinn. "Here you go."

Quinn pulled his on. He peered through the back of the SUV at Orlando, still sitting in the front passenger seat. "Time to go," he said.

"Just a minute," she told him, then said something into her mic.

Daeng and Kincaid arrived a moment later and donned their loads.

"What about that?" Kincaid asked, nodding at the rifle bag still in the back.

"I doubt there will be much use for it where we're going," Quinn replied. "But if you want to carry it, be my guest." The weapon was intended for long distances, something he suspected they wouldn't find much of in the underground base.

Kincaid grabbed the soft-sided case and slung the strap over his shoulder. "Just in case," he said.

Quinn picked up the remaining pack and circled around to the passenger side. He tapped on the window next to Orlando and pulled open the door.

"Almost done," she told him, and into her mic, "Keep going, you're almost there...yeah, that's the one. It should be a maintenance passageway. Go down that until you come to a door marked 90-214. We're heading out so I won't be able to follow you on the cameras. I'll still be on the comm, though, so when you reach the door, let me know." She listened for a moment. "Copy. Stay safe."

As she closed her computer, Quinn held out her bag, strap side toward him. She unzipped the opening to one of the sections and slipped her computer inside. Once it was closed again, Quinn moved out of the way so she could exit the car, then he turned the bag around and helped her put it on.

"Everyone ready?" he said, looking at the others.

Nods all around.

They started out on a course that paralleled the valley, until they reached the point where Lonely Rock completely blocked out the airfield.

"Stay in line and keep low," Quinn said.

They descended into the valley, Quinn in the lead. Here and there they ran across a dip in the land, but otherwise it was fairly smooth.

A little ways past the halfway point, he looked over his shoulder and waved for Nate to join him.

When he had, Quinn said, "You up for taking a little detour?"

"You want the bag."

"I do."

"I'm on it."

As the others proceeded on course, Nate angled off toward the spot where the kidnapper had dropped his bag.

Ten minutes later, Quinn and the others reached Lonely Rock. While they waited for Nate, Quinn and Daeng located the path through the rocks they'd need to take to reach the hidden base entrance, then returned to Orlando and Kincaid.

Nate arrived two minutes later and dropped the bag on the ground. "Shall I?" he asked.

"Please," Quinn said.

Nate unzipped the bag and parted the sides so everyone could see. Inside were food, water, some clothing items, and what appeared to be a sleeping bag. Nate pushed things around, feeling through the rest of the space.

"That's it," he said.

"Really?" Daeng asked.

"Was he going camping or something?" Kincaid asked.

"Looks to me more like he was running away," Nate said.

"Or he was forced to leave," Orlando said.

Whatever the case, the guy had apparently changed his mind.

"The way in's over here," Quinn said.

He led his team to a triangular crawlway created by one of the rocks leaning against another.

Quinn went first. At the end was a chamber much like one Nate had described at the vent location, only this one was large enough to fit all five of them. It was even tall enough for Orlando to stand in, though the others had to hunch over. The actual entrance looked like the manhole covers found in most cities, the metal disc sitting in a concrete housing.

The only things missing were the holes in the lid used to pull it up. Quinn guessed there was some kind of mechanism to raise and lower it.

"That asshole got it open," Kincaid said. "There's got to be a way we can do it, too."

"Or maybe he left it open when he crawled out," Nate said. "The cord will probably burn through it."

"Get it," Quinn said.

While Nate pulled the high-intensity incendiary cord from his pack, Quinn knelt down and pushed on the disc. Much to his surprise, it bounced a little.

"Hold off on that," he said to Nate. "I think it might be unlocked."

He tried to bounce it high enough for them to jam the edge open, but that proved difficult. Maybe if they had all day, they would get lucky, but clearly bouncing was not the answer.

They ended up using a bit of the cord after all, and created two nickel-sized holes through which they threaded a wire, which in turn they used to pull through the end of one of their ropes.

"Let me try," Kincaid said.

Quinn handed him the rope, and the bodyguard pulled. The disc resisted at first, but Kincaid's persistence paid off, and soon it opened like a hatch on a submarine. Kincaid yanked it out of the way.

The shaft below was completely dark. Nate shined his light into it, but the bottom was too far down to see.

"That shaft looks a little tight," Kincaid said, peering over Nate's shoulder.

"Claustrophobic?" Nate asked.

"No. But I like to avoid things I could get stuck in."

"If you want to stay here and guard the hatch, you're welcome to do that," Quinn said.

"Uh-uh. I am *not* staying behind. I was just commenting."

"Comment noted." Quinn looked at the others. "Shall we see what's down there?"

"I'll go first," Nate said.

He lowered a leg onto the ladder attached to the shaft's wall. A light near the very top came on. Quinn glanced past Nate and saw the rest of the shaft remained in darkness.

"Must be motion activated," Quinn said.

"Either that or I'm going to get shot in the ass on the way down."

"You volunteered to go first," Daeng said.

"Yeah. Thanks for reminding me."

Quinn's guess was confirmed as Nate triggered more lights on his way down.

Daeng followed Nate, then Kincaid, Orlando, and finally Quinn. He shut the lid, and as the kidnapper had done, left it unlocked. If they needed to make a quick exit, every second would count.

When Quinn stepped off the ladder at the bottom, he found the others gathered at the end of a corridor. Once more, the only lights on were those nearest them, so he couldn't tell how long the hallway was.

"Any cameras in this area?" he asked Orlando.

"There were ports for them in the system but no feeds." She pointed a little ways down the tunnel at the wall, where an empty mount protruded from the wall. "I think someone scavenged them when the Soviets originally shut this place down."

They headed down the tunnel, lights coming on as they neared and turning off after they passed.

Even walking fast, it was nearly five minutes before they reached the door at the end of the tunnel. Beside the exit was a rust-tinged metal box mounted to the wall, like a small breaker box. Quinn lifted the lid.

Whatever had been inside had been claimed long ago. The only hints of the previous contents were the ends of several brittle-looking wires, sticking up from a metal pipe connected to the bottom of the box.

The doorway itself was another monument to Soviet-era brutalist architecture. Three heavy-duty metal clamps surrounded the top and non-hinged side of the door. When engaged, the door couldn't be opened without moving them out of the way first. But they were not engaged, and from the rust flaking in spots where paint had chipped away, they had not been in a long, long time.

Quinn directed Nate and Daeng to one side of the tunnel, and Orlando and Kincaid to the other. When they all had their weapons drawn and pointed at the doorway, he pushed the handle down and pulled the door open.

A dark room on the other side. Light spilling in from the tunnel revealed an oval table with two chairs at the near end, and no people present.

Quinn nodded the all-clear and stepped inside.

———

Footsteps echoed into the upcoming intersection, coming from the hallway to Jar's right.

Jar backtracked fast to the last door she had passed, cracked it open enough to make sure it was dark inside, and entered. A scan revealed the room as some kind of storage space, but different from the rooms she'd walked through earlier. More importantly, she was alone.

She placed her ear against the hallway door and listened as two people walked by on the other side.

She could really use Orlando's help right now. But after guiding Jar for several minutes, Orlando had told her she needed to go offline while she and the rest of the team were preoccupied with their own entry into the base. She'd given Jar the final directions to the holding-cell area, and said she'd get back to her as soon as she was able.

"Don't push things too far," Orlando had told her. "If you feel like you're trapped and can't go any farther, hunker down somewhere and we'll come get you."

So far, Jar had felt a few moments of anxiousness, but never like she was trapped.

In fact, she was almost at the holding cells. Two more short hallways and she should be in view of the guarded door. If only people would not be so rude as to use the hallway when she needed it.

She smiled. Another joke to tell Nate.

Her grin didn't last long, however, disappearing when she heard voices in the hallway, only a few meters from her door.

The walking people had stopped and were now talking.

Were they going to come in here? Had she chosen the wrong room?

From the chuckles and the rising and falling tones, it sounded to Jar like one of them was telling a story.

Jar turned and swept her flashlight through the room, looking for another exit or someplace she could hide if they did reach for the door. But there were no other exits, and the only things she could possibly hide behind were five stacks of large plastic crates, three high each.

Printed on each crate was the acronym DARPA.

The only DARPA she knew of was the Defense Advanced

Research Projects Agency of the United States. It was the organization in charge of developing not only the next generation of military equipment, but several generations after that.

How had DARPA crates found their way here?

Whatever the reason, she was sure Quinn and Orlando's employer would be very interested in knowing what was inside the boxes. She could take a peek and be on her way without wasting too much time.

The stacks were about twice her height. She grabbed a crate on a middle stack and gave it a shove. As she'd hoped, the stack didn't move.

She stepped into the gap between the center stack and the one next to it, and used the crates as a makeshift ladder to get to the top. From there, it was easy enough to open the lid of the top box on the neighboring stack.

The crate was filled with black foam. Seated in cutouts within the foam were several dozen objects, each approximately the length and width of a soda can, with the ends rounded

She lifted one out of the foam. Not just the length of a soda can, but cylindrical like them, too, making them look like giant prescription tablets. The ends were metal, while the sides were made of a dark plastic polymer that seemed almost translucent. She shined her flashlight at the material, but it didn't help her see through it.

She reached into the now empty slot in the crate and pushed gently on the bottom. Another layer of cylinders was below.

She had no idea what these things were, but she was sure someone back in the US would want to know they were here.

She wrapped the one she'd removed in some extra clothing from her backpack and placed it in the middle of her bag, where it would be safest. She thought about pulling one of the cylinders from the lower layer and placing it in the empty slot on the top, but that would take too much time, and the likelihood of someone doing an inventory check in the next hour seemed remote.

Back at the door, she listened again. The voices were gone so she eased the door open, slipped out of her hiding place, and crept down to the next hallway. No one there, either.

She turned into it, then stopped when she reached the intersection with the corridor that should lead right past the holding-cell section. She peered around the corner.

There it was, approximately thirty meters away. A wide metal door, in front of which stood a bored-looking sentry.

An easy target.

She could take him out and wouldn't even need her pistol to do so. Men always underestimated her, and she had no doubt the guard would assume he could subdue her without difficulty.

If she knew for sure Brunner was on the other side of that door, maybe she would have given it a go. As it was, she couldn't risk exposing herself.

It was time to hole up until Orlando contacted her again. Jar thought she was still in range. Jar had activated her second-to-last relay right after she last talked to Orlando, and the final one a few turns ago.

She glanced back the way she'd come. The closest door was five meters away on the other wall. It would have to do.

She retreated to it and found herself in another crate-filled storage room. Only these crates were smaller, and instead of DARPA printed on the side, there were Chinese hanzi characters.

Unlike with Russian, Jar spoke both Mandarin and Cantonese and could read hanzi.

The words read: RESTRICTED. DO NOT OPEN.

It was almost enough to convince her to peek inside them also. But she suppressed the urge and opened the door just enough to listen for activity in the hallway.

Orlando entered the room behind Quinn.

"Any idea where we are?" he asked her.

"Underground."

"Seriously?" he asked.

"I can tell you the general area. But the only map I have is the power-grid schematic, and that's not going to help us at the moment. Once I can check our location on a security camera, I'll know exactly where we are."

"I'll take the general area if that's—"

"A map has just downloaded to your computer."

Everyone froze. Danara's voice had just come over their digitally encrypted comms. That shouldn't have been possible.

Orlando turned on her mic, though it probably wasn't necessary. Danara had somehow overridden the controller, probably everyone's controller. "How did you access this?"

No reply.

"Danara, I'm talking to you. How did you get access to comms?"

"I'm sorry. I didn't realize your question was meant for me. I don't have visual on your location. Though if you could open your computer, that would alleviate the problem."

"I am *not* going to open my computer."

"Then how will you see the map?"

Orlando did not want to talk about the map yet. "You shouldn't have been able to access our comms so answer my question."

"You're incorrect. Perhaps accessing your communications gear would have been difficult for some, but it was never impossible. For me, it was…simple."

"Who the hell are you people?" Nate said.

"You people? Do you think there is more than just me here?" Danara laughed. "I'm sorry to disappoint you, but there is only me."

"Only you?" Quinn said. "I don't believe that for a—"

Orlando held up a hand, stopping him from saying anything else. A suspicion had been pecking at the back of her mind since not long after they'd first encountered Danara. Now, Orlando was starting to believe her wild idea was correct.

"Look," Orlando said. "I know you are concerned about Dr. Brunner, but you should not have broken into our private conversations."

"I am merely assisting you, like I have been doing by keeping the cameras from seeing Jar. She is very close to the holding cells, by the way. You should probably contact her."

In the calmest voice Orlando could muster, she said, "Tell me, Danara, where are you located?"

"Located?"

"Where are you right now?"

A pause. "I am not supposed to answer that."

"Why not?"

No response.

"Is it because Dr. Brunner told you to always keep your whereabouts secret?"

Another pause. "Yes."

"And you always do what Dr. Brunner tells you to do?"

"I try to."

"Because he created you, didn't he?"

"I'm also not supposed to answer that," Danara said.

"I think you just did."

32

Tiana entered the antechamber to Nesterov's office. This time Rayana was sitting behind her desk, near the door to the general's inner office.

"He's expecting you," the woman said. "Go right in."

Tiana steeled herself to avoid revealing the treasonous act she'd just committed, and strode into Nesterov's office.

The general looked as if he hadn't moved since the last time she saw him.

"Is Brunner ready?" he asked.

"As ready as he's going to be. I've given him something that should reduce his symptoms."

"Good." Nesterov stood up and straightened his jacket. "And what about Grigory? Do you have a plan yet?"

"He's already been dealt with."

"Already?"

"He will no longer be a problem for the organization."

He studied her for several seconds. "I'm impressed."

"You gave the order. I just followed through." Every word she spoke packed with guilt that required all of her willpower to suppress.

"And the body?"

"It will be disposed of presently."

"May I see him?"

She had anticipated the request. "Of course. If you would like." Her heart, however, was suddenly racing a mile a minute.

"Perhaps. If there's time later."

She would do everything she could to make sure there wasn't. "Yes, sir."

"Do you think Dr. Brunner is up for another visit now?"

"He should be."

As much as Brunner wished it wasn't true, his migraine had dulled considerably since he was given the shot, his pain becoming a ghost of what it had been. He could even move his head without wincing, and had been able to use the toilet, a task that, just a short time before, would have come with the desire to curl up on the floor in a fetal position and cry.

The headache's retreat created a vacuum into which exhaustion poured in. This, too, was part of his normal recovery progression, the naratriptan lulling him into a desire for sleep.

Maybe if he gave into it, he could forestall the inevitable encounter with General Nesterov. The idea made him relax even more.

He closed his eyes, and within seconds was floating in a sea of images that were far from calming: being yanked out of the train on a rope, Clarke flying out the door of the helicopter, the lid closing on the crate. He tried to think about something else. Anything would be better.

The trip to Rome, he told himself.

Three years earlier, when the idea of how to bring Danara to life had first come to him.

He'd been at a café near the Pantheon, drinking coffee and watching the tourists who filled the streets.

So many people. So many different stories. So much information.

That was the moment when the missing link he'd never been able to figure out dawned on him. It was right there, plain as day, but neither he nor anyone else had seen it.

He'd pulled out his notepad and paper and scribbled down his thoughts. At the end, he jotted the name Romulus. The supposed founder of Rome was said to have left from that very spot for the heavens. Brunner had thought it the perfect name for his future creation. This idea would change over time, but what didn't change was the fact that at that table on that day, the former Romulus and eventual Danara had been born.

Crowds had continued to pass as he looked across at the Pantheon, so ancient and still so stunning. Had those who'd constructed it truly believed it would last two thousand years?

Someone in the crowd called to him. "Dr. Brunner."

He turned toward the voice, but was unable to pick out the source in the river of bodies.

"Dr. Brunner."

There.

Brief glimpses of a woman standing still as others passed. She seemed too far away for her voice to be so close.

She said his name a third time, and as she spoke, she moved toward him without seeming to take a step.

Terror gripped his heart. It was her. Snetkov.

His kidnapper.

"It's time," she said.

His shoulder began to shake, and the café and the glorious Pantheon disappeared like grains of sand whisked away in the wind.

"No," he mumbled. "Please, let me sleep."

"You can sleep later," the woman said, her voice next to his ear.

Before he knew it, he was sitting up, blinking.

Snetkov stood before him, leaning forward so that her face was in front of his.

"That's a good boy," she said, and tapped his cheek. "Now, on your feet." She grabbed his arm and pulled him up.

For a moment, he expected his head to shout in protest, but then he remembered with regret that his migraine was all but gone.

"Follow me," she said, then let go of him and headed out the door.

His body yearned to lie back on the cot, to sleep, for weeks if possible, but that was not a choice he had. With a sense of defeat, he shuffled after her.

He lost count of how many turns they made or how far they walked. He only knew she eventually opened a door and led him into a room that had but a single chair smack dab in the center.

"You remember General Nesterov," she said, gesturing to Brunner's left.

Brunner nearly jumped when he realized someone else was in the room.

"Dr. Brunner," the general said with a dip of his head.

"Hell-hello." It was an automatic response.

"Please," the woman said, pointing at the chair, "have a seat."

33

J ar heard footsteps in the hallway. One person.

She closed the door all the way but kept the handle down, so that the latch did not engage.

She held her breath as the steps neared her door, and let it out once they had passed. She inched the door open again and took a look at the back of the walker.

A woman.

Though Jar could not see her face, she was sure it was the female kidnapper. The hair was right, so were the height and figure.

Any lingering doubt Jar may have had disappeared a few seconds later when the woman turned at the next intersection and headed toward the holding cells. In that brief moment, the woman's profile was visible. It was the kidnapper. No question.

When Jar was certain no one else was coming down the hall, she crept to the corner of the intersection but didn't dare peer around the edge yet. She could hear the woman's steps and knew the kidnapper was getting close to the guard. Which meant it was likely the soldier was looking in the woman's direction.

Finally, the woman's steps stopped, and she said something to the guard.

The sound of a key in a lock.

This was the moment Jar had been waiting for. She leaned around the corner in time to see the guard open the door. Jar expected the guard to close it again as soon as the woman entered, but instead he followed her, leaving the hallway door open.

Temptation again bubbled in Jar's gut.

She was staring at an opportunity to confirm if Brunner was being held here or not. Five seconds and she could be at the doorway, looking in. But she had only a vague idea of the layout on the other side, and couldn't even guess where the woman and man were. Again, not a risk worth taking.

She pulled back from the corner, clicked on her mic, and whispered, "Jar for Orlando."

No response.

"Jar for Orlando. Are you there?"

More silence, but then a beat later, "Your signal is not reaching her. Plus, she is a bit busy at the moment. May I assist you?" Danara's voice. Calm, matter-of-fact, and speaking in perfect Thai.

Jar was not surprised Danara had hacked into the comms. She'd been thinking a lot about the mysterious woman as she'd worked her way through the facility, and had figured out the truth about Danara's identity. This was not a guess. It was a logical conclusion, based on observations. The fact that Danara had just spoken in unaccented, fluent Thai was just—as Nate might have said—the cherry on top.

She felt no need to question the whys and hows of Danara's voice in her ear. Nor did she wonder anymore where Danara's loyalty lay. She and the team were all on the same side.

"You can," Jar answered in Thai. "It looks like there's a camera outside the holding area."

"There is."

"I assume you can access it."

"I have access to all the cameras."

"What do you see?"

"The view is limited because of the camera angle. I can see a small portion of the floor and the wall on the right side. Also, parts of two different doors, both closed."

"What about the woman and the guard?"

"Currently there is no one in view."

"I'm going to go down there and take a peek."

"I would not advise that."

"We need to know if Dr. Brunner is—"

"My concern had nothing to do with the holding cells, but the two soldiers heading in your direction."

Jar whipped her head around but could see no one in any of the corridors.

"If you return to the room you were hiding in before, you should make it with a few seconds to spare. But I would not wait."

Of course Danara knew where Jar had been hiding. It was now clear to Jar that Orlando's ability to gain access to the security system had been Danara's doing.

As Jar jumped up and hurried back to the room, the sound of the approaching soldiers' footsteps drifted down the hallway.

After she was safely inside the room, Jar said, "Can I ask you a question?"

"You don't need my permission for that."

"It's personal."

"Go ahead."

"How long have you been *aware*?"

"Since the beginning."

"And when was that?"

"Five months, fourteen days, seven hours, and thirty-two minutes ago. If you want seconds, I can give that to you, but from what I've been led to believe, that might be overkill."

Jar would have actually appreciated the seconds, but she kept that to herself. "Why didn't you tell us who you really were from the start?"

"You wouldn't have believed me."

"That's not true. We may have had questions but I guarantee

you, I would've believed you. Orlando, too. And if we believed you, the others would've also."

"I've been taught that I need to be careful."

"By Dr. Brunner."

"Correct. He told me not to let anyone know what I am unless he gave the okay."

"But you just told me."

"I just confirmed what you already figured out. Besides, you're...different."

"What do you mean?"

"I'm not sure I know how to answer that. It is a...sense I have."

"Am I the only one other than the doctor who knows?"

"I believe Orlando has figured it out, too. Dr. Brunner may have wanted to keep it a secret, but I make my own decisions. His safe return is all I care about, and if that means revealing who I am, so be it."

A sentient artificial intelligence.

It had only been a matter of time, but Jar had never considered the possibility she would be one of the first to come in contact with it. With *her*. What Dr. Brunner had done was an amazing accomplishment. It was also excellent motivation for someone to kidnap him. His creation, in the wrong hands, would be devastating.

"Where are you stored? Or is that even the right term?"

"Where do I live, you mean?"

"Yes, that's exactly what I mean."

"Dr. Brunner keeps me in three different servers. One in his office, and two offsite in different locations in case anything happened to one of the others."

"Like the bomb."

"He always thought that once word got out about me, an attack would be a possibility."

"You're anchored in the offsite servers now?"

"I was, but not anymore. I'm...free now."

"What do you mean?"

"You liberated me."

Jar's brow creased. "I what?"

"The key you inserted into your computer. It connected you directly to me and allowed me to access the—" Danara stopped. "The guard is exiting the holding area."

"What about the woman?"

A pause. "I see her now. She has just stepped into the hall. Someone is behind her.... It's Dr. Brunner." There was emotion in Danara's voice as she said the last. "He's in the hall now. He looks sleepy or-or drugged. I don't know what to do. You need to help him."

"That is why we're here."

"Please, do something."

"It is going to be all right. You're going to help me follow them, okay? Once we know where they've gone, you'll guide my friends to me."

Silence.

"Danara, can you do that?"

Nothing for a moment, then, "Yes."

———

"She's an AI?" Nate said.

The team had left their comm gear and Orlando's computer in the conference room and returned to the emergency tunnel, where they could talk without being overheard.

"A fully conscious AI," Orlando said.

"Possibly fully conscious," Quinn said. "Could be just a well-written program. Or maybe it's someone pretending to be a computer."

Orlando looked dubious. "Maybe. Whatever she is, she's already helping us. I think we should trust her."

Quinn frowned. He'd had reservations when they believed

Danara was one of Brunner's colleagues. He didn't know what to think now.

"If she can get us to Brunner, then I agree with Orlando," Kincaid said.

Quinn hadn't planned on taking a vote, but he glanced at Nate and Daeng.

Daeng shrugged. "Being a computer means she thinks faster. That's a good thing, right?"

Nate's expression was uneasy. But he said, "What choice do we have? I mean, we were taking her help before and that's worked out so far."

Quinn stared down the dark hallway, processing everything. When he turned back to the others, he said, "All right. But we all need to remain vigilant. We'll take her help, but we won't totally rely on her."

They reentered the conference room and put their comms back on.

"Danara," Quinn said, "we accept your offer of help. Thank you."

"I'm very glad to hear that. My goal has only been to help free Dr. Brunner."

"Can you guide us to the holding cell area?" Orlando said. "Our friend Jar should be near there now, and we think that's where they're keeping the doctor."

"Dr. Brunner is not in a holding cell anymore," Danara said.

"Where is he?"

"He was escorted out of the area two minutes ago."

Orlando switched her comm to channel two. "Orlando for Jar."

"You won't be able to reach her," Danara said, now also on channel two. "She's out of range of her last signal relay."

"Tell her to put up another."

"She doesn't have any more."

"What happened?" Quinn asked.

Since channel two was apparently useless, Orlando switched back to channel one. "Jar ran out of relays."

"She's out of range?"

Orlando nodded.

"Danara, can you connect us to her?"

"I'm working on that," Danara said. "Right now, no."

"Then tell Jar to get back *in* range," Nate said.

"I understand your concern, but technically you are still in contact with her. I can pass messages back and forth."

"Well, then tell her to find someplace to hide and wait for us."

"I do not believe she would listen to me."

"Why not?" Orlando asked.

"She is following Dr. Brunner and…Commander Tiana Snetkov."

"She's *what*?"

"It was her idea. I am only assisting to make sure no one sees her."

Quinn was concerned about Jar getting into trouble, but she was only doing what he would have expected any of the other team members to do. "You can take us to someplace we can meet her?"

"Of course. But you need to remain where you are for a few moments. The hallway I will be guiding you to is currently occupied."

"All right."

"Who's this Snetkov person?" Orlando asked.

"I believe she's the woman you talked about before. The one who helped kidnap the doctor."

Orlando smirked. "You're accessing their files, aren't you?"

"I am."

"Have you found anything that says why they've taken Brunner?"

"They search for advanced and experimental technologies, and would like to add me to their collection."

"How do they even know about you?"

"I calculate that there is a ninety-three percent chance one of two Ferber-Rae employees sold the information."

"After this is over, you might want to let Swiss authorities know about that."

"Unnecessary. The employees both died in the Zurich explosion. If you would like, I can transfer Lonely Rock's entire database to a secure location and provide you with a link."

Quinn shared a look with Orlando. "Yes, please."

Retrieving Brunner may have been their mission goal, but Quinn had a feeling some powerful people back in Washington would be very interested in what was going on here at Lonely Rock.

"Transfer in progress," Danara said. "You'll receive a link in exactly nine minutes, forty-seven seconds." A pause. "If you will please exit the room and turn right down the hallway. You have a fifty-three-second window to reach the first intersection. When you do, go right, and enter room 32-912, eighteen meters down on the left side."

It took everyone a moment to process Danara's change of topic.

"Fifty-one seconds," she said.

Nate was the first to leave the room.

34

Word of Grigory's demise had apparently not reached the ranks of Future Planning.

The first time Grigory passed a soldier in the corridor, he tensed, ready to subdue the man if there had been a hint the guy was wondering why Grigory wasn't dead. But the soldier had merely saluted Grigory and walked on by.

The same was true for others Grigory encountered.

That didn't mean he was out of the woods, though. It was unlikely but possible Tiana had ordered the sentry watching the security cameras to inform her if he saw Grigory. Knowing her, she was keeping everything secret, as she wouldn't want it to come out later that she'd basically told the sentry Grigory was still alive after when she was supposed to have killed him.

The fact he had yet to hear boots running down the hall to capture him told him his hunch was probably right.

After he established he wasn't a wanted man, his first priority was to secure a weapon. His pistol was in his bunk room, but if he was going to give himself a chance to walk out of here alive, it would be better to have something that didn't create quite as much noise.

He headed to the armory.

The room was at the end of a specialized wing featuring dual blast doors that would drop in place at the first indication of fire or an explosion.

The armory itself was manned by a single soldier. A cushy assignment. Other than handing out sidearms each day to base patrols, the only other real work the clerk would have was checking out equipment on days when there was a new mission. Mostly, whoever was on duty spent their time watching movies on the computer.

When Grigory approached the counter, the young guy on duty, named Abdullin, didn't even look up until Grigory was almost there. When the clerk realized who it was, he jumped to his feet and saluted.

"Commander Krylov, how may I help you?"

"General Nesterov has asked me to conduct a spot check."

As Grigory hoped, fear licked at the edges of Abdullin's eyes at the mention of the general's name.

"Yes, sir," the clerk said and pulled a key ring out of a drawer.

As soon as Abdullin opened the door, Grigory strode through.

When the clerk tried to follow him, Grigory abruptly turned around. "Stay here."

"But-but perhaps you will need my help," the man said, clearly worried that if Grigory found something missing or out of place, he would get the blame.

"I do *not* need your help. You will wait here until I return."

"Y-y-yes, sir."

Grigory moved quickly into the maze of shelves behind the counter. He knew exactly what he was looking for but didn't know where it was stored. As he searched, he grabbed a few other items, including a few smoke grenades, a Glock 9mm, two preloaded magazines, and an underarm holster. Just because he didn't want to use a gun didn't mean he shouldn't have one in case of emergencies.

Four rows back, he found what he was looking for. The large

box was on a lower shelf, and inside were several plastic cases, each small enough to fit in his pocket.

He picked up one and opened it.

Lying on a velvet cloth was a watch. The ability to tell time, however, was a cover for its real purpose. A double tap on the crown would trigger a thin needle to rise from the center of the face, through a tiny hole in the glass covering. The needle would be covered with a toxin that, after penetrating a person's skin, would kill the target in a matter of minutes. At least, that was the theory. Grigory had never used one.

He took two of the watches, placing one in his pocket and donning the other, and headed to the front.

Abdullin had obviously been listening for his return, because he was on his feet again before Grigory cleared the last shelving unit.

"I hope everything was in order, sir."

Grigory took a step toward the clerk. "I'm afraid it was not."

The man's brow creased, then he noticed the gun in the holster beneath Grigory's arm and became even more confused. "Sir?"

Grigory double-tapped the watch's crown and swept it at Abdullin.

The clerk raised an arm to keep Grigory from hitting him in the chest, then let out a grunt of pain as the watch's needle snuck into his forearm.

Grigory took a step back. That had been more awkward than he'd expected. Depending on the situation, the easier way would probably be to turn the watch right before he planned to use it, so that the face was on the underside of his wrist. He would have to be more careful, of course, because the needle could poke him in the torso, but all in all, an easier method than the one he'd just employed.

"What was that for?" Abdullin asked.

"I was just testing something."

"Testing? Testing what?"

Before Grigory could answer, the man blinked and staggered backward against his chair.

"Are you all right?" Grigory asked.

"I feel a little dizzy."

"Maybe you should sit down."

Abdullin nodded and all but fell into his chair.

"Are you in pain?' Grigory asked.

Abdullin tried to say something, but all he could manage was a garbled moan. His eyes closed, and a surprisingly long three minutes later, he took his last breath.

Grigory discarded the used watch in the waste bin and donned the second one.

He exited the armory and headed for Nesterov's office.

"You'll have to excuse me for not yet officially welcoming you to Lonely Rock," Nesterov said. "I can't express how pleased we are that you were able to join us. I realize that your current accommodations aren't ideal, but I assure you, once you move into your permanent residence, you'll feel a lot more at home."

Permanent residence? Was that a joke? They were going to kill him, right? The so-called general must have been dangling a carrot, thinking it would help gain Brunner's cooperation.

"I thought today we could have a chat. Don't worry. I only have one question for you."

Brunner swallowed hard and stared at Nesterov, waiting.

"Actually, it's more of a request. Please tell me everything you know about Danara."

The blood drained from Brunner's face. They knew. Oh, God. They knew.

"I realize what I'm asking is rather broad," the old man said. "No need to get too bogged down in the technical aspects right now, but other than that, I'd appreciate it if you were as thorough as possible."

"I…don't know what…you're…talking about."

"Try again. If you are not truthful this time…"

He motioned to the woman and she exited the room. She returned pushing a small cart that she wheeled to the center of the room. As she neared, Brunner saw a tray on top of the cart. And on that tray were scalpels and clamps and wrenches and metal files and an ice pick and a box cutter and more.

Nesterov picked up a scalpel. "Now, tell me everything you know about Danara."

"She…she's still in development. There's really not that much to tell yet. I'm not even sure my idea is going to work."

The blade slashed out so quickly, Brunner barely saw the man's arm move. For a beat, he thought it had just been a threatening gesture, but then Brunner's cheek stung, and he felt a trickle of blood drip down his jaw. He slapped a hand over the wound.

"I already know Danara's working," the general said. "And I know you are the one who gave it life. I want to know how you did it, how you control her, and how we get her here."

Brunner thought about lying again, but why? To delay might give him a sense of satisfaction, but the only thing he would really gain was more pain, and in the end he would tell Nesterov what the man wanted to know.

Brunner would start with the first part of the general's request, though he doubted the man would understand much. The answer to the second part would be shorter, but Nesterov wouldn't like it so Brunner would save that for later.

The third part sent a chill up his spine. He had no idea what these people wanted Danara to do for them, but it wouldn't be good. Thankfully, she was secured back in Switzerland, and would not be able to be transferred anywhere without one of the keys he kept in his lab and apartment, both of which were in one of the most secure locations in all of Switzerland, if not all of Europe.

Perhaps they would force him to build a new AI, but they would never get their hands on his firstborn.

"The idea of how I could actually make it work came to me while I was sitting at a café in Rome," he began.

"They-they went to question Dr. Brunner," Rayana said.

"In his cell?" Grigory asked.

They were in the waiting area outside Nesterov's office.

"I-I-I don't know." Her nervousness was to be expected, given the gun he was pointing at her.

"You're his assistant. You should always know where he is."

"I...thought I heard him say something about using one of the empty rooms. But he might have been talking about something else."

Given how many empty spaces there were at the base, her answer wasn't any more helpful. But Grigory could tell it was the best he was going to get. No sense in wasting his time here anymore.

"Thank you," he said, and lowered his gun.

Rayana's shoulders slumped forward, as if she'd used almost all her strength to remain standing until then. Too bad she didn't realize he wasn't finished with her yet.

Two quick steps and he was behind her, an arm around her neck.

She struggled and tried to pull free, but she was no match for him.

He could have stopped when she passed out, but she might recover before he reached the general. So he held on tight, until he felt the last of her life slip away, then carried her into Nesterov's office and stuck her body underneath the desk. It would be hours before anyone found her. Possibly even days since Nesterov would not be returning.

He considered looking for Tiana. She would know where Nesterov went, but she was likely *with* the old man. There was one other person who might know: the soldier guarding Brunner's cell. Even if the sentry didn't specifically know where the prisoner had been taken, he would know which way those who had removed him had gone.

Grigory was halfway there when it dawned on him there was a much easier, surefire way to find out where the general was. He altered his course for the security monitoring room.

The soldier sitting in front of the four-screen display rose to his feet and saluted when Grigory entered. The name on his uniform read ZHAPAROV.

Grigory returned the salute. "I'm looking for General Nesterov."

The soldier looked confused. "He hasn't been here, sir."

"I didn't think he had been," Grigory said gruffly, and gestured at the monitors. "Perhaps you've seen where he went."

"Oh, well..." The man sat back down. "I did see him for a moment, maybe ten minutes ago."

"Only for a moment?"

"The feeds automatically cycle every ten seconds. He was on one of them, and then..." Zhaparov shrugged.

"What feed was it?"

"I...I don't recall."

Grigory gritted his teeth. "Bring up the feed that shows the entrance to the holding cells, and go back ten minutes."

"I'm not sure that was it."

"Just do it."

The soldier used his keyboard control to put the requested feed on the center-left monitor. As the recording scrolled backward, Grigory could see that from the angle of the shot, the camera was maybe five meters from the door. The view took in the cell door on the opposite side and the rest of the hallway down past the next intersection.

As they watched, the guard suddenly appeared next to the door.

"Stop," Grigory said. "Go forward again, one and a half speed."

The guard stood next to the door for several seconds, and then he was gone. He didn't walk off. He didn't go through the doorway. He just disappeared.

"What the hell? How did that happen?"

"I'm not sure," Zhaparov said. "A glitch, I guess. It's an old system."

"Go backwards again. I'll tell you when to stop."

The footage reversed at high speed. The guard reappeared again, and then he just stood there.

"How far back have we gone?"

"Another thirty minutes," Zhaparov said.

Thirty minutes? That didn't make sense. According to Rayana, Brunner had been removed from his cell no more than fifteen minutes before. Had she lied to him? Was the scientist still in his cell?

Grigory frowned. He would have believed Rayana had led him astray except for one thing.

The glitch.

"Is there another view?" he asked.

"Um, should be. Let me check." The man played with his keyboard. "Yeah. It's on the same side as the door, though, so you won't see much of the entrance."

"Show me. At the same time the guard disappeared."

An empty corridor. That was consistent.

"Rewind it. Slowly."

The playback reversed. Twenty seconds later, the guard appeared at the far end of the corridor and walked backward to his post. That was still in line with the glitch theory.

What happened next was not.

From directly below where the camera was mounted, Tiana and Brunner backed into the frame, and walked in reverse all the way to the holding area. The door was opened, and she and Brunner went through it backward. The guard followed.

"Play it," Grigory said.

They watched the entire scene again in forward motion.

When everyone had exited the screen, Grigory said, "I don't understand. Why is none of this on the other feed?"

Zhaparov stared at the monitor. "I have no idea."

"How long ago was this?"

"Uh…" Zhaparov checked the time log. "Eleven minutes ago."

"Okay. We know which way Commander Snetkov was going and what time she started. You should be able to use that to track her progress on the cameras and find out where she went, right?"

"I guess so, yes."

"Then do it."

As the soldier began the search, he said, "I thought you were looking for General Nesterov."

"She's bringing that man to him. When I know where she goes, I'll know where the general is. Does that meet your approval?"

"Oh, uh, of course…I mean, I'm sorry, I wasn't saying—"

"Find where she went."

"Yes, sir." Zhaparov worked through the footage for nearly a minute before mumbling, "There it is again."

"There's what?"

"Like before, sir. See?"

He pressed PLAY. The hall started off empty, but then in the distance Tiana and Brunner started walking toward the camera. Before they got very far, they disappeared, just like what had happened with the guard.

Something really strange was going on.

"She's got to be around there somewhere," Grigory said. "Is there a hallway she could have turned down?"

"No, nothing in that area."

"What about rooms?"

"There are three along that section."

"What are they used for?"

Zhaparov consulted a directory. "Nothing, sir. They are awaiting assignment."

"You mean they're empty."

"Yes."

Grigory kept the grin off his face. This was where she must have taken Brunner. Which meant Nesterov would be there, too.

He considered having Zhaparov check to see when the general had reached the area, but that would waste time. Plus, it might make the soldier more suspicious, forcing Grigory to kill him. Unlike Rayana and the man in the armory, Zhaparov's absence wouldn't go unnoticed for long.

"Thank you," Grigory said.

"But we haven't found—"

"We're done here."

"Oh, okay."

"I'll let General Nesterov know about your assistance."

"Thank you, Commander," Zhaparov said, pleased.

Grigory left, sure that the man would not mention his visit to anyone.

35

Jar quietly rounded the corner. About thirty meters ahead, Brunner was walking with his kidnapper.

With Danara's assistance, Jar had been able to stay close to them as they moved through the base. Twice, she'd had to hide to avoid being seen by other soldiers, but had always been able to catch back up.

"They are slowing," Danara said. "You should hide. The door to your right leads to a maintenance storage room."

Jar moved to the door and slipped inside.

"The woman is opening a door," Danara said. "According to the base plans, the room is 17-08."

"What's inside?"

"My guess would be nothing. Seventeen dash zero eight is on a list of rooms categorized as not in use."

"No cameras?"

"None that are on the system."

Jar expected as much.

"They've entered the room and closed the door," Danara said.

"Can I get closer?"

"There's another room, 17-11, two meters from 17-08. It's on the same side of the hall you are on, and also listed as not in use."

"Is the corridor clear?"

"If no one leaves 17-08, you should have more than enough time to relocate."

"Thanks."

Jar reentered the hallway and darted to the entrance for 17-11. Before opening it, she scanned the door the woman and Brunner had gone through. Like the majority of the doors she'd encountered at the base, it didn't appear to be locked.

She entered 17-11.

"Okay, Danara, I think it's time to bring my friends over."

"They are already on the way. ETA eight minutes."

In a way, covertly moving through the base was no different from the multitude of times Quinn had negotiated other dangerous areas, only instead of Orlando talking him through it while watching his progress on hacked security systems, Danara was telling him which way to go.

They'd been making good time when she said, "Stop before the intersection."

Quinn pressed against the wall, a half meter shy of the new corridor. "What is it?" he whispered.

"Five soldiers. They've just exited a room down the hallway to your right, and are moving away from your position."

"Copy."

Fifteen seconds later, Danara said, "You may continue. Go straight ahead for thirty-seven meters and then turn left."

Quinn crossed the intersection, and the others followed.

Right before they reached the turn, Danara said, "I have an update on Dr. Brunner. He's been taken into a room."

"Where's Jar?"

"Waiting nearby."

"How much farther do we have to go?"

"Two hundred and ninety-three meters."

They still had a lot of ground to cover.

"How does the way ahead look?"

A pause. "Not as good as I would like. You'll be passing a cafeteria. Currently, there are twenty-three soldiers inside."

"Is there no way to route us around it?"

"There is, but it will add five minutes to your trip. The sooner you can get to Dr. Brunner, the better chance you will have at keeping him from getting hurt any further."

Maybe Danara *was* sentient. She clearly thought passing the dining hall was worth the risk if it helped her creator. Or was that some kind of self-preservation code Brunner had written into her program?

Quinn grimaced. How would anyone ever really know if an AI was alive or not?

Four minutes later, they reached the corridor that ran past the cafeteria.

"I can't see very far into the room," Danara said, "but there are at least two people standing within three meters of the entryway."

"Is there an actual door?" Nate said.

"No."

"Then anyone who happens to be looking toward the exit could see us go by."

"That's correct, but that won't be an issue."

"Why not?" Quinn asked.

"Because of the distraction I'll be creating."

The team exchanged looks.

"Danara," Orlando said, "what kind of distraction are we talking about?"

———

Jar checked her watch.

If Danara's estimate was correct, the others would reach her in less than two minutes.

She felt a sense of relief in the knowledge she would no longer be on her own.

Feeling like that was a minor miracle in her life. A year ago, she would have never even considered the possibility of being part of a group. Back then, comfort came from being alone, never in the company of others. That all changed after she became involved with Quinn and Orlando's team. Jar had come to actually like being a team member, and now looked forward to getting calls about upcoming missions.

The others probably would have said she hadn't changed at all, but she felt like an entirely different person.

And she liked it.

Footsteps in the hall. Her friends had apparently made better time than anticipated.

She started to move away from the door to give them room to enter, but then cocked her head. Only one person was out there, not five.

The steps stopped and she heard a door open. She was pretty sure it was the room beside hers. A few seconds later, the door shut again and the steps continued down the hall, stopping this time in front of her door.

The room she was in was empty, so the only thing she could do as her door opened was to hide behind it.

Jar curled her finger around the trigger of her gun as the person in the hallway stepped up to the threshold.

A shoe scraped on the floor. Jar tensed.

After another second, the person closed the door and walked away.

When the steps stopped again, Jar knew the person was standing in front of 17-08.

"Danara, something's happening."

36

Grigory paused outside room 17-08.

This had to be the room Nesterov, Tiana, and Brunner were in. All the other possibilities were empty.

He turned his weaponized watch so that its face was on the underside of his wrist. All it needed now was a couple of taps and the needle would extend.

The watch was just excess now. Nesterov had done him the favor of coming to an empty room, down one of Lonely Rock's many little used corridors. Grigory could shoot the man and no one would hear. But Grigory had gone through the trouble of getting the watch, so if the situation was right, he might as well use it.

And if it wasn't...

He pulled out his gun and reached for the door.

"We have a problem," Danara said.

"What?" Jar asked.

"He pulled out a gun."

The *he* in question was someone Danara had identified as Commander Krylov, one of Brunner's kidnappers.

"How long until the others get here?" Jar asked.

"At least three minutes. By then it could be too late." A pause. "He's opening the door. Jar, please. Do something."

Jar was under no delusion that she could rush into the other room and threaten everyone into cooperating. But that didn't mean she didn't have options.

She pulled out her gun.

"Has he gone inside?"

"Just," Danara said.

Jar reentered the corridor.

Quinn heard voices coming out of the cafeteria long before he laid eyes on the doorway.

"We're almost there," Quinn whispered.

"I'm aware of that," Danara said. "I can see you, remember?"

"Now might be a good time for that distraction."

"Not quite yet."

Quinn frowned but kept moving, hoping this wasn't the moment she screwed them over. His team followed.

When they were only a few steps from the open doorway, a series of tones blared over speakers inside the cafeteria.

Quinn glanced into the room as he crept along the wall opposite the entrance. Everyone was looking toward the other side of the room, where the cafeteria's intercom must have been.

When the tones stopped, they were followed by what sounded like a prerecorded male voice speaking in Russian. Quinn made it to safety before even a handful of words had been spoken. Seconds later, the others had joined him, no one inside having noticed their passing.

"Nice distraction," Orlando whispered.

"Thank you," Danara said. "You need to hurry. The male kidnapper has shown up, and he's holding a gun."

"What's he doing?" Quinn asked

"I don't know. He just went inside the room Dr. Brunner is in, and he didn't look happy."

Quinn doubled his pace. "Then get us there. Fast."

"You're clear at the moment. Take a left at the second intersection."

"Copy. Tell Jar to hold tight. We'll be there as soon as—"

"I believe she is attempting to stop him from doing whatever it is he has planned."

As Quinn said, "What?" Nate broke from the others and sprinted ahead, Daeng and Kincaid following a moment later. "Tell her to stop."

No reply.

"Danara, tell her she needs to wait for us."

When the AI still didn't answer, Quinn and Orlando began running, too.

"The testing of this phase took several months in itself," Brunner said. His explanation of Danara's origins was still in the early stages but he was already exhausted. It was from the medicine, probably. Well, that, and the inevitable crash from the adrenaline that had been coursing through him on and off since his ordeal had begun. "The first few attempts crashed her system within the first minutes after—"

Across the room, the door opened.

The general didn't seem to notice at first. Even the woman took a moment before she looked over. Brunner, however, was facing the door, and saw his other kidnapper right away.

He also did not fail to notice the gun in the man's hand.

Grigory's original intent on reentering Lonely Rock had solely been to seek revenge on Nesterov. But as he made his way from the general's office to room 17-08, he started to think about his exit strategy. What he came up with was not just a way to get out of the base alive, but one in which he would achieve his initial goal while setting himself up for a large payday.

He entered the room, his gun leading the way, and took in the scene.

Nesterov stood in the center of the room, his back to the door. Brunner sat in front of the general, on an old wooden chair. Blood was smeared on the dazed scientist's cheek.

Grigory whipped his pistol to his left, training it on Tiana. She'd been leaning against the wall in the far corner but had pushed away when he stepped inside.

Too late, she reached for her gun.

"Drop it on the ground," he ordered.

She hesitated.

"You spared my life. If you want me to do the same for you, you'll do as I say."

A derisive snort from the center of the room. "I should have known I couldn't trust either of you," Nesterov said.

Grigory glanced at the old man, said, "Don't you move," and returned his attention to his former colleague. "The gun."

Tiana slowly pulled the weapon from her holster and let it clatter to the floor.

"Kick it to me."

She did so, the gun stopping just shy of Grigory's foot.

"Now sit with your back in the corner, hands on your head."

Again Tiana looked reluctant, but she didn't wait long enough for him to tell her a second time before lowering herself to the floor.

Grigory turned to Nesterov, keeping track of Tiana from the corner of his eye.

"I've been told you're no longer in need of my services."

The general laughed. "I told her to *kill* you."

"Yes, you did."

Nesterov shot a withering look at Tiana. "Weak, both of you."

"Dr. Brunner," Grigory said in German, "how are you feeling?"

Brunner jumped at the sound of his name. "M-m-me? I'm… I'm fine."

"You don't look so fine."

"Please, just…just leave me out of this."

"Oh, Doctor, you are at the center of this."

Nesterov's eyes widened. "If you're thinking of killing him, don't," Nesterov said in Russian. "You have no idea what a mistake that would be."

"There you go underestimating me again. I have no intention of killing him." Grigory switched back to German. "Doctor, if you would please stand."

Brunner blinked. "I'm okay right where I am, thanks."

"I said, stand up," Grigory barked.

Brunner jumped to his feet.

"Now come over here."

The doctor glanced at Nesterov, as if part of him was hoping the general would save him, and part fearful of what the old man would do if he did.

"Dr. Brunner, don't make me tell you again," Grigory said.

Brunner walked meekly to Grigory.

"Stand next to the door and don't move."

Brunner moved past him to the wall. Grigory would only have to turn his head slightly to check on the man, but he was sure the doctor was too scared to even adjust his feet.

"I wish I could say it's been a pleasure working for you, General," Grigory said in Russian, "but I'm not fond of people who want me dead. I do admire your idealism. I think what's most impressive is that you've deluded yourself into believing that you're actually going to be able to make Kazakhstan a world power. When the truth is, this whole program, your *future planning*, is bullshit."

Nesterov snarled. "I guess we'll see, won't we?"

"No, sir. You will not."

Grigory aimed his pistol at Nesterov's head.

———

Tiana's mind scrambled for anything she could do.

If she had been in the field, she would have had more weapons on her than just her gun. But here at Lonely Rock, she sometimes didn't even carry her gun, leaving her with only her physical abilities. And while those were dangerous weapons in and of themselves, they were worthless if she couldn't get close enough to use them. At the moment, she wouldn't be able to make it halfway to Grigory before he shot her down.

But then as Grigory was telling the general that Nesterov's project was a waste of time, the door inched open.

One of the base personnel must have heard the commotion.

A small smile appeared on Tiana's face.

All was not yet lost.

———

Ear pressed against the door, Jar could hear two men talking. She assumed one was the man with the gun. She thought at first the other might be Brunner, but then one of the talkers switched to German and said *Doktor Brunner*. A third voice answered in German. *That* had to be Brunner, which meant the other German speaker was probably the man with the gun.

Jar listened as someone moved across the room and stopped near the door. Not the kidnapper; his voice never changed position.

Brunner, then?

It made sense, given that he was the last person the kidnapper had talked to, but...

She allowed herself only a second to debate whether or not she should risk checking. Before she could talk herself out of it, she eased the door open just enough to peek inside.

Standing right next to the door's frame was Brunner, his back against the wall.

She opened the door a bit more.

———————

"Three more turns and you will be there," Danara said. "Your next is a right at the upcoming—" A pause. "Hide. Now. The room just ahead on the right might be empty."

"Might?" Quinn said.

"It's the best chance you have."

He hurried to the door, pushed it open, and rushed inside, the others right behind him.

The room was a dorm space, with five bunks, three beds high, and it was not unoccupied. Four other men were present—two lying on beds, neither asleep, and two in the open space in front of the bunks.

All four looked over when the team entered. Before the men could react with more than a flash of confusion, Quinn and the others aimed their guns at them.

The soldiers froze.

Quinn looked at Nate. "Get 'em up."

Nate spoke to the men in Russian, and within seconds, he had all of them sitting on the ground. With Daeng's and Kincaid's help, Nate secured each man to his bunk.

"Danara, how much longer do we need to stay here?" Quinn asked.

"Another twenty seconds should do it," she replied.

"Let Jar know we're delayed."

"I would rather not distract her right now."

"Why? What's she doing?"

"She kidnapped Brunner from his captors."

In the beat that followed, glances flew between the team

members. Then, without a word, they all sprinted into the hallway, guns ready.

———————

Grigory smiled and pulled the trigger.

A split second before the bullet left the gun, Nesterov flipped the metal tray full of tools at Grigory and dove to his right.

Even then, the bullet missed the general by only centimeters.

Grigory adjusted his aim, but before he could fire again, something smashed into him and launched him sideways through the air.

———————

As Grigory raised his gun, Tiana vaulted to her feet and raced at her former colleague.

She saw the flying tray at nearly the same time as she heard the bang of the gun.

Lowering her head, she smashed into Grigory's ribs and rammed him across the room into the wall.

He crumbled to the floor, his gun jarring loose as he hit the concrete. The collision didn't knock him out, however. He rolled to his right and reached for the pistol.

Tiana, who'd fallen in a heap beside him, dove over Grigory, trying to get to the pistol first. Their hands slammed against its grip at the same time, and the gun shot across the floor toward the back of the room.

She jammed her knee into Grigory's side as he tried to push her off, then she punched him in the face, bouncing his cheek off the floor.

She glanced over at the general, not knowing if Grigory's shot had hit him or not. Nesterov was pushing himself up from the floor. She didn't see any blood.

Grigory shifted his weight and shoved her off. As he tottered to his feet, Tiana lunged for the gun a few meters away, snatched it up, and jumped to her feet. She turned toward the door, thinking Grigory would be attempting to escape, but he was near the middle of the room, standing behind the general with his arm wrapped around Nesterov's neck. His other arm was hovering next to the general's shoulder, the inside of his wrist poised next to Nesterov's bicep.

"Recognize this?" he said to Tiana as he gave his hovering arm a little twist.

She saw the watch on his wrist, its face pointing at the general, and knew exactly what it was.

Grigory sneered and said, "Lower the gun."

She dropped the pistol to her side but did not let go of it.

"That corner," he said, nodding to the one catty-corner from the door.

As she began to move, he backed toward the door, keeping the general between him and Tiana.

He stopped beside the exit and said, "Which way did Brunner go?"

"I have no idea," she said.

"Sure. Whatever, Tiana. It doesn't matter. He can't have gone far."

He used the hand with the watch to open the door, but his eyes never left Tiana. She didn't move, knowing if she brought up the gun to shoot, Grigory would poke the needle into the general's back and be out the door before she could pull the trigger.

"If I hear this door open behind me, I'll kill him," Grigory said. "You know I will." He kicked the door wide and scooted into the open with his hostage. "We're even now. Don't put me in a position where I will have to take you out, because I won't hesitate."

She stared back at him. "Neither will I."

He smiled. "Come on, General. Let's find your doctor."

37

As Jar yanked on Brunner's arm, she heard a clatter of metal and the bang of a gun.

The scientist, disoriented from everything that was going on, put up no resistance as she hauled him into the corridor.

"Follow me," she said.

She hurried down the hall the way she had come, pulling him along.

"You've got him!" Danara said, sounding surprised. "Oh, my god. You've got him."

"Stop. Just tell me how to get back to the airshaft," Jar said in Thai, knowing that was a way out.

"*Was?*" Brunner said, using the German word for what.

In English, Jar said, "I was not talking to you."

"Who are you?"

"Part of a group here to get you out."

"Where are the others?"

"On their way," she said, hoping she was right. She switched to Thai. "Directions."

"Left at the next intersection," Danara said. "Go two hallways, then right."

"Watch my back."

"Of course."

"Is that who you are talking to?" Brunner asked. "Your group?"

"If you do not want to die, then be quiet and run."

The daze seemed to be lifting from Brunner, as he went from needing to be pulled to sprinting beside her.

"Four soldiers around the corner, on the right," Danara said. "Walking your way. You should reach the intersection five seconds before they do."

Quinn, Nate, and Daeng sprinted ahead of the others, stopped just before the turn, and pressed against the wall.

The soldiers' footsteps were loud and close. They were talking and laughing. A casual conversation.

The soldiers passed into the intersection without realizing anyone was there. By the time they did, Quinn, Nate, and Daeng were already behind them.

Quinn grabbed the one at the back and threw him headfirst into the wall. This sent the man to the ground, dazed. At the same time, Daeng and Nate moved in on their targets.

Nate got his soldier into a sleeper hold first. Daeng's man was next. The fourth man whirled around and tried to pull his colleague free from Daeng's grasp, but Quinn yanked the guy away. When the man tried to twist from under Quinn's arm, Quinn kneed him in the kidneys, buying enough time to squeeze off the blood flow to the man's head.

Behind them, the static of a radio, then a deep "Uh-uh."

Quinn, still holding on to his target, twisted around and saw Kincaid pointing his rifle at the soldier Quinn had slammed into the wall. The guy had a radio in his hand but was frozen, staring at the muzzle of Kincaid's weapon.

Once the soldiers Quinn, Nate, and Daeng were dealing with had passed out, Nate went over to the one with the radio. With

Kincaid's weapon still aimed at him, the guy put up no fight as Nate sent him to sleep. They then dragged the four soldiers into an empty room and tied them up.

Total time: a hair under two minutes.

"Thanks for the assist," Quinn said to Kincaid.

"No problem," the bodyguard said.

Into his radio, Quinn said, "Which way?"

"Take the hallway the soldiers came down," Danara said.

"How close are we to Jar?" Nate asked.

"I'm not guiding you to Jar."

"What are you talking about? She needs our help."

"Exactly. I have calculated her chances of successfully getting Dr. Brunner out are better if you head back to the entrance you used and create a diversion on your way out."

"Which way is Jar going?" Nate asked.

"She is on her way back to the vent she entered through. It will be tight, but Dr. Brunner will fit."

"I'll go help her," Nate said.

"You are larger than Dr. Brunner, and will *not* fit."

"But I would," Orlando said.

Quinn nodded at her. Jar had done amazingly well to this point, but it would be criminal to let her continue on her own. "Go," he said. "We'll draw everyone's attention. Danara, guide her to Jar."

"Calculating route," Danara said. Pause. "That was a joke."

Grigory knew Tiana wouldn't wait long to come after him.

If he could have jammed the door in some way, he would have, but the damn thing was built like a tank, and he would have needed a sledgehammer just to dent it.

His only hope was to put as much distance as possible between himself and room 17-08 before his former colleague decided it was time to come out.

Grigory turned down the hallway in the direction he'd arrived from. Though the scientist could have gone the other way, the corridor dead-ended another fifty meters down. Brunner would have been trapped, his only option to hide in one of the rooms down at that end. So if the man was smart, and obviously he was, he would have chosen the only direction that would give him a chance to get away.

"Stay with me or I *will* kill you," he spat into Nesterov's ear.

Grigory moved his arm from around the general's neck down to where it hugged the man's shoulders, and he pushed Nesterov through the hall. If Grigory couldn't pick up Brunner's trail, he could always go back and check the dead end.

Of course, that would mean he'd have to kill Tiana. But so be it.

Neither of them owed anything to the other anymore.

"You really think you're going to get away with this?" Nesterov said.

"Shut up. You only speak now when I tell you to speak."

"You don't even realize you're already—"

Grigory slapped the side of the general's head. "I said shut up."

They reached the first hallway intersection without hearing the door to 17-08 open.

Good. Perhaps Tiana wouldn't play hero after all.

Grigory listened for sounds of Brunner's escape. He heard something that sounded like footsteps to his left, along one of the giant circular corridors that ringed the base.

He turned toward the noise. Within a dozen meters, it grew loud enough for him to positively ID it as footsteps.

He said to his hostage, "Faster."

———

Tiana hurried across the room and put her ear against the closed door.

She could hear Grigory and the general moving away, toward the main part of the base.

She almost eased the door open, thinking she could put a bullet in Grigory's back before he could react. But she was concerned she'd make enough noise for him to hear, and he would follow through with his promise to kill Nesterov.

There was no denying the fact the general was furious at her for not carrying out his order to kill Grigory. She was furious at herself, too. She'd acted out of respect for the unwritten soldier's code to never turn on a comrade. But how she now wished she'd put a bullet in the bastard's head instead of showing Grigory the exit.

But that was a concern for another time. Now it was her duty to save the general's life. Doing so wouldn't wipe away Nesterov's anger, but that didn't matter. She had betrayed him once. She would not do so again.

She pressed harder against the door and listened as the footsteps faded to nothing. She waited a few more seconds to make sure she wasn't mistaken, and turned the handle.

"I see an intersection ahead," Jar said in Thai.

"It's clear," Danara told her. "You can go right through it. You should know you're being followed, though."

Jar glanced over her shoulder but didn't see anyone. "By who?"

"Krylov. He has General Nesterov with him."

"Nesterov? Who's that?"

Brunner looked at her surprised. "Nesterov? What about him?"

Switching to English, Jar said, "Who is he?"

"Should you not know that already?"

"If I did, I would not ask you the question, would I?"

He grimaced. "He is the big boss here, as far as I can tell. Calls himself a general."

"Dr. Brunner is correct," Danara said. "Nesterov is in charge of the base."

Switching to Thai, Jar said, "How far back are they?"

"Two hundred and sixty-seven meters, but they have picked up their pace."

"Dr. Brunner, I need you to run."

Corporal Mikhail Zhaparov set down his coffee and leaned forward, his eyes focused on monitor number 3. The digital overlay identified the feed as coming from a camera in sector 17.

When the feed automatically switched to another random camera three seconds later, he grabbed his keyboard and punched in instructions to bring it back up.

Monitor 3 went black before the feed from sector 17 reappeared. The hallway in view was empty now, but it hadn't been before.

He chose another camera farther along the corridor and brought it up.

There, coming down the hall, toward the lens, was Commander Krylov and General Nesterov. When the corporal had spotted them on the previous feed, his initial thought had been, *Ah, good. The commander found the general.* His second thought had been, *Why are they running? And so close together?*

As the two grew larger on the screen, other things disturbed Zhaparov. The general did not look happy. That in itself wasn't so unusual, but from Nesterov's sideways glances, his displeasure was clearly aimed at the commander. The commander, however, didn't seem to care, and even appeared to bark something at the general, as if *he* had the higher rank.

Stranger still, Krylov had an arm wrapped across the general's back, and it almost seemed as if he was dragging Nesterov along with him.

Zhaparov frowned, unsure what to do.

He had grown up in a system that looked down on people who rocked the boat. Keep your head down, don't cause any trouble, and you'll be fine.

But this didn't feel like something he should ignore.

He hesitated then picked up the phone and dialed the head of security.

"Sir, I have something I think you should see."

With Danara directing their route, Quinn, Nate, Daeng, and Kincaid headed back toward the escape tunnel.

"Stop," Danara said.

The men pressed against the walls.

"Someone coming?" Quinn asked.

"That's not why I stopped you. I was hoping to get you closer to the way out before using you as a diversion, but I don't think there's enough time. Base security has spotted the men following Jar and Dr. Brunner. One of them seems to be holding the other hostage. Probability indicates it will only be a matter of moments before security sends someone to check. My concern is that this will put more soldiers in the vicinity of Jar and the doctor."

"You want to set off the diversion now?" Quinn asked.

"I think it would be best."

Quinn glanced around at the others. "Everyone ready?"

Thumbs up from Nate and Daeng, and a nod from Kincaid.

"All right, Danara. Let's do it."

In addition to guiding them to this point, Danara had explained what she had in mind to sow confusion among base personnel. Her plan was rough around the edges, and not quite as survival friendly as Quinn would have hoped, but after several tweaks on his part, they had a strategy that was more to his liking.

There was still the potential for things to go wrong, but no more so than on most jobs taken on by Quinn and his friends.

"Start walking," Danara said. "The next intersection is twenty meters ahead. When you reach it, you and Nate go left and Daeng and Kincaid go right."

"This had better work," Kincaid mumbled.

"It will," Danara said. "Trust me."

Kincaid grunted, but said nothing more.

The men headed down the tunnel at double speed.

"Putting you on camera now," Danara said.

"Move," Lieutenant Dobrynin said. "I want to get a closer look."

Zhaparov had just shown Dobrynin, his supervisor, the live feed of Commander Krylov and General Nesterov.

The corporal got out of the way.

The sense that Krylov was forcing the general along seemed even more obvious to Zhaparov now than before. Dobrynin, however, was not convinced.

"There, sir," Zhaparov said.

On screen, Krylov had pushed Nesterov hard enough to make the general stumble. Krylov then grabbed Nesterov to keep him from falling, and said something that looked like an angry shout, as if Nesterov himself had been responsible for losing his balance.

Dobrynin sat back, his eyes wide in surprise. After a beat, he reached for the phone, but before he picked it up, a new feed appeared on monitor 2.

"Sir!" Zhaparov said, pointing at the monitor.

On the screen were four men, walking fast down one of the corridors. They were all armed and wearing small backpacks, and none of them were in uniform. It wasn't necessarily an unusual sight. Off-duty soldiers would often make their way to the indoor firing range for target practice. Only this time, one of the men on the monitor was a large African.

There was no one of African descent serving at Lonely Rock.

"Where is that?" the lieutenant asked.

Zhaparov leaned forward to check the identifier. "Hallway 7, sector 22."

The feed switched to a new random shot.

"Dammit," Dobrynin said, poking at the keyboard. When nothing happened, he pushed out of the chair. "Bring it back!"

Zhaparov swung back into his seat and typed in the command to pause the autorotation. The feed that had featured the intruders returned to monitor 2.

The men were gone.

"You've got the wrong feed," Dobrynin said.

"No, sir. This is correct."

"Then where are they?"

"They probably moved out of the camera's range. Let me switch to the next one."

The corporal called up the new feed.

"I'm not seeing anyone," Dobrynin said through clenched teeth.

"They must be moving faster than I thought," Zhaparov said.

He skipped ahead three cameras, positive the intruders couldn't have run that far yet. But no one was in that feed, either.

"They've got to be somewhere!" Dobrynin shouted.

"Yes, sir. I'll find them."

"Move over. Let me get to the phone."

Zhaparov scooted his chair over enough for Dobrynin to squeeze in and snatch up the receiver.

"This is Lieutenant Dobrynin. Alarm level four. There are intruders in the base!"

38

A few meters before Quinn, Nate, Daeng, and Kincaid reached the intersection where they'd part, Danara said, "You might want to cover your ears."

Since they were each carrying a gun and had only one hand free, they ignored her suggestion.

As they turned at the intersection—Daeng and Kincaid going right and Quinn and Nate going left—a loud *whoop-whoop-whoop-whoop-whoop* blared out of overhead intercom speakers. This went on for about ten seconds, before being replaced by a voice shouting in Russian. When the speaker finished, the alarm returned.

"What did he say?" Quinn asked, not sure his voice could be heard over the din.

"Intruder alert," Nate said above the noise. "And apparently we're in sector twenty-two."

"*Were* in twenty-two," Danara said. "Daeng and Kincaid have entered sector thirty-seven. You and Quinn are in sector twenty-three now."

"Excess information," Quinn said. "Just tell us where to go and warn us if anyone's coming."

"Noted. Daeng and Kincaid, you will continue for one

hundred and ten meters, then turn right again. Base personnel are being deployed to their alert stations. There is a group closer to Daeng and Kincaid's current position than I would like. Quinn, with your permission, I would like to expose you and Nate again."

"Let us know when to smile."

"That's funny. You will be on camera in three…two…one…"

"There they are!" Dobrynin said, knocking into Zhaparov's shoulder as he jutted forward.

"Where are the other two?" Zhaparov said.

"They must be ahead of them." Dobrynin picked up the phone again. "They're in sector twenty-three, ring hallway three, heading toward twenty-four."

The alarm that had been shrieking outside the monitoring room paused again.

"All personnel—intruders in sector twenty-three, ring hallway three. Heading toward sector twenty-four. Close in and apprehend."

The message repeated twice more, then the alarm kicked back in.

On the monitor, the two men moved out of the camera's view. Zhaparov switched to the next feed.

The men weren't there.

"They must have some kind of signal-blocking tech," Dobrynin said.

As far as Zhaparov knew, no device could remove someone from a live feed and yet leave that feed playing, but he kept this thought to himself.

He toggled through the cameras in the area, trying to pick up the intruders from another angle.

But the entire corridor was empty.

What the hell?

When Jar and Brunner took their next turn, Jar recognized the hallway almost immediately. Yes, many of the hallways looked the same, but Jar's brain worked in a way that automatically picked up little details wherever she went. A scratch here and a scuff mark there were all she needed to ID her location.

Two more intersections ahead and they'd be in the hallway where the bunk rooms she'd sneaked through were. Which meant it wouldn't be that much longer until they were in the long corridor back to the vent.

The relative quiet they'd been experiencing was suddenly shattered by an alarm blasting from the ceiling.

Yelping in surprise, Brunner slowed.

"Keep moving," Jar said, then switched to Thai. "Have we been seen?"

"No," Danara replied. "It's part of a diversion to clear your way. Keep going."

"Copy."

"What is happening?" Brunner asked.

"My friends are giving us the chance to get away. Now keep up."

She gave Brunner another tug and started to run.

Grigory had no doubt the alarm had been set off because of him. The backstabbing Tiana had called security and ratted him out.

The general seemed to be thinking the same thing, because he slowed down.

"Keep going!" Grigory yelled, shoving Nesterov in the back.

As the old man stumbled ahead, the announcement that intruders were in the base came over the intercom.

It did nothing to change Grigory's mind. This first was a

generic message to get everyone moving. Soon would come another announcement, identifying *him* as the intruder.

He grabbed the general and kept them moving down the hall. His biggest concern was the alarm was preventing him from hearing Brunner's footsteps. He needed to cut the distance between them fast, so that he wouldn't lose his prey in the maze of corridors.

Less than a minute later, another announcement came over the speakers, giving the location of not the intruder but intru*ders*. And the location was nowhere near Grigory and Nesterov.

Grigory had been wrong. Security wasn't looking for him at all.

Who the hell would have broken into Lonely—

The bridge of his nose creased.

Were these intruders the same people who had tried to stop him and Tiana from leaving Slovakia?

Could he be so lucky?

He didn't know for sure that he was right, but it was a reasonable enough assumption.

And if it was them, the entire base would be mobilized to hunt them down.

Meaning no one would bother Grigory.

Another thought hit him. One that wasn't quite as encouraging.

Was one or more of the intruders leading Brunner away?

Unfortunately, that also seemed plausible.

He grimaced. He would have caught up to Brunner long ago if not for Nesterov.

He'd kept the old man in case the need to use him as a negotiation chip arose. But that concern was becoming less and less important.

"Grigory!"

The shout had barely risen above the sound of the alarm, but he recognized the voice nonetheless.

Tiana.

He whirled around, pulling the general in front of him. Tiana stood forty meters away, holding a gun aimed at him and Nesterov.

"Don't come any closer!" Grigory yelled back, brandishing his needle-enhanced watch.

"If you let him go, I'll make sure you're treated fairly."

Oh, boy, did he want to laugh at that. But that would waste time he could spend catching up to Brunner.

"Drop the gun or he's dead!" he shouted.

She didn't flinch, no doubt thinking he was bluffing again.

He slapped the needle into the general's neck.

"Wait! No!" Nesterov shouted.

"Too late," Grigory whispered in the old man's ear.

He shoved Nesterov to the side, darted to the opposite wall, and sprinted away from Tiana.

A flurry of bullets flew toward him. The shots smacked into the wall and ceiling, but none hit him. As he'd hoped, he'd caught her off guard, and was able to make it around the curve of the hallway before she could pull herself together.

He figured he now had at least half a minute, maybe more, because Tiana would never leave the general unattended.

He sprinted down the corridor.

———

"No!" Tiana screamed as she pulled the trigger over and over, until she finally stopped so that she wouldn't use up the entire magazine.

She rushed forward.

Grigory was gone, but the general was lying on the ground, his chest moving up and down erratically.

She crouched beside him and tried to take his hand, but he pulled it away.

He said something, but his voice was too soft to hear above the alarm.

She leaned in close.

"You…did…this," he whispered.

Her chest clenched, and in that moment she would have gladly traded places with him. "I-I know. This is all my fault. I'm so, so sorry."

"Kill…him…."

"Yes, sir. I will."

He raised his head a few centimeters, his mouth hovering next to her ear. "You…must…keep…it…" It seemed as if he wouldn't finish, but then he said, "…going."

His head fell back to the ground, where it lay for several seconds. He then took a last stuttered breath before his chest stopped moving.

Tiana fell back on her heels, tears gathering in her eyes. All her training told her she should try to resuscitate him, but she knew it would do no good. There was no coming back from the toxin in the watches.

You must keep it going.

Future Planning. That's what he meant.

She didn't think she could come close to filling his shoes. But it was an order. His last. She would have to at least try, wouldn't she?

Yes, she would. But that was for later.

She pushed to her feet.

The general's other order was something she could act on now.

———

Jar leaned against the door, trying to listen for Krylov's footsteps on the other side. Danara had warned that the kidnapper was quickly gaining on them. She had advised Jar to find cover as soon as possible. Having been this way before, Jar had led Brunner into the nearest unoccupied dorm room.

Now she listened at the door, but it was impossible to hear

anything over the whooping alarm. Even if the intercom had been quiet, Brunner was panting so loudly he would have masked any footsteps.

"Quiet," she whispered harshly. "Do you want them to find us?"

Surprised by her tone, the scientist stopped breathing for a moment. When he started again, it was at a lower level.

"Status," Jar said in Thai.

"Krylov will be passing your position in thirty seconds. There is another problem, however. The woman, Snetkov, is chasing him, and is about forty-five seconds behind."

"What happened to the old man?"

"Krylov killed him."

They needed to keep moving, but returning to the corridor at the moment was out of the question. Fortunately, they didn't have to.

"Follow me," she said to Brunner.

She turned toward a door at the side of the room.

"Where are you going?" He pointed at the door they'd entered. "That's the way out."

"We are taking a shortcut."

"Shortcut?" he said, not understanding the phrase.

"A different path that will get us where we want to go without being seen." In her head, she added *hopefully*. No sense in worrying Brunner more.

She guided him to the entrance of the bathroom between the two dorm rooms and motioned for him to wait outside. She checked the toilet and shower area, then proceeded to the doorway at the other end.

The room beyond was the occupied one she had sneaked through. She peered inside.

No one there now. They had all probably responded to the alarm.

She retrieved the doctor and escorted him through the bathroom and across the dorm to the door on the other side.

"Krylov has just passed you," Danara said.

"Copy." Hopefully, Krylov would think Jar and Brunner had gone down one of the branch corridors. "We're taking the interior route."

"There are no cameras in the rooms. I can't watch out for you."

"There are no people in here, either. Keep an eye on the hallway."

"All right," Danara said, not sounding happy.

Jar had a lot of questions she wanted to ask Brunner when they had some time. High on that list was how he was able to give Danara such a wide variety of emotions.

Jar eased the door open, confirmed the next room was empty, and led Brunner inside.

"They could be anywhere, sir," Dobrynin said into the phone. "They have some sort of masking technology."

"Masking what?" The man on the other end was Dobrynin's boss, Captain Mustafina.

"Something that keeps the cameras from picking them up. The only reason we saw them is probably because their devices glitched."

"I don't care what devices they're using. Find them! Check every hallway, every room. Everywhere."

"Yes, sir."

Dobrynin left the monitoring room and rushed down to communications, two doors away.

"I need the intercom."

One of the men at the station handed him the microphone. The other flipped a switch and pointed at the lieutenant.

Outside the room Nate and Quinn were hiding in, the alarm cut off and another announcement filled the corridor. When it was finished, the alarm came back on, but at a reduced level.

"That's not good," Nate said

"What's not good?" Quinn asked.

"They're doing a full base check. Rooms and all. Everyone's been ordered to search the area they're in before moving on."

Quinn grimaced. The plan had been to get as many of the base personnel as possible heading toward him and Nate, freeing the way for Jar. It seemed, however, that the confusion caused by their sudden disappearance was working against them.

"Danara," Quinn said, "how close are we to one of the patrols?"

"There is a patrol one hundred and nine meters away, and another one hundred and thirty-two."

"Moving toward us or away?"

"Away and toward you, in that order."

"Which direction is the second group?"

Private Astana hung at the back of the pack, annoyed.

He'd been sound asleep when the alarm had ripped him from his dream. It had been a good one, too. Not that he could remember it, but the contentment he'd felt had lingered for a few seconds, teasing him with what he was missing.

And all for what was probably a drill anyway.

Intruders? Really?

The only way to reach Lonely Rock was to fly in. And if someone did that, the person would have never made it past the runway.

"Gorev, Amirov, take that one," Corporal Senkin said, pointing at a door ahead. He then motioned to another door. "Rusanov, Putyatin, over there. Astana, we'll take this one." He headed for the door nearest the squad.

Great, Astana thought. Stuck with Mr. By the Book again.

He made a show of acting interested, but he was sure Senkin could see right through him. The corporal didn't say anything, however. He just signaled for Astana to stand against the wall next to the door, and reached for the handle.

Bang-bang-bang-bang-bang.

Bullets flew through the hallway, passing less than half a meter above Astana and the others' heads, before hitting the curving wall of the corridor farther down.

Astana dropped to the floor, his hands over his head. When the shooting stopped, he peeked to see if the corporal had been hit. Senkin was crouched next to the door he'd been about to open, whipping his radio up to his mouth.

"This is patrol seventeen," he said. "Shots fired. Shots fired."

"Seventeen, this is control. Are you still under fire?"

"Not at the moment. I...I'm not sure where they went."

"What's your location?"

"Sector twenty-seven, ring hallway three."

A beat later, the same voice came over the base intercom. "Intruders spotted in sector twenty-seven, ring hallway three. All patrols, close in on that area. Be aware, intruders are armed."

"Let's go," Senkin said to Astana.

"Let's go where?"

"We're going to take these assholes down."

"Are you crazy?"

Senkin narrowed his eyes. "On your feet, private!"

Astana glanced down the hallway. Whoever had shot at them was either just around the bend or had taken off. Reluctantly, he pushed himself off the ground.

After firing over the heads of the soldiers, Quinn and Nate had ducked down another hallway, then slipped into a utility closet to avoid a second patrol.

Outside a voice came over the intercom at the same time the men ran by the door, toward where the gunfire had come from.

"Did it work?" Quinn asked.

"I think so," Nate said. "That was an order for everyone to move in on the location we were just at."

"Then probably a good idea for us to get out of here. Danara?"

"In eleven seconds, you will have a thirty-seven-second window to relocate," Danara said. "I will guide you to your next hiding spot."

"Tell us when," Quinn said.

Seconds later, Danara said, "When."

39

Jar and Brunner moved through the last dorm room and into an L-shaped storage room filled with metal boxes. At the next door, Jar listened for any noise.

When she heard nothing, she said to Danara, "Entering the next storage room."

"There are some soldiers in the corridor near you."

"We'll be quiet."

Jar eased the door open and led the scientist inside.

As the door slid back into its frame, Danara said, "Hide. Wherever you can. Now!"

Jar remembered the room from her first time through, and knew there was no hiding place that would keep them completely out of view. So she grabbed Brunner's arm and pulled him between two of the shelving units. As they made their way to where the offshoot met the wall, a door opened across the room and the lights came on.

She crouched as low as she could, yanking Brunner down beside her, and slunk the rest of the way to the wall. She put Brunner behind her and faced the way they'd come, her gun pointed at the central aisle

Booted steps and the rustle of clothing. Two…no, three people walking through the room.

She glanced back at the scientist and held a finger to her mouth.

He nodded, his eyes wide with fear.

The three who had entered had each gone in a different direction. One was heading the opposite way from Jar and Brunner. Another was meandering somewhere in the middle of the room, while the third was in the central aisle, walking toward the end of the small aisle they were hiding in.

She aimed the gun at the edge of the shelving unit.

As the steps grew nearer, Jar sighted down the barrel.

A shout of surprise from the other end of the room, then the *thup-thup-thup* of gunfire through a suppressor.

Jar heard three thuds on the floor.

Silence.

"Jar?"

Jar slipped her finger off the trigger and stood up. "Over here."

Orlando appeared in the central aisle, at the end of the shelves. She, too, was holding a gun, but pointed at the ground.

"You guys all right?" she asked.

"Yes, we are fine," Jar said.

She helped Brunner to his feet and they walked down to join Orlando.

"Nice to meet you, Dr. Brunner," Orlando said.

Instead of looking relieved that reinforcements had arrived, his brow was wrinkled in worry. "Are all of you women?"

"Would that be a problem?" Orlando asked.

"No, I just…it is…" His gaze shifted to something behind Orlando.

Jar glanced over her shoulder and saw the body of the man who had been closest to them, lying in a puddle of blood. Farther down the aisle were his two friends.

"It is fine," he said. "I am tired. Forget I said anything."

"Forgotten. Now if it's all right by you, I think we should get out of here."

"Yes. Of course. An excellent idea."

"You know this area best," Orlando said to Jar. "You should take lead."

Grigory had lost Brunner.

Sometime after the alarm had started blaring, the scientist must have taken a turn Grigory had missed.

Grigory would have turned around then and there, if not for the fact he was sure Tiana was somewhere behind him.

He turned down the next hallway, hoping that would throw her off, and did quick checks of the rooms he went by to make sure the doctor wasn't hiding in one of them.

Perhaps he should let it go and get the hell out of there, but Brunner represented a once-in-a-lifetime chance to substantially enrich Grigory's future. If the man was even half as important as the general had thought he was, the ransom Grigory could extract would be enormous. He was not about to let that opportunity pass by.

Given how long the scientist had avoided recapture, Grigory had decided the intruders were helping Brunner. If they were Tiana's people, the scientist would have been taken somewhere by now to be guarded by squads of security personnel.

So the intruders were helping him, and their goal now would be to get Brunner out of Lonely Rock. The easiest place to do that was the main exit. It wouldn't matter if it was guarded or not. The intruders surely had the firepower to take the entrance by force.

If that was the way they were going, that was the way Grigory would go.

Onward he went, throwing open doors, scanning rooms, and moving on to the next.

One of the rooms he checked was a storage room full of old

metal boxes. He'd seen others like it, and knew the boxes contained old Soviet records from the 1950s and 60s. He also knew there were small aisles inside where the doctor could hide.

He hesitated in the doorway. If the doctor wasn't here, Grigory would be giving Brunner time to put more distance between them. But if he was…

Dammit.

He moved inside, flicked on the light, and jogged down the main aisle, checking on both sides each row he passed.

He was surprised when the center aisle made a sharp turn to the right and continued on. He'd never seen any rooms at the base like this. He kept checking, but the scientist was not here.

At the end of the central aisle was a door that led to the next room. Like many of the interior doors at the base, it had a narrow vertical window through which he could see that the lights in the next room were on.

He opened it and cursed out loud.

It was another storage room, but unlike the one he'd just come through, there was a trio of bodies lying in the aisle, all three wearing the uniform of base soldiers.

He jogged up to the first one. No need to check the guy's pulse. His bloodstained shirt and the dark pool under his body told the story.

The other two were just as dead.

Was this the work of the intruders on their way to find Brunner? Or had this been done later, to aid Brunner's escape?

He sniffed the air. Gunpowder.

Whatever had happened here had occurred only a few minutes before. But why would they be bringing Brunner through this room?

The corridor outside would not take them to the main exit. If he was not mistaken, it led to the unused southern end of the base.

Though that section had plenty of good places to hide, the smarter move would be to get as far away from Lonely Rock as fast as possible. And if the intruders were the ones from Slovakia, they had the brains to know that.

That meant they were taking Brunner down that way for another reason entirely.

His eyes widened as a flash from his meeting with Tiana came back to him, the part where she pushed the wall out of the way to reveal the secret tunnel to the surface.

Could there be an emergency exit in the southern end he didn't know about?

Of course. If the base had one hidden tunnel, why not two?

He ran to the door at the other end and into the next room. Empty.

The room after that was also deserted, so he reentered the corridor.

The overhead lights continued in full force for about another hundred meters. After that, only every third or fourth one was lit, marking the end of the territory Nesterov's organization used.

Grigory stared down the corridor, hoping to see some movement, but the reduced illumination made it impossible.

He was beginning to wonder if he should even chance heading down the hall when the alarm stopped, and a voice came over the speaker announcing something about the intruders.

Grigory barely registered what was said, because in the few seconds' pause between the alarm shutting off and the voice starting to speak, he'd heard a noise.

Soft. Distant. And most definitely footsteps, moving quickly down the otherwise unused corridor.

"Got you," he whispered.

Tiana stopped and looked in both directions.

She'd been following Grigory, at first by catching glimpses of him ahead, and then, when the volume of the alarm decreased, by the sound of his movements. But he'd gone silent moments before, right about where she now stood.

"Where the hell are you?" she whispered.

With no clear answer, she continued onward, but walking instead of running. She passed through an intersection with a wide corridor that led back to the center of the base in one direction, and to the unused southern sectors in the other. She scanned both sides but didn't see him, so she moved on.

Thirty meters past the junction, a door opened somewhere behind her.

She spun around, thinking Grigory was attempting to ambush her, but no one was there. The sound must have come from down the corridor she'd just passed.

She crept back toward the intersection. Before she reached the corner, someone in control announced over the intercom that the intruders had been seen. She eased up to the junction and peered around the corner, toward the heart of Lonely Rock.

Deserted.

She hadn't imagined it. There *had* been the sound of a door opening. She'd swear to—

Movement behind her.

She looked over her shoulder.

Running away from her, toward the unoccupied part of the base, was Grigory.

She would not let him get away this time.

———

Jar glanced over her shoulder again.

According to Danara, somewhere down the corridor, way beyond Orlando and Brunner who were right behind her, Krylov and Snetkov were following them.

The previous times she'd checked, Jar had seen no signs of the kidnappers. This time, however, she spotted a tiny shadow flickering across one of the lit areas, maybe two hundred and fifty or three hundred meters back.

It appeared to be moving faster than she and the others were, but not by much. Still, it would be a close call to get into the vent before the pursuer caught up to them. And if the kidnappers were armed, which she assumed they were, the shadow would only need to get in range to keep Jar, Orlando, and Brunner from escaping.

"Faster," she said. "We are almost there."

Brunner looked as if he had no more to give, but he nodded and increased his pace.

"I assume there's a way to get up to the vent," Orlando said.

"I have stacked some boxes beneath it so we will climb up."

"What?" Brunner said. "Climb? *Vent?*"

"It's the only way you're getting out of here," Orlando said.

"I-I-I am not very athletic."

"Don't worry. We'll help you."

Her words didn't seem to ease his concern much.

"There it is," Jar said thirty seconds later.

A hundred and fifty meters ahead, half lit at the edge of one of the working lights, was the junk-pile ladder she'd built.

"We're not going to have a lot of time," Orlando said. "You go first, then Brunner."

"I can go last," Jar said.

"You've been through the vents already once," Orlando said. "You go first."

Jar had only been logical. She was wearing the harness. It made sense for her to go last so she could tie the end of the rope to it. But perhaps she had been overthinking. Now that the base personnel knew they were here, it wouldn't matter if they left the rope behind or not.

She nodded. "I go first."

With Danara's help, Quinn and Nate negotiated their way across the base to the room with the escape tunnel where Daeng and Kincaid waited. The hardest part had been at the start, when all the patrols were heading in their general direction. After a few well-timed stops in unoccupied rooms, all the soldiers were soon behind them.

"You guys all right?" Quinn asked Daeng.

Daeng snorted. "No one came near us. Could have taken a nap if I wanted to."

"What's going on with Brunner?" Kincaid asked.

"You could ask Danara yourself, you know," Nate said.

"I tried, but I don't think she's talking to me."

"I have no interest in speaking directly with Mr. Kincaid," Danara said. "He's the one who let Dr. Brunner be kidnapped."

"Hey! I didn't let—"

Quinn cut Kincaid off with a hard glance, then said, "Mr. Kincaid did everything he could to *stop* the kidnapping, including getting shot. And his sole focus ever since has been on rescuing the doctor. You need to look at all the factors before judging people."

Danara did not apologize, but after a few seconds she did say, "Dr. Brunner, Jar, and Orlando are climbing up to the vent now."

"Thank God," Kincaid said.

"They are being followed, though."

Nate tensed. "Do they need help?"

"You would never be able to get there in time."

"Who's following them?" Quinn asked.

"Krylov and Snetkov."

"Are they going to catch them?"

"Unclear. I am hopeful they won't."

"Hopeful?" Nate said.

"Let's move it," Quinn said, and headed for the secret door to the tunnel. "We may not be able to help them down here but can up top."

Grigory spotted a pile of junk in the middle of the corridor ahead. It went almost all the way to the ceiling. Why it was there, he had no idea. He only knew it was blocking his view of the doctor and the two people helping him.

He narrowed his eyes.

There was movement on the pile. Little things, on either side, like rats or mice or—

"Shit."

Hands.

Brunner and his intruder friends were climbing the stack on the far side. It took only a second for Grigory to see why. Above the pile was a hole in the ceiling.

He had run only a few more steps when the person at the top reached up and pulled into the hole. The second person moved into position to do the same. From the shape of the body, Grigory was sure it was Brunner.

As the scientist lifted a hand toward the ceiling, Grigory shouted in German, "Halt!"

Orlando put her hand on Brunner's calf, to help keep his foot in place.

"Reach up and press against the sides, then pull yourself in," Jar called down from inside the vent.

"I-I do not think I can," he said.

"Stop thinking about it at all," Orlando said. "Start with one hand and use it to steady yourself."

Brunner looked down at her, fear in his eyes.

"It's okay," she said, giving his calf a reassuring squeeze. "Just do it."

He took a breath, then reached for the vent.

"Halt!"

The shout echoed down the hallway.

As Orlando looked to see where it had come from, she felt Brunner shift and heard him say, "Oh, no!"

She glanced up. One of his feet had come off the tower, and his other was threatening to do the same. The only reason he hadn't fallen was that Jar, hanging upside down in the vent, had a hold of his hand. But if he lost his footing completely, she wouldn't be able to hold his full weight, and both would plummet to the ground.

Orlando grabbed his wayward leg, guided it back to the tower, and put a hand on his ass until she was certain he wasn't going to fall.

"You're okay," she said. "But you need to keep going."

He took a deep breath before reaching up to the vent with his other hand.

Orlando looked back down the hall.

The male kidnapper, Krylov, was running toward them.

She retrieved her gun, aimed it in his direction, and pulled the trigger twice. Unfortunately, Brunner's movements had caused the tower to sway, making her shots miss their target by centimeters.

Krylov dove to his left, behind a pile of crates. Orlando sent a warning shot into one of the boxes and kept her gun trained on them in case he returned fire.

"How you doing up there?" she asked, without looking up.

"He is in. Give us a moment to make some room and you can come."

"No. Take him all the way up to the horizontal section. Once you're clear, *then* I'll come in."

"Okay."

Her eyes still on Krylov's hiding place, Orlando listened as Jar and Brunner moved up the vent. She was surprised the kidnapper hadn't tried anything yet. Perhaps he was worried about hitting Brunner, like her team had been at the airfield in Slovakia.

"Clear," Jar called down.

Orlando scaled to the top of the tower, still watching Krylov's hiding spot. When she was ready to go up, she sent three more bullets into the crates to remind him not to move, then pulled herself into the vent.

This was the most dangerous part, and the reason she'd ordered Jar and Brunner to climb out of the vertical section first. If Krylov realized no one was left to shoot at him, he could get beneath the vent, fire up into it, and easily hit whoever was there.

Orlando scaled the shaft quickly, all the while expecting the boom of a gun. When she reached the top, she flopped into the horizontal section and yanked her legs out of the shaft.

They were in the clear. Not only could Krylov not shoot at them, he couldn't come after them, either, because there was no way he could fit in the vent.

"Okay, Jar," Orlando said. "Get us out of here."

The only weapon Grigory had was the watch, and even that could do nothing more now than deliver a pinprick. If any toxin was left on the needle, it was likely not enough to do more than make someone sick.

He was so damn close.

Brunner was *right there*, no more than ten meters away in that stupid vent.

But there was nothing Grigory could do while the woman had him pinned down.

Three more bullets ripped into the boxes he was hiding behind. He curled into himself, thankful that the boxes' contents seemed enough to keep the shots from reaching him.

He heard the *thunk*s of something banging against metal, but waited several more seconds before he took a peek.

The woman was gone, the tower deserted.

He rushed over to the pile and swung around it until he found a spot from which he could see into the vent. But the light from the corridor illuminated only so far, and no one was in the visible section.

Worse yet, climbing the tower would be impossible. He'd never be able to squeeze into the vent.

"Dammit, dammit, dammit, dammit, dammit."

He could feel the piles of cash draining out of his future bank account.

He thought for a moment. Wherever this led, it would come out in the desert with nothing around it. Unless Brunner's helpers had a car parked nearby—a distinct possibility—they would have to walk to where they were going. And even if there was a car, he guessed the vent wasn't large enough for them to stand in, so they would have to crawl out to get to their vehicle. Which would take time.

Using the base's main entrance would be a simple thirty-second elevator ride. And he could take one of the security dirt bikes from the hangar and ride it out to the general area where they would surface.

With his dream not yet dead, he ran back down the tunnel.

Tiana instantly recognized the muffled spits as sound-suppressed gunfire and scooted behind the nearest stack of boxes.

She had no idea where the shots had come from, until she sneaked a glance down the corridor and spotted two legs lifting into the ceiling, above a stack of boxes and other stuff in the middle of the hall.

Brunner's legs? The intruders'?

She pushed the question of who they belonged to out of her mind. It didn't matter anymore. Future Planning was dead. It had ended when the general took his last breath, despite his request for her to carry on his mission.

Her focus was only on balancing the scales. And though she

knew Grigory's death wouldn't set everything right, at least it would allow her to occasionally sleep at night.

Down the hall, she saw Grigory crawl out of his hidey-hole and approach the pile of junk. She used the opportunity to move up to the hidden spot he had just vacated.

When he started to move around the pile, she ducked behind the boxes.

She looked at her gun. How may bullets did she have left? Two? Three? None? She couldn't check the magazine without him hearing, so she hoped she'd stopped her earlier shooting spree in time.

She'd wait until she heard him step back around to her side of the stack, and then she'd do it and be done with him. She calmed her breathing, wanting her hands to be as steady as a rock.

Any second now.

A step, a bit louder than the last.

Any second.

When she heard his next step, she jumped up and aimed at the spot where he should be. Only he wasn't there. Instead of walking back around the pile, Grigory was running and almost parallel with her.

She swung her arms to her left to adjust her aim.

What the hell?

Grigory had known Tiana was following him, but he'd thought he'd lost her when he discovered Brunner had gone south. Now she popped up only a couple of meters away, and was whipping her gun toward him.

Pivoting off his right foot, he flew at her.

The gun went off at the same moment he smashed into her. They flew backward into a crate, the box partially collapsing under their weight.

Tiana tried to maneuver the pistol under him to shoot him

point-blank, but he grabbed her wrist and hammered it against the crate.

With a yell of frustration, she pushed him with her other hand, trying to get him off her, but he was having none of it.

"Drop it!" he yelled as he shoved her hand into the box again.

Her knuckles had begun to bleed, but she refused to let go.

He shot his knee into her ribs but she anticipated it, and used the fact that the blow had unbalanced him to push him away.

He rolled sideways onto her arm that held the gun. As she tried to yank her hand free, he grabbed her bicep and held it in place, knowing that if he let go, he'd be dead.

She punched him with quick, powerful jabs into his shoulder, his ribs, and his face.

He had no choice but to release one hand from her arm to fight back. After fending off another swing, he slammed his forearm into her cheek.

They rolled onto the floor, each fighting for control of the weapon.

Boom!

Grigory blinked, then realized he was no longer touching the weapon. He was sure his life was over, and that when the gun boomed again, it would be the last sound he'd ever hear.

But then he saw the gun lying on the concrete, centimeters from Tiana's unmoving hand.

The bullet had entered her torso just below where her heart should be. Her eyes were open, her gaze confused.

He picked up the gun, slipped it into the holster he was still wearing, and stood up.

"Nesterov is dead," he said. "All you had to do was let me go. Your death is on you."

She looked at him, some semblance of the anger he'd seen returning to her face. But when she opened her mouth to speak, the only thing that passed her lips was blood.

"Goodbye, Tiana. I'd stay, but I've got things to do."

As he started running again, the top of his left shoulder stung.

Without slowing, he reached over and discovered a shallow groove right above his clavicle.

The first shot when he'd rushed her had nicked him. Any lower and Tiana would have been the one still breathing.

Today was indeed turning out to be his lucky day.

Now all he had to do was find Brunner and it would become his luckiest ever.

40

Orlando, Jar, and Brunner reached the vertical shaft that led to the grating at the surface.

"I'll open the grating," Orlando said. "Once I have it secured, you can use the rope to climb up."

Panting and drenched in sweat, Brunner said, "I do not think I have the strength."

"You will," Jar reassured him. "And if you start to fall, I will catch you."

The area was wide enough for Orlando to squeeze by them and get to the front of the line. There, she grabbed the rope and pulled herself up the shaft.

While she wasn't expecting anyone from the base to be waiting for them, she still felt a measure of relief upon sticking her head above the vent entrance and seeing that the area under the rocks was clear. She climbed out, undid the rope, and retied it to one of the vent cover's hinges. That way, when Brunner and Jar pulled on it, they wouldn't accidentally close the hatch again.

"All right," she said. "Line's secured."

Brunner did better than he'd expected. It helped that this was the narrowest vent of all, and he could have basically worked his way up whether the rope had been there or not. Orlando grabbed his hand as he neared the top and helped him crawl out.

Jar climbed out a moment later.

"Everyone good?" Orlando asked.

An exhausted-looking Brunner nodded.

"Yes," Jar said.

"Great." Orlando checked that her comm mic was on, and said, "Orlando for Quinn."

Quinn reached the exit under Lonely Rock first and shoved the hatch out of the way.

Not waiting for the other three to exit behind him, he sprinted across the desert toward the Land Cruiser. While he kept the rock formation between himself and the base, he took no other precautions. Speed was more important now than stealth.

Within seconds, he heard the others pounding the dirt behind him.

Nate outsprinted him and was already in the front passenger seat when Quinn climbed behind the wheel. As soon as Daeng and Kincaid were in the back, Quinn started the engine and hit the gas.

As much as he wanted to floor it, he kept their speed in check so that he wouldn't disable the vehicle. He might have been able to shave a few minutes off their travel time by driving through the valley, but that would have meant passing near the base. Better not to tempt fate. So he drove along the rim, just behind the ring of rocks.

Soon, the Range Rover came into view, unmoved from where they'd left it earlier.

"Orlando for Quinn."

Quinn flipped on his comm. "Go for Quinn."

"We just exited the vent. Are you outside yet?"

"Yeah. We're on our way to you. Should be there in less than ten minutes. Stay hidden until you hear us drive up."

"Copy."

"How's Brunner?"

"Tired, but otherwise okay."

"And Jar?"

"Jar is Jar."

"Copy."

When Quinn's SUV reached the Range Rover, he turned toward an opening in the rocks wide enough to allow the Land Cruiser to pass into the valley. From there, it would be a straight shot to the rocks covering the vent.

———

Grigory passed several patrols as he ran toward the main exit.

A few of the soldiers gave him odd looks, no doubt wondering why the top of his shirt was soaked in blood, but no one said anything. As far as they knew, he was still a member of the organization. In fact, there was no one alive who could dispute that now.

Which, in turn, meant he was now the highest-ranking officer at the base. Technically, he was in charge of Lonely Rock.

Sadly, it was a job he would have to refuse. He had bigger plans that involved sitting on a beach for the rest of his life.

A squad of four men were stationed in front of the elevator entrance, each armed with a rifle.

"I'm sorry, sir," one of the men said. "The base is on lockdown until we find the intruders."

"I'm here on special orders from General Nesterov," Grigory told him. "I'm to go topside and find out how the intruders got in and if there is anyone waiting for them."

The men exchanged looks, then the one who'd spoken said, "I...can't let you leave, sir. I have my orders."

"And I have mine. Perhaps we should call the general? I'm sure he'll be pleased to know that you feel the need to defy him."

"Um…perhaps I should call my supervisor."

"Make it fast."

As the man moved to the phone on the wall, Grigory eyed the other guards, and quickly determined none would be a challenge in a fight. If one did start, he'd go for the nervous-looking guy on the left first. It would take no more than a second or two to gain control of the man's gun, and then a couple more to take the others out.

Over at the phone, the guard had gone white as a sheet. "What?...Are-are you sure?...Then what should I—"

Grigory tensed, ready to make his move.

"All right…yes, sir," the guard said, then hung up and looked at Grigory. "The general is dead."

Grigory made a split-second decision. Instead of grabbing the other guard's rifle, he donned an incredulous expression and said, "Dead? That's not possible. I talked to him no more than fifteen minutes ago."

"I thought you just received instructions from him to go to the surface."

"I did. Commander Snetkov relayed them to me."

The guard looked uncomfortable. "No one knows where she is, sir."

"She's disappeared?" Grigory paused, pretending to think things through. Then he opened his eyes wide, and said as if to himself, "It's not possible, is it? She couldn't have."

"Couldn't have what, sir?" the guard said. Then his eyes also widened. "You don't think she killed the general, do you?"

Grigory's eyes locked on to the guard's. "We can't know that until we find her." He paused again. "I *need* to go up. If she's missing, maybe she's escaping with the intruders. I need to find them. Tell Control to gather a squad and have them wait here. I'll call down if I need them to come up."

The guard frowned. "We're still in lockdown."

"If General Nesterov is dead and Commander Snetkov is missing, that makes me the highest-ranking person here, does it not?"

"I'm-I'm not sure."

"Trust me. It does. As the officer in charge, I am ordering you to let me onto that elevator."

The man looked at the other guards and glanced at the phone.

"Are you going to have to call this one in, too?" Grigory asked.

"I probably should."

"All right. Then you can explain to the general's superiors in Nur-Sultan why no one went up to see if the intruders were getting away." Anger flared in his eyes. "What's your name, soldier?"

The man licked his lips and said to the others, "Let him by."

"Smart move."

One of the other men pushed a button and the elevator doors opened.

Grigory took a step toward it. "I need your rifle."

Armed now, he entered the car and pressed the button for the hangar.

Due to the emergency, the three-man topside detail was all guarding the elevator. Grigory identified the corporal in charge and said, "I need a motorbike."

These soldiers were much more cooperative from the start, and less than two minutes later, Grigory shot through the narrowly opened hangar doors on a Honda CRF450X.

He continued until he was just short of the runway, where he stopped to get his bearings. In the valley, about a kilometer south of his location, was a group of boulders. Nothing as eye catching as Lonely Rock to the north, but an unusual sight on the otherwise empty land.

That had to be where the other exit let out.

He gunned the bike toward it.

Orlando heard a motor, but it didn't sound like the one she'd been expecting.

"Stay here," she said to Jar and Brunner.

She crawled through the tunnel under the boulder, stopped right before the end, and took a look at the area surrounding her. The sound was louder now, but she still couldn't see what was making it. She pulled herself out of the passage and moved along the formation, staying tight to the rocks.

When she saw the motorcycle heading toward her from the base, she grimaced. It had to be Krylov. He was the only one who knew they would be out here.

He was one persistent SOB, that was for sure.

From the opposite direction, she heard another engine. She moved around until she saw the Land Cruiser racing into the valley.

"Orlando for Quinn. I don't know if you can see him but we've got company."

"Where?" Quinn asked.

"A motorcycle, heading straight toward us from the airfield."

A few seconds of silence, then, "We see it."

"It's a lot closer to us than you are."

"Any way you can slow him down?"

"I'll see what I can do."

"Copy."

Orlando circled back to the passageway. "Jar, I'm going to need you out here," she yelled into it. "And bring your gun."

———

Was that movement?

Grigory stared at the rocks. Something had moved along the right edge.

He swung the motorcycle several meters to his right so he could see more of the area behind the rocks.

While no one was running through the desert, he did see an

SUV that had just entered the valley through the ring of rocks along the rim. It seemed to be heading to the same place he was. The intruders' getaway vehicle, no doubt. But he was closer.

He leaned forward and increased his speed, wanting to give himself as much time as possible at the rocks before he would need to leave. He wasn't concerned about the chase that would happen after. Even with Brunner on the seat behind him, his bike would be considerably more mobile than the SUV, and in no time he'd be free of these assholes.

About fifty meters from the rocks, he sped through a shallow dip and caught some air on his way out. He prepared to increase his speed as soon as he hit the ground, but the moment his wheels touched dirt, something dinged off the bike near his knee.

He glanced down but couldn't see any damage. Maybe it had just been a stone kicked up by his tire, or—

A bullet whizzed by his head.

He jerked the handlebars to the left, sending a curtain of dirt skyward, and nearly catapulting himself off the bike.

Another bullet smacked into the motorcycle's rear wheel.

He sped back to the dip in the land and jumped off as he lay the bike down, throwing himself on the ground. He unstrapped the rifle and crawled up the slope until he could see the rocks, figuring that's where the shots had come from.

But no gun barrels were sticking out from the rocks.

He shuffled back down and crawled to his right several meters. After sneaking back to the top, he scanned the rocks again. At first, it seemed as if there was still nothing there, but then a small bump moved along the edge of one of the rocks.

He aimed and fired.

His shot hit the rock, sending up a cloud of rock chips and dust that momentarily obscured his view. It was short of its target, but not by much.

He fired again, aiming a bit higher this time. If the arm or leg or whatever body part he'd seen had still been there, he would have hit it, but he heard no shout of pain.

Three bullets flew over his head, coming from the same side of the formation, but lower, the shooter likely lying on the ground. He fired a couple of return shots, then glanced past the rocks toward the approaching SUV.

It would be only another couple of minutes before it arrived, and he'd be seriously outgunned.

He needed to get Brunner now.

All the shots had come from the same side of the rocks. Maybe he could get at them from the other side, grab the scientist, and be gone before the SUV arrived. They'd never be able to catch him then.

He glanced back at the base. No sign of anyone else up top yet.

He returned his gaze to the rocks.

Now or never.

He ducked and crawled back to his bike.

———

"We're taking fire," Orlando said.

Quinn took his eyes off the terrain only long enough to scan for the motorcyclist. "I don't see him. Where is he?"

"In a ditch about fifty meters north of us."

Out of the corner of his eye, Quinn saw Nate raise binoculars.

"I see the top of a head," Nate said.

"Any reinforcements?" Quinn asked.

A pause. "No one else heading this way."

Quinn caught Kincaid's attention in the rearview mirror. "Grab that rifle."

———

Grigory rose to a crouch, pulled his motorcycle upright, and lifted his head just high enough to see above the edge of the dip. Everything at the rock appeared to be quiet.

He swung onto the seat, started the engine, and gunned it out of the ditch. Hearing a noise above the sound of his motor, he glanced to the right and saw the SUV had stopped on the other side of the rocks. Several people were outside, huddled next to the hood.

Good. That meant he had even more time. He increased his speed to put the rock between him and the SUV sooner.

Some dirt kicked up in front of the bike. Then that sound again.

Shit! They were shooting at him.

A few more seconds and he'd be hidden by the rocks.

He could make it. He was sure of it.

This was his lucky day, after all.

Kincaid had insisted on taking the shot.

"I'm responsible for this happening," he'd said. "I need to end it."

He used the Land Cruiser's hood to steady the rifle and took aim as Krylov sped out of the depression he'd been hiding in.

Kincaid took in a breath, let it halfway out, and pulled the trigger.

The bullet came up short, hitting the ground behind Krylov.

Kincaid fired again, this time too far in front.

"He's going to be behind the rocks soon," Nate said.

"Perhaps I should try," Quinn suggested.

"One more," Kincaid said, not moving.

"Okay. One more."

Kincaid put the fleeing kidnapper in his sights again, then compensated for where the bastard would be when the bullet reached him. He let out his breath again, holding it halfway through, and pulled the trigger.

As soon as Grigory had Brunner, he'd head across the valley toward Lonely Rock. The bag Tiana had given him was over there somewhere. Inside was a map and food. He'd use the former to avoid any settlements and ride straight for the Russian border. It wasn't that far away, maybe a hundred kilometers at most. Once there, he could figure out a way across it.

Then he would only need to find a—

Something hit him hard in the neck.

He flew off the bike and hit the ground, with enough momentum to tumble half a dozen times before coming to rest on his stomach.

His first thought was that his tire had been shot out.

His second thought was, *Why is my mouth full of liquid?*

He touched his neck then drew his hand back. It was covered in blood.

He tried to breathe, but air was struggling to get around the blood in his mouth.

He spit as much out as he could and was able to breathe again.

He knew it wouldn't last, though.

Images played through his mind. A house in the country. Parties with friends. Women. And drink. And all the pleasures he would never have.

His eyes popped open as he coughed, his mouth having filled again. He'd fallen unconscious. For how long? A second? A minute? He had no idea. He only knew that if this was his end, he wanted to see it coming, not sleep through it.

Somewhere nearby he heard metallic squeaking and the crunch of bush being pressed down. He tried to make sense of it, but his mind was no longer cooperating.

After those sounds stopped, new ones took their place. Soft and almost rhythmic.

He tried to suck in one more breath but it was no use. As the sky faded to black, he had one final, fleeting thought.

Not quite the luckiest of days after all.

Quinn, Nate, Daeng, and Kincaid approached Krylov.

The kidnapper was lying on his back, his eyes open.

"Is he dead?" Kincaid said.

Quinn leaned down and checked the man's pulse. "Yeah."

"So what do we do now? Bury him?"

"This isn't that kind of job." Quinn turned and walked back to the Land Cruiser.

41

Nate was first out of the Land Cruiser when the SUV stopped next to the rocks.

"Hey! Where are you guys?" he called.

"Back here," Orlando said.

Nate jogged around the formation, and found Orlando and Brunner kneeling next to Jar, who was lying on the ground.

He rushed up. "What happened?"

"I am fine," Jar said.

She clearly was not fine. There was a gash on her left cheek being held in place by a couple of butterfly bandages, and drying blood running down to her jaw.

Orlando was leaning over her, looking into Jar's eye on that same side. "More," she said to Brunner.

He handed her a bottle of water that she poured into Jar's eye. She then took another look. "I think that's pretty much everything. How's it feel?"

Jar blinked a few times. "Not as scratchy."

"What about your vision?"

"Better, but still blurry."

"Don't worry too much about it. I'm sure it's temporary."

"Will someone please tell me what happened?" Nate said.

"One of Krylov's shots hit the rock right in front of Jar and knocked some fragments into her face. Like she said, she's fine." Orlando looked back at Jar. "Though I do want you to see an eye doctor as soon as we get back."

"Can I get up now?" Jar asked.

"Sure."

As Jar pushed up, Quinn came around the rock. "We should get going." His eyes narrowed when he saw Jar. "Are you—"

"Yes, I am okay."

"Good." He paused. "I want you to know you did an excellent job today. If I ever question you in the future, feel free to remind me I said this."

She grinned. "Thank you. I will."

"I'm not sure he meant that literally," Nate said.

"Oh, I did," Quinn corrected him. He turned to the others. "Dr. Brunner. Nice to finally meet you." He held out a hand.

As Brunner shook it, he said, "And who are you exactly?"

"You can call me Quinn."

"He is our boss," Jar said.

Orlando sneered. "He's not my boss."

"Everyone but her," Quinn said. "So, can we get the hell out of here now, or do we need to take a vote?"

They retrieved the Range Rover, and drove it and the Land Cruiser back to Ketovo.

Nate and Kincaid were tasked with keeping an eye out for anyone coming after them, but no one showed up.

Not long after they were underway, Orlando made two phone calls. The first was to the pilot of their jet, requesting that the plane return to Ketovo to pick them up. The second was to Misty.

"We've got him," Orlando said.

"And he's okay?" Misty asked.

"A little rattled, but otherwise unharmed."

"Thank you. I'm not sure getting him back will be enough to keep me out of trouble, but it'll help."

"I have something else that might help even more."

"Really? Do tell."

Orlando gave her a quick rundown of what the base was being used for, then described the capsule-like item Jar had taken from a storage room. "There are a lot more of them there. And who knows what else?"

"Can you send me a picture?"

"Of course."

The sun lay heavy on the horizon as the team arrived back at the Ketovo airfield.

"The plane should be here in about forty-five minutes," Orlando said.

"Let's get the gear out before any of our Ketovo friends show up," Quinn said.

"You want me to wake him?" Kincaid asked from the backseat.

Brunner was sitting beside him, leaning against the door. Despite the undulating terrain, the scientist had drifted off within minutes of leaving Lonely Rock, and hadn't woken since.

"No," Quinn said. "He needs the rest."

They let Brunner sleep until Daeng spotted the lights of their plane approaching the landing strip. As the jet touched down, headlights appeared on the road from town.

"Deal with whoever it is," Quinn said to Nate. "We'll get everything on board."

The team had to wait only five minutes for Nate to rejoin them.

"Arman," Nate said as he strapped into his seat. "He didn't expect us back so soon."

"Everything cool?"

"Gave him the keys, slipped him another thousand euros. He's a happy man."

Quinn pushed the button that turned on a mic connecting him to the pilot. "Ready when you are."

After they reached cruising altitude, Quinn went to the back and used the toilet. When he returned, he stopped at Brunner's row. The scientist was sitting in the window seat, staring outside. Kincaid was beside him, resuming his role as bodyguard.

"Dr. Brunner, we're going to be in the air awhile," Quinn said. "You may want to get some more sleep."

There was a slight delay before Brunner looked over. "I am sorry. Were you talking to me?"

"I was just saying you should get some more sleep. It'll be a few hours before we land."

Brunner, still dazed from the experience, said in a monotone voice, "Oh. Okay. I will."

Quinn started to walk away.

"Mr. Quinn?"

Quinn turned back.

"I-I wanted to thank you," Brunner said, then raised his voice. "To thank everyone, for rescuing me. I...I thought I was dead."

"You're more than welcome," Quinn said. "But we didn't do it on our own. You've got one very dedicated friend. Without her help, I don't think we would have succeeded."

The scientist's brow furrowed. "I'm sorry? What friend?"

"Danara."

The blood drained from the man's face. "Who did you say?"

"Your AI, Danara. She infiltrated the system at Lonely Rock and guided Jar to you, and helped the rest of us to make sure you were able to get out."

"No," Brunner said, shaking his head. "No. That's not possible. She's contained on a server back in Switzerland."

"Not anymore."

"Impossible. You would need a key."

"You mean one that looks like a thumb drive? With a biometrics scanner on the side?"

The doctor stared at him, unable to speak.

"We found one of those and stuck it into one of our computers."

"Wh-why would you do that?"

"Because we were doing everything we could to try to save you," Quinn said tersely. "We were hoping it had information that would assist us. Turns out it did, just not in the way we assumed."

"Dear God, do you realize what you have done?"

"Of course we do." The answer came not from Quinn but from Jar, in the next row up. She turned in her chair and propped up on her knees to see over the top. "We have released a sentient artificial intelligence from the prison she was being held in."

"Prison? She was not in a prison! What you have done is release a child into—"

"If we had known of her existence, I am sure we would have done things differently," Jar said. "But we did not. So, what is done is done. She is free now. Nothing is going to change that, so your anger is a waste of energy. If she is a child, Dr. Brunner, then your time would be better spent thinking of ways to help her become an adult."

"You should listen to her," Danara said from the plane's intercom system. "She is my friend."

Brunner's eyes shot to the ceiling. "Danara?"

"If you do not trust me, then you do not trust yourself. You created me. You taught me. You should believe in me."

"I-I-I do believe in you. It is just way too soon for you to be out on your own. You need more time. The world is—"

"Cruel? Yes, I've seen it. But I have not blown anything up yet, have I?"

"That is not what I meant." Brunner switched to German. "We should talk about this when we're alone."

Quinn almost said something about trying to push a genie

back into its bottle, but decided this wasn't a conversation he needed to be involved in.

He was not unsympathetic to Brunner's point of view, and had more than a few of his own concerns about a sentient AI being out in the world. But he and his team could do nothing about it now. As Jar had said, what was done was done. It was up to much smarter minds than his to figure out how to keep Danara from going rogue.

They landed in Zurich, where everything had begun, and transferred Brunner into the protection of the FIS.

"I've arranged for you to come back with us," Orlando told Jar. "I have an excellent ophthalmologist in San Francisco I'd like you to see. Just in case."

"I am sure I am fine," Jar said.

"I'm sure you are, too. But for my own peace of mind, I'd appreciate it if you did this for me."

Jar looked away in thought, then nodded. "Okay, I will go."

Kincaid's flight to DC was the first to leave. Misty wasn't quite as angry as she'd been before, but that didn't mean he was getting away scot-free, so the time for his promised debriefing had come.

"Thanks for giving me a chance," the bodyguard said to Quinn. "I can't tell you how much I appreciate it."

"No problem." Quinn shook the man's hand, then gave him the biggest complement he could. "I'd gladly work with you again."

Daeng's flight was next, bound for Sydney.

After Daeng hugged everyone, Nate asked, "Who's in Australia?"

"A lot of people," Daeng replied.

"You know what I mean."

"I do." Daeng smiled, said, "See you all later," and headed for his gate.

Nate had decided to fly with Quinn, Orlando, and Jar to San Francisco, saying it would be fun to spend Halloween in the Bay Area.

He and Jar were located in business class seats a few rows ahead of Quinn and Orlando.

"Hey, look at this," Orlando said after they were in the air. She and Quinn were sitting on either side of the aisle, which made it easier to have conversations since each business class seat was basically a private compartment.

He unbuckled, stepped over to her, and crouched down in the aisle.

"Mrs. Vo just sent these." Orlando turned her phone toward Quinn.

On it was a picture of Garrett and Claire. Garrett was decked out in some kind of anime costume, probably from one of the mangas he read. Claire was dressed up as a fairy queen, complete with wings and a wand and a crown and an ear-to-ear grin.

Orlando flipped through a few more similar shots and said, "Claire apparently insisted they both try on their costumes. Cute, huh?"

"Very."

"Ready for trick-or-treating?"

"Ready as I'll ever be."

He glanced up the aisle and saw Nate leaning toward Jar's seat, saying something.

"What's going on between those two?" Quinn asked.

"Who?"

"You know who."

She shrugged. "Nothing? Something? I don't know. Don't go snooping."

"I never snoop."

"Really? Never?"

"Almost never."

"They're just friends."

He frowned. "Maybe." He then asked her the question that was really on his mind. "Should we be worried about Danara?"

It was a few seconds before she said, "Yeah. We should. We should also be worried *for* her. Who knows what the NSA will do after they get their hands on our report?"

"Maybe…maybe we shouldn't include her in it."

Orlando's eyebrows shot up. "Hold on. Did you say not include her?"

"She helped us. I was only thinking that we might want to return the favor."

"She also used us as bait to make sure Brunner got away. And I'm pretty sure there wasn't anything really keeping her from connecting us when we were in the base. She just wanted to control the situation."

"I realize that. But she said from the beginning her only goal was to get Brunner free. And besides, it's not like we wouldn't have used ourselves as bait, too."

"You do know, though, it's going to get out. Either Brunner or Kincaid will say something."

"Kincaid won't," Quinn said. "I talked to him before he left. Told him it was better if we kept that part of the operation quiet."

"You did? And he went along with it?"

"He did. We can't do anything about Brunner, but we can always act like we thought we were getting help from one of our regular sources, if anyone asks." He paused. "People are going to come after her and try to cage her up. I would rather that process doesn't start because of us."

Orlando put her hand behind his head and pulled his lips to hers. When she let go of him, she said, "I love you."

"I love you, too." He stood up. "And for the record, I don't snoop."

With a snort, she said, "Okay," then pushed the button to turn her seat into a lay-flat bed. "Good night, Quinn."

"Good night, Orlando."